NIGHT
FALL

Amanda Brooke is an internationally bestselling author. Her debut novel, *Yesterday's Sun*, was a Richard and Judy Book Club pick and since then she has written twelve further books which regularly make the bestseller charts. Amanda lives in Merseyside with a cat called Spider, a dog called Mouse, and a laptop within easy reach.

X @AmandaBrookeAB
f /AmandaBrookeAuthor
⊙ @amandabrookeauthor
♪ @amandabrookeauthor
www.amanda-brooke.com

Also by Amanda Brooke

Yesterday's Sun
Another Way To Fall
Where I Found You
The Missing Husband
The Child's Secret
The Goodbye Gift
The Affair
The Bad Mother
Don't Turn Around
The Widows' Club
A Good Liar
The Wife Next Door

Ebook-only short stories
The Keeper of Secrets
If I Should Go

NIGHT FALL

AMANDA BROOKE

HarperCollins *Publishers*

HarperCollins*Publishers* Ltd
1 London Bridge Street,
London SE1 9GF

www.harpercollins.co.uk

HarperCollins*Publishers*
Macken House, 39/40 Mayor Street Upper
Dublin 1, D01 C9W8

First published by HarperCollins*Publishers* 2024
1

A catalogue record for this book is available from the British Library

ISBN: 978-0-00-843194-5 (PB)

Set in Sabon LT Std by HarperCollins*Publishers* India

Printed and bound in the UK using 100% Renewable Electricity by
CPI Group (UK) Ltd

MIX
Paper | Supporting
responsible forestry
FSC™ C007454

This book is produced from independently certified FSC paper
to ensure responsible forest management.

For more information visit: www.harpercollins.co.uk/green

In memory of Matt Valentine

AUTHOR'S NOTE

The setting of my novel is an isolated spot somewhere in North Wales, so isolated in fact that it won't appear on any map. Mynydd Plentyn is a product of my imagination, inspired by the stunning Welsh hills and valleys around Eryri National Park and its highest peak, Yr Wyddfa (previously known as Snowdonia and Mount Snowdon). All I can say is that my little Welsh mountain, Mynydd Plentyn, which translates to 'Child Mountain' in English, should not be underestimated.

When someone dies
it's natural to wonder if anything could have been done
to save them.
We know life is precious.
And we know it can be precarious too.
Which is why we go to extraordinary lengths to help
someone in peril,
even when that someone is a complete stranger.
Or that's what we think we'd do.
In truth ...
Some people simply aren't worth saving.

CHAPTER 1

SUE

The party of five followed a winding trail through the crowded woodland that hugged the mountainside. Sue had lost her footing more than once, and her suede ankle boots were wet right through even though it wasn't raining yet. She didn't own a pair of hiking boots and hadn't thought them necessary for what was supposed to be a short trek from the pub car park, but as bracken snagged the sleeve of her down-filled jacket, she resisted the temptation to complain.

'Are you all right, Nan?' her granddaughter asked.

Paige was ten steps ahead, her dark brown locks tucked into a beanie hat. Sue's hair had been the exact same shade once, but she had never been blessed with Paige's willowy frame, not even in her youth. Her granddaughter was eighteen years old, technically an adult, and from this vantage point, she looked almost as tall as her dad, although that could be because Sue's son-in-law had his head down and his shoulders hunched. Ray's once imposing figure had diminished in recent months, and the cotton tote bag at his side weighed him down far more than it should.

'I thought this was supposed to be a small hill, not a mountain,' Sue replied, sounding more like the child than the matriarch.

'Compared to some of the peaks around here, this one's a baby,' Paige told her. 'In fact, Mynydd Plentyn means "Child Mountain" in Welsh.'

Sue pulled at the neck of her jacket, inviting the icy wind to cool her down. 'So it is a mountain!'

'That's just what people call it, Nan.'

'Officially, it isn't high enough to be classified as a mountain,' offered Ray. 'Not that we'll be climbing right to the top to find out. I promise, Sue, we haven't got far to go.'

Refusing to be mollified, Sue struggled on until she became distracted by a white fleck floating across her vision. She checked to see if the feathery filling of her jacket had escaped where the sleeve was torn, but the inner lining remained intact.

Her youngest daughter, Izzy, came up alongside her. 'Do you want to stop for a rest, Mum?'

At sixty-two, Sue might not be as fit as she used to be, and her ankles had a habit of swelling, but if she could manage a twelve-hour shift on a hospital ward, she wasn't going to be defeated by a so-called hill. Her huffing and puffing was more of a protest against having to traipse up a mountainside in the middle of nowhere in January. Or at all, for that matter. It had been Paige's idea, and Sue was doing her best to respect a grieving child's wishes. It was just that …

'Ignore me,' she said as she glanced to where Izzy's coat strained across her baby bump. 'If you can make it, so can I.'

'She will, even if I have to roll her uphill,' said Olly, who was Sue's newest son-in-law and the expectant father, a situation they were all still getting used to. Izzy's pregnancy, announced on her thirtieth birthday, had come as a surprise to everyone, most especially Olly, who was two years Izzy's junior and in Sue's opinion, nowhere near ready for parenthood.

'No one is going to do any rolling,' she said, glaring at Olly. 'If Izzy doesn't think she can make it up to the viewing platform, we give up. It's as simple as that.'

'We're nearly there,' Paige called back, loosening the scarf around her neck. 'Once we break out of these trees, there's the most amazing view across the valley. You can see as far as Snowdonia.'

'Not if the clouds get any lower,' warned Olly.

Paige scowled at her uncle. 'That was why we were meant to get here early. To avoid the bad weather. It's not my fault *somebody* slept in.'

They had been following the weather forecast for the last week, and there was a cold front bringing wintry showers along the east coast of the UK, but thankfully it wasn't expected to cross the Pennines. North Wales was, however, going to be treated to torrential rain and strong winds later that afternoon, by which point, they had hoped to be back in Liverpool.

Sue checked her watch to discover that the morning had already slipped stealthily into afternoon. She didn't want to be drenched as well as cold, but when she attempted to quicken her pace, Izzy caused her to slow again.

Izzy tipped back her head to peer through the skeletal canopy of trees. 'Anyone notice how the light's gone a weird shade of off-white?' she asked. She sniffed the air. 'It smells like it's going to snow.'

In a flash of panic, Sue realized the white speck floating across her vision had been a snowflake. 'I don't like this. We should head back to the pub,' she said.

Paige looped her arm through her dad's to encourage him onwards as if her nan hadn't spoken.

'We could always come back in the spring,' Sue persisted.

Finally, Paige was forced to respond. 'But it wouldn't be Mum's birthday then.'

'I know,' Sue said, feeling a stab in her chest. It was thirty-nine years to the day since she had given birth to her first child, but Ellen was never going to be older than thirty-eight, not ever. 'But we could still make it special.'

When Ray tried to bring Paige to a halt, she responded by letting go of him and stalking ahead. The pink mobile phone her eyes had been glued to for the entire car journey to Mynydd Plentyn was pulled from her pocket, and she scrolled as she extended her lead.

'She'll be fine,' said Izzy. 'We all will.'

Sue leant into Izzy so their shoulders were touching, needing the reassurance of one child's presence whilst yearning for the touch of the other. She choked back her tears as she stared at the cotton tote bag swinging at Ray's side. It was like a pendulum counting down the seconds until she had to say goodbye to Ellen forever. She could make out the shape of the brass urn she had helped Ellen's husband pick out at the undertakers back in November. This was the last journey she would ever take with both her children. Could anyone blame her for wanting to turn tail and run?

'Look!' shouted Paige. She was standing at the top of an incline, her yellow puffer jacket backlit by a grey light that was no longer broken by the outline of bare trees. 'We made it.'

The final stretch was significantly steeper than any they had tackled so far, and Sue held back so she could watch over Izzy's progress. Her heart leapt into her throat as her heavily pregnant daughter lost her balance, but Olly was there to right her. Sue was the last to tackle the slope, and there would be no partner to catch her if she fell, just as there would be no shoulder to cry on later when she was home alone. It had been over thirty years since she had experienced such a crushing sense of abandonment, and this time was so much worse. At least back then it had only been a wayward husband she had lost.

Sue tested her footing with each step, pressing her hands to her knees as extra leverage. The grip on her boots was no match for the rotting leaves, and her stomach flipped as she felt herself slipping. A hand appeared in front of her and she let Ray help her up.

'Come on, old woman,' he said with a gentle smile.

'If I'm old, you're not that far behind,' she chided as she was heaved onto safer ground.

'Oh, believe me, I feel utterly decrepit,' he admitted.

Ray was forty-seven with a quick smile and dimples that made him appear eternally youthful, or at least they had done. A hollowness had appeared behind his eyes, ageing him significantly since his wife's death. Ellen had been his soulmate, and he was struggling without her.

Once they escaped the tree cover, Sue had her first sight of the viewing platform next to a rocky outcrop. The timber frame was ten metres wide with a guard rail running along two exposed sides. The information board with an illustrated guide to Mynydd Plentyn explained why it had an identity crisis. One side was a steep hill, while the other ended in a sheer cliff face that marked the exposed spine of the mountain rising above woodland and curving around the valley. The viewing platform was on the edge of the cliff and, today at least, was a misnomer because the spectacular view Paige had sold to them was little more than amorphous grey shapes in a world of white.

Away from the protection of the woods, Sue struggled to stand upright against the arctic blast sweeping across the valley, bringing with it the cloud cover Olly had predicted. Tiny pinpricks of pain hit her frozen cheeks.

Izzy opened her mouth to say something, then coughed as snowflakes hit the back of her throat. 'Told you it was going to snow,' she said.

'This is your fault,' Paige snapped, turning on Olly.

'I bet you were up all night playing bloody *Grand Theft Auto*.'

'Hey,' said Izzy. 'We both slept in, and in case you hadn't noticed, I'm eight months pregnant. It's allowed.'

Paige shot more daggers at Olly before turning to face the storm. The ends of her scarf fluttered around her and she had to tuck them into her jacket. 'It was lovely last time we were here. Wasn't it, Dad?'

'As I recall, it rendered your mum speechless,' he said, putting his arm around his daughter.

Ellen had organized a series of trips in the summer with Ray and Paige, wanting to make the most of their time together before her daughter set off to university in Loughborough. They had gone to Alton Towers one weekend and York the next, but exploring North Wales had been their last adventure. Sue hadn't been invited, nor would she expect to be, but she felt excluded now. This place clearly meant so much to her granddaughter, which was why Sue had conceded to the plan, but it meant nothing to her. It didn't feel right leaving Ellen here.

When a flurry of snow hit Sue hard enough to momentarily blind her, she took it as a sign. 'I don't think this is a good idea,' she said. Seeing a flash of hurt dart across her granddaughter's face, she quickly added, 'I'm sorry, love, but if we try to scatter your mum's ashes now, we're all going to end up covered in …' Her chin wobbled. 'We should take her home.' *Where I can still be with her*, Sue wanted to add. She had tried to put Paige's feelings first, but this was too much. *I'm not ready to let my baby go.*

'We just need to wait for the wind to die down,' Paige insisted. She turned to her dad, but the grim set of his jaw made her expression fall.

'Your nan has a point,' he said, gripping the tote bag tighter.

Olly tugged his beanie hat down to flatten the tufts of ginger hair framing his round face. 'And the wind's only going to get stronger,' he warned.

'You just don't want us to scatter Mum's ashes here!' Paige said, turning on her nan. 'You'd rather she was stuck in a graveyard full of dead people so we can leave flowers that'll just rot. I can't ... I won't do it!'

Before anyone could stop her, Paige snatched the tote bag from her dad.

CHAPTER 2

PAIGE

As I pulled the urn from the bag, I was tempted to tell everyone to go away if they were so bothered about the storm. I knew Nan didn't want to be here, even if she hadn't come right out and said as much. She had adopted a more passive-aggressive approach of pointing out all the downsides of not having Mum's resting place nearby. But I wasn't doing this for the convenience of my family.

I clutched the urn to my chest and let a gust of wind whip the empty tote bag from my grasp. It inflated like a balloon and was tossed back over my head towards the treeline where it snagged on a branch. Pulling a glove off with my teeth so I could grip the brass lid, I tried to ignore the deep-set wrinkles on Dad's face which had appeared overnight. Of course he was hurting too, but I had to do this.

The empty glove dangling from my mouth slapped against my cheek, and as I prepared to open the urn, my stomach heaved at the thought of Mum's ashes being flung back into my face.

'It's not fair,' I cried, letting the glove drop.

'None of this is fair!' Dad roared above the cruel wind. No one looked more shocked than Dad by his outburst. He never shouted, and his voice was weaker when he added, 'Not any of it.'

He took his time picking up my glove which had been swept across the viewing platform, then offered it to me in return for the urn. I didn't resist the trade. 'We won't bury her in a graveyard, though, will we, Dad? We will come back?'

After checking the urn's lid was tightly closed, Dad glanced over to Nan, who was holding on to the guard rail as if she expected to be swept away like the tote bag. She refused to look at either of us.

'I want Mum to be free, that's all,' I tried to explain.

I didn't add how Mum had been trapped for too long, and all because of me. I couldn't imagine what it must have been like for her to have a baby at my age, and even with Dad's unwavering support, she had still given up so much. She had put her dreams on hold for years – years it turned out she didn't have to spare.

'Can't you see it's what Mum would have wanted?' I persisted.

Nan's lips trembled with the effort of holding back a sob, and in that moment, I wanted to rush over and give her a big hug. I wanted to say I was sorry for making everything worse when all I was trying to do was make today memorable for all of us, but Izzy chose that moment

12

to speak up.

'For God's sake, Paige. None of us has the faintest idea what Ellen would have wanted,' she shouted above the baying wind. 'She barely knew what she wanted herself.'

'Don't you dare talk about her like that!' I yelled, my anger rising up through my body to scorch my words.

'All I'm saying is we don't have to be so hard on ourselves about giving Ellen the perfect send-off,' Izzy said, her teeth chattering as more snowflakes caught on her bobble hat and refused to melt. 'She wasn't perfect! She was just as flawed as everyone else!'

My jaw dropped. There was a time when Izzy and I had been close. She was twelve when I was born, and we had been more like sisters growing up. But things had changed in the last year, and Izzy had no right to talk about other people's flaws. She was the one fool enough to marry Olly. She was the one who had drained so much of Mum's time and energy when, unbeknownst to any of us, the clock had ticked down to her last days. 'You bitch!'

'Now come on, that's out of order,' said Olly, diving into the argument.

'You'd better keep out of this if you know what's good for you,' I said, my eyes holding his long enough to leave no doubt that this was a warning he would ignore at his peril.

As Olly clamped his mouth shut, Dad spoke up. 'The only thing we know for sure is that Ellen would want us to stick together.'

When Izzy gave a scornful laugh, I could feel my cheeks turning crimson. The storm wailing across the valley was drowned out by the one raging in my head. 'I'm glad you think it's funny Mum died,' I told my aunt. In that moment, I needed to inflict pain and I knew exactly how. 'It's because of you that she's dead.'

'Me?' Izzy blinked hard. 'What the hell are you talking about?'

'Paige, no,' Dad said firmly.

Nan let go of the guard rail and did her best to straighten up. When she spoke, she didn't acknowledge the fresh wound I had just inflicted on a family pretending not to be torn apart. 'Let's get everyone back down to the pub. It should be open by now. We can have a hot drink before we set off.'

'It might be safer heading straight home,' Olly suggested, taking his cue from his mother-in-law. 'The road out of the valley is pretty steep, and if the snow starts sticking, we might get stranded.' He put a hand on Izzy's back, but she shrugged him off.

'I'm not going anywhere until *she* explains what she meant.'

As all eyes fixed on me, I considered my options. We could have this conversation now, or we could have it on the tense drive home. And I wasn't ready to go home yet. I puffed out my cheeks. *Well, you did ask.* 'The accident wouldn't have happened if Mum hadn't been hurrying to answer *your* call.'

Izzy's mouth moved up and down a few times before she could manage to get the words out. 'But I ... It wouldn't ...' She tore her gaze from me to look at my dad, then Nan, who visibly recoiled. 'She was coming downstairs to get to the phone? Why didn't anyone tell me?'

'It wasn't important,' said Olly.

Izzy spun to face him, her voice strangled as she asked, 'You knew? And you kept it from me?'

'We didn't think ... In your condition,' he stumbled. 'And no one's suggesting you caused the accident.'

'Are you deaf? Paige has just fucking said I killed her!' Izzy spat back.

'Stop, please, stop,' Nan begged, but no one was listening.

'You should have told me, Ol,' continued Izzy. 'Of all people, you're the one I'm meant to trust most.'

Despite having caused enough hurt for one day, hearing the words 'trust' and 'Olly' in the same sentence was bait I couldn't ignore. 'Well, you got that wrong,' I said loudly.

'Shut up, Paige!' Olly said. 'Just shut up!'

Izzy looked from her husband to her niece and back again. 'Why, what else don't I know?'

'Nothing!' Olly said in a high-pitched voice. 'She just means I let you down. And it's not like everyone doesn't know that!' He took a step closer to his wife, blocking my view of Izzy, and hers of me. 'There isn't a day that goes by that I don't regret how I reacted to the baby news. I shouldn't have run away, but I am trying to make things right. You believe that, don't you? You wouldn't have married me otherwise.'

15

Olly wasn't telling Izzy anything she didn't already know, but I suspected his little speech wasn't for her benefit, but mine. He was hoping we could draw a line under the past. Quietly, I took little side steps so I was back in Izzy's line of sight.

'Yes, I forgave you,' Izzy was saying, her voice frosty. 'But how many more times will I have to say those words? How many more times will you let me down, Ol? You should have told me about Ellen. You should have prepared me.'

'I know you're upset, but please, we shouldn't be attacking each other like this. I thought I was protecting you,' Olly told her. His voice wobbled as he glanced to where I was now standing. He cleared his throat. 'We do that, don't we? We keep secrets so the ones we love don't get hurt.'

'Until they get out, and then they hurt us more,' Izzy responded. 'I hate liars.'

'Yeah, well, you can't say you haven't done the same,' Olly said, raising an eyebrow.

Izzy's eyes widened, giving away that she had secrets too. Was there no end to the murky depths of their relationship? 'That was ... You want to bring that up now?' she said with a hiss.

'I just meant—' Olly stopped as panic set in. He didn't know how to get out of whatever hole he was digging for himself. I would have felt sorry for him if I didn't know him better. 'I'm sorry. Forget I said anything.'

'And am I supposed to forget how my entire family has been lying to me too?' Izzy asked, a tear slipping down her cheek.

Nan stepped forward, forcing the warring couple apart. She waited until she had Izzy's full attention. 'Can't you see? This is why we didn't say anything. You can't be upsetting yourself like this.'

Izzy gave a mewl that was part anguish, part anger. 'But it isn't right! Why the hell am I getting the blame for Ellen's death? I wanted to talk to her, that was all.' She spat out the snowflakes sticking to her lips and cast her glance wider. Surprisingly, she didn't direct her glare at me, but I felt a knot of dread as she settled on Dad. 'It's not like I was in the next room on a fucking Zoom call while my wife bled out.'

Like a sudden wind change, the force of Izzy's strike against my dad had me gasping for air. 'Take that back!' I yelled.

'No, darling, she's right,' Dad said, his voice quaking. 'I killed her, or as good as. I know that.'

'But it's not true,' I told him. 'It was a freak accident, that's all.'

'Oh, but you're happy to say it was my fault?' Izzy reminded me.

As I shook my head, the wind buffeted my cheeks. Someone up there was trying to knock some sense into me, but I wanted to stay angry. I'd lost my mum and needed to know why.

'If anyone's to blame, it's me,' Nan said, straightening up while simultaneously shrinking into whatever private purgatory she had reserved for herself.

For the last eight weeks, our family had given

a masterclass in how to avoid discussing the circumstances surrounding my mum's death, and it had driven me mad. The police had reached their own conclusions and a coroner was expected to confirm accidental death, but Mum's life was worth more than that. Surely there had to be a villain, and it was easier casting Izzy into the role. It was her persistent calls and distractions that had Mum hurrying downstairs to answer her ringing mobile. I had so far avoided the question of whether the fall would have been fatal if she had received immediate help. Dad was only feet away in his office, on a Zoom call with Nan, who was bending his ear about some local cause. Dad was a newly elected councillor and his mother-in-law expected him to put the world to rights. All the while, Mum was dying.

With the image etched into my brain, I couldn't offer Nan the absolution she needed. Nor did anyone else, but I doubt she would have accepted it if it had been offered. She covered her face with her hands and released a howl that matched the rage of the storm.

'I hope you're satisfied,' Izzy said, turning on me. 'We're all hurting, Paige. We don't need you sticking the knife in too.'

I swear there was an apology on my lips, but anger was my ruling emotion and had been for such a long time. 'You shouldn't have been bad-mouthing Mum.'

'That's enough!' Dad said sharply. 'It's time to go.'

'Fine, I'm gone,' I replied, turning on my heels.

For a second, my heart tugged at the thought of leaving

Mum there too, but ashes were ashes. There were other ways for us to connect. I wanted to know what it was like being her, and more than anything, I wanted to know how she felt when she died.

CHAPTER 3

SUE

Sue felt only momentary relief when her granddaughter stormed off. Paige may have been the one to release what had been a collective pressure cooker of regrets and resentments, but they would all have to deal with the aftermath.

Izzy had her back to everyone, facing the cliff that rose up on one edge of the platform. Her shoulders shook with sobs, but Sue didn't have the strength to go to her. It had been inevitable that someone would point out that Ray's actions, and therefore Sue's too, had contributed to Ellen's death. She just wished it hadn't been Izzy. Was it bad to think that her other daughter wouldn't have accused her so heartlessly?

While Olly busied himself using a broken branch to unhook the tote bag from a swaying tree, Sue didn't think she had the strength to put her family back together again. When Ray squeezed her shoulder, the touch was brief but offered more comfort than any words could have done.

She watched him go over to his brother-in-law, who was still wrestling with the tote bag. Ray stood on tiptoe and recovered the bag with a single tug.

In a silent procession, they left the viewing platform. Once they had returned to the dense tree cover, it offered some shelter from the wind, but the snow kept falling. The ground was dusted white, adding slippery ice to their hazardous descent. Sue was more worried about where Izzy was treading than watching her own steps, her motherly concern still strong enough to override hurt feelings.

'Do you think Paige will make it down safely?' she asked Ray. She hadn't caught so much as a glimpse of her granddaughter's yellow jacket ahead of them.

'She's nimble on her feet,' he assured her.

Ahead of them, Izzy had heard her mum's question, and she mumbled something in Olly's ear that gave him a start.

'What is it?' asked Sue.

When Olly gave his wife a nudge, Izzy stopped. Turned. 'Paige didn't look like she was heading back this way.'

As one, they inspected the path that would take them back down to the pub. The snow highlighted rather than obscured the many footprints left in the mud. Amongst the clearest impressions, Sue could make out where someone had lost their footing during the ascent – it had probably been her. There were some prints pointing downwards, but they had passed other walkers who had had the good sense to abandon their hikes earlier, so there was no telling if any of the footprints had been made by Paige.

'Why on earth didn't you say something straight away?' Ray asked Izzy, struggling to keep the exasperation from his voice. 'You've seen how unstable she's become. Paige shouldn't be out here on her own.'

'I was upset too,' Izzy reminded him before showing the first hint of guilt. 'Sorry.'

Ray looked beaten. He would never survive losing a daughter too. No one could be expected to be that strong. Sue wasn't. She peered back the way they had come, tears blurring her vision. Beyond the trees pebble-dashed with snow, it was getting misty. If Paige had decided to climb higher, she would be walking straight into thick cloud. 'We need to find her, Ray. She won't be able to see in front of her face. She could lose the path. And if she falls …'

'Paige!' yelled Olly at the top of his voice, making them all jump. 'Where are you?'

'It won't do any good. She won't respond,' Ray told him.

He was being polite. What was becoming increasingly apparent was that Paige wouldn't answer to Olly. When Izzy had introduced her new boyfriend to the family two years ago, he had been a hit with Paige. They would chat about music and celebrity gossip as if they were from the same generation, which wasn't too far from the truth – Olly was only ten years older. But their friendship had cooled after Olly's temporary estrangement from Izzy, and Paige had made it known she didn't want him accepted back into the family.

'Paige!' Ray called, only for his cry to be whipped

away by the wind.

'I'll try phoning her,' said Izzy, prompting all four of them to take out their phones.

Calls were made, messages sent, but none were answered. Paige kept her phone on mute, so even if she were close enough, they wouldn't hear it ring. And Sue didn't think she was close. Her granddaughter was getting further away with each second they wasted.

'We need to move,' Ray said, ready to retrace his steps.

'Is that such a good idea?' asked Izzy, rubbing her bump. 'We could all end up getting lost.'

'I won't leave without her.'

'Me neither,' Sue said, taking a step in what her daughter clearly thought was the wrong direction. Her crestfallen expression made Sue reconsider the prudence of their actions. 'But you're right, you shouldn't stay up here. Olly can take you down.'

Olly had been tapping away on his phone, but now he looked up. 'It would be better if I helped with the search. I'll have more stamina,' he said, relying on his age more than any physical prowess. 'Why don't you go with Izzy, Sue?'

'Because I need to find Paige,' she said, as if it were obvious.

'Don't worry, neither of you has to be stuck with me,' Izzy said in a huff. 'I can manage on my own.'

'Please don't, Izzy,' Ray said. He had spent the best part of twenty years trying to navigate their family, and had often been called upon to referee, but he had his limits. 'We need to look after each other, now more than ever.' He turned to Sue. 'Let me and Olly fetch Paige while you take care of Izzy.'

'But if Paige gets hurt …'

'She's eighteen and just as strong as she is strong-willed,' he replied, offering a tight smile. 'If anyone needs the benefit of your nursing skills, it's going to be Izzy.'

Izzy shifted position as if she was about to repeat her argument about not needing anyone, but thought better of it. 'Shall we go then?' she asked.

'OK,' said Sue, without enthusiasm. She looked at Ray and reached for the tote bag. 'But let me take that.'

Reluctantly, Ray gave up his wife's ashes, appearing unbalanced by their absence.

'We won't be long,' Olly promised.

Sue prayed he was right. She didn't think her heart could stand the strain.

***

Sue tried not to look back as she caught up to Izzy, who had stomped off down the path without waiting for her mum.

'Don't say it,' Izzy warned.

'Say what?' asked Sue.

'That it's my fault Paige stormed off.'

When Sue didn't correct her, Izzy stamped her boot onto a fallen twig. The snap sent a shudder down Sue's aching spine.

'She's old enough to take responsibility for her own actions, Mum,' Izzy continued. 'She's not only putting herself at risk, but the safety of those fool enough to go looking for her. She never thinks about others.'

'She's grieving.'

'We're *all* grieving,' Izzy said, her voice trembling. 'But it was Paige who kicked off first. And what the hell are we doing here in the first place? Are we expected to traipse to Wales every time we want to be close to Ellen? And don't say you agreed with scattering her ashes here, because I know you didn't.'

Sue adjusted her grip on the tote bag. 'I just wanted to make it easier for Paige. It's not important what I want. I can still add Ellen's name to Mum and Dad's gravestone.'

'But it's not enough, is it?'

'No, love, it's not,' Sue admitted. 'It's not nearly enough.'

Hearing the crack in Sue's voice, Izzy reached for her hand. With a loud sigh, she let the matter drop. 'I don't know what Olly thinks he's doing playing the hero,' she said. 'If anyone's going to get lost, it'll be him. He doesn't do outdoors.'

'I'm surprised he's brave enough to go looking for Paige given how she talks to him,' Sue replied.

'You'd think she'd give him a break after we lost Ellen. I suppose she needs to be mad at someone, and Olly is an easy target.'

'Hmm,' said Sue, hoping that was all there was to it. 'We do seem to be hitting out at each other an awful lot lately.'

Izzy pressed her chin to her chest. 'Why did it have to happen, Mum? Why did the world have to take Ellen, and do it so casually and needlessly?'

Sue's grip tightened around her daughter's hand. 'I don't have an answer for that. I wish I did.'

'Maybe Paige was right. Maybe it was my fault.'

'You can't think like that,' Sue replied, knowing it was easier said than done.

'We had an argument the day before she died.'

Sue almost stumbled, her foot slipping on the layer of snow that was growing thicker by the minute. Ellen's urn knocked against her leg as she recalled the sound of Ellen's phone ringing in the background during her Zoom call with Ray, not once, but twice. Had Ellen known it was her sister? Had she been irritated by Izzy's insistence on continuing their argument? 'Was it serious?' she asked.

Izzy concentrated on keeping them both balanced as they took a couple more steps. 'Oh, it was something and nothing,' she mumbled. 'I was going to apologize. That's why I rang her.' She left a pause, then continued, 'I just wish you'd told me she'd been rushing to answer my call.'

'It was my idea not to say anything,' Sue admitted, gripping Izzy's hand tighter. 'When Ellen died, I had a job persuading Ray to leave her side at the hospital. He was wracked with guilt. We both were.' Her voice was distant, her eyes unseeing as she looked beyond the swirling snowflakes being carried by the wind. 'He kept going over our stupid Zoom call, dissecting every sound he chose to ignore because I was monopolizing his attention.'

Sue had been complaining for years about the junction at her local supermarket in Hunt's Cross, and after yet another accident, she was convinced that Ray could use

26

his newly acquired powers as a councillor to fix it. He had tried to explain that he served Wirral and not Liverpool City Council, but that hadn't put her off.

'Ray wanted to know what we might have been saying at the exact moment Ellen fell down the stairs. Had we been laughing and joking? Was that why he hadn't heard her cry out?' Sue's voice faded and she blinked away tears. 'Oh, Izzy, it was horrible. Ray was determined to torture himself, and I didn't know how he was going to drive all the way to Loughborough in that state to break the news to Paige.'

'Me and Olly offered to go instead.'

'I know, but it was another form of self-flagellation, I suppose, and I had visions of him running off the road with Paige in the car too. I had to do something, and I'm sorry, but making your phone calls central to the accident helped ease his guilt. And mine too. It was a case of survival to get us through that day. I never blamed you.'

'But it wouldn't have happened if it wasn't for me,' Izzy said, gliding a hand over her protruding abdomen.

Sue clasped Izzy's other hand to her chest. 'You were not responsible, Izzy. If anything, it was your second call that made us question where Ellen was. We didn't get to her in time, but she could have been there much longer. It's not much consolation, but ...'

'It's something,' Izzy finished for her.

'We will come through this,' said Sue, wishing Izzy could accept the comfort she was offering, but just like the path ahead that was disappearing beneath the snow, there was no easy route to redemption.

CHAPTER 4

PAIGE

There was no way I was heading straight back to the pub, but wandering aimlessly in what was quickly becoming a blizzard would be asking for trouble. My options were limited, however, as there were only two routes up Mynydd Plentyn, both of which started along the same track from the pub. We had taken the blue route to the viewing platform, which was where it terminated. The more difficult red route skirted the other side of the woods, taking hikers all the way up to the old fort ruins. We hadn't gone up that far when I'd visited with Mum and Dad, but I had seen the link path that connected the top of the blue route to the midpoint of the red. Even in fog, it was easy to follow because it was nestled between the treeline and the rocky outcrop that cut into the mountainside above the viewing platform.

All I needed was a bit of breathing space, and I doubted the others would notice I was missing until they got back to the car park, by which point I would be on my way back too. But as I took out my phone, it started to buzz. I buttoned the first call from Olly, then the next ones from Dad and my nan. Messages appeared in quick succession, even one from Izzy telling me to stop being a drama queen. The one from Olly was no surprise.

I'm sorry. Can we talk?

'Can't you all just leave me alone?' I said under my breath in case any of them were closer than I would like. I wished I wasn't wearing such a bright jacket.

The wind carried a sound that might have been someone calling out my name so I picked up my pace, my phone still clutched in my hand. I was going to have to shelve today's plan of posting a photo on Instagram of a wild and rugged landscape that could forever be connected to Mum. I'd wanted to memorialize the moment she floated peacefully away, anything to cancel out the image of her last moments – of shattered bones and blood. Had that been too much to ask?

I could definitely hear people shouting now. It was my dad and Olly, who would love making a great show of being part of the family. Why couldn't anyone else see him for the loathsome toad he was? Why was I even wasting my energy thinking about him? I was here for Mum.

I couldn't be sure if it was the snow getting heavier or the thickening mist that gave the illusion of the storm closing in around me. My cheeks were numb with cold, my teeth were chattering and I had to keep rubbing my eyes to clear the flakes of snow sticking to my eyelashes. It was a stark contrast to our first visit to the mountain. I summoned memories of the gentle sway of trees in a

29

warm breeze, the breath-taking scenery, the endless horizon, the vastness of the blue sky, and the stomach-twisting drop to the green valley below as we stood on the viewing platform.

'We could go higher,' I'd suggested to Mum. She had been shielding her eyes to scan the jagged curve of the cliff rising upwards. 'If we cut across the woods, we can take the path right to the top. Apparently there's some old fort ruins up there.'

'I don't think I could take another step,' Dad said with a deliberate rasp to make him sound old. His knees trembled, suggesting he didn't have the strength to stand straight, but he was smiling. 'I was going to ask you for a piggy-back down to the pub.'

I rolled my eyes. 'If you're that decrepit, you're going to have to give up your gym membership, it's obviously doing you no good.'

In reality, Dad was fitter than men half his age. His energy was boundless, which was how he managed to fit in his new councillor duties around the day job. Not that Mum wasn't ambitious too, although I'd only recently begun to appreciate how difficult it must have been for her to put her dream of being an architect on hold to raise me. I'd been oblivious to how hard she must have worked to resume her studies once I'd started school, then find a job she could fit around me, before setting up her own business as an interior designer. I took so much for granted.

'Maybe you two have been conning me all along and actually spend all your time lounging in the sauna,' I said,

30

turning to Mum, who continued to stare out at the vast landscape. The day was sharp and clear and the only shadows were cast by the crowded peaks surrounding the valley. 'Mum?'

She scratched her nose, then swiped her eyes with the back of her hand as if she had been woken from a dream. She thought I wouldn't notice the tears. 'Sorry, I was miles away.'

'We came here to escape the drama,' Dad said, going over to her. From behind, he whispered in her ear. 'You were the one who wanted to make special memories before this one gets corrupted by uni life. At least wait until she's gone before you start worrying about her.'

'I'm not worried,' Mum said with a sniff.

'We don't believe you, do we, Paige?' Dad said, resting his chin on his wife's shoulder.

Mum never did like a fuss and shrugged him off. 'I have every faith in my daughter. Why do you think I picked this place? Mynydd Plentyn means "Child Mountain". That's Paige. Strong and resilient.'

'Immovable and defiant,' added Dad under his breath.

'Able to withstand any storm,' Mum countered.

'There won't be any storms,' I promised, feeling my cheeks glow. I didn't like being fussed over either. 'And if you have to worry about someone, worry about Izzy. Olly only went back to her because Dad made him.'

'No, I didn't!' said Dad with a shocked laugh and a confidence that suggested he was proud of his intervention. He wouldn't be laughing if he knew what Olly had done. 'We had a chat, that was all. I think he was just terrified he'd end up with a high-maintenance daughter who'd never give her parents a second's peace.' He cleared his throat for dramatic effect. 'I know how that feels.'

I poked my tongue at him. 'Well, they're welcome to each other.'

'That's not fair, Paige,' Mum said.

The snow sticking to my scarf now trickled down my neck, bringing me back to the present. 'No, Mum, what's not fair is that everyone gets a second chance except you. Why did you have to die?' I snapped my mouth shut, realizing too late how loudly I'd cried out.

Crouching down beside a tree, I waited to see if anyone had heard me. Visibility was getting worse as my surroundings were slowly erased by snow and mist, but I could see how the solid rock face on one side of the path had been replaced by a steep incline covered in bracken. Behind me, I'd left clear tracks in the settling snow, which wasn't good, but more worryingly, there were other footprints ahead of me that I hadn't registered before.

Above the howling wind, I heard Olly's voice rising up from below.

'Where are you, Ray? Can you hear me?'

'I'm here!' came Dad's reply. 'We need to keep going! Are you OK to split up?'

'Sure!'

My eyes darted from one tree to the next. I couldn't tell how close they were.

'Paige!' Dad shouted.

Just leave me alone for five more minutes, I thought, except it was Mum's voice in my head. How many times had she said that to me when she was trying to work and her demanding daughter kept interrupting? How did that feel, Mum? What was it like being you? We never got the chance to have adult conversations, and now I hate that I don't know who you were outside of being my mum. Did I even know you at all? What was it like dating Dad? Did the age difference matter? What would you think if I messed around with someone much older?

Too afraid to move, I sought comfort from my phone. I was going to send a message, but there was already one waiting for me. It was from him.

I'm here for you, Paige. I'll send you my location.

CHAPTER 5

KELVIN

Pulling his trapper hat over his ears, Kelvin trudged through the snow to his old but reliable Land Rover. It was one of only five cars left in the Resting Place car park. Most of the hikers had made the right decision to head home before lunch, with some strong encouragement from Kelvin. The forecast had been for wet and windy weather, but the arctic blast coming from the east had travelled further than expected and the rain had turned to snow. Red weather warnings were appearing right across Wales and the North West of England.

'Are you sure about this?' asked Sian, ignoring the keys Kelvin attempted to hand over after they had finished clearing an inch of snow off his car.

Kelvin glanced briefly at Sian's battered Corsa, then tipped his head at the Fiesta parked next to his. 'I've got Dee's car.'

'That isn't going to get you very far if the snow gets any deeper. Which it will.'

'So? Being cut off sounds like bliss after the stampede of "new year, new me" walkers we've had. And at least I won't have to drag you out for extra cover any time soon. Please, take the damn keys, Sian,' he insisted, pressing them into her hand. 'If you don't leave soon, even my old Landie won't be able to get you out of the valley. Rob won't be too pleased if he has to tow you home.'

Rob was Kelvin's younger brother, and had been the first to make the move from Yorkshire to Wales to help run Sian's family farm after they married. The couple also volunteered for Mountain Rescue England and Wales, which was how Kelvin had met Dee, another volunteer at the time. Kelvin's regular trips to Wales became so frequent that he eventually forgot to leave. That had been seventeen years ago, fifteen of which he had been married to Dee. He couldn't imagine being anywhere else, or with anyone else.

Sian still hadn't moved. 'What about Dee?' she asked, teeth chattering as she dithered. 'It might be better if she comes back to the farm with me. You could be snowed in for a while, Kelvin.'

'Honestly, she's fine where she is. Now will you please go. Just take care of my baby,' he said, patting the bonnet of the Land Rover.

'I'll drive carefully,' Sian promised, finally opening the driver's door. She was about to get behind the wheel when movement on the far side of the car park drew her attention.

Kelvin followed her gaze towards the tourist information board, not that he could actually see it, or the

35

rising woodland beyond. The car park was a narrow patch of gravel set against the hillside with room for forty cars, and at the far end there were two grey blobs that may or may not have been moving.

Sian stood on the car's foot ledge for a better view. 'Did you see that?' she asked as a strong gust briefly swept away the snow flurries.

Kelvin felt a release of some of the tension he had been holding. 'It has to be our missing hikers.'

'Thank goodness for that,' said Sian, sharing his relief. 'I think the one on the right is the pregnant woman I mentioned.'

It was Sian who had seen the party of five setting off earlier, and with two unaccounted vehicles left in the car park, it was clear they hadn't returned.

'The others can't be far behind. Let me deal with them,' Kelvin said. 'You can get going.'

'Are you sure?' asked Sian, starting the engine.

'Go!' replied Kelvin, closing the car door.

After waving Sian off, Kelvin went to intercept the two walkers who were making a beeline for the pub. It was only as he drew closer that he realized why Sian had been so concerned. These were not seasoned hikers. The older woman's fashion boots looked destroyed, and her padded jacket was torn. The pregnant woman's shower-proof coat was equally unsuitable for the conditions, and they both looked cold and wet. At least one of the group's cars was a Toyota Land Cruiser, which should get them out of the valley safely, but only if they hurried.

'Hey!' he called out when they failed to notice him approaching.

'Is the pub open?' asked the younger woman, knocking a clump of snow from her bobble hat.

'We've closed up because of the storm, but you might as well wait inside for the rest of your group.'

'Thank you. I'm Sue, and this is my daughter, Izzy,' said the older woman.

'Sorry, I'm Kelvin. I'm the landlord,' he replied, hoping they wouldn't hang around long enough for him to need to remember their names.

'We were planning on scattering my other daughter's ashes,' Sue explained as they reached the safety of the pub. 'But things haven't exactly gone to plan.'

'Ah, I'm sorry to hear that,' Kelvin said, now understanding their slow response to the worsening conditions. 'This weather's crazy, even by our standards.'

The pub entrance opened into a narrow corridor leading to a small bar and dining room on one side, and a snug on the other. Grey flagstones covered the floors throughout, and the walls were painted white with black beams criss-crossing the ceiling. The furniture was mostly wooden and utilitarian to take account of their often muddy and wet clientele, and the menu was a simple fare of soup and sandwiches, which suited most visitors. On days like today, people were more interested in warmth and shelter than any culinary delights.

Kelvin invited Sue and Izzy into the snug where the fire his wife had lit earlier that morning crackled and glowed. The heat burned his frozen cheeks, but he added a log to the fire for the sake of his shivering guests, then grabbed a couple of throws from a basket in the corner.

Sue used both to wrap around her daughter. 'We might need to strip you out of those wet things,' she told her.

'My advice is that you head home straight away,' Kelvin said quickly before offering another blanket for Sue. 'The roads won't be passable for much longer. Are the others far behind?'

Izzy shuffled towards the window despite there being nothing to see beyond the undulating waves of snow. 'My niece went off on her own,' she explained, 'and the others are trying to find her. She's not answering her phone.'

'I'll try again,' said Sue.

Steam rose from her damp clothes as she tapped away on her phone, but it took a while for the screen to react to her cold fingers.

'I'm afraid I can't offer you our usual hospitality,' said Kelvin as they waited for the call to connect. 'I'm on my own and the kitchen's closed.' He didn't feel obliged to mention Dee, who had taken to her bed earlier that morning. The only thing his uninvited guests needed to know was that he wasn't equipped to look after them.

'That's OK,' said Izzy. 'We don't want to hang around longer than we have to.'

Kelvin ignored the pang of guilt as Izzy rubbed her swollen belly. His duty of care was to Dee, and while time out from society might be the break she needed, being stranded in a pub full of strangers was not going to alleviate her anxiety, especially when it looked like one of those people might give birth at any second.

Sue had her phone pressed to her ear, but she shook her head. 'Maybe there's no reception.'

'We have a mast over in a corner of the car park,' Kelvin explained. 'Even at the top, you can usually get some signal, although the weather can interfere.'

'She had better not be at the top,' Izzy muttered, returning her attention to the window. 'Now is not the time for a teenage strop.'

'Paige is a bit upset,' Sue told Kelvin. 'Ellen – my daughter – was her mum.'

'And I am so sorry for your loss,' Kelvin said, leaving a respectful pause before adding, 'but you need to get them down here.'

'I'll try the others,' she replied.

CHAPTER 6

SUE

'It's ringing,' said Sue, offering Kelvin some hope that they would be out of his hair soon. She had lost count of the number of times he had told them they needed to set off. He kept glancing at Izzy's bump, but he needn't have worried – Sue didn't relish the prospect of her family being stranded in his pub either.

She had dialled Ray's number first. He was used to his mother-in-law pestering him, but this was one call he couldn't ignore, and after the tenth ring, he answered.

'Hi Sue, any news?' He sounded out of breath. She hoped that didn't mean he was still climbing.

'I was about to ask you the same. Where are you?'

'On my way back,' Ray said despondently. 'Did you make it to the pub OK?'

'The landlord has a roaring fire on the go for us,' Sue said, feeling obliged to paint Kelvin in a good light in case they did have to fall on his mercy. 'But it's already gone two, and he says the roads might become blocked if we don't get moving soon.'

'I'll be as quick as I can. I just hope Paige is ahead of me. It's impossible to find any kind of path in all this snow.'

'You're not lost, are you?' said Sue, turning sideways so she didn't have to look at the falling expression on their host's face. Her feet squelched inside her suede boots.

'Well, I'm definitely heading downhill.'

'Then keep going. And if Paige hasn't appeared by the time you get back, we can figure out what to do from there. And please tell Olly that Izzy's fine.' She had expected to hear him in the background enquiring after his pregnant wife. She was a little miffed that he hadn't.

'Ah.'

'What does that mean?' Sue asked with a sinking heart. She winced for her daughter's sake when she asked, 'Isn't Olly with you?'

Izzy had been staring out of the window, but her head snapped towards her mum. 'Where is he?'

'Where's Olly, Ray?' she repeated down the phone. From the corner of her eye, she could see Kelvin covering his face with his hands.

'We split up a while ago. He was struggling, so if anyone is going to show up first, it'll be him.'

Sue was inclined to agree, but given the choice, it was Paige she longed to see emerging from the blizzard. When she cut her call with Ray, Izzy had her mobile pressed to her ear.

'Where the hell are you?' she bellowed down the phone, leaving no doubt that Olly had answered. After

41

a delay, she added, 'What? … I can't hear you! … Olly?'

Izzy turned the phone to show Kelvin the connection had been lost. Her hand was trembling. 'I thought you said reception was good. I could hear him, but he kept breaking up. And then we were cut off.'

'It can be patchy,' Kelvin said, his face twisting into a grimace. 'It depends where he is.'

'What does that mean?' asked Sue, instinctively going over to comfort Izzy.

'In these conditions, it's easy to get disorientated. So, for example, if he made it up as far as the ruins, he could have tried to come down on the other side. That's where the mobile reception starts to break up.'

'You mean he could be getting further away?' asked Izzy, horrified. She returned her attention to the world outside. 'It's getting worse out there, Mum.'

'The snow isn't that deep yet,' Sue replied, not fooling any of them.

'Shit,' muttered Kelvin, who was looking out of another window. 'You should have all come down straight away. Was *anyone* dressed for this weather?'

'We didn't know it was going to snow. It wasn't in the forecast,' Sue replied, losing patience with the man who clearly saw them as a huge inconvenience. 'And to be blunt, Kelvin, if I had the power to predict the future, we wouldn't be here. I would have done something to stop my daughter falling down the stairs and leaving her family bereft and broken. I know this particular mess is of our making, but can you please show a little compassion.'

Kelvin's neck turned crimson, swiftly followed by his cheeks, but before he could manage any other response, Izzy gasped. She pressed her forehead against the glass as she scanned the car park. 'I thought I saw something,' she said. 'There! Can you see it?'

'Thank God,' whispered Sue, spotting a flash of yellow.

CHAPTER 7

PAIGE

I ran, slipped, stumbled, and at one point, rolled down the mountainside. I should have been grateful for the thick layer of snow that cushioned my fall, but I wanted to hurt, to feel raw pain. I followed the red route back to the pub as best I could, but it was hard to keep to any specific path when everywhere was turning white. It was a good thing I didn't accidentally stumble back onto the blue route as I would have been tempted to jump right off the viewing platform. Then I would have known exactly what it felt like to fall, and to fall DELIBERATELY. That word was tattooed across my mind in capital letters. *Is that what you did, Mum? Was that how bad you felt?*

The only reason I forced myself to keep going was for Dad. I wanted so much to phone him and tell him to come and get me, but I didn't want him wandering around this godforsaken mountain. We had to leave and I prayed he was back at the pub waiting for me.

My lungs were burning and my legs wobbled. I wasn't sure I could make it, but then the trees began to thin and the ground levelled off. Beneath two inches of snow, I could feel gravel underfoot, giving me the impetus to gather the last of my energy and sprint across the car park. Through the snow and mist, the dark shape of the pub slowly emerged. It was the middle of the afternoon, but lights were on and spilled out across the entrance as someone flung open the door.

'Paige!' Nan cried, racing towards me with her arms open wide.

I started to sob.

'Oh, sweetheart,' she said, wrapping me in a hug.

As I buried my face in her warm neck, I felt her flinch with the cold, but she clung on tighter. She guided me inside, steering me towards a small room bathed in the orange glow of a real fire. The air was thick with a cloying heat, and I couldn't catch my breath as I scanned the room. Izzy was there, and a man I didn't know. But no Dad.

Izzy tossed a blanket towards me, but it might as well have been a hand grenade. 'Your dad and Olly are still out there looking for you,' she hissed, delivering the blow that almost brought me to my knees.

'Now isn't the time for recriminations, Iz,' Nan scolded.

My chest heaved as I tried to contain my sobs. Where was my dad? 'I'm s-sorry,' I told Izzy, and I was sorry for so much. I was sorry for being horrible to her. I should never have blamed her for Mum's fall, and I couldn't blame her for hating me. I hated me too. 'I really am sorry, Iz.'

'A lot of good that does,' she replied, only marginally gentler. Her jaw was set firm and she looked about to launch into a lecture when her phone beeped. She almost dropped it as she scrambled to read the message. 'Thank, God. It's from Olly. He says he's found the blue route, and he's not too far away.'

Nan was arranging the blanket around my shoulders when I clutched her arm. I couldn't speak, but thankfully she knew what my next question was going to be. 'I've spoken to your dad. He's on his way back,' she said. 'It's going to be fine, love.'

Izzy turned her back on me so she could watch from the window. I wanted to join her, but I was scared to look. What if I watched for Dad coming out of the blizzard, only to see someone else? What if he never came back? My throat tightened, but I couldn't stop shaking.

'How about I make you all some hot drinks?' said the man who had remained by the door. 'I can put them in disposable cups.'

'So we can be on our way?' Nan asked with a tilt of her head that suggested there was an underlying tension between the two.

'It would be best if ...' he said, his face twisting into a grimace.

'I know, Kelvin. Believe me, I know,' said Nan. 'We need to get going.'

With Kelvin out of the room and Izzy preoccupied, I was once more the focus of my nan's attention. She unwound the scarf from my neck. 'What were you thinking? You could have got lost, or ... or worse.'

'I'm fine,' I said, shivering uncontrollably.

Nan moved a spindly wooden chair closer. 'Here, sit down. Take off your socks and shoes,' she said.

'But we're not staying,' I insisted as Nan guided me towards the chair. My mind was resisting, but my legs gave way and I sat down with a thump.

'We need to get as dry as we can before we set off,' Nan said as she bent down to undo my boots.

My fingers and toes were tingling painfully and maybe Nan was right about getting dry, but I didn't care. I wanted to leave. Now. 'Will you stop!' I blasted at her in frustration. 'I can do it myself.'

Izzy shot me a look, but she didn't say anything. Neither did Nan, who looked like she might burst into tears. I knew I was acting like a child and had to bite down on my lip to stop myself pouting, because I wasn't a child, not any more, not after what I'd been through.

Nan led by example and I kept my head down as she took off her own socks and boots. When I heard her bare feet slap against the cold flagstone floor as she went to help Izzy, I was still fumbling to undo my laces with numb fingers.

By the time Kelvin returned with a tray of five corrugated cardboard cups and a plate of cookies, there was a row of wooden chairs holding steaming coats, gloves, socks and scarves, all lined up in front of the fire next to our boots.

'How much do we owe you?' Nan asked him.

'On the house,' Kelvin said. 'Accept it as an apology for

being so abrupt. Today hasn't gone to plan for any of us.'

'You can say that again,' I muttered from the far side of the room. I was sitting on a bench, my chin resting on my knees, covered in a musty-smelling blanket, my nose an inch away from my phone. To distract myself from the tortuous wait for Dad, I'd rechecked my messages and the location of the person I'd been tracking earlier, but the authorization had timed out. I didn't want to think about where *he* might be. I should never have responded to his message, never engaged with him at all. I thought I could trust him because he was older, but as I went over our lengthy conversation threads shared during sleepless nights, I realized how wrong I'd been.

When a shadow fell over me, I pressed my phone to my chest before Nan could see. I took the cup she offered and inhaled the sweet scent of hot chocolate.

'Here, take a couple of these too,' she said, handing me the cookies.

'Thanks,' I mumbled.

'Are you OK now?'

'Yeah, fine,' I said to send her away. I wouldn't feel better until Dad was back.

I glanced over to the windows, but they were covered in a film of condensation from our damp clothes. The only exception was the small porthole Izzy had made for herself.

'I've had a call from one of the farmers in the valley,' Kelvin was saying to Nan. 'He's already had to help one stranded motorist ...'

'Does that mean we're trapped here?' I spoke up,

suddenly eager to join the conversation.

'No, love,' Nan replied firmly. 'It just means we're going to need to take it slowly.'

'But the snow's getting deeper,' Izzy said, sounding as worried as I was. 'And it won't just be here, but all the way back to Liverpool. I don't want to get stuck on the motorway, Mum.'

'Then we won't use the motorways. We'll be fine,' Nan insisted.

Her assurance was paper thin, but no one pushed the subject further for fear of what conclusion might be reached. Izzy returned to her outpost, and silence fell so completely that there was no mistaking the sound of the entrance door as it creaked open. I held my breath, then released it when the door slammed shut again. I looked to Izzy, who would have seen whoever it was arrive, but she showed no reaction.

I stood up, dread in my heart, and let the blanket fall to the floor. 'Who is it?'

'It's Ray,' Izzy said without enthusiasm.

I sped across the room and almost slipped on one of the puddles beneath our dripping coats. I kept going and didn't stop until I'd ploughed right into Dad. I released a howl into his chest, the melting snow on his jacket stinging my now-warm cheeks.

'It's OK, Paige. I'm here, I'm here,' he said, almost too soft for me to hear above my sobs.

'I'm sorry, I'm sorry, I'm sorry,' I said over and over again as we made our way to the snug. 'I didn't mean to … I'm sorry.'

'Shush, now. It's going to be all right.'

I wasn't sure I could believe him, not when I'd felt his breath hitch as he stopped outside the snug and prepared to greet the others. What had I put him through?

'Am I glad to be out of that,' he announced brightly, peeling me off him long enough to remove his gloves. He rubbed his hands against his frozen cheeks. 'I can't feel my face.'

Nan rushed over, carrying a throw. 'Oh, Ray, am I glad to see you! Take off that coat, we need to get you warmed up.'

Ray did as he was told, nodding a greeting to Kelvin, then to Izzy, who was making another call. Her smile to Dad was brief, then her expression changed as her call connected. She plugged her finger into one ear. 'Hey, where are you now? You sound closer,' she said, her voice hopeful.

Nan continued to fuss around Dad. 'There's a hot chocolate here for you,' she whispered. 'Or do you need something stronger?'

'Best not if I'm driving.'

Dad was wrapping his bright red hands around the cup, and almost spilled it when Izzy gave a screech. 'It's Olly!' she said, rushing past them to the hallway.

I retreated towards the fireplace and adjusted one of the coats as if I was concerned it might scorch, when I was simply fighting the urge to gather up all our belongings so we could leave.

Nan seemed to read my mind, but after promising we could leave, she'd had a change of heart. 'Kelvin says the roads are blocked,' she said to Dad.

'I was saying it's getting more difficult,' Kelvin corrected.

'We just need to be careful, that's all,' I added.

'Here he is,' Izzy said, clinging to Olly as they joined the group.

'Someone get me a stiff brandy,' Olly said with more drama than was necessary. He was smiling like he was the hero returned.

'I take it you're not the other driver then?' Kelvin said when Sue gave him a pleading look.

'Huh, the only cars Olly drives are with his PS2 controller,' I said snarkily. As guilty as I felt for making Dad trek through a storm for me, I wasn't about to offer Olly the same apology.

'No time for brandy, I'm afraid, Ol,' said Dad, stopping him before he could shake out of his snow-covered jacket. 'It's time to go.'

CHAPTER 8

KELVIN

Kelvin held on to his hat as he stepped out of the pub, only to discover the ferocious winds had been replaced by an eerie calm. The snow continued to fall, however, and as it floated softly to the earth, he would have been tempted to catch a plump snowflake on his tongue if he hadn't been in company. He might very well do so once he had waved them off.

He had done all he could for the stragglers, providing them with blankets, shovels and food in case they did get stranded somewhere – just as long as it wasn't on his mountain. He did feel sorry for them, but he sensed there was something more than grief pulling the family in opposing directions. Whatever it was, he was relieved it wasn't going to be his problem for much longer, but as he watched his boots disappear into the snow as they crossed the car park, his pace slowed.

'It must be six inches deep in places,' he said to Ray. 'And there'll be drifts that are much deeper. You might struggle to drive through it. And there are only a couple of hours of daylight left, if that.'

Sue was walking alongside them. 'Are you saying we shouldn't go?' she asked.

Kelvin pursed his lips. He wished he could keep his mouth shut, but in all good faith, he couldn't send these people into harm's way without offering an alternative. 'Look, if you don't mind taking care of yourselves and spending the night in sleeping bags, you could stay, I suppose.'

Sue's steps faltered, but Ray pushed on. 'The snow isn't showing any signs of stopping yet, and the forecasters can't decide if we're going to get rain tomorrow or more snow. So as deep as it is now, it could be deeper by morning. We might end up trapped here for days.'

'At least it would give the highway agencies a chance to clear the roads,' Sue replied.

'They won't prioritize country roads,' said Ray. 'Our best chance is to leave now, Sue.'

Ray marched ahead with Sue, Paige literally following in his footsteps through the snow. Olly and Izzy were slower and held back with Kelvin.

'I have my pregnant wife to think about,' Olly said. 'Would you risk it, Kelvin?'

'Your best bet is to drive slowly in a low gear,' Kelvin said, only then remembering that Olly couldn't drive. 'Who are the drivers?'

'Ray,' said Izzy.

As Kelvin waited for a second name, he watched Ray and the others walk straight past the Land Cruiser and head towards another car parked further along the row.

Ray was shovelling snow off the roof of his Ford Focus Estate when Kelvin approached. 'I know splitting into two cars would give you an advantage of weight distribution, but it might be better taking everyone in the four-wheel drive. I don't mind you leaving this here.'

The family had gathered around the Ford. 'But this is the only car we have,' said Izzy, an unmistakable strain in her voice.

Confused, Kelvin did a quick inventory of the car-shaped mounds scattered across the car park. After Sian had left in his car, four others remained: Dee's, Sian's and the two unaccounted cars he had presumed belonged to the family. 'The Toyota isn't yours?'

'What Toyota?' asked Sue while Ray continued to scrape away snow.

Kelvin rubbed his forehead. 'It doesn't matter,' he said. There were more pressing issues, like how the family was going to make it out of the valley in a loaded down estate.

Kelvin regretted not getting Olly that brandy. They were going to need some Dutch courage, all except Ray, whose confidence hadn't wavered. Even his daughter looked jittery as she held on to her mother's ashes and surveyed the snowy scene around them. At least visibility had improved.

Kelvin helped shovel snow from around the car's tyres while Sue and Paige loaded up the boot with their supplies. Olly and Izzy were the only ones not actively engaged in the preparations, and Kelvin kept one ear to their conversation.

'What if we get stuck miles from nowhere, Olly?' Izzy asked. 'What if there's no phone reception?'

'That's why we're taking supplies.'

'So the five of us can spend the night in the freezing cold. In that tin can?' Izzy's voice had gone up an octave as she pointed a trembling finger at the car slowly emerging from its snowy grave.

Ray stopped what he was doing. 'It won't come to that, Izzy. I've had plenty of experience driving through worse.'

'Do you drive for a living?' Kelvin asked hopefully.

Izzy scoffed. 'Only the commute from Wirral to Liverpool University.'

'I've travelled around North Wales more times than I care to remember,' Ray replied, meeting Izzy's hostility with admirable patience. 'In rain, shine, *and* snow.'

'But only when you had to. And you heard Kelvin, we don't have to,' Izzy said. She took hold of Olly's arm. 'I don't like this.'

'Honestly, Izzy, the only risk we face is wasting more time by prevaricating,' Ray insisted. 'I've checked our route and traffic is getting through. And we'll keep checking, won't we, Olly?' He looked to the younger man to back him up.

Olly rubbed his wife's back in an attempt to slow her breathing. 'I just want to get you back home,' he told her.

'And I want to be home. But this is madness.'

As Izzy's fear spread around the group, Paige took the car keys from her dad and got into the driver's seat. She turned the engine on and dialled up the heaters to demist the windscreen while she waited for the others.

'Like I said,' Kelvin said to break the tension, 'I can't offer five-star service, but if any of you want to stay, you can. And if Ray takes the car, I don't mind taking people home to Liverpool when the snow clears. It's been a while since I was there.' His offer was more genuine this time. He felt responsible, if not for the adults, then the baby Izzy was carrying. He and Dee had made a conscious decision not to have children, but there were rare moments like this when he found himself thinking he would have made a good dad. And in answer to Olly's earlier question, no, he would not be encouraging his pregnant wife to risk a journey in this weather.

Olly rolled his shoulders, aware of Kelvin's gaze. 'What do you think, Sue?'

She chewed her lip as she turned to Izzy. 'I want to keep you safe more than anything,' she said. 'And there are risks to balance, whatever we decide. I'm not trying to tempt fate, but you're thirty-five weeks pregnant, Iz. You could go at any time, and I don't like the idea of you being stranded up here.'

'But I'll have you with me.'

Sue took a moment, swiping away a thin layer of snow that had settled on the car's recently cleared back window. When she looked up, it was Ray she addressed. 'If Izzy stays, I have to stay too.'

Paige revved the engine. 'Well, I'm not!' she shouted. 'Dad? Can we go?'

'Just wait a minute,' he said, raising a palm towards

her. He licked his lips nervously, taking time like Sue to reassess the situation. The sound of the car door slamming and gears grating interrupted his thoughts.

Ray skidded towards the driver's door. There was a brief tug of war where he tried to pull the door open and Paige fought to keep it shut, but Ray's persistence won. Crouching down, he reached for the keys and switched off the engine. 'You can't even drive on a beach, let alone through snow.'

'Then you drive. Please, Dad. We can't stay here. We just can't!' she wailed. 'I want to go home.'

Ray cupped his daughter's damp cheek. 'I promised I'd look after you when Mum died, and I will.' He took his time standing up to address the rest of the group. 'I'm sorry, but I agree with Paige. We should go home. And I'd rather it was all of us,' he said, his last words directed towards Olly.

As Olly shook his head, Sue clasped her hands to her chest. 'You're right, we should stay together, but let's stay here.'

Ray gave his daughter a side glance. 'It's been too much for her, Sue.'

His mother-in-law nodded as if she shared a deeper understanding of Ray's concerns. 'I know.'

'And I will come back when the roads are clear,' he said to Kelvin. 'Look after them for me.'

Paige got out of the car so her dad could get behind the wheel. While he restarted the engine, she went over to her family. Kelvin stepped back, fascinated by the strange dynamics at work in the group.

'Me and Dad are going to be fine,' Paige said, kissing her nan on the cheek.

'You'd better be,' sniffed Sue.

Before returning to the car, Paige stopped by her aunt. 'Can we talk when you're back?'

'Haven't you said enough?' Izzy responded, but relented when her niece's lip trembled. 'Fine, we'll catch up when I'm home. Have a safe journey.'

Paige ignored Olly as she walked back to the car, but Olly followed and grabbed her arm. They spoke quietly and intently before Paige shrugged him off and jumped into the car.

Noticing that he had an audience, Olly plastered a smile on his face and joined the others so they could line up to wave the car off.

'Were you and Paige talking about me by any chance?' asked Izzy.

'What? No, I was, erm, just telling her to keep an eye on the traffic reports, that's all,' Olly replied, his face a picture of innocence.

The estate struggled for traction a couple of times as Ray drove out of the car park. 'I can't watch,' said Sue, a hand covering her eyes as she peeped through her fingers. 'We shouldn't have let them go.'

Kelvin was inclined to agree, but he would be lying if he said he wasn't just a little bit relieved to be accommodating three guests instead of five. And Paige did seem to be central to all the drama.

Sue must have been aware of the impression her family had made, and as they trekked back to the pub, she said, 'She's not a bad kid, Kelvin. It's just that she's been through so much in the last few months.'

'I can only imagine,' replied Kelvin, but he was only half-listening as he paused in front of the Toyota. Whoever it belonged to had arrived that morning. So where were they now? He wiped snow from the front of the car so he could read the registration plate. He had a feeling he was going to need it.

CHAPTER 9

SUE

'Right then,' Sue said, taking off her damp coat while Kelvin stoked the fire. Her stomach would remain in knots until Ray and Paige reached home safely, and there was no telling when that would be. At least Ray wouldn't have the additional burden of dropping Sue and the others home first. 'Tell me what I can do to help.'

'For now, I'd say get warm and dry,' replied Kelvin. 'We keep a supply of donated clothes in our storeroom at the back if you want to help yourself. You're not the first ones to be caught out by the weather, although people don't normally end up staying overnight, so no pyjamas.'

When Kelvin smiled at his own joke, Sue smiled back. They would probably like each other under different circumstances. 'I am sorry,' she offered.

'No need to apologize,' he said with a shrug.

'Where will we sleep?' asked Izzy, peeling off her coat and stepping closer to the fire.

Sue looked around the small, oak-beamed room with its sparse furniture. The snug had felt warm and inviting when they arrived, but was less appealing now they knew they were there for the duration.

'We have a couple of spare rooms upstairs,' Kelvin said when he noticed Sue raise her eyes to the ceiling. 'They're mainly used for storage, but somewhere under the junk, there are beds, and like I said before, I can provide sleeping bags.'

'I could go up and clear some space,' offered Olly. He had been staring at his phone for the last few minutes.

'No,' Kelvin said quickly. 'Stay down here and get warmed up. If you're hungry, I can make sandwiches, and there's the soup we had prepped for lunch service.'

'We don't want to put you to more trouble than we already have,' Sue replied. 'And we will pay for our keep.'

'Unless you're planning on drinking the bar dry, I'm happy for you to be my guests,' Kelvin said. He glanced out of the window and frowned. 'I'd hate anyone to be stranded alone in this weather.'

Sue didn't need reminding that two of the people she loved most in the world were facing that risk. Ray and Paige had only been gone ten minutes, but she checked her phone for messages. No updates yet. She shifted her weight and felt her socks squelch inside her useless boots that hadn't had time to dry earlier. 'How about you show me where the stores are, and I'll sort out what we need?'

'If you're sure?'

'Honestly, I need to keep occupied,' admitted Sue, pulling off her boots and lining them up next to where

Olly and Izzy had placed theirs in front of the fire. After pulling off her socks, she straightened up. 'Are you hungry too, Kelvin?'

'I can make something later for me and Dee, but thanks.'

'Dee?' Sue's eyes widened in shock, and she had to quickly rearrange her features. 'I didn't realize ... I thought you were here alone.'

Kelvin shifted uncomfortably. 'My wife isn't too good at the moment. She might not be up to making an appearance.'

'Is that me you're talking about?' asked a voice from behind him.

The waif-like figure standing in the doorway gave Sue another fright. The woman looked to be about forty and wore an oversized roll-neck jumper that dwarfed her. Her thick, dark hair was mussed, and there was a silver stripe falling like a ribbon from her left temple. Her smudged make-up darkened the shadows beneath her eyes, and it was those eyes that had given Sue a start. For the briefest, heart-stopping moment, she had thought it was Ellen staring back at her. Her misfiring brain looked for her daughter everywhere as if convinced the world had made a terrible mistake, that she would find Ellen again if only she looked hard enough. Today was not that day.

As Kelvin's wife stepped hesitantly into the room, her gaze darted from one corner to the other. 'Is it just the three of you?'

'There were five of us,' explained Sue, 'but my son-in-law and granddaughter have chanced getting home.'

62

Dee tugged at her jumper, drawing it closer to her chest. 'I saw them leave.'

'We opted to stay,' Sue said, making it sound as if the decision had been a simple one, when in reality, it had torn her heart in two. She hadn't wanted to choose between her only surviving daughter, and the family of the one she had lost. She still didn't know if she had made the right choice.

Dee glanced at Izzy's bump and gave a nod before turning to Kelvin. 'There's no one else staying?'

'No,' he said. The sound of rough fingers scraping stubble filled the pause as he rubbed his chin. 'But I am worried about an abandoned car in the car park. A white Toyota.'

'Does that mean there's someone lost on the mountain?' interjected Olly.

Kelvin's frown from earlier returned. 'I really hope not. I don't suppose you saw anyone else while you were up there?'

'There were a few walkers coming down when we were heading up to the viewing platform,' Sue recalled, 'but I didn't see anyone after that.'

'Me neither,' agreed Olly. 'The only footprints I spotted were my own because I was going around in circles, and even those were slowly disappearing under the snow.'

'Is there any shelter up there if they are stuck?' asked Sue, trying to calculate how long someone could survive the elements. Certainly not overnight. 'There's an old fort, isn't there?'

Kelvin's features were grave. 'The ruins are exactly

that. A pattern of half-demolished walls, nothing more.'

'They could have become disoriented and walked back down on the wrong side,' offered Izzy, revisiting the fears she had harboured when Olly had gone missing.

'Or they could have had an accident,' Sue said, careful to avoid the using the term 'fall', for fear of resurrecting her own nightmares.

Kelvin turned to his wife. 'Did you see the Toyota arrive this morning? Do you know how many people there were?'

She wouldn't meet his gaze. 'It was a man on his own.'

'And was he kitted out for bad weather? Did you talk to him? Did he say where he was going?' Kelvin asked, his questions coming thick and fast.

Dee withdrew a step. 'I didn't … No … I don't know.'

'It's OK,' he said quickly. 'I'll phone around the farms, see if anyone has taken him in.'

'If he is in trouble, I'm a nurse. I can help,' Sue said, finding some relief in being able to focus on the plight of a stranger rather than dwell on Ray and Paige's predicament.

'That's good to know, but hopefully it won't come to that,' Kelvin said, taking out his phone to begin scrolling for numbers. 'Dee, can you show Sue where everything is so they can get fed and dry?' He stopped what he was doing to look up at his wife. His features softened, but anxiety remained. 'If you're up to it?'

'Sure, it'll give me a chance to get to know our new house guests,' Dee said, sounding more confident.

'Expect an interrogation,' Kelvin warned Sue. As he slipped past his wife, he squeezed her arm. 'I won't be long.'

Sue turned to her son-in-law. 'Olly, while I'm sorting things out, keep an eye on the traffic reports. If you see anything worrying, you need to let Ray and Paige know straight away.'

'Will do,' said Olly, showing her the mobile that seemed to be surgically attached to his hand.

'And as for you, Izzy,' Sue said. 'Put your feet up by the fire and rest while I sort things with Dee.'

Izzy touched the back of a chair but was reluctant to sit down on the hard wooden seat protected by a thin, removable cushion.

'Sorry, they're not very comfortable,' Dee said. 'We get a lot of muddy hikers so we don't go in for soft furnishings. There are more seat cushions in the dining room if you want to help yourself.'

'We're wet rather than muddy,' said Sue, glancing at the wet prints her feet were leaving on the flagstones.

'Then let's sort out a change of clothes first, shall we?'

'Good luck finding something to fit me,' Izzy said, patting her bump.

'I can always raid Kelvin's wardrobe. Don't worry, we'll find you something,' Dee promised.

Leaving the heat from the open fire, the corridor felt cool and Sue's damp trousers clung to her legs, chafing her skin and making her walk with a waddle. At the far end, there were stairs leading to the upper floor and several doors from which to choose.

'It's amazing how many of our guests can't read,' Dee said when she noticed Sue checking all the signage.

In the stairwell, there was a 'No Entry' sign dangling from a chain that could be hooked onto the opposite wall to bar entry, and if that failed, there was another on the wall further up declaring the upper floor private. Two doors had signs for male and female toilets, and the last door warned 'Staff Only'.

'You get special dispensation,' Dee said, opening the door to a compact but modern kitchen with a stainless-steel island in the middle for food prep.

'Something smells good,' said Sue, noting the two large pans on the industrial-sized range.

'We go through vats of soup, and today it's leek and potato, and Mulligatawny. We're leaving it to cool so we can freeze it, but please, take what you want.' Dee pulled a couple of smaller pans from a rack and set them on the range for Sue to use. 'And there's a coffee machine over there for hot drinks.'

'Thank you so much for this,' Sue said.

Dee wafted her hand as if it were nothing, and headed out through the back of the kitchen. There was another corridor with a fire exit at the end, but she stopped at the first door. 'All the catering supplies are in here, including bread, eggs, cereals, you name it,' she said before continuing. 'And this last room is for pretty much everything else we need to run the pub.'

The long utility room had a sink, washing machine and metal shelving crammed with supplies on one side, and a haphazard mix of cupboards and stacked boxes on the other, leaving only just enough space to walk down the middle.

'The washing machine is a dryer too, just not a very good one,' Dee explained. 'I find it much quicker putting clothes by the fire. And while you're waiting for your things to dry, see what you can find in here to wear.' She had stopped by a large plastic tub, and began rifling through a collection of cagoules, T-shirts and sweatpants. 'Looking at these, there's not much choice for Izzy, so I might have to pinch something of Kelvin's after all.'

'You and your husband are being so kind,' Sue said, feeling guilty about every bad thought she had harboured about Kelvin's initial inhospitality.

'We're happy to help,' replied Dee as she backed out of the room so Sue could rummage through the clothes for herself. As the two women passed each other, Dee touched Sue's back. 'And can I just say … I'm so sorry about your daughter.'

Sue's default response was to thank the person for their sympathies, but there was intense pain behind Dee's eyes that evoked an unexpected connection. 'Her death hit us hard,' she admitted. She took a breath but couldn't fill the void in her chest. 'I don't think I was ever meant to be this strong.'

'But you are,' said Dee, her eyes glistening. 'You have to be.'

'Yes, I do,' Sue agreed. 'But it isn't easy when your entire family is imploding. I worry so much about Paige.'

'Your granddaughter?'

'She should be going back to university next week

67

– it's her first year and they've been so good about her taking time out – but the way she is right now, I don't see how we can let her go,' said Sue, and it broke her heart to admit it. Ellen had wanted her daughter to go to university so much, not just for the qualification but for the experience. It was the dream Ellen had been denied at that age, and now history was repeating itself.

'But surely it should be Paige making that decision,' suggested Dee.

'I wish it were that simple. She's adamant she's going back. She wants to do it for Ellen, but what if she finds it too much? I don't think she'd tell us until it was too late. That's her dad's worst fear.'

'I'm so sorry,' Dee said, dipping her head quickly, but not before Sue caught the tears welling in her eyes.

'Are you OK?' Sue asked, watching Dee swipe a finger beneath her muddied make-up. She immediately regretted talking so openly about Paige's mental health with this stranger, but she had felt like Dee would understand. And perhaps that was the problem. It was becoming apparent that Dee understood mental health issues all too well.

'I'm tired, that's all,' said Dee, keeping her gaze to the floor. 'Do you mind if I leave you to it? I'll go upstairs and see what jumpers we have spare.'

As Sue watched Kelvin's wife leave, she realized she had been wrong to compare her to Ellen. Ellen had grown into a strong, self-assured woman who would have thrived into her forties if fate had allowed. Dee, by contrast, was impossibly fragile, and her life of relative isolation didn't appear to be doing her any good whatsoever.

Sue reminded herself that she had other people to worry about. Ray and Paige would hopefully be heading out of the valley by now, but the idea of them travelling beyond Sue's reach brought a fresh wave of panic that tightened her chest. She grabbed her phone. She hadn't wanted to pester them so soon, not least because the act condemned her to an anxious wait for a response, but she couldn't hold off any longer. She tapped out a message to Paige.

CHAPTER 10

PAIGE

When we drove away, I could hear the snow being churned up beneath tyres that struggled to find traction. I clung to my seat while Dad remained hunched over the steering wheel, peering past wiper blades that scooped away one layer of snow after another. When would it ever stop?

At least we were moving, I had to remind myself. I'd thought for one horrible moment that Nan would make everyone stay. I didn't blame Izzy for refusing to get in the car, and I was glad I didn't have to endure the drive home with Olly. He wouldn't leave me alone, wanting to know what I was going to do, who I was going to tell, pestering me even as I climbed into the car. I told him to shut the fuck up, that I had other things on my mind. And I did. I'd tried not to show any interest in the Toyota Kelvin thought was ours. Thank God I was leaving.

Except our progress down the mountain was slow. I had no sense of how far we'd gone other than it wasn't far enough. On the outward journey this morning, I'd been too interested in my phone to notice any landmarks, and even if I had, the storm had erased them. I wanted to ask Dad how much longer it would take to get off the damned mountain, but I didn't want to pester him. My nan, on the other hand ...

'Have you had a message?' he asked as I took my phone from my pocket after feeling it vibrate. 'Who's it from?'

'Just Nan wanting to know where we are.'

'How far does she think we were going to get?' asked Dad, his jaw tensing. 'We've only just left.'

He was usually good under pressure, but his frustration made him speed up, causing the car to judder then slide. My heart was in my mouth as we veered to the left where the side of the road fell steeply into mist, but Dad quickly corrected our course.

'Sorry,' he said. 'This is a nightmare, isn't it?'

'You're doing great.' There was no way I was going to let him turn back. I didn't actually care if we got stuck somewhere, just as long as it wasn't here. 'I'll text Nan back when we're out of the valley. The hardest bit will be over by then, won't it?'

'I hope so,' Dad replied. He took his eyes off the road to look at me. 'And I'm sorry about today.'

'Not as sorry as I am,' I said, thinking less about the disaster with Mum's ashes, and more about the arguments that had followed. 'I wish we could forget it ever happened.'

'Me too, darling.'

We were approaching a tight bend in the road and my entire body tensed. If we crashed, I tried to imagine what it would feel like as the car rolled into oblivion. How long would I remain conscious? Would it hurt? Or would it make the pain in my heart go away?

'Maybe it's more important to cherish the happy memories we have of Mum,' Dad said as if he could see the picture my mind had forced into my consciousness. Mum lying in a pool of blood at the bottom of the stairs.

'Was Mum happy?'

'Of course,' replied Dad with more of the confidence I was used to. 'You know she was.'

Did I? When she had been standing on the viewing platform, gazing into the distance to some place not visible to me or Dad, I had thought she was wistful, but what if she had been sad, or depressed even? It was a conversation I didn't want to get into with Dad, but who knew her better?

'I caught her crying a few times,' I admitted. 'Even while we were here.'

'You know what your mum was like, Paige. She could cry watching a comedy,' Dad said. He tried to smile, but the corners of his mouth tugged downwards. 'And if she was a bit sad that day, it was because you were about to leave us. I might have shed a tear myself. I still might.'

'I know you don't want me to go back to uni.'

The car skidded again, but Dad kept us moving forward. 'It's totally your decision, and I'll support you whatever you decide,' he said. 'I know you've worked hard to keep up with lectures as much as you can, but I don't think you appreciate how tough it'll be going back. It was already a big adjustment, and that was before you had your grief to deal with too. I'm sorry you only have me to fall back on. I can never replace your mum.'

I bit down on the inside of my cheek. I'd done enough crying for one day. 'I don't need you to replace Mum. You just need to keep on being you,' I said, trying to focus on what I did have. 'And you didn't have *any* family when you went to uni, and you managed fine.'

'That was different. Being in care most of your childhood teaches you resilience,' Dad replied. 'And just because I did it, doesn't mean I'd recommend it. I was constantly aware how different I was to all those students who had parents to escape from, or run back to. And I can guarantee you'll have people complaining about what their mums are, or aren't doing for them. You'll begin to resent them, which will make you feel even more isolated.'

'But I have friends already. They know about Mum. They wouldn't say anything so insensitive.'

'Do you want to bet?' asked Dad, then pursed his lips tight. 'Sorry, I promised myself I wouldn't push you one way or the other. Ignore me. I'm being selfish. It's me who won't be able to cope.'

'You'll be fine,' I said, but I wasn't sure I believed it.

I kept my gaze fixed ahead, struggling for something else to talk about. Daylight was fading and the snow appeared glaringly bright in the headlights. We were approaching another bend where the road followed the outer edge of the mountain. A particularly deep snowbank was impossible to avoid and the car's engine almost stalled. Dad put his foot down to keep us moving and the car jolted forward, but now we were picking up too much speed. I squeezed my eyes shut as the headlights glanced across the snowy mountain wall. We were heading straight for it, and Dad let out a grunt as he jerked the steering wheel to the left. The car was still moving too fast. We began to spin.

CHAPTER 11

KELVIN

'Hey, Sian. Is my car still in one piece?' Kelvin asked, keeping his tone light to counter the dark clouds hanging over his head. Unlike the ones that had heralded today's storm, these clouds had been gathering for months.

'As long as you don't miss having wing mirrors,' retorted his sister-in-law.

He could hear her smile down the line, but it couldn't ease the tension headache that amplified his anxiety and dulled his thoughts. 'I'd believe that if Rob had been driving,' he replied, leaning back against the wooden chair and rubbing his neck. He was in the dining room, sitting at one of the eight tables set for a lunch service that wasn't to be. Sian was his fifth call, having phoned around all his contacts in the valley to see if he could locate the missing man.

'So what's up? Is it Dee?' Sian asked, more perceptive than Kelvin was giving her credit for.

Sian had been spending as much time as she could afford at the pub, and although Kelvin would return the favour at the farm in the spring, her support went above and beyond their normal division of labour. She had been stepping in because Dee had stepped out, mentally speaking.

'Dee's helping our guests settle in,' he replied, and before Sian could express her shock at both halves of that sentence, he added, 'We have three people who couldn't get away in time, but that's not why I'm ringing. There's another hiker missing. His car's still in the car park, but there's no sign of him.'

'Which car?'

'A white Toyota,' said Kelvin.

In the pause that followed, he imagined Sian running through a mental list of the arrivals she had spotted that morning. 'Did he have fair hair? Wore a green Berghaus?'

'All I know is he was alone.' Kelvin was about to swallow back his disappointment when he realized what Sian was intimating. 'Wait, do you know who he is?'

'If it's the man I'm thinking of, he arrived mid-morning. I didn't speak to him, but he was chatting to Dee in the car park for a while. Have you asked her about him?'

Kelvin tilted his head as if he couldn't quite catch Sian's words, even though the phone line was perfectly clear. 'It must have been a different man.'

'He was the only lone hiker I spotted,' said Sian. 'And if he is missing, you need to raise the alarm pretty quick. Rob's already been called out to a search and rescue on Yr Wyddfa, and it's not going to be the last. All our volunteers are on high alert, and I'm worried we're not going to be able to assemble enough teams to meet demand.'

Sian was a local co-ordinator, having been roped into the local Mountain Rescue Service by Rob years ago. Kelvin suspected it was easier for her to be in the thick of it than left to imagine what her husband might be up against during call-outs. Kelvin had felt the same when Dee had been a volunteer, and probably with more reason to worry. His wife had been quite a risk-taker back then.

'If you're stretched, I don't want to add to your burden until I'm sure there's an issue,' Kelvin said.

'Fair enough, but you should still phone the police and log your concerns,' Sian told him. 'They can check the car's registered owner and try to locate him that way. He could have hitched a lift with someone else and just left his car.'

'That's what I'm hoping, but if not, I might go and do a quick search before the light fades completely,' said Kelvin, wincing in pain as the pressure behind his eyes intensified.

'OK, but be careful, and keep me informed.'

'I will. And thanks, Sian,' Kelvin said. 'Tell Rob to stay safe next time you speak to him.'

'Will do.'

Taking on board Sian's suggestion, Kelvin's next call should have been to the police, but he needed to talk to Dee first. Other than their brief exchange in the snug, they hadn't spoken since she had taken to her room that morning, and a conversation was well overdue. He popped his head into the snug, which was filled with the smell of damp and drying clothes. Olly was sitting forward on a chair, too engrossed in his phone to notice Kelvin, and Izzy was next to him, her head lolling on her husband's shoulder as she dozed. They were wearing mismatched and ill-fitting hoodies and sweatpants, as was Sue when he found her busy in the kitchen.

'I sent Paige a message twenty minutes ago, but she hasn't responded,' she said anxiously. 'And she's not answering her phone either.'

'I'm sure they'll be fine. Reception can be patchy in the valley.'

'Yes, that'll be it,' Sue said. She swallowed hard and set back her shoulders. 'Would you like some of the soup? I was just buttering some bread.' The oily knife glinted in her trembling hand.

'Thanks, but I don't think I could stomach food at the moment,' Kelvin replied, rubbing his throbbing temples.

'Me neither.' When Sue put down the knife, she didn't seem to know what to do with her hands.

'You can always help yourself to a stiff drink from the bar in the dining room,' Kelvin said. 'It might settle your nerves.'

'I'd love one, but I probably shouldn't. Not yet.'

Sue was expecting trouble. Unfortunately, Kelvin was too. 'You wouldn't know where my wife is, would you?'

'She went upstairs to find something roomier for Izzy,' Sue said. She held Kelvin's gaze. 'Is she OK? I was telling her about Ellen's death and how Paige isn't coping too well, and she became quite upset. I got the feeling it might have triggered something …?'

78

Her comment was posed as a question, but if Sue was fishing for information, Kelvin wasn't going to bite. 'Don't worry about it,' he said. He could worry enough for all of them.

As Kelvin climbed the stairs, he wondered how he had managed to become responsible for a bunch of strangers at a time when Dee needed his undivided attention. Having grown up on a farm, he was more accustomed to dealing with animals, and could tell at a glance if a cow or a sheep was in distress. People were a mystery to him, and that often included his wife. When they had first met, she had been an expert at keeping a veil over her emotional struggles, to the point that Kelvin hadn't known they were there.

It was Dee's parents who had warned him of what to expect. He and Dee had been dating for over a year before she took him home to Pantymwyn, and Kelvin soon realized why she had left it so long.

'We don't doubt that you care for our daughter,' Dee's father had said while Dee was out of the room, 'but she's more fragile than she likes to let on.'

'Has she told you how she had her heart broken the last time she was "involved" with someone?' asked her mother, drawing the quotation marks in the air.

'It wasn't only her heart that was broken though, was it?' added her father, giving Kelvin no chance to respond. 'It was her mind.'

'She was in a terrible state,' Dee's mother said.

'And all because of an obsession with a man she had only known for a couple of months.'

'If that,' her mother interjected.

Dee's father looked grim. 'The truth is, I don't think she'd survive another break-up.'

'She almost didn't survive that one. She was away at university at the time, and if one of the other girls hadn't found her ...' Her mother choked up.

'An overdose,' Dee's father said bluntly. 'So, you can see why we would be concerned about any new relationship, and why Dee was keeping quiet about you.' The sound of a toilet flushing upstairs made him speak with more urgency. 'If you love her as much as we do, don't put her through that kind of hurt again. Protect her from herself.'

Kelvin had the distinct impression their preference would have been for him to let their daughter down gently, but it had been too late for that. When he had fallen for Dee, he had fallen hard, and that rush of love was as strong as ever as he reached their living quarters. The rooms above the pub had been their home for all fifteen years of their married life. And it had been a happy life, surpassing all of Dee's parents' expectations. There were plenty of times when he had looked back at their dire warnings and laughed, but not now.

As the pressure behind his eyes intensified, he paused on the landing. The upper floor consisted of a living area with a kitchenette, a bathroom and three bedrooms. And because there would always be customers who ignored the 'No Entry' signs, there were combination locks on every door. Kelvin punched in the code to his and Dee's bedroom and found her rifling through their wardrobe.

'How are you doing?' he asked.

She kept her back to him. 'I'm fine.'

It was a lie Dee had been telling Kelvin for the best part of six months, and he had no way of knowing if her dark, despondent moods were rooted in the past, the present or somewhere in between, but the speed with which they could overwhelm her frightened him. She had seemed happy enough this morning, chatting to Sian and helping prepare the pub for opening as usual, but by midday, she had locked herself away. Was that just how it was now, or had something happened? Sue had talked of triggers. Had Kelvin missed one that morning?

'I haven't had much luck with the missing man,' he said, watching carefully for her reaction.

'Do you think this will fit a pregnant woman?' Dee was stretching one of Kelvin's jumpers.

'Maybe.' He left a beat for his wife to respond to what he had just said, but she continued to drag garments from the wardrobe. Kelvin's headache was making him nauseous. 'Dee, they've already changed into dry clothes. If you want to give Izzy a jumper, that blue one will do.'

Dee picked up the cable knit in the middle of the pile she had made on the bed. 'It might be tight.'

When she began searching the wardrobe again, Kelvin snapped. 'Dee, please. Enough.'

The ear-splitting scrape of coat hangers being dragged across the rail continued.

'I suppose we might need extra clothes for the missing man,' he mused, pushing again for a reaction. 'Assuming he makes it back here.'

81

Dee's grip tightened around the sleeve of a shirt. He could hear her breaths, loud and hard as cotton crumpled in her fist. Without another word, she shoved the shirt back into place and shut the wardrobe door. She moved to the window. She still hadn't looked at him.

Kelvin went over to stand close enough for their shoulders to touch. The only sound was their synchronized breaths and the tiny snaps of snowflakes as they hit the window. The world beyond was a featureless landscape of grey and white, the mountainside no more than a dark smear on a blank canvas. The car park was a flat plane of snow with only the occasional bump to mark a fence or a vehicle. One car in particular drew his attention.

'If White Toyota Man is stuck out there, I don't rate his chances,' Kelvin told her. 'Did he tell you where he was going?'

He heard Dee's dry lips part, but her mouth closed again.

'Dee, I know you spoke to him. Did he say something to upset you? Is he the reason you've been hiding away?'

Dee's chin disappeared into the folds of her roll-neck jumper, like a tortoise retreating into its shell.

'Who is he?'

'No one,' she whispered.

'You're not acting as if he's a no one,' he said softly, placing a hand on the small of her back.

Dee turned quickly and pressed her forehead to his chest, letting out a stifled sob. He wrapped her tightly in his arms, his heart clenching.

'It's OK, I'm here,' he whispered. 'I love you, Dee, but

please, you have to tell me what's going on. Do you know him?'

'No,' Dee said. 'Not really.'

A thousand spiders crawled down Kelvin's spine as they neared the truth. There was only one person he could imagine eliciting the kind of pain Dee's parents had feared would revisit their daughter one day. 'What does that mean?'

Dee kept her brow pressed against his chest so he couldn't see her expression. 'He just reminded me of someone, that's all.'

A resemblance to another man? That was all it was? Kelvin willed himself to feel relief, but when Dee looked up at him and he took in her red, puffy eyes and trembling lip, he knew the threat was real, to her at least. 'Why didn't you tell me?' He cupped a hand under her chin, sensing she would drop her gaze otherwise.

'I thought, once he'd gone ...'

'Except he hasn't gone,' said Kelvin. 'And I don't know what to do. If he is stuck somewhere, and we can find him, would you be able to deal with him coming back here?'

Dee's body tensed, and her eyes flitted to the window. 'He's really missing?'

'It looks that way.'

'Then we can't leave him. He'll die if he stays out there.'

'I know. Which is why I need your help finding him,' he said carefully. 'Do you know where he went?'

Dee wiped away snot and tears with the sleeve of her

jumper. 'He would have followed the blue route.'

'Are you sure?' Kelvin asked with surprise. 'Sue's party didn't pass him. I was thinking he must have taken the red route and got into trouble at the top.'

'No. He didn't come here to see the ruins.'

'Then why was he here?'

Before Dee could respond, there was a shout from downstairs. 'Kelvin! We need you! There's been an accident!' Sue yelled, fear choking her words.

CHAPTER 12

SUE

Sue had her phone clasped in her hand as Kelvin raced down the stairs. 'Ray messaged me. He says they lost control of the car and now it's stuck in a snowbank.'

'How far did they get?'

She glanced back at her phone, her brow furrowed. 'He didn't say, but he must be on the mountain because they're on their way back to us.'

'Can you check?'

'I've already tried phoning both of them, but either the call doesn't connect or it rings out. You did say reception was patchy.'

'Further down in the valley, yeah,' Kelvin replied with a sigh. He checked his watch. 'They left over an hour ago, so it must be some distance. Damn. It was madness to even try getting through in that car.'

Sue didn't like the tone of his 'told you so' voice, but she couldn't disagree. She shouldn't have let them go. 'Will they be able to get back here safely, do you think?'

'There's a chance they didn't get as far as you'd imagine,' Olly said. He was standing on the threshold of the snug, listening to Sue's conversation while keeping one eye on Izzy. 'They probably spent some of the last hour trying to dig out the car. And Ray's message may not have sent straight away if there was no signal where they stopped.'

It was the first time in a long while that Sue was grateful for Olly's input. She hadn't found it as easy as her daughter to forgive him for running home to his parents after finding out she was pregnant, but perhaps this crisis was his chance to step up. And what he said made sense. Kelvin was nodding, which was a good sign.

'And the nearer they get to the pub, the stronger the signal will be,' their host said. 'They could actually be close.'

All eyes darted to the wide oak door. There was only one small window of blown glass that looked out onto the darkening day.

'I'll try phoning again,' Sue said as if there was an alternative plan to fall back on. What would they do if Ray and Paige didn't appear soon? She wouldn't be sitting in front of a roaring fire twiddling her thumbs, that much was certain. The soup she had forced herself to eat churned in her stomach as she listened to Ray's phone ring and ring and ring. Kelvin and Olly watched as she shook her head. 'I'll try Paige.'

'The number you are trying to call ...' came a tinny voice down the line.

As Sue cut the call, she fought her rising panic. Why would one phone ring out and the other not connect?

Either they were both in range of a mast, or they weren't. Unless they weren't together. She tried to recall if it had been Paige's phone that had been unable to connect earlier too. What if she wasn't with Ray? What if the snowbank they hit had caused an avalanche that had crushed the car? What if Ray was on his way back alone, preparing to break some awful news to Sue in person? What if ...

'We have to do something,' she said, her heart hammering in her chest.

'But what?' asked Olly.

'I was about to call emergency services to report our missing White Toyota Man,' Kelvin explained. 'If Ray and Paige aren't back soon, I can explain their situation too.'

'But we need to start looking now,' Sue told him. 'They could be ... It could be too late by the time we find them. Isn't there a Mountain Rescue Service we can call?'

Kelvin raked his fingers through his hair. 'My brother and sister-in-law are volunteers, and they're already dealing with other incidents across the region. Unsurprisingly, they're expecting a busy night.' His features remained grim. 'I don't want to draw on their stretched resources until we know what we're dealing with. We keep some equipment here in case of emergencies, and I was going to do a quick sweep of the area anyway. I just wasn't expecting to have to go down the mountain as well as up.'

'Can I help?' asked Olly.

'Actually, I was hoping you'd say that,' Kelvin said, although he didn't look any happier. 'We have extra outdoor gear upstairs, so once you're kitted out, I suggest we make a start before the temperature drops further.' He was looking at Sue when he added, 'We won't be able to go too far now that we have two search areas, but it should be enough to assess the situation.'

'I'll come too,' Sue said, fixing Kelvin with her steely gaze. 'If Ray or Paige are injured, they'll need me. Do you have a first aid kit?'

'You're all leaving me?' Izzy asked. She had appeared from the snug, hands circling her abdomen for fear that anyone should forget her condition.

'You'll be fine,' said Sue, jumping in before Kelvin could use her daughter as leverage to make her stay. 'Kelvin's wife is still here. She can keep an eye on you.'

'It's going to be OK, babe,' said Olly, reaching out to still her hands. 'I won't be too far away, and I'll come back straight away if you need me.'

'But what if you get stuck out there? Who's going to come and rescue you? I don't want to be alone with a stranger if something happens.' Her lip quivered.

Sue caught a shadow crossing the window in the entrance door. Something had moved in front of the spotlights that had come on across the car park, and for one delicious moment, she thought all their prayers had been answered, but the flicker had been just that, and stillness returned. She refocused on her daughter. 'Don't do this, Izzy.'

'Do what?' she demanded. 'Put my unborn baby's needs ahead of two idiots who should have known better than to drive away in a blizzard?'

Sue could almost hear her patience snap. How could

Izzy be so casual about Paige's safety? She was their last link to Ellen. 'Your baby's fine, and no one is putting either of you in danger. I stayed here because of you, remember? Christ, I wish I had gone with Ray now!'

'Shush,' said Olly.

Sue's blood pressure soared, and she was about to explode at her son-in-law when she realized he was looking towards the entrance.

'Did you hear that?' he asked.

Everyone held their breath. There was a soft rasping sound that might be a fox sniffing around, searching out shelter, but the noise grew louder until there was no doubting the soft crunch of boots trampling snow. The footsteps were drawing nearer.

Kelvin went to the door, and Sue fought an impulse to pull him back. It might be Ray and Paige returning, but it could just as easily be the owner of the Toyota. She wasn't sure she could cope with having her hopes dashed. She had no desire to see a faceless stranger whose life might mean something to someone, but not to her.

'I think I'm going to be sick,' she said as Kelvin invited a blast of cold air into the pub. There was only one figure in the doorway: a man.

Ray shook the snow from his shoulders. 'Are you still taking in waifs and strays?'

'Where's Paige?' Sue asked, rushing forward.

Kelvin was smiling as he ushered Ray into the warmth. 'Well, that's two of our missing persons located.'

'Two?' Sue repeated, looking over her son-in-law's shoulder. Paige was hiding in his shadow, snow continuing

89

to settle on her jacket which was now more white than yellow.

'Paige! Oh, sweetheart, I've been so worried,' Sue said, dragging her out of the cold and into her arms.

Kelvin shut the door. 'You didn't see anyone else during your travels, did you? We have one more car than we should in the car park,' he explained to Ray, not giving him the chance to recover from his ordeal.

Ray blew air out of his mouth. 'I was only concentrating on the road when I was driving down, but we certainly didn't see any other footprints on the way back. Sorry.'

'Will he die out there?' Paige asked, eyes wide.

Kelvin turned to Sue. 'I'd better make that call to the emergency services,' he said, avoiding the question. 'They should be able to find out who owns the Toyota and trace our missing man that way. But unless we hear otherwise, I still think a search is necessary. And the sooner the better.'

'If you're planning on calling for back-up, I'm afraid our car is blocking the road,' Ray said. 'We did try to move it.'

'Well, that doesn't make things any easier, but I was going to lead the search myself,' Kelvin explained. He sighed. 'Hopefully, we won't have to call on extra help.'

'What if he needs to go to hospital?' Paige asked, louder this time.

'We don't even know he's out there for certain. It's nothing for you to worry about,' said Sue as Kelvin withdrew to the dining room to make his call. 'Let's get you two warmed up.'

In the snug, Paige covered her face with her hands, but Ray was too dazed to think about hiding his feelings. 'We left Ellen in the car,' he said. 'I thought it would be safest, but I feel like I've abandoned her.'

'Her ashes will be fine where they are,' Sue reassured him as she peeled off his coat.

Olly offered to take Paige's jacket, but true to form, she insisted on doing it herself. Seats were positioned around the fire, including one for Izzy, but Sue's youngest daughter ignored the offer and retreated to a bench in the furthermost corner. She kept her head down and her lip protruded. Sue regretted snapping at her, but apologies would have to wait.

'Shall I make some hot drinks?' Olly suggested once he had rearranged the growing heap of damp clothes.

'That's a good idea. Thanks, Olly,' Sue said. She waited until he had disappeared with their orders before turning to Ray. 'So what happened?'

Ray leant close enough to the fire for the flickering flames to highlight the shadows in his gaunt features. 'I wasn't driving fast, but the turns in the road were tight,' he said. He looked to Paige for confirmation, but she was staring intently into her lap. 'I lost control and for a second I thought we were going to go over the side of the mountain.'

Sue gasped, not liking how her worst fears had almost come to pass. 'Someone was looking down on you.'

'It would be nice to think so,' Ray said with the saddest smile. 'It was still scary as we ploughed into the snowbank, but the impact wasn't too bad. I tried reversing, but the wheels were just spinning on the compacted snow and we couldn't go any further. Our first plan was to keep heading down on foot and search for a farm, but there really was no other choice but to retrace our steps.'

'You're here now. That's the important thing,' said Sue, feeling the knot in her stomach begin to loosen.

'For the time being,' Ray said. 'I was thinking ...' He looked uncomfortable as he considered his next suggestion. 'Maybe there's a way we could break into the Toyota. We'd have to tow our car out of the way to get past, but it's worth a shot.'

'You can't do that!' Paige said, her head jolting up.

'I'm not keen on the idea either,' Ray said, 'but what if the car has been abandoned? We'd give it back and pay for any damage, obviously. It has to be better than being trapped up here for goodness knows how long.'

'How would we start it?' asked Izzy from the back of the room. 'I don't know how to hot-wire a car. Do you?'

'No disrespect, but I thought Olly might be able to give it a go,' Ray replied. 'He's good at the technical stuff. I bet he could find a YouTube video somewhere that would help.'

'No, I'm with Paige. It's still stealing,' said Sue. 'And besides, it's too dark to do anything tonight.' She delivered this last comment as an order rather than a statement. 'With any luck, the snow will turn back to rain tomorrow, and Kelvin might be able to get one of his farmer friends to move your car with a tractor. Please, can we leave the law-breaking until we have no other choice?'

'I hate this,' Paige grumbled.

'We'll be home soon,' said Sue, placing a hand on her granddaughter's knee. 'Gosh, your jeans are sodden. Dee has a big tub of spare clothes. I'll get you something to change into.'

'Dee?' asked Ray.

Sue lowered her voice. 'Kelvin's wife. Don't expect to see a lot of her. She seems quite delicate at the moment, but her heart's in the right place.'

CHAPTER 13

KELVIN

A single candle flickered on the table, leaving the outer edges of the bar and dining room draped in shadow. Kelvin closed his eyes and kneaded his scalp, listening to the rasp of fingernails echo inside his head as he sought to release the pressure. He didn't realize he had company until someone cleared their throat behind him.

'Do you want a coffee?' asked Olly. 'I've been making drinks for everyone.'

'No, thanks,' Kelvin replied, heaving himself out of his chair. 'I don't think caffeine would do my headache much good.'

'Any news on White Toyota Man?'

Kelvin wished they didn't have to keep calling him that. The police had pulled up the registered owner details while Kelvin was on the phone, but they had been unwilling to share much information other than the fact he was married. 'I've reported him as a potential missing person, and the police are going to try to contact his wife.'

'She hasn't reported him missing already?'

'Not that I'm aware of. Which could mean she knows where he is. It's still possible he travelled home from here with someone else. Maybe his car wouldn't start.'

'Is there CCTV we could check?'

'We're in the middle of nowhere. It's never felt necessary.'

'You don't actually believe he left earlier, do you?' asked Olly, watching Kelvin rub his head again. 'Surely he would have let you know if he was leaving his car here.'

'I think you're right,' Kelvin said reluctantly.

Olly bounced from heel to heel. 'So what next? Are we going out searching? Your wife's sorted out a load of outdoor gear for us.'

'You've seen Dee?'

'No, but she left all kinds of stuff at the bottom of the stairs. Backpacks, walking sticks, even a foldaway stretcher. She's been busy.'

Dee had come out onto the landing when Kelvin had gone downstairs to Sue, and would have heard his plans for a search. She would want to help, but her need to hide away persisted. Kelvin could only imagine what memories White Toyota Man had inadvertently evoked to make her fears so tangible. At least he wasn't the actual man from her past. Dee had shared enough with Kelvin over the years to know that this nameless man had been aware that she was suicidal and had turned his back on her anyway. That would be someone Kelvin would gladly leave to his own fate.

'Are you sure you want to do this, Olly?' he asked.

Olly smiled. 'I'll go and get ready.'

While the younger man went to change, Kelvin climbed the stairs. He punched in the combination code to their bedroom, only to find the door bolted from the inside. Dee had upgraded her blockade. He knocked, trying not to read too much into it. 'It's me,' he said gently through the door panels.

He heard the bolt being pulled back and his wife opened the door, just wide enough for him to enter.

'What's happening?' she asked, closing the door again.

Kelvin tried not to dwell on her blotchy complexion. 'We have five guests now. I take it you heard Ray and Paige coming back.'

'Are they staying? Overnight?'

'There's no other choice, Dee. Especially now their car's blocking the road. Do you think you can reorganize our junk to give them space in the spare rooms to sleep?' he asked, hoping the task would take her mind off her anxiety, but Dee's hands fluttered to her throat. Quickly he added, 'If you're not up to it, I can sort it when I get back.'

'Do you have to go?'

'I don't want to leave you,' he said, placing a hand on her cheek and wiping away a tear with his thumb. 'But what choice do I have?'

'None,' she said, because why else had she bothered to root out all the rescue equipment? She turned her face to kiss the palm of his hand. 'I'm sorry.'

'For what?'

'For everything.'

Kelvin wrapped his wife in his arms. He had never felt so out of his depth, and had a sudden irrational fear that it wasn't safe to leave Dee on her own. He was already spending too much time as it was preoccupied with the needs of complete strangers. This was madness.

'I love you,' he whispered. 'And if you want me to stay, I will.' He could feel her about to object. 'No one else has reported this man missing yet, so we could be chasing shadows.'

Dee pulled away and drew herself up straight. 'Whether someone's missing him or not, he's out there.'

'I don't want to leave you,' he said, as their roles reversed.

'And I don't want you to go, but you have to find Jonah.'

Kelvin cocked his head. 'You know his name?' he asked, trying to disguise the suspicion in his voice.

'He introduced himself,' she said, backing away. 'Please, you need to get going. The longer you leave it, the thicker the snow will be.'

Kelvin remained frozen to the spot. 'You will be all right, won't you?'

'I'll be fine,' she said, almost succeeding in offering a smile.

'If anything were to happen to you, Dee, I'd never forgive myself.'

She was momentarily confused, then she did smile. 'For God's sake, Kelvin, I'm not going to do anything stupid.'

Dee's dismissal was so convincing that it made Kelvin feel foolish for even thinking she might harm herself.

That wasn't who Dee was, not any more. He hoped. 'Are you sure?'

She fixed him with her gaze. 'Yes. Go.'

This brief glimpse of the inner strength he knew his wife possessed was enough for Kelvin to break through his paralysis. 'Fine,' he said. 'And don't be worrying about me. I won't take any chances.'

Kelvin changed into his outdoor gear then headed downstairs, but not before he heard the bolt on their bedroom door slide back into place. Determined not to let Dee out of his sight for too long, he hurried to the snug in search of Olly. What he didn't expect was to find three people dressed for an arctic expedition.

'What's going on?' he asked.

'We're coming with you,' said Ray, zipping up an old coat of Kelvin's from at least five years ago. Olly sported an even older jacket that Kelvin used for messy jobs, while Paige wore one of Dee's old ski jackets with matching trousers.

'I've tried telling them,' Sue explained. 'You're just lucky they persuaded me to stay.'

CHAPTER 14

PAIGE

I speared the snow with one of my walking sticks, cutting through an icy crust that had formed since my failed attempt to escape the mountain. To think, I'd been relieved to discover Jonah wasn't waiting for me in the pub when I'd got back. I should have known the minute Dad found out there was someone lost or injured, he would want to help. I couldn't tell him Jonah was the last person he would want to save. But his mind was made up, and so was mine. If Jonah had to be found, I needed to be there.

'It's getting colder,' I said, noticing how white the vapour clouds from my breath appeared against the yellow spotlights in the car park.

'At least it's stopped snowing,' Dad replied, lifting his face to the haze of a full moon that was breaking through the clouds.

'The temperature will drop even further as the sky clears, so we don't want to stay out longer than we have to,' Kelvin warned as he strode ahead, forcing the pace. He didn't seem aware of the heavy backpack he was carrying. We had shared the equipment between us, but his load was the heaviest. He checked we were following. 'Are you sure you two are up for this? You haven't had a chance to recover properly.'

'I couldn't have sat back and watched you and Olly set off on your own,' Dad said. He was slightly breathless, but he kept shoulder to shoulder with Kelvin. He glanced towards me. 'It's not too late if you want to go back, Paige.'

'No way,' I said as we reached the car park perimeter. I could hear Olly lumbering behind me with a folded stretcher strapped to his back, and my skin crawled.

The dense woodland quickly swallowed us up, and the moonlight wasn't enough to compensate. We paused to switch on our torches and I took the opportunity to let Olly go in front so I knew where he was. Kelvin misinterpreted my reluctance for exhaustion.

'Ray, I think you and Paige should restrict yourselves to the lower sections of our search area while Olly and I work our way up.'

Olly arced his torch towards Kelvin. 'You want us to split up?'

'We can keep in contact by phone.'

'But what if something happens?' Olly continued. 'Isn't that asking for trouble?'

'Better than all four of us getting stuck at once,' Kelvin replied. Quickly, he added, 'Not that any of us are going to do anything that puts us in danger. We're going to follow the blue route, so you'll all be familiar with it. Stay on the path, and use your torches to search the wider area.'

'Fine by me,' said Dad.

I was less eager to agree. We weren't going to find Jonah on the blue route, and I wished I didn't care that we would be looking in the wrong place, but I was too much like my dad. If Jonah was injured, I couldn't leave him to die. I just didn't want him talking to Dad.

The others continued to follow the trail that would ultimately divide into the two routes. 'This is wrong; we should be searching the red route!' I said, shouting loud enough to bring everyone to a halt.

Kelvin adjusted the equipment on his back and grimaced. 'If he's here, he has to be close to the blue route. He told my wife this morning that was where he was heading.'

'But we already know he's not there!' I shouted angrily.

'Paige has a point,' Olly said, looking to me as if I should be grateful he had my back. 'Ray and I were searching for Paige all over this side of the mountain earlier, and we would surely have bumped into him then.'

'We managed to lose each other quite easily,' Dad reminded us.

I stabbed my walking stick into the ground and stood firm. 'Fine, I'll take the red route by myself,' I said. If I could save Jonah single-handedly, he would be indebted. This was buying his silence.

'No, Paige, it's too risky to go up there,' Dad said in a tone he had only used when I was a little girl, but I would always be a child in his eyes. 'The best way we can help this man is to not become victims ourselves. We had a close enough call earlier.'

'Then why bother to search at all?' I asked. 'Even a man with two broken legs and enough determination could drag himself back down the blue route. It wouldn't be that hard.'

'Unless he got a foot trapped in a rock, or was knocked unconscious,' Dad suggested. Despite his good intentions, he was more interested in protecting me than finding our potential casualty.

'Look,' said Kelvin, 'maybe you have a point, Paige, but I have to put your safety above anything else.' He paused to collect his thoughts, clouds of vapour circling his face. 'So, if we do split up, and I think we should, Olly and I could take a look along the lower half of the red route. There might be a chance Jonah started off on the blue route but looped across using the link path.'

'You need to search the ruins too,' I said, hoping no one would stop to wonder why I was so certain Jonah had made it to the top.

I couldn't tell them it was the last place I'd seen him. In fact, it was the one and only time we had met. All our interactions up until that point had been via messages. That was how he had won my trust. I shuddered. I'd been so certain I didn't want to see him again. I still didn't, but I'd already tried messaging him when I found out he was missing. I hadn't expected an answer after what had happened, but it might have put my mind at ease.

'I'll assess the conditions once we're up there,' Kelvin

said, making no promises. 'Meanwhile, you and your dad should keep to the blue route as planned so we cover all bases.'

'But I've been on the red route too,' I persisted. 'I came down that way this morning. I should be the one to go with you.' I glanced at Olly. 'I can manage the tough terrain far better than *he* can.'

'No, Paige,' Dad said firmly. 'I want you to stay with me.'

'There is a chance I won't be able to keep up with you,' Olly warned Kelvin. 'I don't want to slow you down.'

'You're stronger than you think, Olly,' Dad said, patting his shoulder.

'We stay as we are,' agreed Kelvin, but he was looking at Olly's back. 'Ray, do you think you and Paige could take the stretcher up to the viewing platform? Then if we need it, I know where to head.'

'Sure thing.'

'OK, let's get moving,' Kelvin said as they resumed their journey. 'It's possible Jonah is unconscious, but it's still worth shouting his name.'

'I thought you didn't know his name,' remarked Olly.

Kelvin chewed his lip. 'Oh, the police checked his vehicle reg.'

My mouth felt suddenly dry. I didn't like how Jonah had wormed his way into our lives. Could this all be part of the game he was playing, or was I being paranoid? My overactive mind was imagining all kinds of things: rocks beneath the snow ready to trip me up; a gust of wind that might be a distant cry for help; the shadows flitting between the trees that could be someone watching us. I was losing touch with reality.

We didn't stop again until we reached the snow-covered signpost. There was one arrow pointing to the blue route, the other to the red.

'I guess this is where we go our separate ways,' said Kelvin.

CHAPTER 15

KELVIN

Kelvin swept his torch in a wide arc, highlighting the base of one tree trunk before moving on to the next as the ground rose higher.

'Are you sure we're still on the path?' Olly asked between loud pants for breath.

'Don't worry, this isn't the first time I've been called out on a rescue mission. That's why we keep all the gear in the pub.'

'I don't know how you do it,' said Olly, scrambling up a particularly steep slope. 'How much longer do you think it'll take to reach the link path?'

'With the snow this deep, I figure it'll take another half hour or so.'

'I'm sorry for slowing you down,' Olly replied, guessing Kelvin had factored in his partner's limitations.

Paige had been right about Olly being less able, but Kelvin had faith in him. He did seem to be the downtrodden member of the group and, like Ray, Kelvin suspected Olly just needed to believe in himself.

'You're doing fine,' Kelvin said, using one of his walking sticks to prod the ground in front of him before taking a step. 'Just follow my tracks.'

'Will we go right to the top, do you think?'

'I doubt it,' Kelvin said despite Paige having argued a good case. Unless he was sure a life was in danger, he wouldn't put an inexperienced team at risk. 'We can decide once we get there.'

'At least coming down will be easier,' Olly said, already sounding excited by the prospect of returning to the pub.

While Kelvin waited for Olly to catch up, he continued to sweep the surrounding area. The glistening snow covered the woodland in a deep blanket that muffled the sounds of their laboured breaths and the occasional twitter of a bird disturbed from sleep.

'Has it been this bad before?' Olly asked.

'Plenty of times, although this one took us by surprise.'

'Aren't you worried about getting cut off living up here? What if the pipes freeze, or there's a power outage?'

'We'd manage,' Kelvin said. 'The problem isn't so much being cut off, it's who you end up cut off with.'

Olly laughed. 'We must come across as the family from hell.'

'Every family has its issues.'

'You'd be hard pressed to find one as messed up as—' Olly's foot snagged on a rock hidden beneath the snow and he stumbled.

'Are you OK?' asked Kelvin.

'Fine.'

106

Kelvin found himself smiling at the way Olly was trying not to hobble even though his discomfort was written all over his face. He didn't want to let Kelvin down.

Eventually, they reached the edge of the woodland where the ground rose sharply ahead of them. The light from the moon picked out the black silhouette of a snowy peak.

'Wow,' said Olly. 'We didn't see any of this earlier, there was too much cloud cover.'

Kelvin pointed out a craggy outcrop. 'You should be able to make out the old fort ruins, and if you follow the ridge down on the east side, that takes you directly above the viewing platform. You can see why the blue route couldn't continue upwards unless you fancy a bit of rock climbing.'

'I'll give it a miss, thanks.'

'Me too,' replied Kelvin.

He kept looking up to the ruins. The time had come to decide whether or not to go on. He had hoped they would have stumbled across Jonah by now, or at least some sign that he had been there. There was nothing.

Lowering his gaze, Kelvin used his walking stick to point out the dark hem of trees they had just emerged from. 'The treeline encircling the hill marks the link path that connects the two main routes. If Jonah was ahead of you on the blue route but you never saw him, it makes sense that's the path he took. Maybe he saw your group and wanted to give you some space.'

'He probably heard us arguing,' said Olly. 'We didn't behave very well, I'm afraid.'

'The question is, what happened to him next,' Kelvin mused. 'We're a little higher than you were this morning, so if he did reach this point, Jonah would have been inside the cloud cover. He'd know there'd be no point going up to the ruins.'

'Maybe he didn't get this far.'

'Then we need to search the link path,' Kelvin concluded, relieved they had a good argument for what still felt like abandoning the climb.

As they set off, Kelvin used the opportunity to find out more about the family he had inadvertently taken responsibility for. 'It can't have been easy for you all to lose a family member so suddenly.'

'Things were a mess before we lost Ellen,' Olly said. Under his breath, he added, 'I fucked up royally.'

Kelvin glanced over his shoulder, a frown forming. 'They do seem to give you a hard time, if you don't mind me saying.'

Olly looked away. Blinked. 'I deserve it. I haven't treated Izzy very well.'

'She seems to care a lot about you,' Kelvin said, recalling how Olly's wife had stood watch by the window.

'And I care a lot about her. I love her,' Olly said, choking. 'It just took me a while to realize how much. We met through work – I'm in IT, she's in design – and I was never going to have the courage to ask her out, so she asked me. Izzy's good at taking the initiative, but … everything just seemed to happen so fast.'

Olly had slowed down and Kelvin had to wait for him to catch up.

'I wasn't expecting it when she said she was pregnant,' he continued. 'We broke up for a while, and I went back to my parents to give us both some space. And you know how one mistake leads to another, then another? Izzy deserved better from me. And if you're thinking I can't be as bad as they make out, you're wrong. If anything, I'm worse.'

'I don't know you very well,' Kelvin said, choosing to continue their trek rather than stare at a grown man on the verge of tears. 'But I think you're a decent bloke.'

Olly released a sigh, and whatever he said next was just out of hearing, but it sounded something like, 'Oh, but you don't know me at all.'

CHAPTER 16

SUE

It was a case of déjà vu as Sue sat by the fire while her daughter paced in front of the window, waiting for Paige, Ray and Olly to return. She watched Izzy move a hand across her abdomen in sweeping, soothing strokes. Sue could remember Ellen being that pregnant. It was hard to believe she would have been around the same age as Paige at the time. It was harder to believe she wasn't there any more.

'How long do you think they'll be?' asked Izzy, interrupting her thoughts.

'Long enough for you to wear a track in those flagstones.'

Izzy stopped pacing and gave Sue a hard stare. 'How can you sit there like you're on a little country break?'

'Worrying won't get them home any faster,' Sue said as if she were immune to anxiety. She was simply better at hiding it. 'Kelvin seems to know his stuff. They'll be fine.'

'Do you still wish you'd gone with them?'

Sue took a breath and held it a moment. Her youngest had never possessed the same level of maturity as Ellen. 'I want to look after you, Iz,' she said. 'I'm sorry for snapping at you earlier, but we're all stressed after the day we've had, and that includes me. None of us are saints.'

'I don't expect you to be a saint, Mum. I just expect you to have my back,' said Izzy. 'I know I'm not Ellen ...'

When Izzy paused, Sue knew this was where she was supposed to say she had always loved both her daughters equally and unconditionally, and she did, but it had been a long and exhausting day, and it was Ellen's birthday. Why did it always have to be down to Sue to soothe everyone else's feelings when her own loss was crushing the air from her lungs? Who had her back?

'It's not just about what's happened today, or the last couple of months,' Izzy continued. 'I've been struggling pretty much from the moment I saw that blue line on the pregnancy test.'

Slowly, Sue found the strength to twist in her chair to give Izzy her full attention. 'I know what you went through, I was there,' she reminded her daughter. She had seen the pregnancy test stick, and she had heard Izzy recount her argument with Olly, which had taken place over the phone, because of course he had been away at one of his silly Comic Con weekends at the time. 'And no one's more disappointed than I that Olly didn't take to fatherhood the way you imagined, but I'm sorry, some men don't.'

111

'Olly isn't anything like my father, if that's what you're insinuating,' Izzy said, immediately picking up the inference.

Sue's ex-husband had walked out when she was pregnant with Izzy, and the only difference Sue could see was that it had taken a second pregnancy before he ran away. 'Maybe he's not like your dad, but he's no Ray either.'

Izzy crossed her arms and rested them on her bump. 'Why does everyone have to compare him to Ray? Maybe he isn't the kind of man who gets down on bended knee the moment he hears he's going to be a dad, but he is trying so bloody hard to make it up to me. I just wish you'd give him a chance.'

'Is it too much to want you to have someone who loves and cherishes you without being heavy-armed into it?' Sue asked. 'That's all I ever wanted for both my girls.'

'Even me? The one who destroyed your marriage simply by existing?'

'You didn't—'

'No, Mum,' her daughter interrupted. 'You've always resented me!'

Izzy had moved closer to the fire, and Sue could see the reflection of the flames flickering across her face. 'Is that what you think?'

Tears were brimming in Izzy's eyes as she shrugged. She had been expecting her mum to immediately deny the accusation, but Sue hadn't, which was as shocking to her as it was to Izzy. Sue did love her daughters equally, but it would be fair to say that she loved them differently.

Had that difference been rooted in the role her second pregnancy had played in the breakdown of her marriage? Before she could find a way of reassuring her daughter and herself that it wasn't true, Izzy continued.

'Having a husband who worships the ground you walk on isn't all it's cracked up to be, Mum. It drove Ellen mad.'

'If you're suggesting her marriage wasn't perfect, of course it wasn't. No marriage is.'

'Perfect?' Izzy made a noise at the back of her throat, not quite a laugh. 'I think you were happier in their marriage than Ellen was herself.'

'Now that's not fair, Izzy. And you can't go trashing Ellen's marriage when she isn't here to speak for herself.'

'I'm not saying anything Ellen hadn't already told me,' said Izzy. 'There's a lot you don't know.'

'About Ray?'

'No, about Ellen.'

When Izzy's face creased with pain, Sue stood up. 'What about her?'

Izzy's lips were pursed tight, her hands balled into fists. She couldn't speak, not even as Sue placed a hand gently on her back and began to rub.

'How long have you been having contractions?' Sue asked.

CHAPTER 17

PAIGE

I let the beam of my torch trace along the entire trunk of a tree as if I were chasing a squirrel. I wasn't looking for Jonah because I knew he wasn't here. The only place worth searching was up by the ruins, and that would only happen if Kelvin managed to drag Olly up that far, which seemed unlikely. I had to consider the possibility that Jonah wouldn't be seen alive again. Was I a horrible person for coming around to that idea?

'You're quiet,' Dad said, coming up behind me.

'Just concentrating,' I replied as I fixed the torch beam back on solid ground.

Dad had his thumbs looped around the straps holding the stretcher to his back, his walking sticks dangling from his wrists. His torch was held at an awkward angle in one hand, making his sweep of the area almost as ineffectual as mine.

'Do you think Mum's ashes will be safe in the car?' I asked, thinking how concerned he'd been about them earlier.

'We'll get her back, don't you worry.'

'But what if another car comes along when the road's clear and slams into ours? They could push it over the edge.'

Dad's sigh came out as a plume of vapour. 'We would have moved our car long before anyone else thinks of driving up here.'

'Not if they send out a proper search party to look for Jonah.'

'Whatever the emergency, Paige, no one is going to be mad enough to drive along an icy road with enough speed to push our car over the edge.'

'I suppose,' I said, which made me think about how fast Dad had been going when we'd gone into a spin. It had felt like an age before he'd slammed on the brakes. I wasn't a driver, so maybe it was some sort of controlled stop, but if we hadn't hit that snowbank, the crash could have been a lot worse. I had a horrible feeling Dad wouldn't have cared, even with me in the car. He was struggling more than he was letting on.

'It might be a blessing in disguise if the car did roll down the mountain,' he said, adding to my fears. 'It's one way of scattering Mum's ashes. She was never meant to come back home with us.'

My legs shook as I shuffled through the snow towards Dad until our paths converged. We were carrying too much equipment to be able to loop arms, so I settled for knocking his shoulder with mine.

'But she is coming home with us,' I said. 'And we definitely won't come back here. I don't think this is the

115

right place for Mum after all.'

'Then we'll find somewhere else,' Dad said, sounding more like the father I knew. He didn't complain about the wasted journey, or the drama, he simply focused on a solution. 'And maybe next time, we keep it to just the two of us.'

'I like the sound of that,' I said as we continued to retrace the path the family had taken that morning. Things were far simpler when other people weren't involved.

Dad and I helped each other as we navigated the steep rise where Nan had struggled, and as we emerged from the treeline, the air felt sharper. The sky had cleared to the deepest sapphire against a landscape of snowy ridges that glowed violet in the light of the moon. The snow covering the viewing platform was pristine, and all signs of our previous visit had been erased. It was like we were starting over with a blank sheet. And then I looked up and followed the curved spine of Mynydd Plentyn to its peak, and remembered why we were here.

Straining my neck, I could make out the silhouetted railings on the old fort walls. On one side was a sheer drop, and on the other a scree slope. Between that slope and the cliff that formed one side of the viewing platform, there was a gentler hillside covered in an undulating blanket of snow, pockmarked by the occasional shadow of a boulder. Or could one of those shadows be a body? Was Jonah really out there? Why did I have to feel so responsible for him? Why couldn't I leave him to his own fate?

'Jonah!' I called out.

If there was a reply, I couldn't hear it above the sound

of my chattering teeth. The temperature had plummeted now that we were out in the open.

There was a clatter as Dad took off his pack. 'Come on,' he said, tugging my arm. 'Now that I don't have to carry that blinking stretcher, we can take a proper look around.'

'Should we try cutting across to the red route?'

'There's little point if Kelvin and Olly are already searching there.'

'But they're not going to go all the way to the top!'

'And if they don't, it'll be because Kelvin considers it too dangerous, so the answer's still no, Paige.'

I knew Dad was right, and I also knew that if I forced the issue, it wouldn't only be me taking risks. What I wouldn't give for the chance to go up there alone, to find Jonah and to swear him to secrecy. I would do anything he wanted just to stop him talking.

For no better reason than to stay warm, I joined Dad in his fruitless search of the area. While he trudged from tree to tree to create a spider's web of tracks in the snow, I stayed close to the cliff face that acted as the first insurmountable step to the top. I recalled from my earlier hike along the snowy trail that the cliff's edge disappeared into the hillside further along the link path. If I could separate myself from Dad …

'Paige, where are you?'

I sighed. 'I'm here!'

'Hello?' called someone else.

The moment I heard Olly's voice, I made a fist with my hand.

'Did I hear someone call?' Dad asked as he hurried to join me.

'It's only Olly.'

Dad leant forward to rest his weight on his walking sticks. 'Good.'

'No, it's not. They're back too soon, which means they haven't been to the top and they haven't found Jonah. We've been out here for nothing.'

'At least we tried,' Dad said matter-of-factly. He straightened up and cupped his hands around his mouth. 'Hello! We're over here!'

Eventually, two beads of light appeared out of the darkness, growing brighter.

'Have you found anything?' asked Kelvin as they drew close. Olly was straggling behind, an oily slick of sweat covering his face.

'Nothing,' said Dad. 'You?'

'Not so much as a footprint.'

'I think it's time we headed back,' Dad said, wrapping his arms around his body. 'I for one am freezing.'

I knew there was no point arguing, and I didn't say a word as we returned to the viewing platform to fetch our things. It was so cold I could feel icicles forming on my eyelashes, but that only made me feel worse about leaving Jonah. Imagining him lying in the snow, cold and injured, I tried to recall what he had been wearing. He had a dark-coloured padded jacket, but I didn't think he had a hat. No, he definitely didn't. I'd noticed how grey his hair was.

As Kelvin helped Dad fix the stretcher to his back, I

aimed my torch one last time towards the distant hillside curving towards the ruins. The beam was never going to be strong enough to shed light on the area we should be searching.

'Come on, Paige,' Olly said.

He tried to put an arm around me, and I immediately pushed him away. 'Fuck off, you creep!'

'Paige!' Dad snapped. 'That's out of order!'

'It's OK, Ray,' Olly said, retreating from me.

'No, it really isn't,' said Dad. 'I know you're hurting, Paige, but you have to stop hitting out at people. Especially family. Especially now. I know you're disappointed we haven't found our missing man, but we gave it our best shot. We can do no more.'

I opened my mouth to reply, aware that I was in the wrong on so many levels, but the apology stuck in my throat. I would not say sorry to Olly and was thankful when the shrill notes of a ringtone broke the silence I couldn't fill.

Olly pulled off a glove and took his mobile from his pocket. 'It's Sue,' he said. His look of puzzlement was quickly overtaken by alarm. He fumbled to connect the call, already bringing the phone to his ear. 'Hello?' There was a pause as he listened, and then he said something none of us wanted to hear. 'But it's too soon.'

'Is it Izzy?' I asked, my anger cooling so fast it turned my blood to ice.

It was Olly's turn to ignore me for once. 'Is she going to be OK, Sue?' He nodded to whatever Nan was saying, but looked no more relieved. 'I'm on my way.'

'Let's go,' said Dad before Olly had the chance to update us. His one-sided conversation had told us all we needed to know.

I could feel my loyalties being torn as Dad herded us off the viewing platform. But was loyalty the right word? Izzy was family. I owed Jonah nothing. Except …

'Come on, Paige,' Dad said, losing patience when he noticed me pointing my torch one last time up towards the ridge.

I could feel my body sag as I prepared to give up. And then something caught my eye. 'Stop!' I cried out. 'Look!'

CHAPTER 18

KELVIN

Kelvin squinted to where Paige was pointing. The blanket of snow covering the land below the old ruins was more blue than brilliant white in the moonlight, and almost completely featureless. 'I don't see anything.'

'There was a light. I swear,' Paige insisted.

'If this is a trick …' warned Ray.

'It's not! Please, just wait a minute.'

Olly had stepped off the viewing platform, but Paige's plea drew him back. He came alongside her. 'We've got time,' he said. 'Sue said Izzy is only in the first stages and not to panic. We can spare another minute.'

Kelvin would hazard a guess that Sue's reassurances were to prevent the soon-to-be father from coming down the mountain at a reckless speed. He also suspected Paige would spin her own story to make them stay. 'What exactly did you see?' he asked her.

'A flickering light.'

'It could have been the moonlight hitting a patch of

121

ice. It's certainly cold enough,' said Ray, dithering loudly to make his point.

'No, Dad, it was something else,' Paige said as she waved her torch from side to side to attract attention from above.

Despite his doubts, Kelvin did the same. 'Jonah!' he hollered.

'There, see!' Paige said. She waved the beam of her torch in wider, more frantic arcs.

Kelvin narrowed his eyes to slits. Was he imagining the tiny pinprick of light?

'Oh, my God, there is someone up there!' cried Olly as the light jerked from side to side in response to Paige's signal. 'But how are we going to reach him?'

'We?' Ray asked incredulously. 'Izzy is about to give birth, Olly, in case you've forgotten. You need to go.'

'Of course. I didn't mean me,' Olly stuttered. 'I should make a move. Will you lot be all right?'

'Yes,' Paige scoffed. 'We don't need you.'

'Wait,' Kelvin said before Olly could take a step. 'No one is going anywhere on their own.' He was loath to suggest it, but they needed to split up again.

'Paige, go with Olly,' said Ray. His daughter was about to argue, but he silenced her with a stare. 'If we can reach Jonah and he needs to be carried, I'm physically stronger. Sorry, this isn't open for debate.'

Paige scowled, but only for a moment. 'Fine, but you'd better not give up halfway,' she warned before setting off in the opposite direction to where she wanted to go.

'How *do* we get up there?' asked Ray, repeating

Olly's question.

Kelvin stepped back for a clearer view of the rising slopes above the cliff directly in front of them. The signal that had alerted them was now a static pinprick, marking their target but not the route.

'Our best shot is to head back along the link path,' he said at last. 'Around the midway point, this wall of rock all but disappears and there's a place we could start our climb. It's not a well-trodden path and there's a lot of bracken to get through, but it will get us there.'

'Wouldn't it be simpler to head to the ruins and climb down?'

'If we did that, we'd have to tackle that slope in front of it. It might look OK from here, but it's covered in scree. It would be far too dangerous, and near impossible to get back up for an inexperienced climber. I'm guessing that's how Jonah ended up stuck there.'

'He must have stumbled off the top of the wall in the fog.'

'That's why we have railings,' Kelvin said, thinking how lucky Jonah was not to fall over the sheer drop on the other side of the ruins. 'I can only presume he's been there all day, so whatever injuries he sustained in the fall, he'll be in worse shape now. We'll definitely need the stretcher.'

Their trudge along the link path was relatively simple as Kelvin retraced his and Olly's tracks through the snow, but every now and again, he heard Ray stumble.

'I can take the stretcher for a while,' Kelvin suggested. It was light compared to Kelvin's overloaded backpack, but nevertheless, it could be unwieldy.

'No, I'm fine,' Ray said through gritted teeth. 'I just keep misjudging my steps. I'm so cold now I can't feel my feet. I know the last thing we need is for me to turn an ankle.'

'How about a climb to warm you up?' asked Kelvin, pointing his torch towards a small gap between low shrubs. 'This is where it starts to get tricky.'

With sparse tree cover on the higher ground, the snow was deeper, and Kelvin shuffled and clawed his way upwards, creating a channel they would be able to follow back down while balancing an injured man on a stretcher. And that was their best-case scenario.

'I should warn you,' he said to Ray. 'We're in trouble if it's not safe enough to move him.'

'But what would be the alternative?'

It was a question Kelvin had been struggling with more and more as the air got thinner and sharper. Despite his thermal gloves, his fingers were already stiffened with cold. 'We'd have to call for back-up, and there's no knowing how long that would take to arrive.' He didn't mention they faced the same stark reality if Izzy or her baby needed urgent assistance.

'I don't want to be the purveyor of doom, but did you notice how the torch stopped moving before we left?' Ray asked. 'It could have been … Well, you hear of people having a last rush of energy before the end. We could already be too late.'

'Or he could be drifting in and out of consciousness,' said Kelvin.

'It's a shame Sue can't be in two places at once; she might have been able to help.'

Kelvin didn't mention that he wished Dee was there too, although not in her current state of mind. When they had first met, she had told him she wanted to save lives or die trying. It took a while to realize that it was the second half of that equation that attracted her most. Dee had had a death wish. But that was then. Time, love and patience had changed her perspective on life. Or so Kelvin had wanted to believe.

They carried on in silence, sharing only the occasional word of support when a boulder or rocky outcrop blocked their path.

'I think we're nearly there,' Kelvin said as the ground levelled off.

His legs were ready to buckle as he fought his way through the knee-high snow, but as they approached the area where he thought the signal had come from, a surge of adrenaline kicked in. His eyes stung with cold as he searched for that elusive pinprick of light in the darkness.

'Shouldn't we have seen something by now?' asked Ray. 'What if it was the moonlight playing tricks on us after all? Either that or we're in the wrong place.'

Kelvin's jaw tightened. As much as Ray might be right, he didn't need to hear it. 'Hello! Are you there?' he called as he pointed his torch from one uneven mound of snow to the next.

No longer interested in creating channels that might lead to dead-ends, Kelvin lengthened his stride, prodding every snow-covered stone in his path with his walking stick. A boulder. A shrub. Another shrub. His foot caught on a hidden root, and without the energy to rebalance, he fell face first into the snow. Spitting snow from his mouth, he was almost tempted to admit defeat, but he dragged himself up and trailed the beam of his torch up towards the ruins. His heart skipped a beat.

'I can see a track!' he cried out.

Ray was searching another area, and Kelvin waited for him to catch up. Staying where he was, he let his torch do all the work. He couldn't tell if the track cutting a channel down the scree slope had been made by someone climbing up or coming down. Was it possible that Jonah had managed to climb up to the ruins after signalling them? What other explanation could there be?

Concentrating on the lowest section, his torch settled on one particular patch of disturbed snow at the bottom of the slope.

'There he is!' he said, lunging towards the dark shape.

When Kelvin reached Jonah, he was lying on his side with his eyes closed. His lips were tinged blue, his face covered in abrasions, and most worrying of all, there was congealed blood around his hairline, indicating a more serious injury beneath his beanie hat.

Ray joined him and crouched down, then shook Jonah's shoulder. 'Hello? Can you hear me?' Failing to get a response, he took a firm grip on the man's arm and prepared to turn him onto his back.

'No, don't,' Kelvin said. Whether it was good luck or sheer willpower, Jonah had managed to get himself into

126

what was a good approximation of the recovery position. 'He's fine where he is. We shouldn't move him more than we have to in case he has a spinal injury. First things first – let's protect him against the worst of the cold.'

Kelvin shrugged off his backpack and retrieved a couple of foil blankets, but as he wrapped them around the casualty, Jonah groaned.

'Is he waking up?' asked Ray.

'Hello? Can you hear me?' Kelvin asked, leaning closer to Jonah's ear. 'My name's Kelvin. We're going to look after you.'

When Jonah's breathing settled into an uneasy series of rasps, Kelvin took a flask from his backpack. 'If he comes around, try feeding him sips of broth while I phone for help.'

'It's bad, isn't it?' Ray asked. 'He doesn't look stable enough to move.'

Kelvin tugged at the sleeve of his jacket to check his watch. It was almost eight o'clock, plenty of time for the temperature to drop further before the night was over. They could all end up with hypothermia if they were forced to stay out. 'Let's see what the professionals say.'

When Kelvin got through to the emergency services, it came as no surprise that he was eventually put through to Mountain Rescue. Sian's voice was taut with stress.

'I wish I could give you a timeframe,' she said after Kelvin had updated her, 'but a lot of our volunteers are cut off in the snow, and what teams we have are already out on calls. I'll keep trying for you, but I'm sorry, Kelvin, I can't make any promises.'

127

'What about the air ambulance?' asked Kelvin. There was nowhere on the mountain for it to land safely, so they would have to land down in the valley, or chance an airlift, neither of which were ideal.

'There just isn't one available. There are three major incidents currently live in North Wales, and neighbouring regions have the same high demand for resources. Do you think you could attempt an evacuation yourself?'

Kelvin watched Ray's attempts to coax Jonah into consciousness with the warm broth, but he showed no response as it dribbled down his chin. 'He could have a spinal injury.'

'Hypothermia is more of a risk to life right now. It might be the lesser of two evils,' said Sian. 'And at least you have a nurse back at the pub.'

'Have you spoken to Sue? Do you know her daughter's in premature labour?'

'We have a call logged.'

'So you'll appreciate she already has her hands full. And realistically, Jonah's going to need more than patching up.'

'Sue works on a renal ward, not A&E,' Ray said, picking up the gist of the conversation.

Kelvin repeated the information to Sian. 'We're going to need assistance at some point.'

'I know, and I'll make sure you're kept on the list of priorities. I wish I hadn't left you now.'

'You're where you need to be, and so am I,' Kelvin said with a deep sigh. 'So, do I move him?'

'Let's take it one step at a time. If you run through

some basic obs, I'll do a risk assessment. Let me make the decision. This isn't on you, Kelvin,' she said. 'Now, what kit have you brought with you?'

'Basic first aid. Some splints, a neck brace and a portable stretcher. No spinal board.'

'Then we work with what we've got.'

The mood was sombre as Kelvin put Sian on speakerphone and followed her instructions, with Ray's assistance. There were no complex fractures visible, but the gash to Jonah's head when they pulled back his hat was deep. The only reason there wasn't blood pouring from the wound was that the cold had slowed his circulation to preserve vital organs.

Slowly and carefully, Kelvin removed Jonah's scarf which was now sodden with cold broth, and placed him in a neck brace. With Ray's help, they positioned the stretcher so they could roll him gently onto it. Jonah's eyes fluttered, and he moaned a complaint.

'What did he say?' Kelvin asked Ray.

'No idea.'

Jonah's eyes snapped open at the sound of their voices, and he made a grab for Kelvin's arm. 'Dee,' he said. 'Dee will …' His eyes rolled back in his head and he was unconscious again.

'What's happening?' came Sian's voice from his speakerphone, snapping Kelvin out of his daze.

He rested back on his haunches and, for the first time, looked at the man and not his injuries. He figured Jonah was in his early forties, the same age as Kelvin and his wife. Dee had said he reminded her of someone, but how

129

did that explain why a barely conscious man would utter her name?

'He mumbled something,' Kelvin said. 'It sounded like "please", but I could be wrong.' He glanced at Ray, who shrugged. 'And he moved his hands.'

'His legs moved too,' offered Ray.

'All good signs,' said Sian. 'From what you've told me, I don't think there's any choice. You need to apply a dressing to his head wound, then get him back to the pub as soon as you can.'

'We'll do our best,' Kelvin said, reassessing their situation now that their casualty was on the stretcher. 'I didn't quite appreciate how tall and broad Jonah is. He's not going to be easy to lift.'

'And we'll be walking back over compacted snow. We're bound to slip,' added Ray. 'I really think we should wait it out. Or ... Couldn't we wrap him up as best we can and go down ...'

Kelvin shook his head to silence Ray before he could finish, not because the idea of abandoning Jonah was abhorrent, but because it made some sense. Could they leave an injured man to die? He felt his heart sinking, only for it to leap into his throat when he heard the sound of a mini-avalanche from above. Reflexively, he covered his head with his hands until he heard a familiar voice.

'I could help,' said Paige.

The eighteen-year-old had used the snowy slope from the ruins like a sled run. Her features were pinched as she rubbed her bottom, but she wasn't going to admit the descent had been painful.

'Paige! What the hell are you doing here?' hissed Ray.

His daughter was only interested in Jonah's motionless body. Her eyes widened. 'Is he … is he dead?'

'No, but he's in real danger if we don't get him warmed up soon,' said Kelvin.

'Hey, guys,' called Sian from the phone lying on the ground. 'I'm glad to hear you've got an extra pair of hands, but do you mind if you take it from here? You can call me if Jonah's condition changes, but otherwise, I suggest you get moving as quickly as you can.'

Kelvin set to work preparing Jonah for the journey while father and daughter argued.

'You were supposed to go back with Olly,' Ray scolded.

'I did, for a bit,' Paige said, sounding breathless, but not in the slightest bit chastened. 'Olly said he was fine on his own, so I came back.'

Suddenly, it made sense why Paige hadn't put up more of a fight when her dad had sent her back to the pub. She had planned this from the start. 'You took the red route to the top?' asked Kelvin, reluctantly impressed.

'I just followed your tracks to the ruins,' she replied with a shrug. 'It was easy.'

Kelvin looked up to the ruins where Paige had come from. Whoever's tracks she had been following, they weren't theirs. When Kelvin and Olly had followed the red route earlier, they had gone only as far as the link path, and there had been no footprints leading further up. Whoever Paige had been following, they had arrived later.

Not willing to consider who that person might be,

Kelvin finished dressing Jonah's head wound and picked up the green thermal hat he had been wearing. It looked very similar to one he himself owned, the one Dee was always pinching off him. He pulled it over Jonah's head, and tugged up the zip of his Berghaus. As an afterthought, he checked Jonah's pockets, but found only a tube of mints. He stood up to check the ground around them.

'Lost something?' asked Ray.

'I thought Jonah might have a phone,' Kelvin said. He didn't add that there was no sign of a torch either, or any means of shining the light that had attracted their attention earlier. He would keep his questions to himself for now.

'He must have dropped it in the fall,' said Ray dismissively. 'Come on. If we're going to save this gent, we need to get moving.'

'OK,' Kelvin replied, but it was concern for someone else entirely that made him desperate to get home.

CHAPTER 19

SUE

Glancing out of the window yet again, Sue saw the unchanged tracks through the snow where four people had left the pub two hours ago. She was trying not to let her anxiety show for Izzy's sake, but she let out a huge sigh of relief when she spotted a lone figure appearing out of the gloom.

'Thank goodness you're here,' she said, rushing to the door to greet Olly. 'Where are the others?'

'Still out there,' he said, attempting to unzip his coat while taking off his gloves at the same time in his haste. He failed at both. 'How's Izzy? Is the baby here yet? Have I missed it?'

'No, not at all. Her contractions have slowed again.'

'Do you think it's Braxton Hicks, like a false labour? I read up on it,' he said. 'It's too early for the baby, isn't it?'

Sue's stomach hollowed. At thirty-five weeks, yes, it was too soon, although there was never going to be a good time to give birth in the middle of nowhere with only a vague promise of help on the way.

'If she were in hospital, I wouldn't be too worried,' Sue said, leaving Olly to fill in the gaps.

'Then I'm glad she's got you.'

Sue wanted to hug him for that. 'She'll feel better now you're here,' she offered in kind. Izzy had been pining for her husband, their argument that morning overridden by a simmering tension between mother and daughter.

'Can I see her?' Olly asked, freeing himself from his coat. 'Where is she?'

Izzy was in the snug and had pulled herself up from her chair. 'Did they make you come back on your own?' she asked, her face twisting in annoyance.

'Paige followed me part of the way, but you know what she's like,' he replied, rubbing his hands together briefly by the fire before continuing over to his wife. 'She wanted to go back to help. We saw a light higher up. It must have been a signal from Jonah.'

'Jonah?' Sue and Izzy asked in unison.

'The missing man. The police traced his vehicle, so we know his name now.'

Izzy let out a moan and turned to the window, resting both hands on the sill.

'Is it a contraction?' asked Olly, rubbing her back.

'Give me a minute. I'll be fine.'

'It's time we found you somewhere more comfortable,' said Sue. 'Olly can look after you while I sort out that guest room we were promised. Shout me if you need me.'

Sue felt like an intruder sneaking upstairs past the 'No Entry' signs. 'Dee?' she called out halfway up, then once

134

again when she reached the landing. There were seven doors to choose from, all with their own combination locks. Panicking that they may not have a room at all, she knocked on the first door, not knowing if it was a bedroom or a cupboard. 'Dee! We need help.'

Only the creak of floorboards cut through the silence as she moved on to the next door, then the next, knocking louder and more persistently each time. It was possible Dee could have taken medication to knock herself out, or else she had a pillow over her ears to block out the calls for help. The only thing Sue knew for sure was that Dee wasn't going to answer.

Fortunately, the fifth door had been left ajar, and Sue searched along the inner wall until she found a light switch. The solitary bulb hanging from the ceiling revealed a crowded room full of supplies. Somewhere beneath a collection of boxes and bags was a bed. The place looked ransacked, and was presumably where all the equipment for the search and rescue had come from. It was lucky their hosts had left the room unlocked.

Sue worked fast to clear the room, transferring boxes to one corner where she created a precarious tower shored up with bags and other paraphernalia that couldn't be squeezed into the limited space available in the solitary wardrobe. The cleared bed revealed a single bare mattress. There was no linen to be found so she improvised with sleeping bags she had seen in a huge polyurethane bag under the bed. She used the plastic as the first layer to protect the mattress, then placed an unzipped sleeping bag on top as a sheet. Another couple of sleeping bags became pillows and others could be used as blankets. She put her hands on her hips and surveyed the room. What else?

Taking a pair of scissors and a scalpel from a large first aid box she had set aside amongst the jumble, Sue headed down to the kitchen. She found a suitable knife and some clamps before heating a pan of water to sterilize her 'equipment'. All the while, she prayed she wouldn't need to use them. It could be a false alarm. She hadn't examined Izzy yet.

As Sue waited for the water to boil, she raided the storeroom for some bottled water and took out a box of chocolate brownies from the freezer in case anyone needed an energy boost. Wondering how the others would be getting on, she went to the back door to make sure it hadn't started snowing again. An icy gust stole the breath from her lungs, but it was the clear set of boot prints leading away from the door that caused a shudder to run down her spine. They were too pristine to have been made while the snow was falling, and whoever had left them, hadn't come back. Could this be why Dee hadn't responded to her calls?

Sue had an uncomfortable, irrational feeling she had seen something she shouldn't have, but she didn't have the time or inclination to ponder. She closed the door quietly and went to check on her daughter.

Izzy complained about the new room being too cold and the mattress smelling of must. She also fretted about being crushed under an avalanche of boxes and whined about there being no scented candles or birthing balls as per the plan she had agreed with her midwife, but this birth wasn't going to be anything like any of them had hoped.

'Did you hear that sound?' Izzy asked as she sat on her nest of sleeping bags. 'I think it was a door slamming. Are the others back?'

Olly stuck his head out into the corridor. 'Hello? Is anyone there?'

Sue checked the window. The only returning footprints she could see were Olly's. 'Nothing,' she said. She hadn't mentioned the prints leading out the back door, so she alone was left to imagine Kelvin's wife creeping back into the pub. Maybe Dee had just needed some fresh air. She wouldn't be the only one feeling trapped.

'What's taking them so long?' asked Izzy.

Another hour had passed, enough time for Olly's fingers to transform from corpse-white to baby-pink. 'I'll try phoning,' he said.

'And if they don't answer,' Sue told him, 'call the emergency services too. They might be able to update us if by some chance the missing man has been found, or else we can update them.' She felt sick at the thought that the others might have gotten into trouble. Hadn't they endured enough stress for one day? She turned to her daughter. 'Any more contractions?'

Izzy checked her watch. 'Not for the last half-hour, so they're definitely slowing down. I think it's just the stress of today. My body thinks I deserve a practice run,' she said confidently.

'I'm sure you're right, but don't think that means

you're getting out of bed any time soon,' warned Sue.

'Fine. But I am feeling a bit peckish,' Izzy said, this time looking to Olly. His phone was pinned to his ear, but he was yet to talk to anyone. 'Could you find me something?'

'There are some brownies in the kitchen,' said Sue.

'OK, and I'll make us all a cuppa too,' he said. 'I won't be long.'

Once Olly had left, Sue turned to her daughter and chewed her lip. 'Maybe I should examine you,' she said. She knew the basics of midwifery, but her training had never prepared her to examine her own daughter.

'Can't we leave that for now?' asked Izzy, as reluctant as her mother. 'I don't want to have my baby here.'

Sue sat on the edge of the bed and took Izzy's hand. 'You may not have a choice, but if this is it, I can promise you there's no one more determined than I to make sure this baby arrives safely. And I have half the staff at the Royal ready to take my call if I need advice.' She squeezed her daughter's hand tighter. 'I do love you, Izzy.'

'And I love you too, Mum,' she replied. 'I never meant to give you a hard time. I'm only just finding out how hard it is being a mother – hopefully.'

'Hope has nothing to do with it,' Sue said vehemently. 'I won't let anything happen to you, or my grandchild.'

'Grandson,' Izzy corrected.

Sue's eyes sparkled. 'It's a boy?' Izzy nodded. 'But you said you didn't want to know the sex. I should have known you'd find out!'

'We wanted to keep it to ourselves given everything

that went on, but I can't tell you how many times I've nearly slipped up,' she said just as pain creased her face.

'Another one?'

Izzy gritted her teeth, took a couple of deep breaths, then as quickly as the contraction had come, it was gone. 'It's OK, it wasn't a bad one. It could still be stopping, couldn't it?'

Sue arranged the sleeping bags around her daughter, not meeting her eye. 'It could.'

Neither of them believed it and Izzy let out a soft mewl. 'Oh, Mum, what if he really is coming? What if he needs an incubator or something?'

'There's a very good chance he won't. I've felt his kicks, he's a strong little boy,' Sue replied. She dared to smile. 'It's nice thinking of him as a *him*.'

'It feels more real, doesn't it? That's why I decided to find out – to give Olly a chance to bond with him,' Izzy said. She tilted her head when Sue scowled out of habit. 'Don't judge him, Mum. If you have to think badly of anyone, it should be me.'

'Oh, no,' said Sue, stiffening. 'Don't you dare put the blame on yourself.'

'Why not? It's all my fault.' Izzy picked at the open zipper of the sleeping bag covering her lap. 'I knew Olly didn't want kids straight away. He went from living with his parents to living with me. He's never had to look after himself, let alone a baby.'

'But none of us are ever fully prepared for parenthood, and that baby is as much his responsibility as he is yours.'

'That's where you're wrong. I chose this, Olly didn't.'

Again, Sue was ready to come back with an argument, but something in Izzy's tone stopped her.

'It wasn't an accident, Mum,' she said quietly. 'I got pregnant on purpose.'

'What?' Sue spluttered. 'But why?'

'To test him, I suppose,' Izzy said, scraping a fingernail along the zipper hard enough for it to hurt. 'I needed to be sure he wasn't going to turn out like my father.'

'Except he almost did,' Sue said, unwilling to let Olly off the hook. Whatever the circumstances of Izzy's pregnancy, he had still left her.

They could hear the clink of teaspoons and cups downstairs. Olly would be back soon. 'Does he know what you did?'

'Yes, I told him as soon as I knew I was pregnant.'

'So that's the secret you were arguing about this morning?'

Izzy bit down on her lip. 'No, Olly's too kind and decent to use that against me. He knows how messed up I am, and why I did what I did.'

'You're not messed up,' Sue said weakly.

'Aren't I?' Izzy asked, then added, 'Aren't *we*? Just a little bit?'

As much as Sue didn't want to confront Izzy's earlier allegation of her resenting her own daughter, neither of them was going to relax until the air was cleared. She lifted her gaze to the ceiling to give herself a moment. There was no doubting that Sue's unplanned pregnancy had been the catalyst for the break-up of her marriage, and that her husband's desertion had devastated her. She hadn't trusted another man with her heart since, but she had never blamed Izzy, not consciously at least.

'If I blamed anyone for your dad leaving, it was me. I was convinced that if only I'd been attractive or interesting enough, he might have stayed. I felt like I'd let you and Ellen down, and it took far too long for me to realize we were better off without him. I didn't want to be with someone who didn't have the capacity to love our children as much as I did. I'd like to think I would have come to that conclusion anyway, even if he had stuck around.'

Sue shuffled along the bed so Izzy could rest her head on her shoulder. They both sniffed back tears.

'I know I didn't give you the same attention I'd been able to give Ellen in the early years, but it was that much harder on my own,' Sue continued. 'There were times when I was so mentally and physically exhausted that I would have killed for just one day off, not just from work, but from being a mum too. I'm sorry if that showed. I know I wasn't perfect.'

'None of us are,' agreed Izzy, letting her mum rock her gently. 'We all wear masks from time to time, but eventually we have to be who we are. Ellen taught me that.'

CHAPTER 20

KELVIN

The burn of Kelvin's calf muscles was surpassed only by the pain in his fingers. His gloves prevented the stretcher poles from cutting through skin, but after an hour of lifting, pulling, heaving, and on one occasion, almost dropping a man who must weigh at least sixteen stone, Kelvin was reaching the limit of his endurance.

He and Ray were taking it in turns to be the single prop at the back, allowing the other to join Paige at the front where they could hold one corner of the stretcher and use a torch with their free hand. It was Kelvin's turn to hold up the rear.

Having got as far as the link path, they opted for the easier blue route, but it still presented challenges. 'This might be a bit tricky,' Kelvin warned as they approached the dip near the viewing platform. 'Do you want to stop to catch your breath first?'

'I'm fine,' Ray called back, 'and surely every second counts.' He looked to his daughter. 'Unless you need a break?'

Paige's features were set in grim determination. 'Let's keep going.'

Despite their fortitude, the pair at the front hesitated at the edge of the slope. The tracks in the snow where their search party had already passed had become solid ice, and Kelvin was about to suggest they lay the stretcher down and drag it when Ray and Paige started to move again. The stretcher dipped at the front and Kelvin's legs trembled as he crouched to level it. Just when he thought he had the balance right, the stretcher lurched to one side, and then to the other. Paige cried out.

'Be careful!' her dad shouted.

Ray dropped his torch so he could reach over to catch Paige as she slipped, but rather than helping, his movement pitched the stretcher violently to the right. All three of them instinctively tipped it back to the left, but the overcorrection caused them all to lose their footing. The stretcher began to flip over, and with a yell, Kelvin catapulted himself forward to stop Jonah from crashing face down into the snow, or worse still, hitting a hidden boulder. The stretcher bounced off his shoulder and toppled backwards again, landing the casualty on his back with a thump.

'Is everyone OK?' Kelvin asked when he could speak.

Ray was helping Paige to her feet, but she looked embarrassed. 'I'm fine, Dad. I was fine before,' she said, brushing snow from her ski pants.

Kelvin crawled over to Jonah, who was the only one not to have made a complaint. Ray aimed his torch at

143

the man's face, creating ghoulish shadows across his hollowed eye sockets and gaping mouth. His complexion was unnaturally pale.

'Is he …?' Paige gulped.

Kelvin shook the man's shoulder. 'Jonah?'

Receiving no response, Kelvin took off a glove and slipped his hand inside the neck brace. His fingertips found no warmth as they touched flesh. He pressed harder, but couldn't be sure if he had enough sensation left in his fingers to be able to feel a pulse.

'Anything?' asked Ray impatiently.

Kelvin shook his head. How long had they been carrying a corpse?

'No! He can't be dead!' wailed Paige, dropping to her knees.

Ray lowered his torch out of respect, and shadows moved across the dead man's face. Kelvin wasn't sure if it was a trick of the light, but he thought he caught Jonah's blue lips move. 'Point the torch back,' he demanded.

Jonah's face became a Halloween mask once more. His cracked lips remained parted, but his mouth was no longer a dark hollow. His tongue was moving.

Kelvin leant over, his ear above Jonah's mouth, and felt a shudder as he recalled the stranger uttering his wife's name. Afraid of what else might come out of Jonah's mouth, Kelvin clenched his jaw and listened. There were no words, only the rattle of a man dangerously close to death.

'He's still alive,' he said. 'But we need to get him back. Fast.'

Once they hoisted the stretcher up again, they kept to a steady pace. There was some way to go, but gradually the inky blackness they were heading towards gave hints of home. The silhouettes of tree trunks appeared set against a canvas of grey, that turned blue, then orange, until they could see the spotlights from the pub car park shining like beacons.

'We made it,' Paige said, panting harder as they pushed on.

Lighted windows on both floors of the pub welcomed them home, but notably not from the bedroom Kelvin shared with Dee. His gaze travelled to one of the spare bedrooms where a figure was watching them, quickly followed by another. Kelvin guessed the shorter one was Sue, and the taller, wider figure was that of a man. The halo of red hair was unmistakable.

'Olly made it back,' Kelvin said with relief he hadn't been aware he needed to feel. He wouldn't rest until he knew they were all accounted for, and that included his wife.

'Help!' Paige called to her family.

'They're too far away,' Ray said. 'And I imagine they won't want to leave Izzy's side.'

'Help!' his daughter called out again.

It was impossible to tell if Olly had actually heard her cry, but he acted nonetheless. His form disappeared from the window and they had only taken a dozen more stumbling steps when the front door opened and he came charging out, his jacket flapping as he tried to thread his arms into its sleeves.

145

'You found him then,' he said, joining Kelvin at the back to take one corner of the stretcher.

Kelvin flexed the fingers in his free hand, welcoming the pain as sensation returned. 'I just hope it won't be for nothing. How's Izzy?'

'Not too bad. Her contractions have eased, and we're hoping she won't go into full labour.'

'That's good news,' said Kelvin. 'And how's everyone else? Have you seen Dee?'

'No, not really,' Olly said in a way that made Kelvin examine his expression. He looked shifty when he added, 'I noticed wet footprints coming from the back door, so I guess she's been out and about.'

'Footprints?' asked Kelvin, but they had reached the open door where Sue was waiting to greet them.

'I can't tell you how happy I am to see you all back safe,' she said, stepping out of the way so they could manoeuvre Jonah inside.

The stretcher wobbled as it was lowered to the floor with as much care as their weakened limbs would allow. Three of the stretcher-bearers were running on empty.

'How is he?' asked Sue, crouching down to examine Jonah for herself.

'Not good,' said Ray. 'It was a miracle we got him off the mountain.'

'He was briefly conscious when we found him, but he's been unresponsive ever since,' Kelvin explained. He closed the door and leant against it. Snowflakes melted on his jacket. Of course it would start to snow again. The storm wasn't over.

CHAPTER 21

SUE

Sue wore a frown as she knelt down on the hard corridor flagstones and pressed her fingers against Jonah's wrist. The lines on her brow deepened in concentration. 'His pulse is thready, but he's still with us,' she said.

The group that had gathered around her remained silent as she continued to examine the stranger whose life was now in her hands. She counted Jonah's heartbeats, pinched the skin on the back of his hand, pulled back each eyelid in turn, and examined the deep violet of his gums. When she placed an electronic thermometer inside his ear, they all jumped when it beeped. She shook her head when she saw the reading.

'It's going to be a challenge warming him up without shocking him,' she said. 'I think the snug would be best if we can get some ventilation in there.'

'We can open windows,' Kelvin confirmed. 'Would it help if we moved a couple of tables from the dining room to use as a makeshift bed?'

'If you can find something to help strap him down in case he does move, that would be perfect,' she said as she struggled to her feet with Ray's help. She may not have been out searching with the others but she was bone-weary. 'And we can use sleeping bags as a mattress, and foil blankets for now to cover him once we've stripped off his outerwear.'

'I'll get the sleeping bags,' Izzy called from the top of the stairs.

'You need to stay in bed,' ordered Sue. 'I can only deal with one patient at a time. Paige, go and fetch the sleeping bags, then stay with Izzy.'

'But I need to be here.'

'I should be the one to stay with Izzy,' Olly volunteered. 'Unless you need me down here?'

'Yes, we do,' Sue said before anyone else could respond. She didn't want Paige to stay downstairs and experience what could possibly be another death so soon after her mother's. 'Paige, please do as you're told. You can just throw the sleeping bags down the stairs.'

'Let's get those tables,' Kelvin said to Olly as Paige stomped off.

'Anything else you need?' Ray asked when they were alone.

Sue looked down at Jonah and the bandage peeking beneath his beanie hat. She hadn't even checked his head injury yet. She shook her head. 'Oh, Ray, I don't know where to begin. I've been in stressful situations before at work, but there's always been a team around me. It's bad enough having to face the prospect of delivering Izzy's baby five weeks early, but this is something else. I'm out of my depth.'

There was a brief interruption as Olly and Kelvin shuffled past with a five-foot dining table. Olly noticed Sue sizing it up. 'Don't worry, there's a smaller one we're going to grab too.'

Sue tried to smile as she turned her attention back to Ray. 'That's OK then,' she whispered. 'We have *two* tables. And there I was thinking I'd have to manage without any equipment.'

'You'll do fine.'

'I can but try,' she conceded. 'But I will need back-up. I'd better make some calls.'

'I can watch Jonah if you want to go somewhere quieter,' suggested Ray.

'For now, I don't dare let him out of my sight,' she said, feeling torn by thoughts of her daughter upstairs, waiting anxiously for the next contraction they hoped wouldn't come.

'Then why don't we drag him into the snug?' Ray said as Olly and Kelvin made a return trip for the second table. 'This floor is almost as cold as the ground outside.'

'Give us thirty seconds and we can help,' Kelvin promised.

'And if you need a stiff drink, Kelvin's kindly supplied a bottle of brandy,' Olly said, his cheeks already aglow from what Sue presumed was an alcohol buzz. 'Shame we can't give one to Jonah.'

The casualty was going to need a lot more than a tot of brandy, and showed no outward signs of reaction

149

when they moved him. Kelvin and Olly had positioned the patient's 'bed' to the side of the fire nearest a window that had been opened a crack. The fresh air would have to make up for the lack of an oxygen mask, and would also bring the room temperature down a degree or two to help Jonah's body acclimatize.

'Let's get him out of his damp clothes before we put him on the tables,' Sue said, already unzipping his jacket. To Kelvin, she added, 'Do you have a pair of heavy-duty scissors? We're going to have to cut him out of his polo shirt so we can keep his neck brace on.'

As Kelvin headed out the door, he almost bumped into Paige. 'Here are the sleeping bags, Nan,' she said. 'How is he? Has he said anything?'

Sue didn't look up from what she was doing, nor did she point out that she had asked Paige to stay with Izzy. She was too exhausted to begin another battle. 'No, he's still unconscious. Now when you get back to Izzy's room,' she said pointedly, 'there are some hot water bottles we could use. Just throw them down the stairs, and I promise, we'll keep you updated if there are any changes.'

Kelvin returned with the scissors, crossing paths again with Paige as she left. Once Jonah was stripped and on the table, Sue instructed Ray, Kelvin and Olly to wrap him in fleeces and foil blankets while she stepped aside to update the emergency services.

Eventually, she was patched through to someone she trusted. Kim was an A&E doctor at the Royal, and a very good friend. They had already been messaging each other as the situation evolved, and although it didn't take long to get Kim up to speed, it wasn't the kind of handover where a paramedic could reel off the patient's vital statistics and leave.

'He's unresponsive, but he's reacting to stimuli and his pupils are equal and reactive,' Sue told her. 'His pulse was forty-two when he arrived, and …' Her voice acquired an unwelcome note of dread when she added, 'his body temperature was thirty-two point six.'

'Damn,' said Kim. 'What's his blood pressure?'

'I haven't got a clue, we don't have that kind of equipment, and before you ask, nor do we have a pulse oximeter, a saline drip, or morphine.'

'His pulse has gone up to forty-five,' Olly said. He had hold of Jonah's wrist, but rather than pressing his fingers against a pulse point, he had been tapping at a sports watch. 'Hold on, now it's forty-one. Forty-three.'

'Did you get that?' Sue asked Kim. 'We have a pulse monitor.'

'It's better than nothing.'

Sue laughed even though she wanted to cry. 'And I could always see if there's a power drill lying around in case you need me to perform brain surgery.'

'You may laugh but …'

'Don't even think about it, Kim,' Sue warned. 'I'll do what I can to raise his body temperature, but if his head injury is significant, wrapping him up like a Christmas turkey isn't going to do him much good.'

'It's a start,' said Kim. 'I wish I could be there to help, but I'll liaise with the Ambulance Service, as well as

Mountain Rescue, and a team of Olympic cross-country skiers if I have to. We'll get you the back-up you need, but for now, you're going to have to be an extension of me. If you switch to video, we can start our assessment and get Jonah in the best possible shape ready for the evacuation when it happens.'

They worked quickly and methodically until they had formulated a plan of action, if you could call watching and waiting any action at all. When Kim signed off, Sue cleaned and re-dressed Jonah's head wound, using butterfly stiches to help close the deep gash above his left ear. There were multiple contusions on his face, but it was the risk of concussion and internal bleeding that worried Sue – things that would only become apparent over time.

Kelvin had slipped away while she was busy, but Paige had returned, carrying the hot water bottles. She couldn't take her eyes off Jonah.

'Your nan told you to stay with Izzy,' Ray said, his clipped tone perfectly reflecting Sue's growing frustration.

'She doesn't need to,' said Izzy, who appeared in the doorway behind her niece. 'We brought some thermal socks too.'

'Izzy, what the hell are you doing down here?' Sue demanded, wondering if her family was determined to send her stress levels soaring.

'I'm fine, Mum.'

'You look peaky.'

'Please, stop fussing. I've tried to sleep, but I can't relax with all this going on.'

'Well, you should still be resting while you can,'

Sue replied, wishing she had that chance, but with two patients to watch, it was going to be a long night. She was exhausted just thinking about it.

'I will go back upstairs,' Izzy promised. 'I just wanted to see …' Her voice trailed off as her gaze settled on Jonah. She crept closer to the man on the table as if approaching a sleeping tiger. '*This* is Jonah?' she asked.

'Do you know him?' asked Ray.

She blinked hard, her trance broken. 'No, I've never seen him before. It's just … it's a shock seeing someone in such a bad way. That could have been any of us. If you and Paige hadn't made it back to the pub this morning, or if Olly had lost his way in the fog … It doesn't bear thinking about.' She placed a hand on her flushed cheek. 'Is he going to make it?'

Sue wished people would stop asking her that. 'He's alive thanks to Ray and the others, but he's got a way to go yet.'

'He's out of the woods, literally, but not out of the woods,' said Olly, seemingly proud of his little quip. When no one laughed, he assumed a more serious tone. 'I suppose the next thing to do is find out what we can about him.' He grabbed the set of keys and a wallet balanced on top of the heap of discarded clothes. He examined the keys first, showing the others the Toyota logo. Next he opened the wallet.

'That's a breach of privacy,' Paige said, making a grab for it.

Olly twisted away from her. 'But we need to give the police all the information we can. Apparently he

153

has a wife.'

Paige gasped. 'Who said that?'

'The police told Kelvin. They were going to track her down, but any extra information will surely help,' Olly said as he searched the folds of the wallet. He took out a driving licence. 'His name is Jonah Pearson. He's forty-three years old, and he lives in Chester.' He checked for anything else. 'That's it. No photos of kids, no membership cards. It's a shame you couldn't find his phone.'

'We're assuming he lost it in the fall,' said Ray.

Olly dropped the wallet back onto the pile. 'Then how did he signal us? There isn't a torch.'

Ray scratched his chin. 'We must have missed it when we found him.'

'At least we know he was conscious at some point,' said Sue as her attention was caught by her daughter. Izzy was staring intently at Jonah and rubbed her eyes as if she didn't trust what she was seeing. 'What is it, love?'

'I don't know. I thought maybe his lips moved.'

Stillness fell as the family gathered around the casualty. Sue wanted to believe his breathing sounded louder than it had before. She put a hand on his shoulder and shook him gently. 'Jonah? Can you hear me?'

It was just short of a miracle when Jonah's lips peeled away from each other, pulling strings of torn skin and dried saliva. 'Where?'

'You're in the pub. We brought you down from the mountain. You're safe.'

Jonah's eyes fluttered open. 'What ... What happened?' he asked. The foil blanket rustled as he tried, then failed

154

to lift a hand. They had bound his arms and body to the table with rope in case he woke up and panicked.

'We were hoping you could tell us,' Sue replied. 'There was a storm. You had a bad fall.'

Jonah's neck brace prevented him from turning his head, but his eyes flitted from side to side, and he became more and more distressed. Paige was the first to step back. 'We shouldn't crowd him,' she whispered. Ray nodded, and he, Izzy and Olly retreated to a safe distance.

'Dropped phone ...' said Jonah, his tongue moving sluggishly.

'So he fell trying to retrieve it?' suggested Olly.

As Jonah moved his lips again, Sue leant in closer. 'No,' he said. There were more guttural sounds, and his final words were as quiet as a sigh. His eyes rolled back in his head and his mouth slackened.

'Is he dead?' Ray asked.

'No, he's passed out again,' replied Sue. She kneaded her temples with her fingers. Had she heard Jonah right? She looked to the door and hoped Kelvin hadn't been within earshot. 'Did anyone else hear what he was trying to say?'

'He just wanted to know how the accident happened,' said Ray.

'If it was an accident,' Sue replied, even though every fibre in her being was resisting what other conclusion she could reach. 'That last thing he said, it sounded like "pushed me".'

'No!' Paige said, clamping a hand over her mouth.

155

CHAPTER 22

KELVIN

Kelvin's legs almost gave way with the simple effort of climbing the stairs. His body had nothing left to give, but his mind wasn't ready to rest. The number of people relying on him had increased yet again, and help couldn't come soon enough. Sian's latest message had been to tell him Rob's team had rescued one group of climbers and were currently recovering another. His brother had promised to get to Kelvin next, knowing he would never log a request unless it was critical. But would they arrive in time for Jonah, and for Izzy?

With nothing to do except wait, Kelvin set about settling one form of anxiety at least. He stifled a yawn as he stepped into the darkened bedroom, but his mind was very much alert. From the fingers of light stretching from the landing, he could make out the shape of Dee's body, curled into the foetal position beneath their king-size quilt. The usual scent of laundered bedlinen and perfumed body sprays was absent, replaced by that of damp clothes and sweat.

Choosing not to switch on the main light, he approached his wife as he might an injured fawn and imagined her heart beating as fast as his. His foot caught on something, a discarded pair of socks or the sleeve of a jumper, and he flicked it away.

When he switched on his bedside lamp, his eyes quickly adjusted to the light. Dee took longer, blinking away the sting of tears that had dampened the pillow she was lying on. Kelvin gave her a moment, using the time to unlace his boots and drop them at the side of the bed. He clenched his teeth to contain the pain each movement caused his aching bones, stiffened muscles and blistered hands. Lifting his legs up and over the duvet, he lay down next to his wife. Her cheeks were now dry, but her despair lingered like a ghost.

'You went out to search for Jonah,' he said, leaving no room for a lie. The tracks Paige had followed up to the ruins; the hat that bore a striking resemblance to the one he owned; and the mystery of the light signal that Jonah had no means of making. Dee was the missing link.

'I wanted to help.'

'And you did.' Kelvin pursed his chapped lips. 'We wouldn't have found him without you.'

'How's he doing?'

'It's too soon to tell. Sue's trying to warm him up, but there's no knowing how bad his head injury is yet. Was he conscious when you got to him?'

'No,' she replied, her eyes flicking away before settling on Kelvin's face again. 'Why? Did he say anything to you?'

'Just your name.'

Nervous fingers worried at the seams of the quilt. 'I told him help was on the way. He must have heard me.'

As much as Kelvin wanted to believe her, he struggled to accept that two strangers who had met only that morning should have such a marked effect on each other. Dee had to be keeping something to herself, if not outright lying to him.

'Why didn't you stay with him?' he asked, recalling the channel through the snow marking Dee's retreat back up to the ruins.

'Because you were coming for him.'

The answer was a weak one, but he was more interested in why she had been there in the first place. 'You know better than to go out alone in those conditions, especially without telling anyone what you were doing,' he said. What he actually wanted to say was that it had been a crazy idea, that she was mad for attempting it, but those were loaded words he couldn't bring himself to use when describing his wife. 'You broke every rule you preach to other hikers. It's basic safety, Dee.'

'I work better alone.'

There was more truth to this than Kelvin would like. Dee had her own agenda, and Kelvin had been excluded from not only her actions but also the reasoning behind them. Frustration was getting the better of him. 'And why take the red route? You were so convinced Jonah wasn't planning on going up to the ruins,' he challenged.

'I just thought what Paige said made sense.'

'You heard us? You were that close?'

'It was obvious that Jonah must have swapped across to the other route,' she replied, ignoring Kelvin's comment. 'He wouldn't have wanted to hang around if there was a group of mourners about to scatter ashes.'

'You know him that well, do you?' Kelvin asked. When no answer came, he shook his head. 'What aren't you telling me, Dee? One minute you're hiding from Jonah because he reminds you of someone you'd rather forget, and the next, you're going off on your own in the middle of the night – in the middle of a storm – to save him. Why?'

Dee pressed her face against the pillow. 'Don't do this, Kelvin. I can't …'

Kelvin sensed that veil of hers coming down, separating him from the woman he loved. It almost broke him. He reached over to pull a damp coil of hair from her cheek, encouraging her to look at him again.

'Don't shut me out, Dee,' he said. 'You must know you can trust me with anything.'

'I do,' Dee said, her chin wobbling. 'I love you, Kelvin. You know that.'

'And I love you too. I'd be lost without you, Dee,' he added. Except he already felt lost. 'You've been closing down for months now, and it's scaring me.'

Dee's chin wobbled. 'It scares me too, more than you can imagine.'

'Oh, I don't have to imagine,' he said. 'I can feel the whole bed shaking. Please, I need to know what's happening. I think Jonah is more than someone who simply triggered bad memories.' He swallowed hard, unsure if he had the strength to get the words out. 'I need to know. Have I just brought home the man who got you pregnant, then broke you?'

CHAPTER 23

PAIGE

After the adrenaline rush of the last few hours, I could feel the energy draining from my body. Nan had closed the window so the snug was warming up again and my eyes felt tired and gritty. Not that I was going to risk closing them. What if Jonah woke up again?

I honestly don't know what I had expected to happen when we went out looking for him. I could have kept quiet about where I knew he would be, and I could have pretended not to notice the signal for help, but even though my contact with Jonah up until now had been virtual, he was a real-life person. He had the capacity to love and be loved, and that had to count for something. Except, he also had the capacity to damage my family, not to mention his own. I hadn't known he had a wife. How messed up was that?

Why did he have to say I pushed him? Not that anyone knew he was blaming me, but it didn't look good. Yes, I had been up there with him, and we had argued.

I'd shouted at him, and I'd hit him more than once, for all the good it did. He just stood there and took it. He was immovable. So whatever Jonah might recall, that's my truth. But who would believe me? More importantly, who would do the asking? The police? I hadn't thought this through. I was never going to convince Jonah to keep quiet because he didn't want to stay quiet. That was, after all, why he'd come here.

As I stared into the flames of the open fire, I heard the rustle of foil blankets and my heart leapt into my throat, but it was just Dad checking Jonah's heart rate on his watch. He had taken over from Olly, who had been sent upstairs with Izzy over an hour ago. None of us had heard a peep from them since, which had to be a good sign.

'Still forty-four,' Dad said, letting Jonah's hand flop down lifelessly onto the table. The patient's face remained pale, but the blue tinge to his lips had faded to lavender, and the cuts on his face glistened as if his blood had remembered to start flowing again.

Nan had a notepad to record Jonah's vitals, but she didn't reach for the pen behind her ear. It had been less than five minutes since Dad last checked. He just wanted something to do. Waiting was exhausting, but none of us could let our guard down. Things could change in a matter of moments.

My stomach rumbled loudly and I pulled my legs up, hooking my feet on the hard edge of the chair to rest my chin on my knees.

'Why don't you go and make yourself something to eat?' Nan suggested. She hadn't given up trying to get me out of the way. She clearly thought Jonah was about to die, but death didn't scare me as it once had. And if Jonah did die, at least he wouldn't be alone. That was more than Mum had.

'Do you think Jonah was awake after the fall? Do you think he suffered?' I asked, ignoring her question.

Nan groaned as she shifted position, adjusting the extra seat cushion protecting her back against the unforgiving spindles of her chair. She shared a guilty look with Dad before answering, knowing the parallels I was drawing with Mum's death. 'I doubt he would have been lucid enough to understand what was going on.'

'But was that just because the cold got to him?' I asked. There had been no snow to numb my mum's pain.

I heard a sigh. 'I really think you should go and get something to eat, Paige,' Dad said.

'I've put a load of containers of soup in the fridge,' Nan quickly added.

'Soup again?' As hungry as I was, I wasn't going to abandon my post for soup.

'Or how about an omelette? There are plenty of eggs, and Kelvin said to help ourselves,' Nan continued. 'In fact, you could make something for all of us. Go on. Be a love. I'm starving too.'

I could see this wasn't an argument I was going to win, but there was no way I was leaving my dad alone with Jonah. 'Will you come, Dad?'

'That's a good idea,' Nan jumped in before he could refuse. 'Go on, the pair of you. I'm wasting away here.'

Dad was standing over Jonah's body, and I had to tug

163

his arm to get him to move. 'Fine, I get the message,' he said. 'We won't be long, Sue.'

We worked as a team as we snooped around the unfamiliar kitchen and storerooms gathering supplies. Dad set down boxes of eggs and a slab of cheese onto the worktop while I figured out how to use the range. I heard him patting his trouser pockets.

'I left my phone in the snug,' he said. 'Do you have yours?'

'What do you want it for?' I asked, pulling my phone from my back pocket, but keeping a tight hold of it.

Dad managed a laugh. 'Don't worry, I don't need to see whatever weird stuff you have on there,' he said. 'Just take it off silent mode. We need to know if your nan or Olly call for help.'

It wasn't the first time Dad had given me a lecture about turning on the alerts on my phone in case he needed to get in touch, and up until a few months ago, I would have rolled my eyes at whatever non-existent risk he feared might happen. Not any longer.

'Fine,' I said, flicking the mute button off and placing it on a shelf at eye level. It wasn't as if Jonah could message me, and Olly had learnt the hard way not to write anything that might be incriminating.

'Right, let's get to work,' Dad said. 'You grate the cheese and I'll start cracking eggs.'

'I'm not *that* hungry,' I said when he picked up the largest measuring jug he could find.

'Your nan said make enough for all of us. That includes Izzy and Olly. I'd hate for them to come down searching

164

for sustenance and find we'd only looked after ourselves. If they're asleep or not hungry, they can leave it,' he said. 'If today has taught us anything, it's that we have to pull together.'

While Dad sorted out plates and cutlery, I set about making omelettes just like Mum had shown me. When I plated up the first two, Dad looked impressed.

'How about you take those up to Olly and Izzy,' he said, 'and I'll see if I can do as good a job with ours. Oh, and while you're up there, if it looks like Kelvin's still awake, ask him if he and his wife want one too.' He could tell by my face that I wasn't keen on the idea of us being separated. 'Please, Paige. After that hike, I don't think my legs will carry me upstairs.'

On the landing, I could hear voices coming from two of the rooms, and headed towards Izzy's voice. With a plate and cutlery in each hand, I kicked rather than knocked on the door.

'It's me,' I said in a stage whisper. 'Do you want food?'

Olly pulled open the door. 'That's so good of you, Paige,' he said far too brightly. 'They smell delicious.'

I took a short step into the room. 'I'll just leave them here,' I said, setting the plates on the stack of boxes nearest the door.

'How's Jonah?' asked Izzy, sitting up in bed and rubbing her eyes.

'The same,' I answered. 'So I'd better go.'

'No, wait. Why don't we have that talk?'

'My food'll be getting cold.'

'Let her go, Iz,' Olly said, skirting cautiously around

165

me to pick up the plates. 'You're supposed to be relaxing.'

I wanted to punch him, I really did. I don't know where the anger kept coming from, but it was better than feeling dead inside. I glared at him. 'Worried it's you we'll be talking about?'

Olly tried and failed to hold my gaze. 'No, I'm worried about the fact that even a simple comment can have you jumping down people's throats. I don't want you upsetting Izzy again.'

His wife cleared her throat. 'Izzy is here, in case either of you hadn't noticed,' she said. 'And you don't have to worry, Ol. I can give as good as I get with this one.' She gave me a measured look. 'Paige, what is it you're having to eat?'

I tipped my head towards the plates trembling in Olly's hand. 'Omelette, same as you.'

'Well, that's easy then,' replied Izzy. 'You can stay and eat with me. Olly, go downstairs and have Paige's serving.' When neither of us moved, she spoke more forcibly. 'Go on. If you're so concerned about not upsetting me, you'll do as I say.'

I think I only stayed because I could tell how much Olly wanted me to storm off. He took a step towards the door, thinking it would provoke me to leave, but instead, I took the plates from him.

'Oh, and knock on Kelvin's door while you're passing to see if they want food too,' I said with a smirk that lasted only as long as it took Olly to skulk off and close the door behind him.

'Right,' said Izzy. 'Sit down.'

CHAPTER 24

KELVIN

Kelvin was waiting for Dee to answer his question. If Jonah was indeed the man he had feared for so long, someone he could now put a name and a face to, he wasn't sure he could be held responsible for whatever he did next. 'Just tell me,' he pleaded.

'I'm sorry, but I can't,' Dee said. 'Please, you just have to trust me.'

'I promised your parents I'd protect you, but how can I do that if I don't know where the threat is?'

'Kelvin, I don't need your protection,' she said, but her voice sounded painfully weak. 'I only need your patience.'

'For how long? Until Jonah leaves? Or dies?' asked Kelvin, fumbling for answers. 'What if he wakes up and asks for you again?'

Dee shrank back beneath the covers. 'Don't let him,' she whispered.

Kelvin twitched as if struck by an electrical current. 'What?'

'Nothing.'

'It was more than nothing, Dee,' Kelvin replied as one by one the connections lit up. Her fears, and his, were real. 'Jonah isn't a random stranger, is he?' he asked, sinking his head into his pillow. 'Oh, God. What have I done?'

Before Dee could respond, there was a knock at the door. 'Hey, it's Olly. We're making food downstairs and wondered if you'd like something?'

'Thanks,' Dee called out, attempting to sound normal as she rubbed her husband's back. 'Kelvin will be down in a minute.'

Hearing the soft whisper of stocking feet moving away from the door, Kelvin lifted his head wearily from the pillow. 'I'm not hungry.'

'I know, but you need to be down there. We have guests to look after whether we like it or not, and I'm sorry, but I can't do it, so you have to.'

'I don't know if I can face *him* again,' he said, frightened by his own honesty. 'How did he find you, Dee?'

When they had first met, Dee had already established a life of partial anonymity. Her dad had inherited the pub from an elderly relative and she had jumped at the chance to take it on. On the face of it, she was an involved member of the community, volunteering in her spare time, but it was the isolation of the mountain that drew her. Once they had married, the change of her surname was the final step in severing her ties with the past. There were no old uni friends to link her to her new identity, no social media presence, and her parents knew better than to point anyone from her past in their daughter's direction.

So how did he track her down?

'It was just one of those things,' Dee said. 'A chance meeting.'

'Damn the bastard, I wish I'd left him on the mountain,' Kelvin hissed.

Unlike Dee's parents, Kelvin hadn't been so quick to assume Dee was the architect of her own downfall. The man they imagined as some unwitting student who had become the object of their daughter's obsession was far from innocent. Dee's memories were fragmented, but she had shared enough with Kelvin to convince him that the relationship wasn't one-sided. Jonah had found the break-up just as painful, and on the night it came to a head, he had known Dee was going to take an overdose. He didn't try to stop her, or even raise the alarm. He walked away hoping she would die because it was a neat way to end a problem, if only for himself. But unbeknownst to either of them, Dee had been pregnant, and the damage he had inflicted continued to this day. Because of *him*, Dee had miscarried. Because of *him*, she thought she didn't deserve to be a mother, and that meant Kelvin had also been denied the possibility of ever being a father. Kelvin had accepted that willingly because he had fallen in love with Dee, not her ability to bear his children. And now the woman he loved was disappearing before his eyes.

'I can't believe you actually wanted to save him,' he said, only for his body to give another jolt. He swallowed hard. 'Dee, answer me truthfully. When we saw your flashlight, were you trying to get our attention? Or did you give away your position by accident?'

'I don't know what you mean,' she said.

Kelvin prayed her confusion was genuine. 'Christ, I can't believe I'm saying this. Did you go out there to save Jonah, or were you intending to make sure he didn't come back? Is that why you went alone? Is that why you're scared about Jonah waking up?'

'No, Kelvin, that's not it at all,' she said, sounding determined rather than shocked or offended. 'Please, I'm trying so hard to hold it together, and not only for me. There are other people we need to consider. That poor girl, for one.'

It was Kelvin's turn to be confused. 'Do you mean Paige? What does she have to do with this?'

Dee leant over to kiss his forehead. He could feel her lips trembling when she said, 'Let's just get through the next few hours. Help will come soon, and then I'll tell you everything. I promise. Now go.'

Rather than move away, Kelvin pressed closer to Dee, wrapping his arms around her and holding on tight. He wished he could stay there until dawn. 'I'd do anything for you. You know that.'

'You don't have to do anything, my love,' she whispered in his ear. 'You just have to go downstairs and get something to eat. Please. It'll be fine.'

When Kelvin left their bedroom, his aching muscles strained with a tension that knew no release. His mind was elsewhere when he entered the kitchen, and although his eyes were drawn to the two men standing on the other side of the kitchen island, it took a second to register what he had just seen.

170

Ray had had his back to Kelvin, so it was Olly's reaction he saw first. The younger man had actually released a tiny squeak as his body jerked in surprise, and his hand shot behind his back, hiding whatever he was holding.

'Is everything OK?' Kelvin asked as Ray twisted around, looking just as shifty as Olly. What was it with this family?

'Yeah, good,' replied Ray.

'Yeah,' parroted Olly. 'All good.'

Kelvin had to stop himself from laughing, or did he want to cry? No, things were not good, not good at all.

CHAPTER 25

PAIGE

Sitting on the end of the bed opposite Izzy, I cut and stabbed at my omelette in silence, forcing chunks down my throat without tasting it. The sooner I cleared my plate, the sooner Izzy would say her piece and I could leave. I wiped my mouth with the back of my hand in preparation for my exit when I noticed Izzy crease her brow and shift position.

'Is it …?' I said, not daring to ask.

'A contraction? No, I just find it a bit cumbersome having this great big mass of baby and amniotic fluid to manoeuvre.'

'That's all?'

'Yep,' Izzy said, setting her plate down on the mattress, her meal half-eaten.

'Sorry,' I said, to which Izzy raised an eyebrow. She would be wondering which of my many misdeeds I was apologizing for. 'Was it my fault your contractions started?'

Izzy looked about to dismiss the suggestion, but she sighed away the lie. 'Finding out Ellen had been rushing to take my call was bad enough, but realizing everyone had kept it from me was what hurt the most.'

'You can't blame me for that,' I said. Personally, I'd wanted Izzy to know what part she had played, but now I wasn't so sure. What if it wasn't an accident? What if Mum was depressed and had been pushed to breaking point? I shuddered, thinking about Jonah's mumbled words, claiming he was pushed too – only in his case, it wasn't in the metaphorical sense. I needed to get back downstairs.

'You do need to take some responsibility for your actions though, Paige,' Izzy was saying. 'It was your choice to tell me the way you did. You wanted to inflict pain. Well, congratulations. It damn well hurt.'

I concentrated on pulling a loose thread on one of my socks. 'I know I can be a bitch sometimes.'

'Lately, it's been a lot more than sometimes,' Izzy said. 'From the way you treat Olly, I'd say I've got off lightly.'

I rolled my eyes, knowing she couldn't see my expression. If I really wanted to hurt Izzy, now that would be a story to tell.

'Look, I'm sure everyone thought they were protecting me by not mentioning my part in Ellen's accident,' Izzy continued, thankfully keeping to the original subject. 'But that only made it into a bigger deal because it implied my guilt. Lies to protect people are still lies.'

My head shot up. Izzy spoke as if she would never stoop so low, but she was a liar too. I wasn't supposed to know, but she had told some pretty big lies for Mum. I could see a flicker of guilt cross her face. She swallowed back her hypocrisy. 'You could have handled it better, is all I'm saying,' she finished quickly.

'I know.' I reached over to pick up our plates to signal the end of the discussion, but Izzy grabbed my hand.

'Can I tell you something?' she asked.

She didn't let go of my hand until I nodded. The plates remained on the bed. There was no escaping yet.

'Me and your mum had a bit of a falling-out the day before she died,' Izzy said. She pursed her lips. 'It was nothing bad, nothing we wouldn't have worked out, at least. I'd told her I wouldn't do something for her, not any more, but after sleeping on it, I felt bad about letting her down. I hate that I thought she was ignoring my calls on purpose. And I hate that those very calls caused the accident that stopped me from ever making it up to her. So you see, you don't need to torture me, I can do that well enough on my own.' Izzy squeezed her eyes shut as they filled with tears.

I didn't know what I was supposed to say to that. I'd spent most of the last day on the mountain trying to figure out how Mum might have felt on the day she died. I was almost ready to absolve Izzy of blame, and now she had thrown this at me? Why did everyone have a confession to make?

'What was it you wouldn't do for her?' I asked, the ice in my veins giving my voice the force of an arctic blast.

'It's not important now,' said Izzy, sniffing back her tears.

174

'Oh, I think it is,' I said. I already suspected what it was, but me being me, I decided to play along for a while. 'Did you fall out over Olly?'

'No, not at all,' she replied, thinking she was on safer ground again. 'I wish you'd been able to come home for the wedding; you would have seen how everyone else was happy for us. Maybe you wouldn't be so hard on Olly now.'

Oh, I would, I thought. The wedding had been in October and I'd only been at university for a few weeks so I had my excuse. Witnessing their nuptials was never going to change my mind that Olly was a shit.

I shrugged rather than give an answer. I really couldn't care less about Olly right now. 'So if that wasn't why you argued, what else could it have been?' I tapped my finger on my chin as if contemplating other possibilities. 'Was it Dad?'

'No, not exactly. Please, Paige, let's just leave it. I shouldn't have told you.'

'And to think you're usually so good at keeping things to yourself. Like what Mum was doing behind Dad's back.'

Izzy licked her dry lips. 'I don't know what you mean.'

'I think you do. Lies to protect people are still lies,' I said, repeating her mantra. 'I know what Mum was up to, and I know you were covering for her.'

Izzy's jaw dropped as her face flushed scarlet. She looked as if she were about to deny it again, but her features became pinched. 'How did ... Who told you?'

'Does it matter?' I said, determined to keep my secrets too. 'Was Olly in on it as well?'

'He knew, but—'

'Yeah, of course he did!' I said, aware my voice was getting louder. I gritted my teeth as I tried and failed to rein in my anger. 'To think it was Dad who got you both back together, and all the time, you were laughing behind his back. How could you? How could Mum?'

Izzy placed a hand across her forehead as if shielding herself from my glare. 'I promise you, no one was laughing at Ray. Your mum was worried about him more than anyone. They'd spent twenty years building a life together, and Ray was expecting another twenty more.'

'But not Mum,' I said bluntly. 'She only built that life because getting pregnant buggered up her first plans. Did she die thinking it had all been a waste?'

Izzy's eyes darted to the door. 'Please, can you keep your voice down? What if your dad comes upstairs? Do you want him to hear?'

'Of course I don't,' I said in a hoarse whisper as I fought back my emotions. 'I have to lie to him like everyone else has been doing.'

'Yes, you do. And I'm so sorry.'

'Why didn't you stop her?'

'She would have carried on whether I helped her or not,' said Izzy. 'And I just wanted her to be happy.'

'Happy?' I spat at her. 'Did she sound happy when you argued about it? Or by some chance, did she sound suicidal?'

176

Izzy gasped. 'What on earth …?' She blinked hard. 'But she wasn't.'

'Are you sure about that? What if the fall wasn't an accident, Iz? What if she'd just had enough of all the pretence?'

'Your mum *did not* kill herself, Paige. There was nothing remotely suspicious about her death.' When Izzy reached over for me again, I wanted to believe her. I wanted to collapse into her arms and cry and cry and cry, but there were too many reasons to keep my aunt at arm's length. I arched my spine backwards, and as I pressed my lower back onto the mattress, I was mindful of the phone in my back pocket holding too many secrets. Except I couldn't actually feel it. I jumped off the bed and shoved my hands in both pockets. My phone wasn't there. I pictured placing it on the shelf in the kitchen and my stomach plummeted.

'I have to go,' I said.

Izzy shook free of her sleeping bags so she could get up too, but she was struggling to stand. 'Wait, Paige. You need to calm down first.'

'After everything that's happened, there's absolutely no chance of that,' I said, yanking the bedroom door open and flying down the stairs.

CHAPTER 26

KELVIN

Kelvin had wanted to turn around and leave the kitchen the moment he saw the worried looks on Olly and Ray's faces, but if he left he would have to go back into the snug to at least pretend to be interested in Jonah's condition. 'How's our casualty?' he asked.

'Stable,' said Ray, collecting himself. 'I've just taken some food in for Sue, but I don't think she has the energy to eat. Between watching him and worrying about Izzy, she's already exhausted.'

'But Izzy's doing fine,' Olly added quickly, pre-empting Kelvin's next question. 'No contractions. Just a bit of discomfort now and again. I think we can all relax on that front.'

Kelvin had heard raised voices coming from Izzy's room at one point, and doubted there was any relaxation going on. 'I might give Sian a ring just to let her know. It won't be easy getting a team here, and I'd rather they didn't take any unnecessary risks if there's no immediate threat to life.'

'Agreed,' said Ray.

'And they definitely shouldn't put themselves out for that bloke in there,' added Olly, sharing a sideways glance with Ray.

Kelvin couldn't agree more, but he was surprised that Olly and Ray should feel the same kind of antipathy towards Jonah. 'Is there something I should know?' he asked.

As Olly went to pull his hand from behind his back, Ray stopped him. 'It's family stuff,' he said.

'But it's got something to do with Jonah?' Kelvin persisted.

Before either could answer, Paige crashed into the room. Olly almost jumped out of his skin. He changed direction twice before hiding himself behind Ray.

'Hey, Paige,' said Ray, coming forward to block his daughter's path. 'How's Izzy?'

'She's fine,' Paige said sullenly. 'I just wanted to grab my phone.'

Olly reached up to a shelf, and with a sleight of hand, held aloft the bright pink mobile he had been holding all along. 'Is this it?' he asked as if there were any doubt.

Paige sidestepped her dad to snatch it from Olly. No one dared speak another word until she was gone.

'Phew, that was close,' Olly said, wiping a slick of sweat from his upper lip. Then his body tensed as he realized his potential mistake. 'She has gone back upstairs, hasn't she?'

As they listened, Kelvin heard soft footsteps retreating.

'Yeah, I think so.'

'Do you want to go and talk to her about ... you know?' Olly asked Ray.

'I'd rather leave that until we're away from here.'

Ray looked to Kelvin as if he were expecting him to leave, but Kelvin was more inclined to stay. He assumed Olly had been looking at Paige's phone, but what might he have found? It seemed likely it had caused Olly's sudden change of opinion of Jonah. Recalling what Dee had said about watching out for Paige, Kelvin could see the beginnings of a connection forming that he didn't like much.

'I'll update Sian,' he said, taking out his phone. 'Or should we check with Sue first?'

'Make the call,' Ray said.

'And I'll make some coffee,' added Olly.

'Great idea,' replied Ray. 'Sue could definitely do with one.'

Kelvin moved over to the sinks, still close enough to eavesdrop should Ray and Olly strike up a conversation while he was busy.

'Hey, Sian,' he said brightly as if it wasn't past midnight. 'Have you heard from Rob lately?'

There was the sound of a teaspoon tinkling against a cup. 'Actually, I was just about to ring you. The team's currently retrieving a casualty north of Eryri, and an air ambulance is on the scene. They're hoping for a quick handover so they can make their way to you, and we already have paramedics on standby. I don't want to speak too soon, but things have started to get a bit quieter. The

180

roads are pretty much deserted.'

'I'm not surprised. It's been snowing heavily up here again,' Kelvin warned, checking the view from the window. They were at the back of the pub so there wasn't much to see beyond the snowflakes floating past the window in the dark.

'Down here too,' said Sian. 'But temperatures are definitely going to be up come morning, and heavy rain should wash the worst away.'

As Sian talked, Kelvin refocused his eyes so he could see Ray and Olly's reflection in the window. Olly appeared to lean in to say something to Ray, but the older man lifted his hand in warning. Whatever conversation they needed to have wasn't going to happen in front of Kelvin.

'So how are things there?' Sian asked.

'Well, I have good news and bad news. The bad is we have an abandoned car blocking the mountain road,' he said, noticing how Ray turned his head at the mention of the obstruction he had caused. 'So unless Rob can find a way of moving it, they might have to complete the last section on foot.'

'Damn. That's not going to help us get your man down again either.'

Kelvin bristled at the suggestion that Jonah was his man. Not in this lifetime, he thought.

'So what's the good news?' asked Sian.

'Both our patients are stable. Izzy's contractions have stopped and our other casualty isn't showing signs of deterioration,' he said, feeling only a slight pang of guilt that he spoke with unwarranted authority. Only Sue could make that sort of assessment about Jonah. 'We're all pretty much agreed that you can bump us down your list of priorities. If Rob needs to catch forty winks, tell him not to rush on our account.'

'I'll tell him, but you're his last call out, and you know what he's like. He won't rest until he knows he's done as much as he can. I'll tell him to take it easy, but to be honest, I don't think he'd be there much before dawn either way.'

'Fair enough,' said Kelvin.

Closing the call, Kelvin continued to look out into the bleak night. When was this ever going to end?

'Here's your coffee,' Olly said from close behind him.

Kelvin turned and was about to take the cup when they heard a yell.

'Ray!' Sue was calling. 'I need you!'

The cup slipped from Olly's hand and crashed to the floor.

CHAPTER 27

SUE

After being left alone, Sue had switched to a chair that didn't have arms and removed the seat cushion to make it as uncomfortable as possible. She needed to stay awake, but with everyone else gone, the sound of Jonah's steady breaths was soporific. Every time she blinked, it took longer to open her eyes again.

And what harm would it do if she did just close her eyes for a moment? She would spring into action if she was needed. Her phone was in her lap, and there was nothing more she could do for Jonah except wait for him to gradually warm up and open his eyes. The fact that he had talked was a good indication that his head injury wasn't causing any significant harm – yet. There was still the risk of a brain haemorrhage or internal bleeding, but there was nothing she would be able to do if that was Jonah's fate. She could only treat the hypothermia, and there was no doubt that his vital signs were improving. She could relax. A little.

It felt like she had only closed her eyes for a second when Ray shook her shoulder. 'I'll put your food here,' he said.

Through half-opened eyes, she watched him place the plate on the side table next to her. Struggling to lift her head, she turned in Jonah's direction.

'I can see more colour in his cheeks,' said Ray.

'Good,' Sue replied, doing her best to change her posture so it looked like she was more awake than she felt. She heard Ray put another log on the fire, and as soon as silence returned, her head fell back, her mouth gaped open and she began to snore.

The warm air encouraged her mind to melt away their snowy prison, and the bum-numbing chair transformed into one of her more comfortable dining chairs. Her iPad was in front of her, but there was no one on screen. She glanced out of the window at the old apple tree that was clinging on to the last of its autumn leaves. She should ask Ray to help her prune it back, but where had he wandered off to? There had been a phone ringing, she remembered, and he had gone to investigate.

'No!' she heard Ray cry out, making her blood run cold. 'Ellen! Please. Oh, God, no. No!'

'Ray!' Sue screamed, except her mouth wasn't moving. And why were her eyes suddenly closed? Why couldn't she open them? She had to do something, but none of her limbs were working. No, no, no! This couldn't happen again.

Concentrating harder, Sue was aware of every nerve ending carrying messages to her unresponsive body.

184

Finally, her head lifted a fraction, then her fingers twitched. Her eyes snapped open and, realizing it was far too late to save Ellen, she let the wave of grief wash over her.

She took deep, steady breaths to slow her heart rate and still her mind. She could hear the crackle of the fire. All else was quiet. Unnervingly so. She noticed the rubbery omelette Ray had left for her before turning her attention to Jonah lying on the table. He was perfectly still. There was no movement. Not one little bit. Not even the rise and fall of his chest.

Standing up, it took Sue a moment for her vertebrae to realign, a painful process, but one that pushed away the last remnants of sleep. She stepped closer to her patient. The colour that had been returning to Jonah's cheeks had given way to a deathly pallor.

With trembling hands, she lifted the foil blankets covering his body, revealing the restraints that were meant to keep him safe. That had been Sue's job too, but the moment she placed her fingers on the cold and waxen skin of his wrist, she knew there would be no pulse. She stepped away and went to the door.

'Ray!' she yelled along the corridor. 'I need you!'

There was the sound of something breaking in the kitchen and a yelp, quickly followed by the soft thud of running feet. Sue was already back at Jonah's side, her arms wrapped around herself. Whatever limited powers of healing she held in her hands were of no use to Jonah now.

'What is it?' Ray asked, coming to a stop on the threshold. Two more figures appeared on either side of him. No one attempted to enter the room.

'Is he dead?' asked Olly.

Sue nodded.

'Are you sure?' Ray asked. 'Shouldn't you try CPR or something?'

'It wouldn't do much good,' she replied. 'I don't suppose there's a defibrillator you failed to mention, Kelvin.'

'No. Sorry.'

The adrenaline rush that had forced Sue to wake up was receding, and what little energy she had in reserve for emotions had been spent on her dream of Ellen. She looked from one face to another, needing to see some reaction so she could work out how she should feel. All three men were unreadable.

'What happened?' asked Ray eventually.

And there it was, the first emotion to hit Sue, and it was guilt. 'I, erm, I don't know,' she said. 'It was so warm in here and, you know, you saw me, it was so hard to stay awake.' She licked her lips to stop them sticking together. 'I thought he was stable, and I knew Olly would phone if Izzy …' Her voice trailed off as she looked to her son-in-law. 'Have you left her on her own?'

'No, Paige is with her. She's fine,' Olly assured her.

Ray was looking at her untouched omelette. 'You were drowsy when I brought you your food, you must have fallen asleep,' he continued for her. 'That was maybe half an hour ago, probably more.' He was looking to Olly now.

'Sounds about right,' Olly replied. 'I was in the kitchen

when you came back from the snug.'

Ray rubbed his cheek. 'Actually, I'd been in the toilets for a while swilling my face,' he explained. 'You weren't the only one struggling to stay awake, Sue. It's been a tough day for all of us. You shouldn't feel guilty.'

Olly nudged past Ray so he could get a better look at the corpse. 'Do you know what killed him?'

'It's impossible to say since we didn't know the full extent of his injuries. It could be hypothermia, a brain haemorrhage, heart failure …' Sue could continue with a longer list, but her voice cracked. Had it been inevitable? Or would Jonah still be alive if she had only stayed awake? 'We won't find out until the autopsy.'

'It's safe to say we were fighting a losing battle,' Ray said to reassure her. He too had moved closer to the body. 'Let's cover him up.'

'He should be moved somewhere colder,' Sue said.

'We have some tarpaulin we could use to wrap the body,' Kelvin suggested. 'Then we can leave it in the snow for now.'

Sue didn't like the way Jonah had quickly become a thing and not a person, but these were the practicalities they had to consider, and she still had a daughter to care for. There would be no more casualties on her watch. She went to pull the foil blanket over Jonah's face, but Olly stopped her.

'What's that around his nose?' he asked. 'Is it bruising?'

Sue had seen plenty of dead bodies, but it took a concerted effort for her gritty eyes to focus on the tiny purple dots around Jonah's nostrils. 'It's petechiae.

187

It's where tiny capillaries have haemorrhaged,' she explained.

Olly didn't appear satisfied with the answer. 'It wasn't there before.'

'We did knock him around when we were carrying him down,' Ray reminded them. 'Maybe he hit his nose, and the hypothermia delayed his body from reacting to the injury.'

'I don't know,' Olly began unsteadily. 'Maybe I've been watching too much *CSI*, but isn't that a sign of suffocation?'

Sue straightened up fast. 'I don't know, Olly,' she said, wishing he hadn't looked. 'It's possible his airway became blocked with saliva, or vomit, or his own tongue. He might have had a fit while I was only feet away, fast-a-bloody-sleep.' She ran out of breath and gasped for air. Jonah's death was her fault.

'It's pointless speculating how he died,' Ray said, giving Olly a stern look. 'We just don't know. And let's face it, Jonah brought this on himself. He chose to come here.'

Sue knew he was trying to make her feel better, but it wasn't working. 'No one expects to die for setting off on a little walk!' she cried. 'I was just so tired. I heard him breathing. I thought he was getting stronger. What if he did wake up? What if he couldn't breathe? We'd strapped him to the table so he couldn't move. I let him die! I ... I killed him.'

There was a stunned silence where no one knew how to respond until Sue's body began to shake and her legs buckled.

Ray and Olly caught her before she collapsed, but as they tried to steer her towards the chair she had been sitting on when she had forsaken her duties as a nurse, Sue fought against them.

'We need to get her out of this room,' Ray said above Sue's sobs.

Without further discussion, Sue was half-led, half-dragged into the dining room where it was distinctly darker and cooler. Kelvin pulled out a chair at one of the round dining tables where a single candle lit the room. While Ray and Olly gathered around Sue, their host grabbed the bottle of brandy and glasses he had left on the bar for them earlier.

There was the glugging sound of a shot glass being filled. 'I think you need this,' Kelvin said, handing her the brandy.

With the residual light spilling from the corridor, and the flickering flame from the candle, the dark crimson liquid looked to be on fire. Sue shook her head violently. 'No! Not while Izzy might need me. If something happened ... No,' she repeated.

'Maybe the rest of us might need one,' Olly said. He looked to Ray. 'We should tell her.'

'Tell me what?' Sue demanded.

Ray took both of Sue's hands in his to steady her. 'I'm afraid it was no coincidence that Jonah came here today – sorry, I should say yesterday now – but he knew where to find us, Sue.'

Glass clinked as Kelvin continued pouring drinks for the others. He was the only one who remained standing, not part of the family discussion, but invested nonetheless, having opened up his pub to them.

'Find us? Why would he want to find us? We don't know him,' Sue insisted. No one had given the slightest hint of recognition. Or had they? Goosebumps pricked her arms as she recalled Izzy's reaction to seeing Jonah lying on the table. '*Do* we know him?'

'Paige does,' Ray said solemnly. 'He befriended her after Ellen died.'

Sue pulled away from Ray's grasp and sat upright. She wiped away her tears with the back of her hand. 'Then why didn't Paige say something?'

There was the scrape of a chair as Olly moved closer, for now ignoring the brandy Kelvin had set down in front of him. He kept his voice low. 'It was their little secret,' he whispered, but not gently enough to stop Sue recoiling. 'We think Jonah was grooming her. What other explanation could there be for a man in his forties striking up a relationship with a vulnerable teenager who had just lost her mum?'

'And he followed her here?'

'I think he was the one who convinced her to come here in the first place,' said Olly.

'But why? So he could spy on us?' Sue asked. She knew she was awake, but it was as if she had entered a fresh nightmare.

'It seems that way,' Ray said, his features grave. 'Jonah had told Kelvin's wife he was going to the first viewing point, but we never saw him there. But he saw us.'

'And Paige ran straight into his clutches, I bet,' Sue

concluded, fighting to catch her breath. 'Do you think she was with him all that time she was missing?'

When her granddaughter had run away, the worst danger Sue had imagined was that she had gotten lost. That had been horrifying enough, but she felt sick as a vision formed of Paige in the middle of a storm, cowering from the advances of the man who had lured her there.

Ray placed his hands on his knees to stop them jiggling. 'It's possible,' he said.

'Paige hasn't said?'

'No, we haven't spoken to her yet. We're still putting all the pieces together.'

Sue looked longingly at the brandy on the table. Her body sagged. 'Of course she met him. That's how she knew where you should go looking for him. That's why she reacted like she did when Jonah tried to speak. He said he'd been pushed.'

The sharp intake of breath came from Kelvin who hadn't been there when Jonah had tried to talk. Sue had forgotten he was listening, but Ray hadn't. 'We don't know what he said,' he prompted his mother-in-law. 'He was incoherent.'

'Maybe we'll never know,' Sue said, picturing the dead man in the snug. How did she feel about Jonah now? As a nurse, she treated every patient without judgement, but surely there were limits.

'I hate to think what he might have done to Paige, or intended to do,' Olly said, echoing Sue's fears.

'We won't know anything for certain without speaking to her,' Sue said as her thoughts finally caught up with her. 'But how on earth do you know any of this if she didn't tell you?'

In the pause that followed, it was obvious that Olly had the answer, but he knocked back his brandy first. 'So … Well … I was worried about Paige. I thought her reaction to Jonah was off, so I looked … I checked her phone. She'd given me her passcode ages ago when we were sharing videos … You know, for TikTok. She'd changed it since, but I knew she liked using special dates. Anyway, I figured it out and that's when I saw the messages from Jonah.'

There was a rustling sound from the furthest corner of the room. At first Sue thought it was Kelvin, who had retreated to the shadows, but he looked just as confused as they did.

'You've been looking at my phone?' screeched Paige, jumping up from behind the bar. 'You bastard!'

There was a clatter as Olly knocked over his chair in his haste to stand up. He almost fell over it as he backed away from the slender but fearsome figure kicking off the woollen throw tangled at her feet.

Olly yelped. 'I didn't mean to, Paige.'

CHAPTER 28

PAIGE

'You bastard!' I screamed, lurching towards Olly. With his mouth gaping open and his features contorted by candlelight, Izzy's husband – and soon to be ex-husband if I had anything to do with it – had become a real-life version of *The Scream*. It would be funny if I hadn't been so incandescent with a rage that eviscerated all other feelings. With every cell of my being, I hated this sad excuse for a man who had proven time and time again that he couldn't be trusted.

I shoved the heel of my hand against his chest. 'You're going to pay for this!'

Olly reeled backwards. 'I … I'm … I'm sorry,' he stuttered.

Raising a balled fist this time, I was ready to punch him right in the face when an arm glided through the narrowing space between us. Kelvin blocked my advance.

'Paige, just take a breath,' he said.

'Who the fuck are you to tell me what to do?' I

screeched. 'This has nothing to do with you!'

'Paige, that's enough!' my dad shouted.

I could have ignored Dad too, but it was seeing Nan's gaunt face that forced me to lower my fist. She looked so old all of a sudden, and I knew she must be upset about what sneaky Olly had been telling them, but she had been upset before they came into the dining room. I had heard her calling for Dad's help, and knew it must be something bad to do with Jonah, but I hadn't wanted to go and find out. Instead, I'd huddled behind the bar with only a thin throw for warmth. I hadn't been hiding deliberately. I'd just wanted some time by myself, but trouble had found me.

I jabbed a finger at Olly. 'You're going to regret this! If you can go around sharing private messages, so can I!'

'I didn't mean to, Paige,' Olly snivelled.

'Oh, so you hacked my phone by accident, did you?'

'What I mean is, I didn't know you'd been messaging Jonah.'

'And why would you? Why *should* you?'

When no one answered, the rush of anger was replaced by crushing despair. Could my life get any worse? As the first tear trickled down my cheek, my nan stood up. I might be taller, but there was no way I was going to resist her embrace. I bowed my head and pressed my eyes against her shoulder to staunch what was now a flood of tears. How had I ended up in this mess? It wasn't my fault. Not any of it. Well, not most of it.

Nan rubbed my back in a circular motion. 'It's OK, love.'

I felt another shadow moving closer. 'We're going to get through this,' Dad promised.

Were we? I asked myself. How many of my messages had Olly read? I tried to recall the thread of conversations that had zipped back and forth in the last couple of months. Admittedly, it did look odd. Jonah was so much older than even I had realized, but the messages in themselves had been innocuous. It wasn't as if he had made his motives obvious. Even I hadn't worked out what Jonah was up to, which was in my favour now. I didn't have to explain anything. I could bluff my way out of this.

Dad picked up the chair Olly had knocked over. 'Sit down, Paige.'

I wiped my nose with my sleeve and, feeling more confident, went to join him and Nan at the table. 'How's Jonah?' I asked, forcing the question from my lips.

My heart knocked against my chest, counting down the seconds it took for the others to decide who would speak up.

'He's dead, Paige,' Dad said.

I covered my face with my hands, but I wouldn't cry again. I had no tears left, not for him. I was sorry he was dead, sorry I'd made the foolish mistake to meet him up by the ruins, but I couldn't pretend not to be glad our secrets had died with him.

Grabbing one of the shot glasses of brandy, I knocked it back before anyone could stop me.

'Are you ready to talk about who he is to you?' asked Nan.

'There's nothing to tell,' I replied, my eyes sliding towards the scumbag who was still hiding behind Kelvin. 'I'd rather talk about why Olly decided to hack my phone.'

'Please, Paige,' he replied, peeking over Kelvin's shoulder to meet my gaze. 'I'm sorry.'

Kelvin looked uncomfortable in the firing line of my glare. He cleared his throat. 'I'll leave you to it,' he said. 'I should check on Dee.'

Nan gripped the table, needing to pull herself to standing. 'And I should go up to Izzy,' she said, about to follow Kelvin out of the room. 'She'll be on her own.'

'Then I should go too,' Olly said as one distraction followed another.

Olly hurried to the open door, with Nan close behind him. My audience was about to reduce to one, and I couldn't face Dad on my own. He'd know I was hiding something.

'Izzy's fine,' I said. 'She would have phoned if she needed us. If we're going to talk, I need you all to stay.'

The offer stopped Nan in her tracks. She raised her hands in exasperation. 'And if we do, will you tell us what happened?'

I could certainly tell them something. I just hadn't decided what.

'But I have to go,' whimpered Olly, opening the door an inch wider.

'For God's sake, Olly, sit down!' Nan snapped. 'The sooner we do this, the sooner we can be with Izzy.'

When the four of us gathered around a spluttering

candle, it was reminiscent of a séance. What would Mum have made of it all? What would she want me to do?

'Is it just Olly who read my messages, or was it a free-for-all?' I asked, needing to know what I was dealing with.

'I didn't read them,' Dad admitted, unable to look at me. 'But from what Olly's said, it looks like Jonah put a lot of effort into building your trust.'

'And I only read snatches,' mumbled Olly. 'It was the way he was so familiar with you. Like you'd been friends for ages when obviously you hadn't.'

'He used your mum's death as a way to get you to open up,' Dad added. 'That's how these things work.'

'You're not in any trouble, Paige,' Nan interjected, 'but you do need to be honest with us.'

My dad was nodding. 'Whatever is said in this room doesn't have to go any further.'

The comment was laughable. For a family that delighted in its secrets, there appeared to be no boundaries when it came to my privacy. But of course I didn't laugh, because this was far too serious. I had a choice. Unburden myself and hurt those I loved, or bury myself in the slow death of lies.

'Did you see Jonah while you were separated from us?' Nan asked, opening up the interrogation.

'It was really foggy up there,' I said, lifting my chin haughtily. 'I could have been within a couple of metres of Jonah and not seen him.' I clenched my hands and relived the sensation of beating my fists against his chest.

'Don't play games, Paige,' Dad warned. 'This is

197

serious. If you won't talk to us, it could be the police asking questions next. They'll need to conduct some sort of investigation.'

My heart skipped a beat. 'Why? I didn't push him, Dad,' I said without thinking. 'And I heard you saying a minute ago that Jonah was incoherent. He could have been trying to say anything.'

'I said that because Kelvin was here. I'd do anything to protect you, Paige. I still will.'

Tears stung my eyes again. *I would do anything to protect you too, Dad*. Izzy could attest to that.

'We know you arranged to meet him here. There's no point denying it,' Nan said.

'Actually,' Olly interjected, 'I don't think Paige knew he was here until he messaged her. He probably wanted to keep it as a surprise.'

I turned to him slowly. 'You really don't know when to shut the fuck up, do you?' I said through gritted teeth. When Olly opened his mouth to speak again, I had to make him stop. He had given me no choice. 'If that's how you want to play it, maybe I should check my phone for some other messages.'

The rushing of blood to my head blocked out Olly's whimper as I took my phone from my pocket and unlocked it. Magicians call this misdirection.

198

CHAPTER 29

KELVIN

Kelvin took the stairs two at a time. He had no idea how Dee was going to react to the news that Jonah was dead, but then he didn't know how he felt about it himself. He wasn't the kind of person who would wish anyone dead, but Jonah was as close as Kelvin had come to an exception, and he allowed himself to feel a certain sense of relief.

Unlocking the door to their bedroom, he took a couple of steps into the darkened room. Within the strip of light falling across the carpet from the window, he could see the silhouettes of snowflakes falling ever downwards. The crumpled bedlinen was a series of mountains and valleys, but there was no human form beneath the covers. The room was empty.

As he turned on his heels and entered the corridor, his mind spun with countless possibilities.

'What's going on?' asked Izzy, appearing next to him.

'Shit!' Kelvin said, bringing his hand up to his chest.

'Sorry, I didn't see you there.' After a breath, he realized Izzy was still waiting for an update. He wasn't about to explain the horrifying situation unfolding with Paige, but there was some news he felt obliged to share. 'I'm afraid Jonah died.'

Izzy's eyes opened wide. 'Oh, no.'

'There really was nothing anyone could do, and maybe you should concentrate on looking after yourself and the baby for now. I think your mum's on her way up to see you.'

'Right,' said Izzy, still looking dazed.

'Do you need anything?'

'No, I'll be fine. You carry on doing whatever …' She wafted her hand distractedly. 'I'm good.'

Kelvin moved towards the second room that made up his and Dee's private quarters. He hoped he wouldn't have to broaden his search for his wife, but he could already picture her downstairs in the snug standing over Jonah's dead body.

As soon as he opened the door, he could smell freshly brewed coffee. The open-plan living room was awash with warm light from a lamp next to a large, over-stuffed sofa. The place was modern but homely, not least because Dee was sitting there waiting for him. She was wrapped in a fleece, her hands curled around a mug. She had made a poor attempt to tame her dark hair, pulling it into a topknot, and the corners of her eyes were scored red from salty tears.

'Who were you talking to?' she asked.

'Izzy. She's restless.' He paused to check her expression.

'Did you hear what we were talking about?'

Dee pursed her lips. Shook her head. 'But I heard shouts before,' she said. 'Is it Jonah?'

Kelvin took Dee's cup and set it on the coffee table before slowly sinking into the sofa cushions next to her. 'He died a while back.'

His wife didn't move for the longest time. He watched her blink. Once. Twice. 'How?' she asked.

'The honest answer is we don't know,' he replied, trying to analyse Dee's lack of response. 'He was in bad shape so it could be anything. Sue was on her own with him, and she fell asleep. She blames herself.'

'It wasn't her fault.'

'She's struggling to see it like that. There's a chance he suffocated, choked on his own tongue or something. We'd strapped him down to stop him falling off the table, and with his neck brace, he wouldn't have been able to move. Sue's convinced she could have helped if she'd been awake.'

'Why?' asked Dee, twisting to look directly at Kelvin. 'Why does she think he was suffocated?'

Beads of sweat pricked the base of Kelvin's neck. He didn't want to dwell on Jonah's death, or his last hours of life, but the force of Dee's question compelled him to answer. 'Erm, there was bruising … No, it was little haemorrhages around his nose.' He couldn't remember the word Sue had used.

'I see.'

'Either way, he's gone now, Dee,' Kelvin said. 'He's out of our lives.'

'And what are the others doing?'

'Rob should be here by dawn. They can evacuate Izzy, and as for the rest, according to Sian, the forecast is for heavy rain tomorrow, so it won't be long until we have the place to ourselves again.'

'Tomorrow,' Dee repeated in a way that made the future sound unreachable.

What little relief Kelvin had felt earlier was pumped away with every thump of his heart. 'Technically, later today,' he tried.

'Can you stay here with me?' she asked. 'Until help comes.'

'Of course,' he promised. 'I just need to organize moving the body somewhere colder, but I can come straight back. I don't think the family want me hanging around anyway. There are conversations they need to work through,' he added. As his blood pressure rose, his head pulsed, marking the return of his tension headache. 'About Paige and Jonah.'

He waited for a question, but it didn't come. Although Dee's pupils dilated just a fraction, she betrayed no hint of surprise that those two names should be connected.

'You already knew about them, didn't you?'

'Knew what?' Dee asked feebly.

Kelvin had been horrified to hear how Jonah had been grooming Sue's granddaughter, but not shocked. Dee's warning to watch Paige had prepared him for there to be some kind of link. But what horrors had Jonah visited upon a young and vulnerable woman? Had Sue heard right about his last words? Had Jonah been pushed? Ray had been quick to dismiss the suggestion, but he would want to protect his daughter if he suspected she was involved. In the space of an evening, Kelvin had wrestled with the possibility that his own wife had wanted Jonah dead, and now he wondered if a teenager was capable of pushing this predator off the edge of the ruins. Only one thing was certain. Both women had their secrets and whatever Jonah had done to them, he was never going to answer for his crimes.

Kelvin sighed. 'Why are you still protecting Jonah even now he's dead? How can you still be in his thrall?'

Dee shook her head from side to side. 'I'm not protecting Jonah. I'm protecting us,' she insisted. 'I don't want to have this conversation now.'

'I know you don't, but I need to understand, Dee. It's driving me crazy,' Kelvin exclaimed, matching her frustration. 'Please. Give me something. Trust me.'

'I do trust you,' she replied, reaching for him.

When Kelvin refused to respond to her touch, Dee slipped an arm around his waist and rested her head on his chest. Her body was as taut as his.

'Jonah isn't as bad as you think,' she said. 'Or at least he wasn't bad to me, not intentionally.'

Kelvin rested his chin on the top of her head. He couldn't accept that. 'Then where does all that fear come from?' he challenged. 'If you're so sure he never meant to hurt you, why hide away all these years? Why lock yourself up here? I can't bear this, Dee. I can't bear it for another second.'

The rise and fall of Kelvin's chest as he took deep

breaths seemed to lull Dee into submission. Her shoulders sagged. 'You're right, I have been hiding, but as much from myself as anything. For over twenty years, I refused to confront my past. I accepted the story others had built around me because my own recollections were pure madness.'

'But something changed,' Kelvin said because he had witnessed that change. 'Last summer.'

'I realized I should have trusted my memories,' she admitted.

'About what happened at university.'

'About what happened when I met *him*,' she said. 'I'd actually thought he was helping me, but our relationship moved frighteningly fast. And then it got out of control.'

These were things Kelvin had heard before, but his heart beat a little faster when he asked, 'How did it get out of control?'

'I know I've said it was intense, but what I've never really acknowledged before is that it was almost entirely driven by him, not me. It was pure devotion – an insatiable need to be with me that quickly became suffocating.' Dee's hand tightened around the folds of Kelvin's jumper. 'And I didn't know how to end it. In that sense, what happened was my fault.'

'He was an expert at manipulation,' Kelvin said, for the first time being able to offer his own insight into the man, if only based on Jonah's actions in the last twenty-four hours.

'It was more than that. Being worshipped like a goddess can be intoxicating. You know it needs to stop, but each time you try, he offers you another fix that's even more addictive,' Dee said as if reciting something from memory. 'He makes you believe that a world without him is bleak and colourless. He makes you think life isn't worth living without him. And he absolutely didn't want me to live without him.'

'Which is why he didn't intervene when he realized what you were planning to do,' Kelvin concluded.

'There was no planning, Kelvin,' Dee said, pressing her face to his chest. 'It all happened in the space of one night. He told me I was cruel and heartless for breaking up with him, made me feel worthless. And maybe I am. I'll never forgive myself for not protecting my baby.'

'You didn't know you were pregnant,' Kelvin said, sharing the pain of this wound.

'That might be so, but bad things have happened because of me. Terrible things.'

'And what about the good things?' Kelvin reminded her. 'What about us?'

'You truly are the best thing that ever happened to me,' she told him. 'I hate putting you through this.'

'You're not putting me through anything, Dee. We've got the rest of our lives to look forward to. Whatever hold Jonah had over you, it's gone. He's dead. It's over.'

Dee looked up into his eyes. 'No, Kelvin. It isn't.'

CHAPTER 30

SUE

When Paige began taunting Olly with whatever was on her phone, Sue's emotions reached saturation point and she felt her mind detach so she could watch the scene unfold dispassionately. Olly was letting Paige run rings around him, and to think he was about to become a father. At least he had recognized he wasn't up to the task, which was something Izzy was yet to discover. And then there was Paige, who didn't seem to be taking the situation seriously at all. Was she in denial about what Jonah had been doing to her? Or had she seen him for what he was while they were alone at the ruins? Had she pushed him?

There was a pressure around Sue's chest that tightened as she considered the possibility that her granddaughter's actions, together with her own desertion of duty, had caused a man's death. But not an innocent man. What had their family been reduced to? And how was she meant to fix any of it?

'Now, what have we here?' Paige was saying as Sue forced herself back into the squabble. Her granddaughter's finger swiped across her mobile. 'Ooh, I do have a long list of contacts, don't I, Olly?'

'I think you need time to calm down,' Olly said. 'Maybe we should take a break.'

'Take a break?' Paige replied in a squeak. 'Oh, no. You started this, so I'm going to finish it. Now, let me see who's been messaging me. Beth. No. Chris. Uh uh. Clara. No. No, no, no.' And on it went as she skimmed through more of her contacts.

'I don't know what you're doing, Paige,' Ray said, 'but can you please stop. We're only interested in what Jonah was filling your mind with.'

'Oh, you'll be interested in a minute,' Paige promised, beaming a smile that darkened rather than brightened the mood. 'Ah, here's an interesting read. It's from my friend Hannah. You remember Hannah? We weren't that close at school, but you know how it is when a common interest unites you.' She was smirking now. 'Well, she sent me an interesting message in the summer, and when I say message, it's actually a load of screenshots of other messages. Now, where are they?'

Olly's hand shot out across the table, but his fingers glanced off Paige's phone as she pulled it close to her chest.

'Olly, stop that!' Sue said. 'You're both acting like children.'

'I know, shocking, isn't it?' replied Paige. 'Especially when you think Olly is twenty-eight. Unlike Hannah, who's the same age as me.'

Olly's lip quivered. 'It's not what it looks like. I told you that,' he said. He twisted in his chair, turning away so they couldn't see his face as he stood up. 'But fine, show them anything you want. I'm sick of this.'

'Sick of what, for God's sake?' Ray asked, his patience snapping.

'You can't blame me, Olly,' Paige snarled at him as he slunk towards the already open door. 'It's not my fault that of all the girls you picked, it should be someone in my friendship group. I never wanted this to be on me.'

When Olly turned, it wasn't for a counter-attack, but self-sabotage. 'You're right. It shouldn't be on you. I need to own up to what I did.'

There was a part of Sue that wanted to shut down the conversation there and then. She had enough to deal with. More than enough. The invisible band around her chest tightened further. 'And what exactly did you do, Olly?'

'OK,' Olly said, taking a shaking breath. He looked down at his feet, then up again, his jaw set firm. 'When I left Izzy last year, I was running scared. I was a coward who couldn't face up to my responsibilities, but staying away was harder than I expected. Izzy should have hated me, but she didn't. She felt guilty about …'

He stopped to consider what to say next. It was possible that he had told Ray, and even Paige, how Izzy had planned her pregnancy without his knowledge, but he didn't know Izzy had told her mum. There was no end of ways he could tangle himself up in his family's web of lies.

'She understood why I was scared,' he continued. 'She

208

understood me.' His voice cracked. 'And my response was to find a way for her to hate me as much as I hated myself.'

'Which was?' demanded Sue, needing him to get to the punchline. She didn't think she was having a heart attack, but even so, she was struggling to breathe through the pain.

'I messed about on a dating site, and got chatting to Hannah,' he said. He looked to Paige, no longer angry, simply broken. 'Her profile said she was twenty-four, and we only swapped messages for a couple of weeks.'

'Please don't say you sent her dick pics,' Sue said, recoiling from the phone clutched in Paige's hand that apparently held the evidence of his treachery.

'No!' Olly said, his face a picture of horror that he should be having this conversation with his mother-in-law. 'But I did say things I wouldn't have dreamt of saying in person. We never actually met.'

'But I bet you wanted to, didn't you?' asked someone on the other side of the door.

Olly shrank into the shadows as Izzy stepped into the room. They all stood to attention as Izzy stormed past her husband and headed straight for her niece. 'Show me.'

'No,' Paige said, twisting away as Izzy barrelled into her. 'I'm going to delete everything.'

Despite her condition, Izzy wasn't holding anything back. She reached around Paige. 'Give it to me, now!'

To Sue's relief, Paige had enough sense not to fight a pregnant woman, and in the end, she didn't need to.

'Give it to her,' Olly said, his voice full of resignation.

The screen glowed in Izzy's hand as she devoured the messages that had come into Paige's possession. Her breath quickened.

'The things I said,' Olly began, 'you know that isn't who I am. I pretend to be a different person online.'

'Hardly a defence when you're online even more than Paige,' Sue said. She approached Izzy and tried to look over her shoulder. 'Is it bad?'

'Olly says, "You look so sweet. I bet you taste good too."' When Izzy looked up, Olly flinched. 'And did she taste good, Ol?'

'I told you, I never met her,' he said, his voice the squeak of a mouse faced with a lion. 'Ask Paige.'

'He didn't,' Paige mumbled, her rage long forgotten. 'Hannah shared Olly's profile with one of my other friends who'd met Olly, and that put an end to it.'

'It was already at an end,' Olly maintained. 'I never would have gone through with it.'

Izzy returned to the messages. 'Hannah says, "What exactly would you like to do to me?"'

'Maybe you shouldn't read any more,' said Sue, resting a hand on Izzy's arm. 'We get the gist.'

Izzy laughed as she continued to read out the messages. '"I'd tie you up," he replies. Hannah then asks for details, but poor Olly is already out of his depth,' she mocked. '"I'd smother you in chocolate and lick you ALL over." Nice use of capitals, Ol.'

'What about the other messages I sent her?' asked Olly, turning to Paige to back him up. 'What about the ones where she asks to meet me and I keep putting her off?' Back to Izzy, he added, 'Yes, I was out of my depth, and you're only laughing because you can see I was never going to go through with it.'

'I'm laughing,' Izzy corrected, 'because otherwise I'd cry, and if I cry, I won't stop until I've no more tears to shed, and if I use up any more tears on you, Olly, I swear there'll be nothing left, and I'll be on my own again.'

Sue couldn't bear to hear the pain in her daughter's voice. 'You're not alone, Izzy. Never think that.'

However well intended, Sue's reassurance ignited a fury deep within Izzy that would put Paige's tantrums to shame. 'Don't go telling me it'll be OK, Mum, because you know better than anyone it won't be. It just won't!'

Izzy released a howl of despair that stopped abruptly. There was a gushing sound as something splashed onto the stone floor at her feet. 'No!' she yelled, fear taking over her anger.

'Is it the baby?' Olly asked, rushing forward.

Izzy groaned as she straightened up, but she slammed her hand against his chest. 'Keep the fuck away from me!'

Sue manoeuvred herself between her daughter and son-in-law, but Izzy had already set her sights on Paige.

'And you can have this back,' she said, flinging the phone at her niece. 'I hope you enjoyed the show!'

Sue expected Paige to lunge for her mobile, but she stepped back and let it smash against the flagstones. Turning on her heels, she fled from the room, taking with her the dark energy that had been suffocating all of them. Sue's reaction was to puff out her cheeks and release a slow breath. Izzy was her only concern for now.

'I'm not ready, Mum,' her daughter whispered. 'It's too early. The baby won't be strong enough.'

'That's where you're wrong. He's obviously heard all the commotion and thinks an early appearance is necessary to keep all of us in check,' Sue assured her. 'I'll admit it's not great timing, but we can do this. Trust me.'

'Trust?' Izzy repeated. 'Do any of us know what that word means any more?' She let out a moan and squeezed her eyes shut.

'Is it a contraction?' asked Sue.

Izzy nodded. 'I've been getting them for a while,' she said between gasps. 'They didn't really stop. I thought if I ignored them ...'

'We should get her upstairs,' said Ray.

'Can you manage, Iz?' Sue asked, putting an arm around her daughter's waist.

'I can try.'

As Izzy took the first faltering steps, Olly moved to her other side to help support her, but she batted him away.

'I'll help,' Ray said, taking his place. 'Olly, why don't you go and clear up the coffee you spilled in the kitchen, and make some more. I think we're all going to need it.'

Olly reluctantly obeyed, but he waited at the kitchen door as they passed. 'I love you, Izzy.'

'Just make yourself useful, Olly,' Sue said as she felt her daughter resist moving away from her cheating husband. 'Phone for help. All the numbers are on a pad in the snug. Tell them Izzy's waters have broken and she's in active labour. I'll update them as soon as I know more.'

After waiting for another contraction to pass, Izzy managed to climb the stairs where another challenge awaited. The door to the spare bedroom was firmly shut. 'I'm sure I left it open,' Izzy said.

Ray put an ear to the door. 'Paige? Are you in there?'

'Go away!'

'Paige, it's your nan! Open this door immediately!' Sue yelled. She waited as long as her patience would allow, which wasn't long at all. 'Paige, Izzy is about to have her baby. We need that room! Now!'

Ray sighed. 'Paige, did you hear that?'

'The little bitch,' Izzy hissed. She took a deep breath and bellowed, 'I'm not giving birth on the landing so you'd better get out here now!'

A catch turned and a door opened further down the corridor.

'Did I hear right?' Kelvin asked as he joined them. 'Are you in labour?'

Izzy pursed her lips. Nodded.

'I can let you in,' he said. He was reaching for the combination lock when he paused. 'Or you could use the other room. It's the one I would have offered you as a first choice. It's bigger, and has less clutter.'

'I honestly don't care where I go,' Izzy said. She grimaced, waiting for the next contraction. 'As long as I can rest somewhere.'

Kelvin unlocked the door at the end of the corridor, and Sue popped her head inside to inspect the room. It was bigger, with a double bed and wardrobes that could be opened without having to move boxes first. 'Thanks,

Kelvin. It looks fine,' she said, returning to Izzy's side. 'But we'll need more bedding, plastic sheeting, and towels. Oh, and a soft blanket to wrap the baby in when he arrives, and maybe some cloths to improvise as nappies too.'

'I'll see what I can find,' said Kelvin.

They were about to shuffle inside the room when another door creaked open. Paige appeared, holding the stainless-steel bowl containing the equipment Sue had sterilized earlier. 'Do you need this?' she asked. 'Or you can still come in here, if you like.'

'Too little, too late,' Izzy told her. 'Thanks for nothing.'

'Paige, I'll come and talk to you in a bit,' promised Ray.

There was a clatter as Paige abandoned the bowl on the floor before slamming the door shut. The sound of her sobs reverberated in Sue's aching chest, but she continued in the opposite direction.

'This isn't so bad,' Ray said, following them into the new room after collecting the bowl and equipment.

Izzy looked less impressed with what was to become her birthing suite. 'I can't believe this is happening,' she said. 'I should have known there was something more going on between Paige and Olly. I've been so stupid.'

Ray closed the door. 'If I'd known how he'd betrayed you, Izzy, I would never have tried to get you two back together.'

'You don't think I should forgive him?'

'What message does it send if you do?' Sue replied, jumping in before Ray could offer his usual balanced and considered view. 'How many more times is he going to break your heart?'

'I agree that a relationship can't be built on lies,' said Ray, 'but we all make mistakes, and if Olly can learn from this, there's a chance he can redeem himself.'

'Do you think so?' Izzy asked, her eyes pleading for him to convince her.

'I'm not saying you shouldn't be angry with him,' Ray continued, the angel on Izzy's shoulder to counter Sue's devil. 'But when you broke up, you let him go because you didn't want to trap him. And whatever stupidity he got up to during that time, he did come back to you. That has to count for something.'

Izzy sagged. 'I can't think about it now,' she said, eyeing the bare mattress. 'I need to sit down.'

'We should get you out of those clothes first,' Sue said, glancing at her daughter's wet jogging bottoms.

Ray's cheeks reddened as if he expected Izzy to strip off there and then. He grabbed a newspaper from a dresser. 'Here, she can sit on this for now while I go and find something else for her to wear.'

'To be honest, Ray, Izzy isn't going to need another pair of pants just yet. But we could do with that bedding.'

'I'm on the case,' he said, looking relieved to have an excuse to leave.

CHAPTER 31

KELVIN

'Here's everything Sue asked for,' Kelvin said, meeting Ray in the corridor. 'Is there anything else she needs?'

'I'll find out.'

Ray was about to head back but hesitated outside the room Paige had barricaded herself inside. The poor man looked as if he had been hollowed from the inside out. Kelvin paused too. 'How is she?'

Ray pressed his fingertips to his eyes then rubbed his face. 'Confused, I think,' he said. 'I don't know what kind of nonsense Jonah was filling her head with, but it explains why she's been so angry lately.' He looked back to Kelvin. 'You might find this hard to believe, but she was always a gentle child. This last year has been incredibly tough with one thing on top of another, and I feel like I've let her down.'

Kelvin pressed a hand to Ray's back. 'As an outsider, you seem to be the one holding this family together.'

Ray nodded and pulled back his shoulders. 'A family that's about to get a little bit bigger. I'd better get these to Sue.'

'I'll be downstairs if you need anything else.'

Leaving Ray to deal with his particular challenges, Kelvin went to face his own. He grabbed a tarpaulin from the storeroom, and when he could think of no other excuse to delay him, he made his way to the snug. The glowing logs on the fire were turning slowly to ash, but the room was still warm and he wasn't sure if the smell of decay was imagined or real.

Olly didn't seem to notice the dead man lying on the table. His eyes were glazed as he stared off into the distance, and the sound of Kelvin opening a window startled him. 'Have you seen Izzy?' he asked.

'Sue's making her comfortable.'

'Good,' Olly replied, then nodded at whatever internal monologue was continuing in his head. 'Good. Right. Well, I've made some calls.' He checked the notepad Sue had been using to record Jonah's vital signs, and tapped it with his pen. 'I managed to speak to Sian. She's going to try for an air ambulance again, but I don't know …' He glanced towards the figure hidden beneath foil blankets. 'Now we only have one patient, do you think they'll come?'

'Technically they have two people to consider,' Kelvin reminded him. 'There's your baby too. Do you need to go up to Izzy?'

Olly's head drooped. 'I'd love to, but … No, I need to keep busy.'

Kelvin couldn't imagine staying away if it were Dee, and he was about to try again when they heard a gurgling sound coming from the corpse. 'In that case, do you want to help me move Jonah outside?'

'Sure.' As Olly set down the notepad, he added, 'I told the emergency services he'd died. They're going to inform his wife.'

Kelvin shuddered. It was hard to imagine there was a woman somewhere about to receive devastating news about her missing husband. But would she be devastated? She might actually feel liberated from the type of obsessive and suffocating relationship Dee had described.

As both men stared towards the table, the breeze from the window made the foil sheets tremble, giving the impression that the corpse had life left in him yet. The thought gave Kelvin goosebumps, but he edged closer.

He pinched the flimsy foil sheet covering Jonah's upper body and, with one tug, let it float to the floor. The restraints had been left in place, and the thin blanket protecting Jonah's torso was twisted beneath his pinned back arms. Had Jonah struggled against his bindings as he choked to death?

'I don't suppose we need these now,' Olly said, starting to untie the rope around Jonah's legs.

Kelvin unknotted one of the other restraints, and glanced at the white fingers of Jonah's left hand. There was no wedding ring. Perhaps his marriage wasn't something he had wanted to advertise.

As they worked silently, Kelvin scrutinized the body as he might a specimen under the microscope. The man didn't look anything like the villain he had imagined over the years. Jonah's five o'clock shadow accentuated a strong chin and granite features. A feathering of wrinkles around his eyes had softened in death, and despite the bloodied scratches and scrapes marking his waxen complexion, Kelvin could see how Dee might have fallen for him twenty years ago. It was harder to conceive how Jonah had ever thought he could entrap an eighteen-year-old in the present day. He had preyed on the vulnerable, that was how. This was a man who had conditioned a young Dee into believing that if she couldn't give him the adoration he expected, her life was worthless. How could she still think he hadn't intended to harm her? She had often said how marrying Kelvin had been healing, but some of that earlier conditioning had surely persisted.

'Shall we?' Olly asked as they spread the tarpaulin out on the floor ready to transfer the body.

Olly took the legs and Kelvin the shoulders as they hauled the dead weight from the table. Jonah dropped heavily to the floor, his neck brace cracking as it hit the flagstones. Kelvin snatched up the sides of the tarpaulin to cover the corpse so he didn't have to look at his face ever again.

'Sorry, I just need a break,' he said, putting an arm across his mouth to avoid breathing in the fetid air filling the room. He moved to the open window to take a couple of deep breaths.

'I'm sorry we ever brought him back here,' Olly said. 'If we'd known what he'd done ...'

Kelvin had thought the same, but begrudgingly, he was

glad they had rescued him. 'It's right that we tried,' he said, returning to the body. Jonah had cast a shadow over his life for long enough. His death wasn't going to haunt him too. 'We're better than men like him.'

'You might be,' Olly said under his breath as he tied the discarded rope around the tarpaulin.

'Look, I can handle it from here if you want to go up to Izzy. Or is childbirth not for you?' asked Kelvin, trying to make sense of Olly's reluctance.

'I'm not allowed. Izzy told me to stay away,' Olly said. He kept his head down. 'We had an argument. It's why her waters broke. It was all my fault. I don't deserve her.'

Kelvin appreciated that Izzy's wishes should be respected, but he had seen the way she had waited anxiously for her husband's return when he was missing in the storm. They loved each other, and it wasn't every day that you became a father.

'Something this important is worth fighting for, Olly,' he said as he began gathering up the sleeping bag Jonah had been resting on. 'Talk to Izzy. Tell her you need to be there, if that's really what you want.'

'It is. More than anything,' Olly replied. 'But what if she does let me in and I mess it up? What if I pass out at the sight of blood? Izzy's got enough reasons to think I'm not ready for this. And I wouldn't blame her if she never wanted me near her or the baby again.'

'That might be true, but what if it's not?' Kelvin asked as he tossed the sleeping bag by the door, ready to be thrown out. It wasn't something he wanted left in his pub. He might build a bonfire later to burn everything

Jonah had touched, tables included.

'But she's so angry at me.'

'What if she's waiting for you to prove yourself?' Kelvin suggested. He began moving chairs to the far end of the snug so as not to be further contaminated. 'This could be your best chance.'

Olly picked up one of the seat cushions lying on the floor. 'You're right,' he said, turning the cushion in his hand.

A smile was forming on Kelvin's face as Olly puffed out his chest. He was glad to see this downtrodden man growing in stature before his eyes, but his attention was caught by the cushion Olly was holding. Cream cotton covers had been Dee's idea and were always showing up the dirt, but at least they were washable. He was used to seeing smudges of dried mud, but the smudges on this cushion were the colour of rust. It might not have occurred to him that it was dried blood had he not registered the pattern of the stains.

Noticing Kelvin staring at the cushion, Olly turned it around. 'It looks like a face,' he said with a laugh. It was only when Kelvin failed to respond that he examined the marks in more detail, then glanced over to the tarpaulin covering a man who had apparently died from suffocation. He pressed the cushion into Kelvin's hands as if it were a bomb about to explode. 'I should get Ray.'

CHAPTER 32

SUE

'We can't put it off any longer. I'm going to need to examine you,' Sue told her daughter.

Izzy was sitting awkwardly on the bed, propped up on one elbow. Her posture suggested she wasn't fully committed to going through with the birth, but the baby was going to arrive whether they wanted him to or not. The only babies Sue had seen delivered had been her own, and she prayed there would be no complications. She had already lost one patient tonight.

'It will be OK, won't it, Mum?' Izzy asked, seeing fear and doubt drain the colour from Sue's face.

Sue was gripped by a vision of her little grandson being born cold and unresponsive. She knew the torture Izzy would put herself through, thinking if only medical support had arrived in time ... If only. If only. If only. Sue wasn't going to put another mother through that. She swallowed back the panic that made her fingers tingle.

'Childbirth is the most natural thing in the world,' she said.

'But I didn't want a natural childbirth,' Izzy complained. 'I wanted drugs, an epidural, the lot.'

'I can check with Kim, but I should think we'll be able to give you some paracetamol. I'm sure Kelvin must have some.'

Izzy clawed at the sheet. 'Paracetamol?' she cried, then began to pant.

Sue checked her watch. The contractions were just over six minutes apart. She sat down on the bed so Izzy could rest against her for support. She rubbed her daughter's back.

When the contraction eased, Sue whispered in Izzy's ear, 'I think it's time I checked the business end.'

'Can I have some water first?'

Sue passed her a bottle of water, and Izzy drank slowly.

'Izzy,' prompted Sue when her daughter wasted more time adjusting her position.

'Fine,' Izzy replied, and lay back as her mum directed. 'Just don't speak. Let me imagine you're Margie.'

'No problem, Mrs Malone. Or can I call you Izzy?' Sue asked in an approximation of Izzy's midwife's Geordie accent.

'Just get on with it,' Izzy said, squeezing her eyes shut.

As Sue was examining her daughter, there was a tap on the door. 'Whoever it is, go away!' she hollered, breaking her vow of silence. If it was Ray offering help or information, she knew she could rely on his good sense to announce his presence. No one spoke, so she ignored whoever it was. A tense minute later, she pulled off her gloves. 'You're about five centimetres dilated, so you've got a while yet.'

Izzy scooted up the bed and covered her bare legs in a sheet. 'Who was knocking?' she asked in a way that suggested she was secretly hoping it was Olly. 'Can you check?'

Sue opened the door to find both her sons-in-law talking outside Paige's room, and her simmering fury was reignited. She wanted to slap Olly – to cause him physical pain to make up for the hurt he had inflicted on her daughter – but the grave look on his face stopped her in her tracks.

'What is it?'

'How's Izzy doing?' Olly asked quickly.

'Fine,' she said, looking at Ray for an answer.

'Paige still won't let me in,' he explained with a roll of his eyes. 'So I'm going down to help Kelvin move the body.'

'Good,' Sue said coldly. She was finding it hard to shake the guilt of having fallen asleep, but it was quietly dawning on her that they wouldn't be in this mess if it weren't for Jonah. He was the one who had brought them here, and because of him, every fracture in her family had been exposed and magnified.

'Mum!' moaned Izzy.

'I have to go,' Sue said, slamming the door on Olly just as he made to move towards her.

Holding her daughter's hand, Sue helped Izzy breathe through the contraction. She wiped a film of sweat from her brow. 'We've got this,' she soothed.

'Have we?' Izzy asked. 'What a mess we've made of everything. And poor Jonah.'

'Poor nothing,' Sue said. 'Don't waste your breath on him.'

Izzy continued to breathe heavily even after the contraction had eased. 'How can you say that?'

'I'm sorry, but he was a bad man, Iz,' Sue told her. 'We don't know exactly what his game was, but he came here to spy on us. Or Paige, to be exact. Ray thinks he'd been grooming her.'

Izzy was shaking her head. 'No,' she said. 'No, that can't … that can't be. He was in contact with Paige?'

'Olly found messages on her phone,' Sue replied. 'They'd been in touch since Ellen's death, apparently, and we think they met up by the ruins after Paige wandered off. I don't know what he did to her, Iz, but he must have tried something. I'm just glad she got away.'

She didn't mention how Paige would have been the last person to see Jonah before his fall, or remind Izzy of what Jonah had said in his semi-conscious state. Ray was right. He had been incoherent.

Izzy's breathing began to slow. 'But he wasn't here because of Paige.'

'You don't know that.'

'Oh, but I do.' Izzy's brow creased as her eyes flicked to the door. She kept her voice low when she said, 'I know who he is, Mum. I should have worked it out when I heard his name, but it was only when I saw him in the snug that I realized.'

225

'You know him too?'

'Not really. Not as well as Ellen,' Izzy said. 'He could only have been here because of her. He would have wanted to see Ellen's ashes being scattered.'

'And why would he want to do that? I don't understand. Why the secrecy?' Sue needed to keep talking because if she allowed herself to stop and think, the answer was plain to see. Izzy had tried to tell her how Ellen had been unhappy, that her life wasn't as perfect as everyone presumed. It was obvious what Izzy was suggesting, and yet Sue's mind refused to make the link. Her body tensed as she prepared for the next blow to strike. How much more could one family withstand?

'Ellen was having an affair,' Izzy said. 'With Jonah.'

'No! No, she wouldn't,' Sue replied, backing away. Ellen's family – her happy marriage – were her legacy. She needed Izzy to stop talking. 'You're wrong. Ellen would never do such a thing, and certainly not with a man like that. He was *grooming* Paige.'

'He wasn't grooming Paige,' Izzy insisted, but weariness overtook her. 'Or at least I hope to God he wasn't. I only ever met him once. He turned up at my house the week after Ellen died, and he seemed genuinely heartbroken. He couldn't accept she was gone. He must have thought he'd get sympathy from me because I knew they were planning a life together, but I sent him packing.'

'Ellen was going to leave Ray?' asked Sue, her hand clawing at her throat. 'I don't believe it! She wouldn't …'

'I couldn't believe it either,' Izzy said. She bit down hard on her lip, turning the skin white. 'In fact, that's what we were arguing about the day before she died. She'd been using me as an excuse when she wanted to slip out to see Jonah. She'd turn up at mine, but he'd be waiting around the corner to pick her up, and I just had to hope Ray didn't try ringing me.'

'Poor Ray.'

'She was going to tell him and Paige after Christmas,' Izzy said. 'I was hoping that secret had died with her, but from the things Paige has been saying, she obviously knows too. And now it makes sense how she found out. Jonah must have got in touch with her after I turned him away.'

'No wonder Paige is a mess. Why couldn't he have left us in peace?' asked Sue. 'And to think Ray risked his own life to save him. If only he knew.'

Sue automatically looked to the door, and her heart leapt into her throat when she saw a shadow move along the gap above the floor. When she jumped off the bed, Izzy didn't question why. Her wide eyes confirmed she had seen the movement too. Sue took hold of the door handle and jerked it open. Olly almost toppled into her.

'What are you doing?' Sue snapped.

'Waiting in case you need me.'

'We don't …' Sue checked the landing. 'Where's Ray?'

'He's gone downstairs,' Olly said.

Sue would have liked the chance to go down too. She wanted to phone Kim for advice out of earshot of her daughter. She needed to be prepared for the worst should it happen.

'Is there anything I can do?' asked Olly when he noticed her hesitation.

'No thanks, we'll wait for Ray.'

To her surprise, Olly squared his shoulders. 'No, if anyone should be helping, it should be me,' he said loud enough for Izzy to hear. 'I want to be here.'

'And I said no. We'll manage fine without you.'

'Mum, let him in,' called Izzy. 'We need to talk anyway.'

'But I don't want you getting upset more than you already are,' said Sue, but as she was turning to face her daughter, Olly slipped past her into the room.

He hurried to Izzy's side, kneeling on the floor in supplication. 'I'm so sorry, Iz,' he said, grasping her hand. 'I know I'm a coward.'

'And an idiot,' she told him.

'And any other name you want to throw at me, and I can't promise you I'm not going to mess up again.'

'Hardly an apology,' Sue muttered.

Her daughter silenced her with a single look. This was not her fight. And what did she know about the perfect relationship? She had clearly got it wrong about Ellen's marriage. Was it too much to hope that the truth wouldn't come out? Could she count on Paige to keep the secret when it was already eating her up inside? And even if they could keep what they knew to themselves, would an inquest into Jonah's death need to establish what he was doing at Mynydd Plentyn? What a godawful mess.

'Do you think we could have some privacy, Mum?' asked Izzy.

Sue surprised herself by nodding. She was all out of

arguments. 'There are a few things I could be getting on with, but I'll be as quick as I can. Olly, rub her back, hold her hand, and let her punch you if she has to,' she added with a malicious glint in her eye. 'But if she feels like she needs to push, you holler for me straight away. *Straight* away. Do you understand?'

'Yes, absolutely.'

Sue rested her hand on the door handle. 'Izzy, the thing about Ellen. Can we keep it to ourselves for now?'

'Funnily enough, I have other things on my mind,' Izzy said with an exhausted smile that quickly twisted her features as the next contraction took hold.

Sue checked her watch. They were running out of time.

CHAPTER 33

KELVIN

Kelvin stared at the smouldering fire as he waited for Ray. When he had seen what looked like the bloody imprint of Jonah's face on the cushion, he had refused to believe the evidence of his eyes. His weary and overworked mind must be imagining things, or else the cushion had come innocently into contact with Jonah's face at some point. What other explanation was there?

If he had been holding the cushion at the time, he might have tossed it straight into the fire before Olly had seen it too. He still might. There was a cold breeze cooling his neck, but he could still smell death. Or was it murder? And if it was, that meant there had to be a murderer. He thought back to just before Jonah had died, when he had left Dee in their bedroom and gone downstairs. How long was he in the kitchen with Ray and Olly before Sue raised the alarm? Long enough for someone to sneak down and smother Jonah?

No, he told himself. It couldn't have been Dee. There hadn't been enough time. His grip on the cushion tightened. It could be turned to ash in a matter of moments.

'Can I see?' Ray asked, striding into the room.

'It's definitely blood,' Kelvin said, needing to establish some certainty.

Ray rotated the cushion, looking at it from every angle. 'Is that so surprising considering how much we were handling Jonah? I know I had blood on my hands.'

'Me too,' said Kelvin as he crouched down next to the body. He had to be sure. Gritting his teeth, he pulled back the tarpaulin. 'Look at the pattern, then look at Jonah's face. The grazes, the blood along his hairline, in his eyebrows. It's a perfect match.'

'Tell me what you're thinking,' Ray said.

'The same thing you are,' Kelvin said, reading Ray's grim expression. One of them had to say it. 'I think that cushion was used to smother Jonah.'

'Sorry?' Sue asked. She had entered the snug just as Kelvin finished speaking. 'What on earth is going on? Why would you say that?'

Ray tried to pass the cushion to Sue but she wouldn't take it. 'We found a bloody imprint of his face.'

'Then it must have happened when we were transferring Jonah from the stretcher,' she said. 'We rolled him on his side a few times.'

'But he was never face down,' Kelvin said. 'The only way that cushion could pick up marks like that would be if it was placed over his face. And you said yourself he suffocated.'

231

Sue reached for the back of a chair to keep herself upright. 'I said it was a possible explanation for the petechiae, but there will be others. Maybe we warmed him up too fast and the haemorrhaging was because his blood pressure shot up. I don't know. I'm not a pathologist.'

Ray kicked his socked toe against the flagstone floor. 'None of that would explain the stains on the cushion.'

'What if the pattern is just a coincidence?' Sue persisted. 'They might be old marks. It could have been from someone on their period.' There was a flash of inspiration behind her eyes. 'It could have been Izzy. She was in here for ages, pretending not to be in labour. She might have had a small discharge and tried to hide it.'

'I suppose we'll only know when the police send it off for analysis,' said Kelvin. Despite his best efforts, he wasn't reassured. He covered Jonah's body and stood up. 'There will have to be an investigation.'

'Investigation?' Sue asked, her voice rising. 'No, no, we've all suffered enough. We don't need an investigation.'

'Kelvin's right,' Ray conceded. He placed the cushion onto a chair and took two measured steps back. 'We should leave it to the professionals.'

'But they'll go through everything that's happened, in detail. Do we really want strangers picking over our lives?' Sue replied. 'And your wife, Kelvin. She would need to be interviewed too, and I can't imagine that being good for her mental health.'

While Kelvin was as sure as he could be that Dee hadn't had the opportunity to kill Jonah, Sue had a point. How would his wife fare during a police investigation? What would her actions look like to an outsider? She had gone into hiding the moment Jonah made an appearance, only to sneak out alone to rescue him. She had told Kelvin he wasn't a bad man, but she had been terrified of him waking up. There were so many inconsistencies, and the police would pick her story apart.

'Then what do we do?' he asked, hoping the family had their own reasons for not wanting anyone to look too closely at Jonah's death.

Sue put a hand against her chest. 'I don't know. I can't deal with this right now.'

'Do you want to sit down?' asked Ray, stepping towards her.

'No,' she said, warding him off. 'Thank you, but I'm fine.' Her voice shook. 'Sorry, but I just can't … I have a call to make, and I need to get back to Izzy. I'll go with whatever you decide is the right thing to do.' She picked up the notepad Olly had left on the side table. 'I'm sorry, I just can't do this.'

'I understand,' Ray told her. 'It's complete madness. We'll sort it. I promise.'

After Sue left, Kelvin and Ray retreated to the far end of the snug. They slumped into chairs, bodies bent over, elbows resting on knees. It was the early hours of the morning, but the night was far from over.

'I have to be honest,' Kelvin said. 'As much as I want to believe Sue's alternative theories, I do think Jonah's death was deliberate.'

Ray puffed out his cheeks before releasing a long sigh. 'In that case, can we call it what it is, Kelvin? Murder.

233

There are seven people under this roof, and one of us took matters into our own hands.' He covered his face briefly to hide the pain that was already in his voice. 'We could be talking about someone I love.'

'At the time of Jonah's death, we were spread throughout the pub,' said Kelvin, needing to approach it systematically. 'I was upstairs with Dee, and when I came down to the kitchen, there wasn't enough time for her to sneak down after me. It takes minutes to suffocate someone, and she couldn't have got back upstairs without being seen.' He relaxed his shoulders, relieved to offer an alibi for his wife. 'However, just to be perfectly open and transparent, I could have gone into the snug before I joined you and Olly in the kitchen. But I didn't.'

Ray gave the slightest nod. 'And if I'm being open with you, I did go into the snug to give Sue her food. I could see she was sleepy, and I could have waited for her to drop off. But I didn't,' he said. His shoulders sagged. 'I went into the toilets and, well, I cried like a baby. It had been an exhausting day and it was meant to be this perfect send-off for Ellen. Did we mention it was her birthday?'

'No, I'm sorry.'

'So, yeah, I was too busy bawling my eyes out. And when I swilled my face and returned to the kitchen, Olly was in there checking Paige's phone.'

'And I think we can both discount Izzy. She was upstairs the whole time.'

'You're right,' agreed Ray. 'I don't think she was left alone. Olly had gone up with her, and then Paige took over until ...'

'Until she came down to the kitchen,' said Kelvin. 'And like Dee, there wouldn't have been time for Paige to go into the snug and do – whatever – after leaving us. Unless ...' He rewound the scene. 'Unless she went downstairs before me, and went straight to the snug. By the time she came to fetch her phone, Jonah could already have been ...'

'No, I don't think so. No,' Ray said firmly.

In the silence that followed, the only sound was the logs on the fire collapsing in on themselves. If it wasn't Paige, as Ray wanted Kelvin to believe, the only other people left to consider were Sue and Olly, and whilst Sue had more opportunity than most, it didn't feel worth considering her as a suspect given her reaction to his death. It was hard to imagine Olly killing him either. Ray was being too quick to dismiss Paige.

'Forgive me,' Ray said when he found his voice. 'I can't believe I'm even saying this, but what justice are we seeking by pursuing this? Jonah would have died anyway if we hadn't rescued him. Doesn't that give us some entitlement to decide his fate?'

'But Jonah's fate isn't in question,' Kelvin said. 'He's dead.'

'And his death needs to be investigated, I know that, but we don't have to lead the police to any particular conclusion,' explained Ray. 'If we were to carry on as if foul play had never crossed our minds, what would we do? We'd move the body and clear up. It would be natural to wash the sleeping bag, and anything else that might have come into contact with a bleeding patient.'

His gaze travelled across the room to the seat cushion. 'Don't you think?'

'Ray, even if we did all of that, there's still the evidence on the body. What if Jonah inhaled fibres from the cushion? I don't know if that would prove he was suffocated, but it would surely raise questions.'

'Even so,' Ray said. 'I know it's a lot to ask, but can we try? Whoever did this isn't a murderer in the real sense of the word. This is someone who, for whatever reason, felt trapped. Not by the snow, but by Jonah's presence.'

Kelvin's thoughts turned to Dee. Was it possible to get through this without revealing her links to the dead man? Needing to keep the pressure on Ray, he said, 'It sounds to me like you're describing your daughter.'

There was no energy behind Ray's words when he said, 'It does, doesn't it?' He rubbed at the deep shadows under his eyes. 'Can I trust you, Kelvin?'

'Yes,' Kelvin said without hesitation.

'When I mentioned before how we knocked Jonah carrying the stretcher, it got me thinking. We lost our balance a few times, and I know I tried my best, and I'm sure you did too, but what if …? What if …' He choked on his words.

'What if Paige wasn't being so careful?'

Ray gave an imperceptible nod. 'Kids that age don't always know their limitations, and I'd assumed she had overestimated her strength. But what if she'd done it deliberately?'

Kelvin recalled how they had all lost their balance after the stretcher began tipping from side to side. It had seemed to come out of nowhere. 'It's possible,' he said, not liking the conclusion being drawn. How much more difficult must it be for Ray?

'And I'm afraid that's not all,' Ray continued. 'Sue was right when she said Jonah had been talking. I wanted to believe it was incoherent mumblings, but I heard what he said too. He was quite clear when he told us he hadn't fallen. He said he was pushed, which explains why Paige was so eager to get off this mountain. If only I hadn't failed her.'

'This isn't on you.'

'Oh, but it is,' replied Ray. 'All the time Jonah was grooming my daughter, I wasn't there emotionally for her. I'd checked out after my wife's death, as it were, but I need to protect Paige now. And whilst I absolutely believe in justice, isn't it possible that Jonah's death, in its own way, is justice served?'

It wasn't as if the thought of destroying the evidence hadn't already crossed Kelvin's mind, but this wasn't a simple act of throwing the cushion into the fire before anyone noticed it. These people had been complete strangers twenty-four hours ago, and now they were talking about a conspiracy to conceal a crime.

Ray stood up, taking time to unfold his body. 'It's your decision, Kelvin,' he said. 'I'm not going to pressure you one way or the other. Now then, do you want help moving the body?'

'Sure,' Kelvin said. 'Just let me put some washing on first.'

CHAPTER 34

PAIGE

As I lay curled up on the bed stolen from Izzy, I heard someone punch in the combination code and unlock the door. I pulled the sleeping bag over my head. I should have known I couldn't hide away forever, but my dad's patience had lasted well. God love him. He still thought Jonah was some creep who had only been interested in young girls. It would break his heart if he knew the truth. Hopefully that wouldn't happen now.

Above the sound of Izzy's cries in the next room, I listened to the door closing softly. Careful footsteps drew closer. I don't know why, but I was suddenly convinced it wasn't Dad. And it wasn't Nan because I could hear her talking to Izzy, who was shouting expletives that could only be intended for Olly. Which meant he was in there too.

I snapped back my covers just as a strange woman loomed over me. Her clothes were crumpled and her hair was piled on top of her head at freakish angles.

'Get away from me!' I yelled, scooting up the bed.

'Sorry, I didn't mean to scare you,' she whispered, raising both hands as if she knew I was worried she might be carrying a knife. 'My name's Dee.'

With my back pressed against the headboard, I drew my knees up to my chest. So this was Kelvin's wife. With her pale complexion and red eyes, she matched the description of a character in a gothic novel who had been locked away for her own good. 'What do you want?'

My uninvited visitor sat down on the edge of the bed. 'Just to talk.'

'Why?'

Dee appeared to give this some thought. 'Because Jonah is dead.'

I pulled up the sleeping bag so Dee couldn't see my chin wobble. 'I know.'

'We need to talk about him.'

Yes, I did need to talk about Jonah, but preferably with a qualified therapist, not this weirdo. 'I'm sorry, but I don't see what he has to do with you.'

Dee looked puzzled. 'He didn't tell you about me?'

'No, but then there was quite a lot he kept to himself,' I said. 'I didn't know him. Not really.'

Dee plucked at the bobbling on her leggings. 'Neither did I.'

'Then what do we have to talk about?' I asked impatiently. It was the middle of the night and I was too tired for riddles.

'I'm sorry about what happened to your mum,' Dee said, looking away. 'I wish there was more I could have done.'

I watched as she wiped her eyes even though there were no tears. Was she all cried out, or was she faking an emotion she didn't feel? I glanced at the door. I couldn't reach it without passing her first. 'You make it sound like you knew her.'

'I met her once,' Dee explained. 'It was last summer, when you were all here. We talked briefly.'

'So you didn't know her.'

'I saw enough to know she was lost,' Dee said, fixing me with her stare.

I began to shake violently. How had this stranger taken one look at Mum and seen what I couldn't back then? 'Mum claimed she was sad about me going off to uni, but it was so much more than that.'

'She believed, wrongly, that Jonah could offer her a new life.'

I gasped. 'You know about the affair?'

'Yes. Considering our chat was all too brief, your mum trusted me with that,' she said. 'I had hoped we would meet again. I didn't know until yesterday that she'd died. It was Jonah who told me. He felt guilty.'

'Guilty!' I screeched. 'Of course he was fucking guilty. She's dead because of him. He messed with her head, just like he tried to mess with mine.'

The sob that rose up through my chest couldn't be swallowed back, and I pulled the sleeping bag over my face. I wanted so much to go back to that summer's day when we were standing on the viewing platform. I needed to know what Mum had been thinking. Had she felt so lost that she couldn't find her way back to us? How many lies had she told to cover up her affair? And why cheat on Dad in the first place, and with a creep like Jonah?

'If I'd known who he was,' I wailed, 'I would never … I never would …'

As I gasped for air, I heard the mattress creak then felt it dip right beside me. A hand rested on my knee, another on my shoulder.

'None of this is your fault, Paige,' Dee said. 'And it's not your mum's either. Never think that.'

'I don't know what to think any more,' I cried.

Dee's voice was right next to my ear. 'I can help,' she whispered.

When I felt two arms wrap around me, I wanted to push this creepy woman away, but I didn't resist when Dee began rocking me like a mother might a child.

'We can work through this together,' Dee told me. 'I can't promise it'll be easy, or painless, but you have to trust me.'

'But I can't trust anyone, not ever again!'

Dee pulled back the cover I was hiding beneath so she could look me in the eye. 'I know that feeling all too well, believe me.'

Despite myself, I rested my head against Dee's chest. Above the whoosh of blood pressing against my eardrums, I could hear her heartbeat too, slower and steadier. I let the sound calm me.

'I know some of what your mum went through, Paige,' Dee said. 'I tried telling her she needed to be careful, but in the end, I don't think she recognized the real threat.

She thought she was in control.'

I raised my head. 'Jonah said she killed herself.'

Her body jerked in shock. 'When did he tell you that?'

'When we were up on the ruins.'

Dee gave me a puzzled look. 'Do you think it's possible?'

'It was probably more lies,' I said, wishing I believed that. I wiped my nose on the sleeping bag. I needed to stop crying. 'Mum wouldn't do that to me. She did everything she could to help me get into my first choice uni. She wanted to see me graduate more than anything. And she'd hate that I only lasted one term.'

Dee appeared almost as horrified as Mum might have been receiving the news. 'You mustn't give up!'

'But if recent events have proven anything, it's that I'm not to be trusted on my own.'

'Don't underestimate yourself,' Dee pleaded. 'I only lasted one term too, and I regret it to this day.'

'What happened to you?'

Dee thought on it a while. 'I will tell you, Paige, but first, you need to explain what happened up on the ruins. Between you and Jonah.'

'But what's his connection with you?'

Dee held my gaze. 'Your mum,' she said. 'Now, please, tell me everything.'

I sat up straight, no longer a crumpled mess, and just like that, I obeyed. If Mum had trusted her, so should I.

'Jonah got in touch on Messenger back in November,' I began. 'He'd heard about Mum, and said he used to work with her. Loads of people had been getting in touch to offer their condolences, so it didn't seem out of the ordinary at first. But he kept messaging, sharing memories about Mum, and it was nice hearing more about that side of her life. It never crossed my mind that they were having an affair. Mum had just started freelancing as an interior designer, and Jonah had his own business, so it was understandable that they'd talk a lot. But ...' I slapped a hand across my eyes. 'He actually made a point about me not telling Dad, saying it might not go down too well if it came out how much he and Mum had chatted. I was so stupid not to see the red flags.'

When I let my hands drop, I was aware that Dee was watching me. Here was someone else asking me to trust them. Was it another mistake?

'How did Jonah persuade you to come here?' Dee asked when I didn't continue.

'I'd mentioned how we were planning on scattering Mum's ashes, and he said it should be down to me to pick where. So I persuaded Dad to let me choose, and of course he said yes, anything to make me feel a little less sad. Mynydd Plentyn wasn't even on my shortlist until Jonah suggested it. And that's when things got a little more intense. I'd said I wasn't so sure it was the right place, that Mum had been sad here, and he said she'd talked about that day a lot, and yes, she was sad, but she had been sad a lot. She was just good at hiding it.' I gave a pitiful laugh. 'And she was, wasn't she?' I asked Dee, because how the hell did I know? I was just her daughter.

'Like most people, I imagine there were parts of Ellen's

life that made her sad, and other parts that brought her joy,' Dee said diplomatically. 'And I don't doubt that you were the part that brought her joy.'

I raised an eyebrow. 'I can tell you've been locked in your room all day. Clearly you don't know me.' Before Dee could make another embarrassing attempt to shore up my ego, I continued. 'When I pushed for more information, Jonah backed off and would only make these cryptic comments about Mum, like he knew something I didn't, but couldn't tell me.' I sighed. 'Which obviously he did. And after re-reading some of his messages, I can see how he dropped just enough hints about how Mum was feeling before she died to make sure I kept coming back for more. I was trying everything to gain his trust. I wanted to please him, and so naturally I went with his suggestion of where to scatter Mum's ashes.'

It had taken me too long to see Jonah for the manipulator he was. First impressions could be deceptive, which was why I took another, more considered look at Dee. She didn't look nearly as threatening as she had when she first came into the room. If anything, she looked more like a victim than a villain.

'He brought me here because of you, didn't he?'

Dee nodded slowly and deliberately, but said nothing.

'I'd promised to send him photos of where we scattered the ashes,' I continued. 'I didn't know he was going to be here until the storm came in and the whole family started arguing. And that was my fault. I've been the most awful person to be around.'

'I can be guilty of that too,' admitted Dee. 'If you're

anything like me, you ran off by yourself so you could contain your emotions without anyone else seeing the real you.'

I nodded. I liked the way Dee had listened and more importantly, understood me. 'When I left the viewing platform, I didn't think about where I was going, but the minute I was on my own, Jonah sent a message. I didn't understand how he could possibly know what was going on – until I realized he was close enough to have heard us yelling at each other. He told me to make my way up to the ruins.'

'That wasn't his original plan,' Dee told me. 'He wanted to crash your family gathering on the viewing platform, but that was when he thought he could convince me to go with him.'

'But why?'

'I promise, I will get to that,' said Dee. 'The thing is, I refused point blank to go with him, and my guess is his next best option was to get you on your own.'

'Which is exactly what happened,' I said. 'Except it was a complete white-out up there, so he came to find me.'

* * *

'You need to watch your step,' Jonah had said as he appeared through the mist.

It was the first time I had seen him in the flesh. His profile picture had been an indistinct figure standing on the keel of a boat holding a huge fish, and the real-life version

245

was taller, broader and older than I'd expected. I wasn't stupid, it had crossed my mind that our conversations might be leading towards a romantic relationship, and I was curious about what it would be like to have an affair with an older man. Mum had fallen for Dad at my age and he was eight years older, but there was over twenty years' difference between me and Jonah and it wasn't going to happen as far as I was concerned. Jonah's only attraction for me was that he knew my mum. I was facing a future where I wouldn't get to make any more memories with her, so I wanted to gather up other people's.

The snow at that point was only a light dusting, but as we ascended into the clouds, it was disorienting to have the entire landscape painted white. I took his hand.

'I'm sorry about this, Paige,' Jonah said, keeping his head down against the snow flurries whipping around us.

'It's not your fault,' I replied, but I scowled as I thought about the rest of the family scattering below us. I'd wanted Mum's final send-off to be a memorable one, but not this kind of memorable. I couldn't believe Nan had waited until now to say she wanted Mum's ashes buried. And how dare Izzy be so snide about Mum? And as for Olly, he had no right to be there at all after the way he'd treated Izzy. If I felt guilty about leaving any of them, it was Dad. He would be worrying.

'I wasn't apologizing about today,' Jonah continued. He was a little out of breath. 'It's about ...' He squinted through the cloud. 'Look, there's the steps to the ruins. Let's talk up there.'

I stayed behind Jonah, using him as a windshield as

we followed the remnants of the inner walls of the fort to the highest point. Buffeted by the wind, I grabbed hold of the railings that ran along the edge of the fort's exposed foundations. It was only from memory of seeing the ruins from the platform that I knew one side was a sheer drop, while the other fell away down a steep but less deadly incline covered in scree. I didn't know which side we were on. We could have been looking out into oblivion for all I knew.

Jonah rested his back against the rail next to me. He folded his arms, his broad shoulders braced against the wind. 'I haven't exactly been truthful with you, Paige. There's a reason I wanted to get you here.'

My stomach did a somersault. Jonah hadn't mentioned 'getting me here' at all, and now I was stuck in the middle of nowhere with a man whose opening line had been an apology for lying to me. Letting go of the rail, I let the wind push me an inch or two away from him. I pressed my chin into my scarf. 'You're not some psycho, are you?' I asked with a nervous laugh.

'No, but I am scared you're not going to like me very much when I tell you how much I loved your mum.'

'That's fine. Everyone loved Mum,' I said, deliberately misunderstanding him.

'I was in love with her, Paige,' he clarified. 'And she was in love with me.'

I lifted my head as if in a daze. Heavy snowflakes stuck to my eyelashes. 'The only man Mum ever loved was Dad.'

'I'm sorry, but that's just the lie she lived. She didn't

love him.'

I released a sigh that was more like a grunt. All of the anger I'd been directing at my family surged through my body as a burning fury to be aimed at a new target. 'You know nothing about them!' I erupted. 'You're just saying that because you're jealous!' Jonah's expression remained hard and stubborn. He was delusional. 'That's it, isn't it? You fancied Mum and you hated the idea that she might actually be happily married.'

'Ellen and I were seeing each other for almost six months. Ask Izzy.'

I didn't like the way he was bringing up family members as if he knew them intimately. What if everything he'd said was a lie, and he didn't know Mum at all? Had I overshared personal details with a complete stranger? But I couldn't remember giving him my aunt's name. 'What does Izzy have to do with anything?'

'Ellen kept telling your dad she was going to see her sister when she was actually with me, and Izzy played along.'

'No!' I shrieked. I was shaking my head, but Jonah had got to me. Could it be true?

'The day she came here,' he continued, 'was the day she decided she had to leave Ray. She wanted to be free, and I promised her I'd do everything I could to make that happen. We were going to have this amazing life together.'

'I don't believe you!' I screamed, too angry to cry.

Had everyone been lying to me? Mum had spent the summer taking me and Dad on little trips, making memories to mark the end of my childhood, not the end of our family. Not that. How could she?

In the heat of my fury, the mist around me could almost be smoke, the flakes of snow ash. Everything was burning. I loosened my scarf. It was so hot.

'I'm sorry, Paige, but it's true. She'd been miserable for such a long time and she was sick of fighting for snatches of happiness here and there. She wanted to be free, but she was worried about you. She was going to wait until after Christmas to tell Ray, giving you time to settle in at uni, but I knew it was a mistake.' Jonah's voice was edged with bitterness. 'He'd trapped her once and he would do it again.'

'Trap her? You mean break the spell you had her under! You're a manipulator, Jonah. You want to take every nice thing between Mum and Dad and turn it into something horrible! It might have worked on Mum, but it won't work on me!'

'I'm not trying to manipulate you, Paige. I want you to hear the truth.'

'Then why didn't you tell me who you were from the start instead of pretending to be one of Mum's friends?' I asked. I wanted to turn and run, but I was too afraid to turn my back on this monster.

'I didn't like deceiving you, but it was necessary,' Jonah said. 'You have to believe me.'

'Yeah, that hasn't exactly worked for me before,' I mocked.

'Hate me if you must,' he said, 'because I damn well hate myself. Ellen would be alive if it wasn't for me.'

'Don't flatter yourself. Mum's death had nothing to do

with you. It was an accident.'

'That's where you're wrong, Paige. Her death was a deliberate act.'

I had to catch his words on the wind, and still couldn't make sense of them. And then it hit me like the storm. Jonah had convinced Mum she was trapped, expecting it to be enough to tear her away from her family. But Mum hadn't been able to choose. She kept putting him off until she couldn't take it any longer, and that was when she had removed herself from the equation.

I balled my hands into fists. This pathetic man had taken over Mum's life, and now he wanted to monopolize her death. He wanted to be the man she would rather die for than live without. He was the one who had trapped her.

I screamed as I punched his chest, again and again and again, until my cold hands turned numb. Snot and tears dripped from my nose, my ears buzzed with a fury I couldn't contain, and all the while, Jonah stood his ground. His arms remained folded, his feet shoulder-width apart. He refused to react and so I barrelled into him hard enough to make him stumble backwards.

'I hate you!' I cried before spinning on my heels.

If he called after me, I couldn't hear above the storm, not least the one howling inside my head.

CHAPTER 35

SUE

Sue sat next to Izzy on the bed while Olly acted as a prop behind her. He was actually doing quite a good job of supporting his wife, in every sense of the word, while Sue kept to the role of reassuring midwife. It was much easier to remain focused that way. She didn't have to be Olly's judgemental mother-in-law or Izzy's terrified mum. Most importantly, she didn't have to think about whether or not Jonah had been murdered. Or by whom.

'Why are you looking so worried?' Izzy asked when the latest contraction eased.

'I'm not worried,' replied Sue, telling her face muscles to relax. 'You're progressing exactly as you should, and I have Kim and your midwife waiting for my call if I have the slightest concern.' With that, she took her mobile from her pocket and placed it on the bedside table. 'Look, I don't need to phone anyone.'

She didn't mention that she had already gone through the most likely complications with the experts. There

251

were difficulties she needed to watch out for, but she was prepared. She had scissors and a scalpel, a straw to clear the baby's airways if necessary, and a food bag clip for when she cut the cord. What else did she need? She looked around the room as if sheer will alone could conjure an incubator for the baby's premature lungs, bags of blood should Izzy haemorrhage, not forgetting a surgeon in case an emergency caesarean was necessary.

Izzy pursed her lips tightly and began groaning.

'Another one?' Olly asked, only to receive a nudge from his wife's elbow for asking a completely redundant question. He had been bearing the brunt of his wife's wrath, another reason Sue was grateful for his presence.

'Can you breathe through it?' Sue asked.

Izzy shook her head, panic in her eyes.

'Do you need to push?'

'Oh, God. Yes.'

'Well don't, not yet,' Sue said quickly. She grabbed a pair of rubber gloves. 'I need to check to see if you're fully dilated, so pant through this one.'

Izzy's eyes grew wider. 'Whoa, no, I can't,' she cried, her knuckles turning white as she gripped Olly's hands.

'Yes, you can,' said Olly. 'Come on, breathe with me.'

Olly was the only one panting as the contraction came and went, mostly from the pain of having his hands crushed. Meanwhile, Sue examined her patient. This was it. It was time.

Mother and daughter worked as a team, Sue shouting instructions, Izzy screaming expletives. Olly was the cheerleader and when he said, 'You can do this,' he could have been talking to Sue as well as his wife.

It went on and on, contraction after contraction, until suddenly the head was crowning.

'Stop pushing!' Sue yelled. 'His head's out. I just need to …' She checked to make sure the umbilical cord wasn't around his neck, and that he was in the right position. 'It's all good. This is it, Iz. You need to push. Push!'

'Push!' hollered Olly.

With a sudden gush, Sue's little grandson entered the world. He was covered in gunk and hair, but he was pink and perfect.

Except he wasn't moving.

Sue grabbed a towel and wrapped him in it. She didn't look up at Izzy or Olly who had also fallen silent. She turned the baby over and rubbed his back vigorously. 'Come on, sweetheart. Come on.'

Olly followed suit. 'Come on, son,' he said. 'Please. Just cry.'

Sue's heart fluttered and her vision blurred while her ears strained for the sound of the baby's first breath. She let out a gasp that was more of a cry. 'Did you hear that?' she asked, turning him back over. When she wiped his tiny nose and mouth, his face scrunched up as he let out a mewl.

'Hello, sunshine,' she said, before laying her grandson on her daughter's chest.

CHAPTER 36

KELVIN

Closing the entrance door behind him, Kelvin shook the snow off his boots. He and Ray had dragged the corpse to the side of the pub entrance, then covered the tarpaulin with snow. They had done it with humanity and respect because they were decent human beings, unlike the deceased.

'I could do with a brandy,' said Ray, eyeing the dining room. 'Care to join me?'

'Maybe we should see if there's any news first?' replied Kelvin, unnerved by the silence that had descended inside the pub.

'I'll come with you,' said Ray as Kelvin made for the stairs.

They paused on the landing and listened. There were no cries, no words of encouragement. Just silence. And then they heard a baby cry.

Ray released the breath he had been holding. Tears welled in his eyes. 'What a relief,' he whispered. 'I can remember the day Paige was born, and the feeling of completion it gave me.' He offered a wan smile. 'There I was thinking the sleepless nights would only be for the first few months. It's worse now than ever.'

Kelvin couldn't return the smile knowing what would be keeping Ray awake from now on. Could murder ever be justified, or overlooked? Ray wanted to protect his daughter, and wouldn't Kelvin do the same for Dee? Was he doing the same for Dee? Could he be absolutely certain she hadn't had time to reach Jonah in the snug?

Ray walked towards the sound of the baby, but the door opened before he could reach it. Olly slipped out carrying a bundle of used bedlinen. He wore a smile that made his cheeks glow.

'How's Izzy?' Kelvin asked.

The new dad's eyes sparkled. 'She's good. Really good, and the baby too. He's perfect. Sue let me cut the cord. Then they delivered the placenta. I can't believe people actually eat it. But Sue says it looks intact, so no problems there,' he rambled. 'But honestly, it was amazing. *He's* amazing. We just need to decide on a name now. Maybe something Welsh. I don't know. I'm just glad he's here and he's healthy.'

'Congratulations, Olly,' said Ray. 'I'm very happy for you both.'

'Has anyone updated emergency services yet?' asked Kelvin.

'Sue's on the phone now. They've said they still want Izzy and the baby to be checked over properly so they won't call off the rescue.'

255

'How long before they're here?' asked Ray, sharing a look with Kelvin.

'An hour or two, they said.' Olly blew air between his lips. 'What a day.'

'It's not over yet, Ol,' Ray warned him.

Olly seemed to expect Ray to say more, then the spark disappeared from his eyes. 'God, yeah, sorry. Did you see the cushion? What do you think?'

'Didn't Sue tell you?'

Olly shrugged. 'We've been a bit preoccupied.'

'We need to get our stories straight,' Ray explained.

A sense of unease crawled down Kelvin's spine as he imagined having to give statements. How likely was it that they could give reasonable accounts of what happened without mentioning how Jonah was in contact with Ray's daughter, and knew Dee too? How hard would it be for each of them to behave as if there was nothing to hide?

'Does that mean you think it might have been murder?' Olly said with a gasp. When Kelvin glared at him, he lowered his voice. 'But why would someone do that?'

'We were hoping you might know, Ol,' Ray said. If he saw the look of confusion in Kelvin's face he ignored it. He had already concluded that his daughter was most likely responsible, but Kelvin supposed it was natural to clutch at straws.

'Me?' asked Olly, aghast. 'How would I know?'

It was possible his apparent shock was feigned, just like his reaction to seeing the marks on the cushion may have been from guilt rather than surprise. Perhaps Ray was right to be suspicious.

'I know you care a lot about Paige,' Ray said, putting forward his argument. 'You didn't have to mention the messages you'd found on her phone. You knew there was a good chance Paige would retaliate the way she did, but you still wanted to protect her. What else might you do in her name?'

'I wouldn't kill a comatose man, if that's what you're suggesting,' Olly said, his voice becoming higher in pitch. He hugged the dirty bedlinen closer to his chest. 'You know I couldn't do something like that.'

'The fact remains that Jonah *was* murdered,' said Ray carefully. 'And you had the perfect opportunity when you came downstairs.'

'But I didn't go into the snug. And you were down here too, you would have seen me.'

'I was in the toilets for a while.'

'Well, we only have your word for that,' Olly said. He jutted his chin out. 'The kitchen was empty when I got there, and I spent all my time hacking into Paige's phone. I was still skimming through her messages when you came in.' His breath caught as his face lit up with inspiration. 'Which means I couldn't have killed Jonah beforehand because I had no reason to. I didn't know he'd been stalking Paige until then.'

'And Ray didn't know either until you spoke to him,' Kelvin added, relieved to have found a solid alibi for both men. He needed allies, not suspects.

'Then if it wasn't us, who was it?' asked Olly. 'Who would put a cushion over the face of defenceless man strapped to a table? It has to be someone with some serious issues, that's for sure.' His face fell suddenly as he glanced towards Paige's door.

Anticipating where the next accusation would be aimed, Ray attempted to deflect him. 'Maybe it was a terrified woman in labour who's just lost her sister?'

Olly held Ray's gaze. 'More like someone who's just lost her mum and is mightily pissed off with the world in general and more specifically, with the man who's been grooming her. You can't tell me you haven't considered it might have been Paige.'

Kelvin raised a hand. He was still concentrating on the door that had drawn Olly's attention. Was that Dee's voice he had heard? 'I don't think we should be talking here,' he whispered.

CHAPTER 37

PAIGE

After making my confession, I'd broken down in sobs. 'I killed him,' I'd said, over and over until I let exhaustion wash over me. Dee had pulled the sleeping bag over my shoulder, and I didn't remember anything else until I woke up to find an empty space where my visitor had been.

Rubbing my sore and crusted eyes, I pulled myself up, and realized I hadn't been left alone. Dee was standing with her ear pressed to the door.

'What is it? Are the rescuers here?' I asked, unsure if I wanted to be saved.

Dee jumped with fright then looked at me. 'No, it's … it's your family,' she explained in a whisper.

'What are they saying? Is it Izzy?'

Dee raised a finger to her lips and we both listened. I could hear people talking, but before I could zone in on the voices, they stopped. Dee re-joined me on the bed.

'What's happening?' I asked, fully awake now.

'Your dad was outside talking to Olly,' Dee said, then couldn't continue. Her chest heaved as she tried to control her breathing. Noticing my growing concern, she smiled to reassure me. 'Izzy's had the baby. It sounds like they're both OK.'

'That's good,' I said, still confused as to why Dee should look so serious. 'I don't think I could have lived with myself if I'd harmed them as well.'

'*You* didn't harm anyone,' Dee said with unexpected force.

'But I did,' I said. How many more times did I have to say it? 'I killed Jonah.'

'Paige, look at me,' Dee said, cupping my face. Her eyes fixed on mine. 'What happened to Jonah is not your fault, not any of it.'

'But it is,' I countered. 'I was the only one up there hitting him. He fell because of me. He said so himself.' There was no point in denying it now that everyone knew I'd met him. 'He said he was pushed.'

'But he didn't blame you.'

'How can you know that?'

'Because Jonah told me.'

I should have felt relief at that, but my mind was whirring with new questions, ones that made me feel less comfortable in Dee's company. As far as I was aware, Dee hadn't been downstairs since they had brought Jonah back. 'But how? When?'

'I was the one who found him. It was my torch signalling you last night. I'd followed the red route, like you suggested.'

260

Realization dawned. 'So when I backtracked after leaving Olly, it was your footprints I was following?'

'Yes, and when I reached the ruins, I could see where the snow had been disturbed immediately below me where Jonah had tried climbing back up.'

'Jonah was awake all that time?'

'He told me that the bump on the head had knocked him out for a while, and when he eventually came to, he was lost in the fog. He knew it was safer trying to get back up to the ruins than risk stumbling over the cliff edge, but the slope was too steep and unstable, and he was too weak. He was barely conscious by the time I found him, but he told me about you running away before he fell.'

'What exactly did he say?' I demanded.

Dee rubbed a palm against her chest as deep scarlet patches flamed her neck. 'He told me to talk to you. That was why he got you here in the first place.'

CHAPTER 38

KELVIN

Kelvin took the bedding from Olly and discarded it in the utility room where the washing machine was running through its latest cycle. The others had disappeared into the dining room, and while he would rather return upstairs, he knew he wasn't going to find Dee in their living quarters. Rather than dwell on why his wife would want to talk to Paige, he went to join the others.

'I need a drink,' he said as he took his seat at the table.

Ray poured him a brandy, and as Kelvin took his first gulp, Olly resumed their conversation from earlier. 'You don't really think it was me or Izzy who killed Jonah, do you?' he asked, his voice quavering. His earlier bravado had given way to the same kind of fear that was twisting Kelvin's insides.

'No,' Ray said, the effort almost too much for him.

Kelvin agreed. Izzy had been too busy hiding the fact that she was in labour, and as for Olly, he may have killed

262

hundreds of gangsters, assassins and invading troops in his time, but only with a game controller.

'And I don't think anyone is ready to contemplate the possibility of it being Sue,' Ray offered, swigging back his brandy.

'Like you, she wouldn't have had a motive,' Kelvin told him. 'She didn't know about Jonah's messages to Paige until after he'd died.'

'What about you and your wife?' Olly asked Kelvin, voicing logic rather than hostility. 'Dee could have gone into the snug while we were in the kitchen, or you could have done it when you came downstairs after me.'

'Again, there was no motive,' Ray said, relieving Kelvin of blustering his way through an answer.

The neck of the brandy bottle rattled against glass as Kelvin topped up their drinks. His silence about Dee's connection with Jonah condemned Paige to being the prime suspect. He downed his drink. It did make sense that it would be her. 'Paige is the one who had ample opportunity if we can assume she went straight to the snug after leaving Izzy.'

'But why? What exactly did he do to her?' Olly asked, then continued to answer his own question. 'Maybe Jonah tried to attack her up on the ruins. She could have pushed him away, and that's when he fell.'

'No,' Ray whispered, head shaking in denial.

'It would explain why Paige was hell-bent on getting you to take her home when we all knew the sensible thing was to stay put,' Olly persisted.

'But then why help with the rescue?' Ray asked. It was

more of a plea.

Kelvin swallowed back another slug of brandy, along with a good dose of self-loathing. He needed to believe it was Paige. 'You said it yourself, Ray. She could have deliberately dropped the stretcher. Her whole reason for joining the search could have been to hinder his recovery. And when that failed, she used the cushion. I'm sorry, but it all fits.'

Ray continued to shake his head. Tears glinted at the corners of his eyes. 'No.'

'From what I read of Jonah's messages – and I only skim-read a few,' said Olly, 'he was using Ellen's death to get Paige to open up to him, reflecting her grief like it was his own.'

'No!' Ray cried out, openly crying now. 'I can't listen to any more of this!'

'I'm sorry, Ray,' Olly said. 'As much as we all want to protect her—'

Ray slammed his fist on the table, rattling the glasses and almost upending the bottle. 'It was me!'

Chair legs scraped against flagstones as Kelvin and Olly jerked backwards. Silence sucked the air out of the room just as quickly.

Olly licked his lips. 'But we've just agreed you and Sue didn't have a motive.'

'It was me, damn it!' hissed Ray. 'I was the one who went up to the ruins. It was me who pushed Jonah. Just like I was the one who dropped him on purpose when we were carrying him down. It was me, me, me.' He stabbed a finger to his chest. 'And I put the cushion over the

264

bastard's face. I killed him.'

While Ray ranted, Kelvin rearranged the glasses on the table. He should feel relief at the confession, but first he had to actually believe it. With a sinking heart, he said, 'You didn't know Jonah yesterday morning, Ray. Why would you fight with him?'

'Maybe I did know him,' Ray countered. 'I could have looked at Paige's phone long before Olly did.'

'Then what's her passcode?' asked Olly.

'It's her birthday,' he answered.

'No, it used to be your birthday, Ray. That's the one she shared with me ages ago, but she'd changed it again. Probably because she knew she couldn't trust me,' Olly replied. 'It almost caught me out, but I took a lucky guess. It was the date Ellen died.'

Ray sank his head into his hands. 'It can't be Paige,' he said, his shoulders shaking. 'What will happen to her? I can't lose her too.'

As the door swung open, Olly leapt to his feet, his earlier confidence evaporating at the sight of his mother-in-law scowling at him.

'Where's the cup of tea you promised Izzy?' Sue scolded, only to be pulled up short by the sight of Ray sobbing. 'Please God, what now?'

CHAPTER 39

SUE

Sue felt the tightness in her chest return as Olly pulled out a chair for her. She had done a good job of pushing thoughts of Jonah to the back of her mind, hoping that as long as she didn't look in that direction, their collective fears would simply vanish. Her daughter and grandson had been her priority. They still were. She raised an eyebrow at Olly as he attempted to return to his seat.

'Izzy shouldn't be left on her own,' she said. 'And she's still waiting for that cup of tea.'

He jumped up again. 'Yes, sorry. I just … Sorry.'

'It's our fault,' Kelvin explained once Olly had left. 'We needed to talk to him about Jonah.'

'Are we any nearer understanding what happened?' she asked, giving Ray only a side glance. His head was no longer in his hands, but he was staring off into space.

'I'm not sure,' said Kelvin.

Sue put her hands on her chest and rubbed hard.

Whatever stress she felt was about to intensify. It was perfectly obvious some conclusion had been reached.

'I don't suppose you want that drink yet?' asked Kelvin, indicating the brandy.

'No,' she said, not quite as firmly as her previous refusals. 'Any idea how long it will be until help arrives?'

'Rob sent a text not long ago. They had to pick up a paramedic en route whose vehicle had been stuck in the snow, but they should be here within the hour,' Kelvin explained. 'Olly said you've updated emergency services. Did you talk about Jonah's death at all?'

'I explained he died while I was asleep and I didn't know the cause of death.' She looked from Kelvin to Ray and back again. 'What else is there to say?'

'Ray has told us he's responsible for everything,' Kelvin replied. 'From pushing Jonah off the ruins to smothering him. I, for one, don't believe him.'

'Oh, Ray,' Sue said, touching his arm. He was shaking even more than she was. 'Why would you say that?'

'He's protecting his daughter,' Kelvin said when Ray made no attempt to speak up for himself.

'You think Paige did it?' Sue asked, swaying from a sharp stabbing pain to the heart. 'No, it can't be.'

'She's going to need help, Sue, even if we're the only ones who ever know Jonah was murdered,' Kelvin continued. 'Whatever damage he did while grooming her won't go away simply by ignoring it. Paige will have to come to terms with what she did eventually, whatever the provocation.'

Sue couldn't contemplate any scenario where Ellen's

little girl would take someone's life, no matter what the circumstances, and unlike Ray and Kelvin, she knew it wasn't because Jonah had been grooming her. It was Paige's mother that Jonah had seduced. Sue stared at the broken man next to her. How was she going to tell Ray that?

'I've already lost Ellen. Please, let me do this. I have to, for Paige,' Ray mumbled.

Reaching for the brandy, Sue topped up Ray's glass, then waited patiently for him to take his medicine.

'What if it wasn't her?' she asked Kelvin. 'It could have been Olly.'

'That's why he was here with us,' he replied. 'It wasn't him, Sue. Or Izzy.'

'Well, of course it wasn't Izzy,' Sue said, bristling at the idea that another member of her family should fall under suspicion. 'But someone placed that cushion over his face. What about you and your wife?'

'We've been through this,' Ray said, his words slightly slurred. 'We keep going around and around in circles, and it always comes back to the same thing, as much as I wish it didn't.'

'So that's it? You're willing to accept it was Paige?'

'I don't want to,' Ray said, his voice choked as he fought back another sob. 'But what other explanation is there? She killed him, Sue. She killed him in cold blood.'

CHAPTER 40

PAIGE

'I need to tell you about what happened to me,' Dee said, her back pressed against the headboard while I squeezed alongside her on the single bed. I didn't like the way she had to take deep breaths before continuing. 'How was Freshers Week for you?'

'Erm, I don't know,' I answered, thrown by the question. What did this have to do with Jonah? She obviously wanted to take it slowly, so I played along. 'It was great. Lots of drunken parties and a constant hangover, but I met some really nice people. I thought we'd see each other through the next few years. And then shit happened.'

'For me too,' said Dee. She was staring straight ahead, but she was also looking back in time. 'Except I was never a party animal. So while everyone else was out dancing on tables, or so it seemed, I was lonely in my need to be alone. I felt different, and somehow less of a student, so I spent most of my time hiding out at the library.'

'I've always loved hanging out in libraries too,' I said, finding momentary comfort in revisiting my childhood ritual of going to the library on Saturday mornings with Mum. Dad would already be there and would have a stack of books set aside for me. 'My dad's a librarian.'

'Yes, I know,' Dee replied before taking another gulp of air so she could continue the story she needed to tell. 'During those first few weeks, the library was my safe space. And that's where we met. He was a bit older than me, but I liked him.'

I imagined Dee as an eighteen-year-old, wide-eyed and delicate. It was more difficult to picture Jonah in his youth. His grey hair would be dark, but his eyes just as piercing. He would have attracted a lot of attention.

'He was my first proper boyfriend,' Dee continued. 'I couldn't understand what he could possibly see in me, but he made me feel special. We kept it low key because I was a student and he wasn't, but that made things more exciting. I'd sneak into his place or he'd slip into the halls of residence when my flatmates were out. He bought me things, clothes that weren't my style but he claimed suited me, and books he wanted me to read when I already had a huge reading list. His initial interest in helping me with my archaeology degree quickly fizzled out, and I felt out of my depth when he started up conversations on subjects I knew nothing about. And so there would be more books he'd pile on me to broaden my mind.'

'It sounds like he set out to make you feel stupid,' I said, thinking how Jonah had made me feel foolish too.

'I didn't see it that way at the time. He told me I was the

love of his life, and that was overwhelming. Frighteningly so. I wasn't ready for that kind of intensity and tried to slow things down, create some space, if only to catch up with my studies. But he refused to keep away. He told me he couldn't live without me. He couldn't eat or sleep at the thought of not seeing me, or so he said. And this was all in a matter of weeks.'

Dee pressed her fingers to her eyes, but there was no sob. She was deep in concentration as if the memories didn't come easy for her.

'It was suffocating,' she confessed. 'I did have feelings for him, it was hard not to, but eventually, I accepted that I could never love him the way he wanted me to, and it was unfair to give him false hope.' The bed creaked as she shifted position. 'The first time I suggested we break up, he took it so much worse than I could possibly have imagined. He told me in graphic detail how he was going to end his life, leaving me convinced it wasn't some idle threat. So of course I backed down.'

'That's awful,' I said, turning to face Dee properly. 'Do you think Mum had to put up with threats like that too?'

For a second, Dee seemed to sway, but she met my gaze. 'Yes, I'm sure she did.' She cleared her throat. 'It came to a head the week before the Christmas break. We'd argued because I had plans to go home, whereas he expected me to stay. I broke up with him, for good this time, but he turned up late one Saturday night, knowing I'd be alone. He'd brought along his suicide letter for me to read.'

'That's just sick.'

'When I refused to even look at it, he read it out loud between heart-wrenching sobs. His, not mine, or not at first. He'd brought a bottle of vodka, so I poured him a drink and one for myself just to calm things down. I didn't have any mixers. I'd usually keep some cartons of orange juice because he preferred vodka and orange, but I'd had a clear-out. My bags were almost packed for going home for the holidays the following week.'

I pictured Dee and Jonah in a tiny room just like the one I wouldn't be returning to in Loughborough. A single bed on one side of the room, a fitted wardrobe, desk and shelving on the other, with just enough space for a rug in between.

'He sat on the bed, so I chose the chair. I was determined not to engage with him. I watched him sob, wiping trails of snot across his cheek with the back of his hand. He was a mess, but I didn't go to him. I didn't plead with him. He slurped his vodka, and I drank mine. I refilled our drinks, more than once, as I let him cry it out. This was a man I'd been in awe of when we'd first met, but in less than three months, his displays of adoration had become deeply uncomfortable, embarrassing even. I wasn't going to give in to his emotional blackmail this time.'

It was hard to imagine a man as tall and broad as Jonah pulling off being the tormented victim of a broken heart, but wouldn't it be more impactful to see a grown man cry? 'You must have been so strong to withstand that kind of manipulation.'

Dee looked sad. 'I thought so too, which was why I let my guard down. He'd got up to leave but then collapsed and, naturally, I reached out. The sobbing resumed, and we both ended up sitting on the floor, our backs against the bed and a half-empty litre of vodka between us. I filled our glasses again. I didn't realize how much I was drinking, and how much he spilled before it reached his mouth.'

'You were the one getting drunk?'

'My thoughts had become dulled, but I was aware that I was out of my depth. I suggested calling someone, but he didn't have family, and wouldn't hear of involving the uni counselling services. So I tried to talk him down myself. I wanted him to see that he had a future, just not with me. And at some point, the conversation shifted. It was so subtle that I didn't notice.'

'What did he do?' I asked, aware I was getting closer to understanding how Jonah might have driven my mum to despair.

'He told me not to blame myself. He said I wasn't to know what effect I'd had on him, and he was sorry that I was going to carry that guilt for the rest of my life,' Dee said. A laugh caught in her throat. 'He was almost right. For twenty years, I never doubted that what happened was my fault. What was worse, he made me believe that I would destroy whoever dared to love me. "You won't do it intentionally," he'd said. "You're too sweet for that, but you will crush them with your heartlessness."'

I felt a shudder run down my spine. What words had he whispered into Mum's ear?

'My head began to swim,' Dee continued. 'He encouraged me to drink more vodka because I was the one crying now, and I must have finished the bottle. I was inconsolable. Even *he* claimed not to want me at this point. He said there was no going back for us. He had seen me for what I was, and he was repulsed.' Dee rubbed her temples, easing the pain I could hear in her voice. 'On and on it went until I had a panic attack. I thought I was dying, and I remember him trying to soothe me. He had anti-depressants, and he gave me two.'

I watched in horror as she extended a hand in front of her, palm up as if accepting the pills.

'Later, my memories were so disjointed. I could remember seeing the pills sitting in the palm of my hand, and wanting to die. I recalled him leaving. And the next thing I knew, I was being shaken awake by a paramedic. I was covered in vomit and one of my roommates was crying. There were empty sleeves of pills on the floor. I was rushed to hospital and that's when I found out I was pregnant. Or at least, I had been. The overdose caused a miscarriage.'

'Oh, Dee. I'm so sorry.'

'When my parents arrived to take me home, they thought the best medicine was to never talk about it again. One of my roommates had helpfully told the paramedic that I'd been quite secretive, that there had been a boyfriend of sorts but it was all very strange. They assumed it was a case of unrequited love after a brief fling. He disappeared into the woodwork, and I was left believing a half-told story. The blame was on me, and rightly so. I killed my baby.'

'You can't blame yourself for any of it!' I cried.

Dee rolled her shoulders. 'I don't, not any more,' she said. 'After seeing him again last year, I dared to revisit what had happened that night, and all those gaps in my memory fell into place. The picture I pieced together was very different to what I had once accepted.' Slowly, she held out her hand again, palm upwards. 'That image I had of him placing two pills in my hand wasn't one single memory, Paige. I was too upset and too drunk to figure out it was the same scene on repeat. He fed me maybe two whole sleeves, and I'm only alive today because I threw up after he'd left me for dead.'

'He tried to kill you,' I said.

'No one ever asked where the pills came from,' Dee said. 'He'd brought them with him. And I don't think they were ever intended for him.'

'At least he's dead now,' I said, suddenly freed from my own sense of guilt.

The knock on the door wasn't loud but it made me jump, and I almost toppled Dee out of bed. She righted herself and we stilled, neither of us saying a word. There was another knock.

'Paige, I've brought you a cup of tea,' Olly called. 'I need to talk to you. It's important. Please.'

'I think you should speak to him,' Dee encouraged.

After listening to what Dee had endured, I felt better about facing whatever challenges lay ahead of me. 'OK,' I said.

We both got up, and Dee stood behind the door as I opened it. She pressed a finger to her lips.

***

Teaspoons rattled as the tray trembled in Olly's hands. I could tell I must look shocking by the horror on his face. Self-consciously, I smoothed my hair and rubbed my eyes, any traces of yesterday's make-up long gone. 'What do you want?'

'Can I come in?'

I drew the door closer so I filled the gap. 'Shouldn't you be with Izzy?'

'They're good. She and the baby are sleeping. It's a boy.'

I felt warmth spread across my chest at the thought of my tiny cousin. I wanted to see him, and I wanted to make amends with Izzy too. I had reached the conclusion that there was only one person responsible for Mum's death, and it wasn't my aunt. I missed how things used to be between us, but our relationship was something to work on in the future. Right now, I had to hear more from Dee. She hadn't told me everything yet. I needed to know more about what Jonah had said after his fall, and why she was so convinced it wasn't my fault.

'Just say what you have to say, Ol.'

'I want you to know that no one's angry with you,' he began. For clarity, he added, 'I'm not angry with you. I deserved to be publicly shamed for what I did, and in a way, I'm glad it's all out in the open.'

'You shouldn't have looked at my phone,' I said, trying to hold on to my hate even though he'd made a good point. Divesting myself of one horrid little secret had been liberating, but there were so many more I had to keep.

'I know it was wrong,' Olly said. 'But if anything, I

wish I'd looked sooner. Things might not have gone as far as they did.'

'That's some apology.'

'It's too late for apologies,' Olly said with a finality I didn't like. 'The damage is done, Paige.'

My mouth went dry. As much as I'd despised Olly in recent months, it was only because I was hurt by how much he'd let us all down. He'd been like an annoying elder brother, and I missed our old relationship. Was he saying there was no way back? I curled my lip to disguise a tremble. 'If you say so.'

'The thing is, Paige,' he continued, 'we're going to face a lot of questions about what happened to Jonah, and I want you to know that I've got your back.'

'You've got my back?' I asked, thoroughly confused. Was he giving up on me or not?

'We know what you did.'

I continued to stare at him.

The teaspoons rattled again. 'We know you killed Jonah.'

Ah, I thought. *I should have been prepared for this.* If I'd thought Jonah had been trying to say I'd pushed him, the rest of the family were bound to reach that same conclusion too. I glanced to my left, catching Dee's eye. She was the only one arguing my innocence. 'Well, that's where you're wrong, Olly. Yes, I saw Jonah on the ruins, but he didn't fall because of me,' I said, repeating what Dee had said.

'That's hardly the point,' Olly said as if he were scolding a child. Fatherhood had clearly gone to his head.

'Jonah didn't die because of his injuries. We found the cushion.'

'The what?'

'The seat pad you used to suffocate him,' Olly said carefully. He was gripping the tray tight enough to turn his knuckles white.

The shock should have sent me reeling, but I was convinced Olly was the one confused, not me. 'But he—'

Olly didn't let me finish. 'An autopsy could establish his death had nothing to do with his head wound, or hypothermia, or any other natural cause, and we need to be ready for that.'

'Are you messing with me?'

'I wish I was. Your dad's downstairs, and he's in bits. He tried taking the blame just so you wouldn't get into trouble.'

I took a step back so this time when I looked at Dee, I could see her clearly. 'But I didn't do it,' I whispered.

'Listen,' Olly said, bringing my gaze back to him. 'I don't know what Jonah was up to, but my guess is he did something bad.' He blushed, clearly uncomfortable with whatever possibilities he was conjuring. 'And when we brought him back here and he started talking, you got scared. Maybe you saw him as a threat again. That's why you wanted to help with the search in the first place. You wanted to silence him. Ray says you kept unbalancing the stretcher on purpose so you'd drop him.'

The accusation was like a punch in the gut and I almost doubled over. 'My dad said that?'

'We want to help, Paige. I know you're not a murderer.'

'I'm NOT a murderer!' I yelped. 'And I can't believe anyone's suggesting I am. Where's Dad?'

'He's downstairs with your nan and Kelvin. We haven't got much time, but we will figure this out. You just have to be truthful.'

'*Truthful*?' I echoed, tapping into hidden reserves of anger I thought had been extinguished. 'In that case, maybe I should go downstairs and tell Dad that Jonah was never interested in me. It was Mum he'd been having an affair with. And don't say you don't know about it because I know you do.'

Two mugs of tea slopped their contents onto the tray as Olly struggled to keep it balanced. 'That was Jonah?'

'Doh!' I said, mocking him. 'And just to be absolutely clear, I don't know anything about a cushion. It's true I didn't want Jonah talking, but only in case he told Dad about the affair. I didn't want him to find out Jonah was connected to us at all, but you cocked that up by sharing my messages! I didn't kill Jonah!'

'Then who did?' demanded Olly.

'I don't know!' I cried. It didn't make sense.

I felt Dee's hand come to rest on the small of my back. It was such a gentle touch, full of knowing and sympathy. She held the answers to all the questions I'd been harbouring since Mum's death. That was why Jonah had brought me here. But why on earth would he want me to speak to Dee when she had such a horrific tale to tell?

I shook my head. Two women. The same man. So where was the anomaly that stopped the pieces fitting together?

Dee was a university student, away from home for the first time. She had sought sanctuary in the library. Jonah had seduced her. He'd got her pregnant. He wanted to control her, and when that had failed, he'd tried to kill her. And then he'd run.

Mum had met Jonah when she was much older. He had seduced her too. He'd said they were going to make a life together, but maybe Mum had rejected him too. He hadn't been there when she died, but he could have influenced her actions. But wouldn't he want to disappear again? Why bring me here where I would find out about Dee, and with all the family around?

'Paige, what's wrong?' Olly asked, glancing to where I kept looking as if he had figured out someone else was there.

'I can't ...' I said.

I couldn't breathe. My thoughts had become tangled. Or had they? I was thinking of all the other similarities between Mum and Dee. Mum had been a university student too. She had been away from home for the first time, and had warned me not so long ago how overwhelming it could be in those first weeks. Like Dee, she had sought solace in an older man. She had fallen pregnant. She had become trapped. Hadn't she met Dad in a library too?

'Paige, please,' Olly said. 'Come downstairs. Talk to your family.'

There was a whooshing sound in my head as if I had been dropped into the centre of a cyclone. I remained still while the world spun around me. 'I didn't unbalance the stretcher, Olly,' I told him. 'If anything, it was Dad who made it tip over.'

'But not on purpose sur—'

Before Olly could finish his sentence, I barrelled past him. The tray crashed to the floor.

CHAPTER 41

SUE

Sitting around the table in a darkened room with dancing shadows cast by candlelight, Sue felt as if the storm had picked her up and tossed her into a horror story. This was her granddaughter they were talking about.

'Paige needs to admit what she's done before we decide anything,' said Kelvin. 'I don't want to start lying to the police only for her to contradict whatever we might want to say. She's traumatized, I get that. Whatever he did to her ...'

'But we don't know he did anything,' Sue interrupted, her words strangled.

What she didn't add was that she suspected the hurt Jonah had inflicted had been emotional rather than physical. It was hard enough for Sue to process that the bruised and broken stranger she had tended had once been her daughter's lover. How difficult must it have been for Paige? And how much more painful would it be for

Ray? Ellen would want her secret to be buried with her, except Ellen wasn't buried. They hadn't even managed to scatter her ashes, and now her secret had been cast into the four winds. Jonah had told Paige, and it seemed inevitable that Ray would find out too. How else could they protect Paige without speaking of the real reason she had been thrust into a battle with Jonah?

'I think Paige's behaviour speaks for itself,' Ray said. 'And I'm sorry, Kelvin, but knowing my daughter, she isn't going to take responsibility for what happened.'

'You're right, Dad, I won't.' Paige was silhouetted against the open door, her hair an unkempt mane. 'I'm not going to confess to something I didn't do. I can't believe you're setting me up for a fucking murder.'

Ray shot up out of his seat. 'I know you're scared, I am too, but we'll get through this, Paige,' he said, holding out his hand as he approached her. She batted it away.

'Olly says Jonah was suffocated with a cushion. Are you absolutely sure?' she asked, looking to Sue. 'None of you are experts in forensics, or coroners, or whoever else decides these things.'

Sue stood up, but her jelly legs wouldn't carry her to her granddaughter. 'We're as sure as we can be without the person responsible owning up,' she said pointedly. 'We've got rid of the cushion, but it might not be enough to disguise the fact that Jonah didn't die naturally. There's other tell-tale evidence on his body that can't be erased.' A sob tore at her throat. What had her granddaughter done? 'But you wouldn't have known that.'

'I didn't need to know it!' Paige growled.

283

Ray made a grab for his daughter again, and this time succeeded in pulling her to him. 'It's too late, darling. If we can't cover this up, we have to make sure you say the right things. No court would want to see you punished if you acted out of fear.'

Gasping for air as if she were the one suffocating now, Paige shoved her dad hard, and he staggered backwards. 'For fuck's sake, let me breathe! Let me think!'

Sue's blood ran cold. She could only imagine how tortured Paige must feel trapped by her mother's lies. There was no time to spare feelings. The rescue team would arrive soon and they needed to get their story straight. The plan was to keep as much to the truth as possible so they wouldn't accidentally trip each other up. They wouldn't mention the cushion, obviously, and Jonah's phone had been lost, so all they needed was for Paige to agree not to mention knowing Jonah at all, or at least not unless his autopsy made a full investigation necessary. Their secrets could stay in this room, but first they had to be aired. All of them, however painful.

'It's time to tell the truth, sweetheart,' Sue said softly.

Paige shook her head. 'You don't know what you're asking.'

'Oh, I do,' Sue replied, placing a hand on Ray's back.

Kelvin cleared his throat, the last to get to his feet. 'Would it help if you talked privately?' he asked.

'No,' Paige answered. 'You need to hear this.'

'Hear what?' Ray asked, the last to realize there was more going on than he could possibly imagine.

Sue began rubbing his back, soothing him for what

would be a devastating blow. But Paige being Paige, her opening shot was a curveball. 'Why did Mum have me?'

'What kind of question is that?' asked her dad. 'She wanted you. She wanted us to be a family.'

Paige raked her fingers through her tangled hair. 'But that wasn't what she planned, was it? She went to uni to study architecture but had to give it up because of me.'

'It wasn't the sacrifice you make it sound,' Ray insisted.

'And she hadn't got that far with her studies. She was only there for one term,' offered Sue.

She understood Paige was trying to justify why Ellen had felt the need to set herself free from her family, but now was not the time. Sue was about to press the conversation on, but the energy in the room shifted. Paige was in control, not them.

'One term at Aberystwyth university,' her granddaughter said without emotion. 'There's a coincidence.'

'A coincidence?' Sue repeated as she followed Paige's gaze towards Kelvin. His Adam's apple bobbed up and down as he swallowed.

'What university did Dee go to?' Paige asked him.

Kelvin shoved his hands into his pockets. He didn't look comfortable having his wife drawn into their conversation. 'Aberystwyth.'

Sue looked again from one to the other. 'What does that have to do—'

'Stop this, Paige,' Ray interjected, his impatience showing. 'We need to settle this now, because at some point you will have to talk to the police. Think about how it's going to look if you go off on a tangent. They'll know straight away you have something to hide. And you do have something to hide.'

As her father's eyes bored into her, Paige looked away.

'This is for your own good. Can't you see that?' Ray pleaded.

When Paige looked back at him, there was defiance in her eyes. 'What I see is you trying to control me. Just like you did to Mum.'

Sue had never heard her granddaughter speak to her dad like that before, and it was her attitude rather than the accusation that shocked her most. 'Paige!' she snapped.

Paige held her body tense and didn't flinch at the reprimand. She had always idolized her father, and it would tear her apart to tell him about Ellen's affair. Was she trying to dismantle her parents' marriage, hoping to lessen the blow? It was gut-wrenching to watch, and as she became aware of her own cowardice, Sue took a step forward. She was about to tell all when the shadows cast in the light from the corridor shifted. They all looked to the door.

Dee stepped into the room and linked arms with Paige. She stared straight at Ray.

286

CHAPTER 42

ELLEN

Ellen stared at the mottled swirls of Artex on the ceiling. It was quite warm for November but miserably damp – perfect conditions for the spots of mould to grow and multiply. She drew the duvet up to her chin as if she hadn't given up all rights to defend her modesty a long time ago. The man lying naked beside her had spent the last six months exploring every inch of her body. She felt sick with guilt, not least because of her argument with Izzy.

It had been unfair to place her sister in such an impossible position. Ellen had tried to explain how suffocating being married to Ray could be, but it had sounded petty complaining about how she couldn't even take out a gym membership without Ray deciding to join too. It was her own fault. For too many years, she had gone along with the pretence that theirs was a happy marriage. Did that justify an affair?

'This is wrong,' Ellen said, repeating what Izzy had said to her earlier.

Jonah propped himself up on one elbow and slid his hand across her waist. 'What's wrong is you going back to that bast—'

'Don't,' Ellen interjected. She would not tolerate Ray being called names, not when she was the transgressor, not even if what Dee had said about him were true.

Ellen had taken her family to Mynydd Plentyn on a whim after spotting the translation of its name. Child Mountain. It felt like the perfect description of Paige as she faced the next phase of her life. Her daughter had the potential to be strong and resilient as long as she was allowed the freedom to make her own choices and correct her own mistakes. Waving her off to university had been a wrench, but Ellen wanted her daughter's experience to be everything that hers wasn't.

It had been a series of missteps that had led Ellen to abandon her degree, and with it the exciting future in architecture she had envisaged. Although a relationship had been amongst the possibilities she had considered while at uni, it was never meant to result in a pregnancy, a marriage and the abandonment of her studies. She had accepted her fate, however, because she had thought it was her choice. If she felt trapped, she only had herself to blame for building the cage. Or so she had believed until Dee had caught her crying in the pub toilets after a trip up to the viewing platform where she had already been struggling to keep her emotions in check.

While Ray and Paige tucked into sandwiches and soup in the sweet little dining room, Ellen stared into the faded mirror and wondered if she would ever summon the courage to leave her husband, and what the price of her freedom would be. Ray would make it difficult to leave while Jonah was making it harder to stay, but this wasn't about what either of them wanted.

As she rinsed her blotchy face, she heard a toilet flush and a woman appeared from a cubicle. Ellen's cheeks reddened. She had thought she was alone. 'Sorry,' she said, moving to the side to let the stranger past.

'Is there anything I can do?'

Ellen kept her head down. 'Allergies,' she explained.

'I suffered the same way too,' the woman began. 'It was a long time ago, but I remember what it was like.' When Ellen gave her a quizzical look, the stranger offered a tentative smile. 'I'm Dee.'

'Ellen.'

'And is it your daughter waiting for you in the dining room? With Ray?' asked Dee.

'You know my husband?' Ellen queried, feeling suddenly on edge. She glanced at the exit.

'I won't keep you,' Dee said. 'I never expected to see him again. I never really considered that he might have a family. I'm guessing your daughter's in her late teens? Which means you must have met Ray only a few years after I left Aberystwyth University.'

'I was at Aberystwyth too. And yes, Paige is eighteen,' Ellen said, surprised she should offer the information so willingly. Her pulse was rising. Fate had brought her to this mountain.

When Dee continued talking, she talked fast, aware that they could be interrupted at any moment. Ellen was transfixed by the story of how Dee had met Ray during her first term at university. He had spotted her alone in the library where he worked and their relationship had intensified quickly.

'That does sound familiar,' said Ellen, her eyes glistening. 'Except with me, I fell pregnant, so our lives were bound together after that.'

'I fell pregnant too, but I had a miscarriage,' said Dee. 'Doesn't it seem odd? Two students getting pregnant during their first term, by the same man. It shouldn't have happened. We used condoms.'

'So did we. I presumed it was a faulty pack.'

'So did I,' Dee said. She shook her head. 'Another coincidence?'

Before Ellen could consider an alternative explanation, Dee continued. 'You'll have to forgive me, I haven't confronted these memories for a long time, but I have a horrible feeling I need to tell you what happened when Ray and I broke up.'

And so Dee told Ellen about the suicide letter Ray had read out to her when she dared to end their relationship. She spoke with a confidence that soon trickled away as she described drinking glass after glass of vodka, and the pills that appeared in her palm, over and over. It was as if Dee were telling her story for the very first time, and it made her weep.

'I can understand how you must have felt,' said Ellen because she knew how painful her own near-break-ups with Ray had been. 'Being worshipped like a goddess is intoxicating. You know it needs to stop, but every time you try, he offers you another fix that's even more addictive. And when you finally see it through ...' This was where their paths diverged. 'I can only imagine how disorienting that would be. The regrets and recriminations, the guilt. And I can certainly believe Ray wouldn't have handled it well, but it's not like he made you do it.'

'Ray fed those pills to me, *all* of them,' Dee said as if the thought had only just struck her. 'And then he left me to die. So, yes, I do blame him.'

'No, you must be confused,' Ellen said, horrified by the accusation. 'I'm sorry you had such a rough time, but you said yourself you were drunk. What you're suggesting, it would be ... No, I refuse to believe it.'

'For years, I refused to believe it too,' Dee confessed. 'But in a way, you've given me the courage to remember. What he did to me wasn't a one-off. He coerced you too, didn't he? Marrying him, having his baby. Staying married. You did those things because he guilt-tripped you into it.'

Dee's assertions were harsh, but unnervingly accurate. 'Maybe I have given Ray more years than I should have done, but I am my own person. And now my daughter's moving out, it's time I got my independence back.'

Dee tilted her head. 'You're leaving him?' she asked. When Ellen refused to answer, it was all the confirmation Dee needed. 'Please, be careful.'

'Don't worry,' Ellen insisted, surprised to see genuine concern staring back at her. Or was it fear? 'Honestly, I've got someone looking out for me.'

Ellen didn't know why she had gone on to tell Dee

about Jonah. It was instinctive. Perhaps she wanted to share the affair with someone who, rather than judge her, would be happy, or at least hopeful for her.

Since that meeting, she had tried not to dwell on how fearful Dee had been for her safety. Ray could never be so cold-hearted as to feed a young girl pills. It was unthinkable. He wasn't the cruel and callous one. She was.

'Stop it,' said Jonah, his chin resting on his hand as he waited for Ellen to look at him. 'Stop feeling guilty. If you ask me, Ray should be grateful that he had your unquestioning loyalty for this long.'

'I had his too,' she tried.

'What you had, Ellen, was a coercive relationship,' he corrected. 'He love-bombed you so you felt under pressure not to reject him. Your whole marriage was built on a foundation of being obligated to a man you didn't love.'

'But I did love him,' she said, too weakly to sound convincing. She had been flattered by the intensity of Ray's love, and felt lucky to have a husband who wanted to satisfy her every need. Except Ellen's original needs had been to get her degree and forge a career ...

'You *did* love him,' Jonah repeated, focusing on her use of the past tense. 'You've given enough. It's time to get out of there.'

'Not yet.'

'Doesn't it worry you what his ex-girlfriend said?' asked Jonah. 'She could have died.'

'Even if that's true, I can't believe Ray played the part

she says he did,' Ellen said, regretting having told Jonah about the conversation. 'Dee dated Ray for a few months; I've known him for half my life. He would never hurt me. If anything, I'm the one doing the hurting. The least I can do is give him and Paige a nice Christmas.'

'But what if he finds out about us? The longer you wait, the more chance there is that something could go wrong. I want to look after you, Elle,' Jonah said. 'And the best way of keeping you safe is for you to be here, with me.'

'No, Jonah. I'm not moving in with you,' Ellen said firmly. She could see right through him. This was the reason he was overplaying the threat Ray posed. 'If I do leave—'

'When you leave,' he interjected.

'When I leave, I want a place of my own. Paige needs to know she can still come home to me.'

'I can find us a nicer place,' he promised. 'This flat was only ever meant to be a temporary stopgap until my divorce comes through.'

'It's not the state of the flat that's putting me off,' Ellen began, only to stop and smile when Jonah pulled a face. 'OK, maybe it is a bit, but the break from Ray needs to be clean. He has to realize that I've not had my head turned by some devastatingly handsome, annoyingly charming, knee-tremblingly sexy, middle-aged man. I'm leaving because I want to be the kind of woman you think I am. I want to find out who she is.'

'You mean a beautiful, charismatic, confident, knee-tremblingly sexy …'

'I was thinking more like independent,' Ellen responded before realizing what he had just said. Her smile broadened despite the knot of anxiety tightening her stomach. 'And if you do have to describe me, use your own words.'

'Can I help it if our feelings are mutual?'

'They are, aren't they?' she said, her resolve strengthening. It was nice to be in a relationship where their affection for each other was perfectly balanced.

'I love you, Elle. And if anything happened to you ...'

'It won't.'

'You don't know what he's capable of, not really. You've never gone against his wishes before,' said Jonah.

That wasn't exactly true. Ellen had stood up to Ray once or twice, like when she had resumed her studies after Paige had started school. Her husband had come around to the idea when she settled on an Open University course, and he had even occupied their daughter so she could complete her coursework – at home, obviously. Putting her interior design degree to good use had been a little trickier, but when Paige moved up to senior school and became more independent, Ray's past arguments about being a full-time mum had passed their sell-by date. He had sulked, but only until Ellen suggested they might need to consider separating if they didn't make each other happy any more.

'If you left, there would be nothing else to live for,' he had warned her. 'I'd probably end up driving my car into ongoing traffic just to stop the pain. I'd try not to hurt anyone else on the road, but you don't think of these things when you're hurting that much.'

She had heard similar threats over the years, including that first time when she discovered she was pregnant and thought they should consider a termination. 'If you kill our baby, you'll have two deaths on your hands because I'll kill myself too,' he had told her.

It had sounded shocking when she repeated it to Jonah once he had earned her trust, but back then, Ray's threats had been bookended by endless hours of gentler persuasion. He talked of how much he loved her, how he would devote his life to making her happy, massaging her ego enough to make her feel all-powerful, and his suicide threat had been just one more declaration of love, albeit an extreme one.

She had never acknowledged it as controlling behaviour because even if she had, there had been no one to tell. Her mum adored Ray and would be more concerned about his state of mind than her daughter's career. And Izzy had only been twelve when Ellen married. Even now, Ellen found it difficult to admit to her little sister how gullible she had been, but she was starting to open up, although clearly not enough judging by Izzy's recent ultimatum.

As Jonah's fingertips began exploring her naked body, Ellen forced herself to check her watch. 'I'm sorry, I don't know how long this council meeting of Ray's will last. I need to head home.'

'I don't want you to go,' he said, his hand moving lower.

'No, I have to leave – now,' Ellen said, peeling Jonah's arm from her waist so she could get up. When he went to resist, she gave him a warning glare. She could stand up for herself.

'I don't want to make it harder for you. I just hate letting you go,' Jonah said, getting out of bed too. 'I'll drop you back off at Izzy's.'

'Thank you,' she said, pulling on her underwear. She went over to him, missing his touch already. 'It won't be for much longer.'

He kissed her long and hard before pulling away. 'I'll do this for as long it takes, Elle,' he said. 'Just promise me you'll be careful.'

He was worrying too much. She *was* being careful.

CHAPTER 43

KELVIN

Kelvin had at first been relieved when Dee appeared in the dining room, giving him an excuse to return upstairs where they would wait for the authorities to take control of the guests he no longer wanted in his pub. His willingness to involve himself in their lives had evaporated the moment Paige brought his wife's name into the argument. He didn't know why she had asked which university Dee had attended, and he didn't want to know.

'I don't think you should be here,' he said, taking a step towards his wife.

Dee shook her head imperceptibly, acknowledging him only briefly. She wouldn't stop staring at Ray.

'This is Dee,' Paige announced, directing the comment at her dad.

Ray ignored Kelvin's wife. 'I love you, Paige,' he said, 'but I swear, I don't know what to do with you.'

'Don't you remember me, Ray?' Dee asked.

Her voice was surprisingly clear with no trace of the anxiety that had kept her locked in her room. In fact it was strong enough to send a shock wave that rocked Ray's body.

'Everyone calls me Dee these days,' she continued, 'but my given name is Danielle. It was Dani to my friends back in uni, but I think you know that.'

Kelvin felt a rush of adrenaline that derailed any thoughts of extracting his wife from the unfolding situation. 'What's going on?'

Dee held Kelvin's gaze for just a second, but it was enough to remind him that she was stronger than he was giving her credit for. She had this.

'I recognized you, Ray, when you came here last year with Paige and Ellen, but there was no way I wanted to renew our acquaintance.' Her voice caught, but she regained her composure quickly. 'I did speak to your wife though. She told me a bit about her life, including her affair with Jonah, and I told her some things too.'

The ground beneath Kelvin's feet became shifting sands as all the lines connecting Jonah to Dee and Paige no longer made sense. Jonah was the abuser, they the victims, but had he heard right? Jonah had been having an affair with Ray's wife. Did Ray know?

Sue was rubbing Ray's back, expecting him to react, but there was no time. Dee was still talking.

'There was a lot for us both to process,' she continued, 'so Ellen promised that when she'd left you, she would come back so we could talk properly.'

'That's utter nonsense,' Ray said, his voice like steel.

'Ellen would never have left me. It was a fling, a mid-life crisis. Our marriage had its share of wobbles over the years, and Jonah was one we could have easily overcome.' He paused, his eyes boring into Dee. 'I don't know who you are, and I certainly don't remember you. All I see is a delusional woman going through a crisis of her own, and you'd do well to keep out of my family's affairs.'

'Believe me, I wanted to,' Dee said. 'It was Jonah who pushed for this.'

'And what exactly is *this*?' he snorted.

'Justice, I suppose,' she told him. 'And it looks like I'm the only one left to make it happen. I've been scared of you for too long.'

The candle flickering on the table sucked the oxygen from the room. Kelvin couldn't trust himself to speak, but his hand formed into a tight fist. Jonah had been the accuser. Which meant ...

Dee hadn't finished. She pulled back her shoulders, growing in stature. 'So tell me, Ray, if you'd known I was here amongst your family, would you have killed me too? It wouldn't be the first time you'd tried.'

'This is ...!' Ray began, his eyes darting around the room while he adjusted his response. His features had hardened by the time he refocused his attention on Dee. 'Oh,' he said with a sneer. 'I do remember you now. You were the girl who stalked me.' He turned to Sue, and almost conversationally, added, 'When I was in Aberystwyth, I used to dread the fresh intake of students each year. You could guarantee there'd be a handful of social outcasts who would hide in the library. It only took the smallest act of kindness, and suddenly you couldn't get rid of them.'

Sue didn't appear to share his amusement. She withdrew her touch. 'Is that how you saw Ellen?'

'God, no, not at all,' Ray said, placing a hand over his wounded heart. 'But Dani here misread all the signals, and before I knew it, she was professing her undying love. I felt sorry for her, but I couldn't give her what she wanted. She was emotionally unstable, which led to a suicide attempt, and her parents had to remove her from uni. I was shaken by what happened, but I pitied her. I was glad she survived. Or at least I was until now.'

Kelvin flew at Ray and grabbed him by the collar. He raised his hand, tensing his arm muscles, then paused just long enough to see Ray squirm. A hand curled gently around his closed fist.

'No,' said Sue. 'I want to hear what he has to say.'

Reluctantly, Kelvin lowered his hand. He needed an explanation too, so he manhandled Ray towards a dining chair and pushed him into it. The others remained standing.

'This is crazy. I can't be held responsible for someone else's actions twenty years ago,' Ray spluttered. 'Did I feel responsible? Yes, in a way, but I didn't put the pills in her hand!'

'Oh, but you did, Ray,' Dee corrected. 'You got me so drunk I didn't know what I was doing. And afterwards, I couldn't trust my memories. How could I possibly accept that someone who loved me as much as you claimed, could also want me dead? Not when you were the one saying you couldn't live without me.'

'He used that trick to keep Ellen from leaving,' said Izzy from the doorway.

Sue gasped at her daughter's sudden appearance. 'What are you doing down here? You need complete bed rest, Iz. What about the—'

Before she could finish, Olly appeared behind his wife. He was holding a tiny bundle swaddled in a fleece blanket. 'We're good,' he said.

'No, you have to take them back upstairs,' ordered Sue.

'Izzy is staying,' Olly replied. 'We all are.'

Sue looked about to argue again, but Olly reflected her glare with one of his own. Her shoulders slumped. 'At least make her sit down.'

Izzy took a seat a safe distance away from her late sister's husband. 'When did you work out who Jonah was, Ray?'

'I didn't until now,' he said innocently.

'I don't think so,' said Kelvin, no longer seeing Ray as the good and honest man he had been foolish enough to respect. 'I was more shocked to hear your wife was having an affair than you were.'

'Perhaps I knew Ellen better than you,' Ray said smugly. 'He meant nothing to her.'

'She was in love with him, Ray,' Izzy said, sounding too tired to be angry. 'For the first time in her life she was with a man because she chose to be, not because there was an unplanned pregnancy, not because she pitied him. There was no pressure to love someone back just because they loved her too much.'

'Liar!' Ray hissed. 'The Jonah thing was an infatuation, pure and simple. It's not like she cared enough to want to move in with him.'

'Because she wanted to leave on her own terms, for herself, not for anyone else,' Izzy replied, sounding proud of her sister. 'I'll be honest, I didn't approve of what she was doing at fi—'

'Oh, but you were happy to go along with the charade,' he snapped.

'I'm not proud of that, but I'm glad Ellen got to experience what it was like to be loved in the right way,' said Izzy, leaning in as Olly reached to wipe the tear trickling down her face.

'Rubbish,' Ray snarled.

'But it's not rubbish, is it?' Paige asked. The anger had gone, and she sounded utterly forsaken. 'Did you smother Jonah, Dad? Is that why you tried to set me up for it, to protect yourself?'

'To protect you!' Ray cried, extending a hand to his daughter. She was too far away for him to reach, but still she leant back. 'I love you, Paige. You're all I have left.'

'And so the cycle continues,' said Dee. 'First it was me, then Ellen, and now it's Paige you expect to give up her dreams, all so you don't have to deal with your abandonment issues. You expect unconditional love, and when you don't get it, you coerce and manipulate.'

Kelvin shook his head. 'Why didn't you tell me it was him, Dee?'

'I was scared about what might happen while we were

all trapped here,' she explained. 'But it happened anyway, or at least it did to Jonah.'

'And was that why you didn't want him waking up?' Kelvin asked. 'Because he knew about you and Ray?'

'Ellen had told Jonah everything, and he wanted to expose the truth. He engineered it so we would all be here together, but he didn't warn me, and up until yesterday, I didn't even know Ellen had died. There was no way I was going to agree. I couldn't face Ray,' she said. She blinked hard then stared at the man who had stolen her dreams. 'But you've given me no choice. I can't sit back and let Paige take the blame for Jonah's death when it was you who silenced him for good.'

'He could have done it. There was definitely an opportunity while he was down here alone,' Olly said quietly so as not to disturb the baby. 'He said he was in the toilets when I came down, but that was just a lie.'

Ray rolled his eyes. 'So what are you suggesting? That after giving Sue the food that was meant to keep her awake, I waited around for her to nod off? Don't you see how ridiculous that sounds? Much as this mad cow would like you to believe her fantasies, I didn't kill Jonah.' His eyes fluttered with self-satisfaction.

'I remember you coming in and shaking my arm,' Sue said, her brow furrowed. 'You said later that you didn't realize I was about to doze off, but I was already asleep, wasn't I? You shook me awake.'

'Because I was concerned about you abandoning *your* patient,' Ray said. 'Why would I wake you up otherwise?'

'But if Sue was asleep when you entered the snug,

303

that's when you could have done it,' Olly said, to which Ray responded with a tut.

Sue closed her eyes briefly as if to visualize the scene. 'I asked Ray if Jonah was OK and he said his breathing was steady. I didn't check for myself. I hadn't woken up properly, and I just fell back to sleep. I couldn't honestly say if he was alive at that point.'

'And the reason you didn't wake up properly was because Ray didn't try too hard. He didn't want you going over to Jonah,' Olly said. 'Was it you who pushed him off the ruins too, Ray? Was that what Jonah was trying to tell us?'

'I didn't get that far up,' Ray said looking to Paige. 'Maybe if I had, I could have done something to prevent all of this. What kind of man entices a child to a deserted spot just to tell her that her mum had been lying to her? I'm sorry you ever had to find out she was going to abandon us. You had every right to be angry with him, darling. I wish it had been me who had pushed him.'

Paige shook her head, tears slipping down her cheeks. 'Why are you doing this to me?'

'It's OK, Paige,' said Dee. 'We can all see what he's up to, and unfortunately for Ray, I had a chance to speak to Jonah when I found him up on the ridge.' For the benefit of those who hadn't yet heard, she added, 'It was me who signalled where he was, and he was barely conscious when I got to him, but he did talk. He said Paige had run off, and he'd been leaning on the railings, about to message her, when someone came up behind him and shoved him over the top.'

'*Someone?*' repeated Ray.

'You,' Dee clarified.

Ray released a sigh of exasperation. 'He would need eyes in the back of his head to have seen who pushed him, assuming we're to believe the ramblings of a semi-conscious man with a head injury.'

'Hold on,' Olly said to Dee. 'If Jonah confirmed he and Ray didn't speak, how did Ray find out about the affair?'

'He must have overheard me and Jonah arguing. It was so foggy, he could have easily sneaked up without us seeing,' Paige said. She bit her lip, waiting for her dad's response.

'What do you want me to say?' Ray asked.

'The truth would be nice,' answered Kelvin.

When Ray remained tight-lipped, Dee spoke up. 'Admit it, Ray. You already knew.'

For a moment, Kelvin was too busy scrutinizing Ray's expression to register the keening sound coming from Sue. He leapt forward just as her legs went from under her.

CHAPTER 44

ELLEN

Ellen left Ray asleep in bed and headed downstairs. It was Saturday morning, and once she was armed with her coffee, she went into their home office to catch up on admin. She was surprised to find a stack of papers on the printer for Ray's council meeting the previous night. They looked freshly printed, with no staples, no scribbled notes on the agenda page, no doodles. She didn't give it much thought until she went to make breakfast an hour later. It was unusual for Ray to sleep in so late, and he didn't reply when she called.

It had been harder than ever to tear herself away from Jonah the night before, but she had managed to arrive home before her husband. She had been relieved when Ray had gone straight to bed, but now she wondered if he might be unwell – or at least she hoped that was all it was as she went to investigate.

The curtains in their bedroom were drawn, and it took a second to make sense of the shadows on the bed in the dim light. She felt a jolt when she realized Ray was lying on his back, duvet tucked under his armpits, his hands resting at his sides. He was staring up at the ceiling, and hadn't reacted to her arrival.

'I've been calling you, Ray. Didn't you hear me?' she asked as the quickening beat of her heart sounded an alarm.

'Sorry. I was just wondering what it would be like to be dead,' he said, his tone robotic.

Ignore him, she told herself. 'Don't be silly. I'm making breakfast. Do you fancy a full English as a treat?'

'Like a final meal for the condemned man?'

Ellen's mouth was dry as she crossed the room and pulled open the curtains. 'Someone's in a funny mood today,' she said. Her thoughts were racing, but not fast enough.

'Only if you find it funny that your spouse has been cheating on you.'

Ellen clung to the curtain. 'I don't—'

'Don't know what I'm talking about?' Ray guessed. He continued to stare at the ceiling. 'I followed you, Ellen. I saw you go into Izzy's house, and then I watched you leave a couple of minutes later to get into a white Toyota parked around the corner. Very flash. I hope you'll be blissfully happy together.'

Ellen's breathing was fast and shallow. She hadn't wanted nor expected to have this conversation today, but in some ways, she had been preparing for it for years. *Say what you have to say*, she told herself. *It doesn't matter what he threatens, you deserve to live the life you choose.*

This is non-negotiable.

'I never wanted to hurt you,' she said, 'but I can't give you what you want, Ray. It's as simple as that.'

'Don't tell me what I want. I want you. I *need* you. There can never be anyone else.'

Ellen had expected lots of pleading, wringing of hands or wrenching sobs from her husband, and Ray's lack of emotion scared her. 'Can't you at least look at me?'

'No. I don't want to see your pity. You think I'm pathetic.'

'I don't think that at all,' she said, but even she could hear the lie. She overcompensated by adding, 'You're intelligent, generous, dependable, and very good-looking. You'll have no problem finding someone who appreciates you more than I ever could.'

'And what qualities does Jonah have that make him a better catch?'

Ellen's body rocked with the force of another shock. 'You know his name?'

'Someone kindly sent me an email. A concerned citizen who thought I might like to know my wife is about to sabotage my fledgling political career. As if I care about that,' he said, continuing to direct his conversation at the ceiling. 'When I decided to stand as a councillor, I stupidly thought your enthusiasm was because you believed in me, but all you were ever interested in was keeping me occupied so you could fuck someone else.'

Ellen opened her mouth to tell him that she was proud of him and that the affair hadn't been planned, but that would bolster his argument for her to stay, which would surely be his next tactic. *Let him think badly of me*, she told herself as she pulled down a carry-on case from the top of the wardrobe.

It might have been simpler to flee with nothing, but Ellen felt it important to set the tone from the start. Ray should be left under no illusion that his emotional manipulations wouldn't work this time.

'You're right,' she said, unzipping the case at the foot of the bed. 'I was praying that you'd get elected. Do you have any idea what it's like living with someone who makes it their business to be involved in every single aspect of your life? All I ever wanted was for my free time to be just that, *mine*.'

'Then maybe I should give you what you want. A life without me.'

Refusing to react to the veiled threat, Ellen carried on gathering up bits of make-up and underwear. 'Would it be so bad if we found other people?'

'Try telling that to Jonah's wife. Will all three of you be moving in together?'

'I have no intention of moving in with anyone. And besides, Jonah and his wife have been separated for over a year.'

'Still messy,' Ray said. 'At least our break will be swift and clean.'

Ellen had been picking out some clothes from the wardrobe, but she turned towards him. She knew she shouldn't ask. 'What does that mean?'

Keeping his arms tight by his sides, Ray unfurled his fingers to reveal a sliver of metal. It was a razor blade.

'Did you want to keep this bedding? I could use plastic sheeting if you prefer.'

Ellen tried to suck air into her lungs but found she couldn't. Her chest was constricted, her legs felt like jelly, but her mind remained clear. She stopped herself from moving closer to the blade. For the first time, she contemplated that she might be the one in danger.

She hadn't wanted to believe Dee's story, nor did she like how Jonah was using it as leverage to get her to leave sooner. It felt a little too close to the kind of trick Ray might pull, but what if Jonah's fears were justified? She had to admit that what Ray was doing now – what he had done many times before – wasn't a normal response. She couldn't predict what would happen if she kept to her resolve. Or could she? Hadn't another woman been in this exact same position? What if Dee's story had been true?

Ellen glanced at the door, then gave a yelp as Ray sprang up onto his knees. Balancing on the mattress, he tugged at his pyjama sleeve and held the razor blade above the purple veins threaded through his wrist.

'Would you like to watch?'

A teenage Ellen would have given in to his needs, a younger Dee would have sat down and talked him out of it. Neither of those options had worked out well for either of them. Ellen shoved one last sweater into her case and zipped it up. 'No, thanks. I'm going,' she said, calling Ray's bluff.

The mattress creaked as Ray sank down onto the bed again. 'Have you ever stopped to think what the last nineteen years have been like for me? I'm the fool who has given more, loved more, and hurt more while you've enjoyed one big power trip.'

'Hardly.'

'So that's it then? You're leaving me?' he asked, a tremor betraying the first signs of emotion.

Ellen bit her lip. 'Yes, Ray, I am.'

'And you don't care if I live or die?'

'No,' she said, no longer believing he would go through with it. 'But I hope you don't for Paige's sake. She adores you. You still have her.'

There was a glint in Ray's eyes that Ellen didn't like, and she wanted to cram the words back into her mouth. Ray loved their daughter, but he had never kept her on a chain the way he had his wife. If anything, he had encouraged her to spend time with her nan or Izzy, preferring to have Ellen to himself. What if he transferred his dependencies onto Paige? He didn't need a lover or a sexual partner to replace Ellen; he simply craved an object to love and consume.

'This is going to crush her,' Ray said, his shoulders shaking as the first sob issued from deep within his chest. 'But fine, you go.'

Ellen managed to get to the landing before Ray caught up with her.

'Paige has always been so sensitive,' he said. 'I wonder if we've protected her too much. She doesn't have the emotional tools to deal with this. I can't imagine how she'll cope when she finds out what I've done – and why. I doubt she'll be able to carry on with her studies.'

Ellen attempted to drown out Ray's wheedling by doing a quick mental audit of what she needed to take. Her laptop was in the home office, and her phone was in the hallway on top of the post she had intended to pick up on her way back to the kitchen.

'I'm sorry,' Ray continued. 'I wish I was strong enough to carry on for Paige's sake, but there's only one person with the power to stop this. Are you really going to destroy all our lives, Ellen?'

CHAPTER 45

SUE

Sue would have smashed her knees against the hard dining room floor if Kelvin hadn't rushed to keep her upright, and even then she had needed Paige to help her too. If she had been watching from the sidelines, she might have suspected a stroke or heart failure, but the chest pains that had been worrying her were the least of her troubles. There was nothing wrong physically. It was all in Sue's head. All of it. The pain. The grief. The despair. The *hate*. So much hate. Little wonder she had no mental capacity left to tell her body to stay upright.

Her feet scraped along the flagstones as she was dragged to a chair. Izzy drew up a seat next to her, and Paige crouched by her side. Sue leant on her granddaughter for support, and Paige offered a tearful smile.

'I've got you, Nan,' she said.

Oh, but who's got you? Sue wanted to ask as tears flooded her throat, drowning her words, but not her thoughts.

313

What a fool she had been not to see it before, but Ray had been a false god that she had helped create. The mortal man she glimpsed behind the mask filled her with abject horror. Dee was right. Ray had known about the affair. She could see that now, and so much more.

'I'm sorry,' she whispered to her granddaughter.

'Don't worry about me, Nan,' Paige said. Her eyes were full of love and concern, but her expression hardened as she turned to face her father. 'Can't you see what you're doing to us? Admit it was you who smothered Jonah with the cushion, Dad, or I swear I'll walk away from you forever.' As she spoke, she sought out Sue's hand.

'No, you won't,' he answered. His eyes narrowed. 'I won't let you.'

'And that's always been your problem, hasn't it, Ray? You don't know when to let go,' said Sue. Her voice shook, but she spoke clearly. The horror that had almost paralysed her had been replaced by steely determination. She had to do this for her family. She had to do this for Ellen. 'You were everything my husband wasn't, and I often thought Ellen didn't know how lucky she was. You never accused her of getting pregnant to trap you, but why would you? It was exactly what you wanted. You were the one doing the trapping.'

'He got me pregnant too,' Dee said.

'No, I didn't!' Ray yelled, losing his composure.

'You didn't know, and neither did I,' Dee said, facing him. 'You once told me I was destined to destroy those who might love me, and after the miscarriage, I saw it as proof that you were right. I might have gone through the rest of my life believing you if I hadn't been blessed to have a man like Kelvin in my life.' She stopped to share an unspoken moment with her husband before turning back to Ray. 'But I'm not the killer, Ray. You are.' She turned to Sue and Paige, holding her body so tense she was barely breathing. 'That's what Jonah came here to tell you.'

'It's OK,' Sue reassured her as she gripped Paige's hand fiercely. The child was going to need an anchor. 'You don't have to explain. I can imagine all too easily what he came here to say.'

CHAPTER 46

ELLEN

As Ellen reached the landing, she rounded on her husband. 'Stop it, Ray! Just stop it! No marriage can survive on threats and coercion.'

There, she had said it. Ray was coercive, and as long as his constant wheedling gave him the results he was after, he would carry on controlling her. If only she had been as strong as Dee, her ordeal wouldn't have stretched over decades.

'If you love our daughter as much as you claim, you'll carry on protecting her,' she said. 'Our divorce will come as a shock, but we can make it relatively painless for her. And that will be *your* choice.'

'Oh, no, you don't get to put this on me. You're the one abandoning us.'

'I'm not abandoning Paige. Just you.'

Ray's tears evaporated as hate burned in his eyes. 'You'd be nothing without me. Not many men would have stood by you after you got pregnant.'

'Because you got me pregnant on purpose!' she hissed. This was something she had never contemplated at the time, but after comparing notes with Dee, it was one coincidence too far. 'Admit it, Ray. The condoms you used weren't defective. You either damaged them or removed them without me knowing. They call it stealthing these days.'

'Who's been filling your mind with all this nonsense? Jonah?'

Ellen would love to see the look on Ray's face if she mentioned Dee, but she wasn't going to send him off in pursuit of a previous victim just so she could make her escape. 'I've reached my own conclusions, and now I see you for what you are.' She glanced at the razor held carefully between his thumb and forefinger. 'I know you're not going to use that.'

When Ray lifted his hand, Ellen flinched, giving away her fear. He smiled. 'You're right,' he said, tossing the razor to the floor.

Before Ellen could enjoy the relief, Ray made a grab for her case. She should have let him take it, but she clung to it with both hands. If she could win the small battles, she might win the war. Unfortunately, Ray had no intention of letting go either. He lifted the case, forcing her to raise it until it was at chest level. She couldn't figure out what he was doing until he began to use the case as a prod, pushing Ellen backwards along the landing.

Sunbeams played across the walls as the narrow space around them opened up. Aware they were getting dangerously close to the top of the stairs, Ellen reached one hand behind her, but before she could grab hold of the banister, Ray pushed. Not hard, but enough to unbalance her.

Ellen stepped back, hoping to plant her foot firmly on the floor, but it wasn't there. Reflexively, she let go of the case and her arms windmilled. Finally, she found the banister, but it was the back of her hand that smacked uselessly against it. Her toes crunched as her foot landed on a stair two steps from the top, her shoulder bounced off the wall, and her feet lifted into thin air. For a split second, she saw Ray immobilized at the top of the stairs, the case firmly in his grasp. And then her head thwacked against the handrail. Down she went, and as other parts of her body smashed into immovable objects, her momentum continued to build, splintering wood and breaking bones. It was over in a matter of seconds although Ellen had blacked out long before the pain signals reached her brain.

When she came to, she assumed she was waking up in bed as normal, and was confused to see spotlights in the ceiling in place of the chrome fitting in her bedroom. Slowly, the jigsaw pieces of her memory fitted back together and she let out a whimper. Her body felt cold rather than broken, but she knew better than to move her shattered limbs.

She could hear Ray's footsteps slow and steady as he came down the stairs. 'Oh, Ellen, what have you done?' he asked with no suggestion of alarm. 'I really wish I could help, but ...' He pondered for a while. 'Well, you've made it abundantly clear you don't need or want me.'

Carefully, she turned her head towards the man who had told her again and again that life wouldn't be worth living without her, but before she could focus on his cold stare, a blinding pain consumed her and she blacked out again.

Ellen awoke to the sensation of blood congealing on her cheek. She licked her lips, tasted more blood and tried to swallow, but it was difficult when she was panting so hard. She tried to call out but made only a rattling noise. Was Ray leaving her to die? And then she heard his voice, tantalizing her with the briefest glimmer of hope. He was in the home office only feet away, the door ajar. She could see his profile as he sat at the desk, his face awash with the blue light from his iPad perched on a stand.

'Are you sure this is a good time, Sue?' he was asking.

'Yes, of course. It's sweet of you to call. You must be so busy.'

Ellen felt her slowing pulse skip a beat. 'Mum!' she called out, or at least her lips parted, but there was no air in her lungs. She couldn't breathe. She closed her eyes and concentrated as if force of will alone could transfer her unspoken words. 'Mum, please help me. I need you. Please come. I have to stay alive. I have to protect Paige.'

As she struggled to open her eyes, the chatter from the home office continued uninterrupted by her death. And she was dying. She knew that. She just wanted to sleep, but she fought to keep her thoughts clear. Even though her family would never know what was going through her mind as she slipped away, Ellen was determined that it would be filled with love. She rejoiced at the good fortune of having a daughter who, despite being cocooned by her parents' seemingly happy life, was strong and smart and determined. She would figure out her father. And Izzy would help. Beautiful Izzy, who always felt second best, but had found someone who would make her happy on her terms, as long as she and Olly could forgive each other for their misdeeds. And her mum, whose voice she could hear in those last moments. *Don't trust him, Mum*, Ellen warned her. *Don't trust him.*

Her phone began to ring close by. Ellen didn't hear it.

CHAPTER 47

SUE

'You know?' Dee asked Sue, resting against her husband who had moved to join her.

'It was wrong of Jonah to drag you into this,' Sue said. 'This was never about you, or him for that matter.'

She considered closing down the conversation there and then. No one else needed to know the awful truth. They would have to deal with Jonah's murder, but that was nothing compared to what else she believed Ray had done. She would give anything for Paige and Izzy not to hear it. If Dee could agree to stay quiet …

Goosebumps pricked Sue's skin as she turned to her son-in-law. When she had welcomed Ray into their family, he had filled the patriarchal role with ease. He was the cornerstone they all depended on. Take Ray away and the family would collapse, just as it had when her husband had left. That was what she had thought, and it was a fear that persisted. It wasn't as if Olly could breach the gap.

'Nan?' Paige asked, noticing how tightly Sue was holding her hand.

No, she told herself. It wasn't Ray who had kept their family together. He hadn't raised two children alone. She had done that. The patriarchy was dead. It had only survived this long because she had been foolish enough to submit to it. Not any more. She leant over and kissed the top of Paige's head. 'I'm sorry, but this is going to hurt,' she whispered. 'Be brave, like your mum.'

Sue stood up, unsure whether her legs were willing to support her or not. 'Ray relied on his powers of suggestion to mould my memory to fit his narrative, and I've been a willing participant. I didn't challenge him when he told you how I'd just been sleepy when he came into the snug when in actual fact I'd been well away.' She shook her head. 'I've never challenged anything he's said.'

'So you do think he killed Jonah,' said Izzy.

'If only that was the worst of it, love,' Sue said to her only surviving daughter. She breathed in through her nose, out through her mouth. Her heart beat like a drum in her chest. She had to do this. 'He killed Ellen too.'

A wave of disbelief sent gasps around the room, but Ray showed no reaction. Dee, the least surprised, sniffed back a tear. 'Jonah was convinced of it too,' she confirmed.

'Then why didn't he go straight to the police instead of involving you?' demanded Kelvin.

'He knew he couldn't prove it.'

'Hmph,' muttered Ray, his chest puffing out. 'Could that be because there's absolutely no foundation to this vicious accusation? Of course I didn't kill Ellen. How could I?' he asked Sue. 'It has nothing to do with powers of suggestion. You know exactly where I was when Ellen fell. We were on a video call. You saw me with your own eyes.' He overemphasized his words as if Sue were suffering from some temporary mental impairment.

Sue had gone through their Zoom call more times than had been good for her, but as she replayed it again through the lens of the past, she tilted the angle. No longer listening to her inane chatter about traffic flows and council procedures, she checked the view from Ray's perspective. He had been sitting in his home office facing the door.

'When Izzy phoned that first time, we heard Ellen's phone ringing from the hallway,' she said. Her brow furrowed as she concentrated harder. 'It was quite loud, but I didn't hear anything else to strike alarm, and you didn't react other than to roll your eyes at the intrusion. That was when Ellen supposedly fell, but if I could hear the phone ringing, why didn't I hear her fall? Why didn't I hear her scream?' She shuddered at the thought. It was almost too much to bear, but she had to continue. 'You didn't go and investigate until Izzy's second call because you already knew what you'd find. You initiated our Zoom call to give yourself the perfect alibi. I bet the door was open the whole time. It would explain why I heard the phone ringing so clearly. My Ellen was lying at the bottom of the stairs, and you ...' The contempt in her voice twisted her features. 'You were looking at her the whole time.'

Paige folded in on herself. 'That's what Jonah meant when he said it was a deliberate act. You— you left Mum to die?'

'No, Paige, never,' Ray said earnestly. He was so believable. 'I was devoted to her, you know that.'

'Even though she was going to leave you?' asked Sue.

'How many more times do I have to say this? I didn't know she was having an affair!'

'Yes, you did,' Dee said quietly, but her voice was lost to the cries from Ellen's family.

'Ellen had no inkling that you might have known,' Izzy was saying, 'but that means nothing. I think we've all worked out you're a good actor. You've played a convincing part in this family for years.'

Ray shook his head in disdain. He was never going to admit to his crimes, even if Sue tried to throttle the truth out of him. And she wanted to so much.

'Stop lying, Ray,' Olly said as he rocked his baby son. 'You've already given yourself away. You knew all about Ellen's plans not to move in with Jonah, and you knew about Izzy covering for her too. No one here offered that information, which means you had to have heard it from someone else. So who was it?'

'It was Jonah,' Dee said, speaking louder than before.

'So he did hear him talking to Paige up by the ruins,' Olly said, nodding.

'Did you, Dad?' Paige asked with a trembling voice.

Ray held her gaze. He looked as though he was getting tired of lying to her. Somewhere in his blackened soul, he had a conscience after all.

'He knew before then,' Dee said without waiting for Ray's response. 'Ray received an email from an anonymous source telling him all about his wife's infidelity months ago.'

'But you've just said it was Jonah,' Sue replied.

It was Olly who worked through the logic. 'Jonah sent the email?'

'He told me yesterday. He was wracked with guilt. That's why he was so intent on exposing the truth.'

'But why would he do something like that?' cried Sue.

'He hoped it would be a catalyst, forcing Ellen to act sooner rather than later,' Dee explained. 'He was worried that the longer she stayed, the more chance there was of Ray realizing something was wrong and manipulating her into staying.'

'Look, I received no email,' Ray insisted. 'Or if I did, it must have ended up in my junk folder. I think the only thing you've proven is how contemptible Jonah really was. And you dare to attack me?'

'Why don't you just come out and admit it, Ray?' Olly said. 'Tell us what you did.'

Ray sneered. 'I don't have to answer to *you*.'

'No, but you will answer to the police,' said Kelvin.

'And why would that be?'

'Sorry?'

'Who says there's been any wrongdoing whatsoever?' Ray asked. 'Ellen died from a fall. Her mother has already vouched for my whereabouts when it happened, and her body is now ashes. There is absolutely no evidence to suggest it was anything other than a freak accident.'

His eyes flicked to Paige. 'Which it was, darling. I would never ...'

Paige took a couple of shallow breaths. 'I don't believe you.'

'Even if we can't get justice for Ellen,' said Sue, anger tensing her jaw, 'we can still have you locked up for what you did to Jonah.'

'Can you?' Ray challenged. 'Again, where's the evidence?' He addressed Kelvin when he added almost casually, 'I'd say that boil wash will have finished by now, and even if the body indicates something other than a natural death, the only thing we know for sure is that you knowingly destroyed incriminating evidence.'

'What's he talking about?' asked Dee as the mood around the room changed.

'Your husband washed the cushion that had marks on it suggesting it could have been used to cover Jonah's face,' Ray told her. 'Although, I have to say, I wasn't convinced.'

'You were convinced enough to blame your daughter,' said Sue, but her case was weak. Ray had weaselled his way out of every harm he had inflicted. He wasn't going to answer for his crimes, and although he would never get back the family he had clung to so obsessively – not even his daughter if Sue had anything to do with it – it didn't feel like justice. It wasn't even close.

'It does make me wonder what was going through Kelvin's mind,' Ray said, clearly enjoying his musings. 'He had no reason to protect a family he'd never met before, but now you've crawled out of the woodwork, Dani – sorry, I mean, Dee – it all makes sense. Your husband thought he was covering up for you. And maybe he was. If Jonah could have an affair with one married woman, why not two?'

'I—I never met him until yesterday!'

Ray shrugged as if he was bored with the argument.

Kelvin turned to his wife. 'I believe everything you say,' he began. 'But Ray makes a good point. Why would I help a group of strangers conceal a crime?' There was a crooked smile on his face that he aimed directly at Ray. 'My problem is, I like to assume most visitors who come here are good, honest people, and if it was up to me, I'd take everyone at face value. Dee isn't so trusting. You've all seen the 'No Entry' signs, and I guess some of her scepticism must have rubbed off on me.' His features hardened. 'I didn't put the stained cushion in the washing machine, Ray.'

CHAPTER 48

KELVIN

Kelvin didn't know Ellen, but he grieved for her family. He could feel their anger, and absorbed it into his own. Appearing out of the storm, they had been a group of stragglers he had wanted to turn away, but now he would fight for, and with them.

The blood was draining from Ray's face as it dawned on him that he couldn't talk his way out of this one. He appeared paralysed by fear, but then he rolled his shoulders. Kelvin felt prickles on the back of his neck as the atmosphere changed, and he took a step forward. Olly sensed it too, and just as he handed his sleeping son to Izzy, Ray jumped to his feet.

'You're all mad!' he yelled, turning in a circle to face each one of his accusers. He pointed a swaying finger at Dee. 'Especially *her*. Do you honestly think the police are going to take *that* seriously?'

Kelvin launched himself at Ray. 'You piece of sh—'

Olly stepped into the narrowing space between

the two men. He was shorter than both, but he had acquired a presence that forced Kelvin to a temporary halt.

'The police will take Dee seriously because we'll be backing her up all the way,' Olly said as Kelvin prepared to push past him if Ray so much as looked at his wife again. 'And if the evidence confirms that Jonah was murdered, we can damn well show there was only one person with a true motive.'

'Who the fuck would listen to you?' snarled Ray as he looked Olly up and down.

Kelvin felt Olly's shoulder twitch. He wasn't going to be cowed, but before he could respond, a phone started to ring. It was Kelvin's. 'Shit,' he muttered.

This was not the time for an interruption, but the call had to be an update from the rescue team. He checked his phone and saw it was his brother, and while he took the call, Olly raised his hand, palm facing towards Ray – a warning for him to stay where he was.

'Hey, Rob,' Kelvin said, his voice shaking with emotions he couldn't quell. 'Where are you?'

'Put the kettle on, we'll be there in five minutes. That car was a bugger to move,' replied Rob. There was the sound of a straining engine in the background. 'How is everyone? How are mother and baby doing?'

Kelvin's eyes flicked to Izzy. 'She's fine, the baby's fine, so take it slowly. See you in a bit.'

'Where are they?' asked Sue when he had finished.

'They've managed to move Ray's car, so they won't be lo—'

Before he could complete the sentence, Ray gave a yell and spun towards the door.

Olly made a grab for his sleeve, but Ray tugged his arm away and kept moving. He had to cut past Izzy to reach the door, and as he did so, he used the back of her chair as leverage to propel himself faster. The chair tipped, and Izzy let out a cry. She couldn't right herself without letting go of the baby, and instinctively turned her body so that she would land on her side. Olly caught them both.

'Are you all right?' Kelvin asked, coming up behind them.

'I'm fine,' Izzy panted. 'Just get the bastard.' When both men hesitated, she howled, 'Go!'

Rushing for the door, Kelvin and Olly bumped into each other as they tried to get through it at the same time. Kelvin was knocked against the doorframe.

'Hurry up!' shouted Sue who was right behind them.

They piled into the corridor only to find it empty. The main entrance door remained firmly closed. He hadn't escaped that way.

'Where's he gone?' asked Sue.

While Olly took the stairs, Kelvin bounded towards the kitchen with Sue close behind. Pots and pans rattled as he skirted around the island, heading to the rear corridor. It was empty, and even before he opened the back door he knew there would be no new footprints in the snow.

'He didn't come this way,' he panted to Sue.

Kelvin didn't believe Olly would have any better luck upstairs because it didn't make sense for Ray not to head for an exit. Unless ... His heart stuttered as he turned to the utility room and swung the door open. There was the smell of freshly washed laundry, but he wasn't interested in the damp cushions in the washing machine. Checking the racking, he spotted the cushion he had wanted to preserve peeking out behind a box. Ray hadn't tried to destroy the evidence. So where was he?

They checked the storeroom if only to be thorough before making their way back to the main corridor, where they stopped to catch their breath. Olly crept back down the stairs and put a finger to his mouth. He had heard something and was heading towards the snug. Above the crackle of the fire's dying embers, there was the clink of metal against metal.

Kelvin and Sue followed, and watched as Olly took a step into the snug. Without warning, his body jerked and his head snapped back. A hand had been thrust palm first into his chest, and knocked him back into the corridor. As Ray came racing out of the snug, Olly rebounded off the wall in time to grab hold of him by his newly acquired ski jacket. Ray spun around. He was holding a pair of boots by the shoelaces, and aimed them at Olly's head. Olly ducked, and it was Sue who howled in pain as she took the full impact on the side of her head.

Olly released a cry of his own as he let his closed fist fly, but it glanced off Ray's cheek.

'You stupid fucking moron!' Ray yelled, pulling back his arm and landing a punch square on Olly's nose. 'You'd be out of this family if it wasn't for me!'

There was the crunch of bone, and Olly's cry was

tempered only by a blast of cold air as Ray pulled open the front door. Kelvin was only vaguely aware of the door slamming as their quarry slipped away. He had been behind Sue and supported her by her elbows, fearing she might collapse. There was a nasty red mark along one side of her face and her eye had started to puff out.

'I'm fine,' she said and they both turned to Olly who was scrambling to his feet, his face covered in the blood gushing from his nose.

'You're just letting him go?' came a trembling voice. Paige was standing at the door to the dining room, her eyes as wide as a fawn caught in headlights. 'But he left Mum to die.' She was struggling to breathe as she looked from her nan's swollen cheek to Olly's bloodied face. 'Are you OK?'

'What's happening?' called Izzy from out of sight, having remained in the dining room.

'We're fine,' Olly shouted back, his voice nasal. 'Just give me a minute.' He pressed his fingers to the bridge of his nose.

'We can't let him get away,' Paige persisted.

'He won't get far on foot,' replied Kelvin. He glanced at the boot print on Sue's face and added with a wince, 'Even if he does stop to put those boots on.'

Paige stepped towards her nan. 'I don't know who he is any more.'

'None of us do, love,' said Sue. 'All I can say for sure is that our family is going to be stronger without him. I promise you that.'

The way Sue lifted a hand in Olly's direction to include

him in their number made Olly straighten his spine. 'I won't let Ray near you ever again, Paige,' he said with a snuffle. 'If that's what you want?'

Before Paige could answer, they heard the roar of a car's engine and the screech of tyres fighting for traction in the snow.

'They're here at last,' said Sue.

CHAPTER 49

PAIGE

As Olly pulled open the entrance door, we crowded around him, vying for our first glimpse of the new arrivals. The car was turning in a wide arc through the snow, its headlights highlighting a set of fresh footprints leading away from the pub. In the gloom, the reflection of brake lights glistened off a patch of wet gravel, and it took me a moment to heed the flash of red as a warning. The rectangle of wet ground I was staring at with tired and swollen eyes was where Jonah's car should have been.

'Is that Dad driving?' I asked in disbelief.

'Damn, that was the rattle of keys I heard!' Olly said. 'He must have taken them from the snug.'

'He's leaving us?' I asked as if the father who had promised to protect me still existed. Then my thoughts caught up and I wanted to cry.

I hadn't chased after Dad when he ran out of the dining room because even though Dee had exposed him as a monster, he still looked like the dad I had worshipped as my hero. The dark world I had been plunged into didn't feel real, but neither did his love. For my entire life, I had simply been a weapon Dad had created to force Mum into a life of servitude, the daughter he had been prepared to let take the blame for killing Jonah.

'I need to warn Rob before he meets Ray coming the other way,' Kelvin said, his voice frayed with worry as he took his phone from his pocket. 'The snow will have made the road dangerously narrow, and the passing points won't be visible. One of them could go over the edge if they're not careful.'

I watched as the Toyota's red tail lights dipped out of view, but a moment later, another set of headlights rose upwards, playing across the car park gates. 'Is that them?'

The vehicle was a similar model to Dad's getaway car, but it had an orange and white chequered pattern on its sides, and bar lights on the roof as opposed to a foot of snow. The driver pulled into the clear stretch of gravel left by Jonah's car. Two men clad in orange all-weather suits, and a third in green, exited the vehicle. Gathering up heavy holdalls, they tramped through the snow to the welcoming committee.

'It's good to see you, Rob,' Kelvin said, giving one of the men a hug.

'Sorry we couldn't get here sooner,' Rob said, glancing to the side of the entrance where shovels were resting next to a heap of snow.

I was confused by what they were looking at until I noticed the tarpaulin peeking through the snowy grave. Despite what Dad had said, I had wanted to help bring

Jonah down safely from the mountain.

'Who the hell was that driving past?' continued Rob. 'If he isn't careful, he's going to run off the road.'

'An unwelcome guest,' Kelvin replied cryptically.

'You need to warn him about the estate car. We had to push it up against a boulder, but it's still a tight squeeze getting past. The last thing we need is another car blocking our route or, God forbid, something worse.'

'Is he going to crash into it?' I asked, having visions of losing another parent to an accident. My brain stalled. No, that was wrong. Mum's death hadn't been an accident. Dad had sat in his chair chatting away as he watched Mum die, and all because giving nineteen years of her life wasn't enough for him.

'Leave us to deal with Ray,' Nan told Rob, shaking me from my thoughts.

'What happened to you two?' the paramedic asked, looking from Sue's injuries to Olly's.

Kelvin ushered the new arrivals inside. 'Long story. First things first, you need to check on the new mother and baby.'

'They're in here,' said Dee. She was standing outside the dining room and nodded to Rob.

Her brother-in-law gave her a worried glance. Presumably Dee didn't normally look so ghostly. 'Not the peace and quiet you were expecting, is it, Dee?'

'I'm just glad you could join the party,' she said, raising an eyebrow before turning to Olly. 'Izzy's a bit upset. She needs you.'

'You might want to wash your face first,' Nan warned

him. 'We don't want her getting any more shocks.'

'In that case, Sue, you might want to put some ice on your cheek too,' he replied.

Nan appeared to agree, but after the paramedic and the second member of the Mountain Rescue team disappeared into the dining room, no one else moved. If there was going to be a discussion about what to do next, everyone wanted to be involved.

'I imagine it's been rough,' Rob said, 'but I'm sure you did all you could for the fall victim.'

There was an awkward silence in which no one rushed to correct Rob's assertions.

'What should we do about Ray?' asked Nan.

'We can't have him blocking the road again,' said Dee, who must have overheard Rob's warning. She gave him an enigmatic smile and held out her hand expectantly. 'Can we borrow your car?'

'Seriously, Dee?' Rob said, his shocked expression entreating her to tell him it was a joke. Her hand remained extended. 'It's been years since you were a volunteer.'

'And yet only last month I was unofficially helping with one of your rescues.'

'Only because it was on your mountain.'

'So is this,' she said.

Rob rubbed his eyes. 'You're not insured. Can't you just phone him?'

'He won't answer.'

Realizing Dee wasn't going to back down, Rob sighed. 'Fine, but I'll have to come with you,' he said, sounding bone weary. 'I'll drive.'

'You've been working through the night,' Kelvin said.

'You don't need this.'

'And we won't be long,' added Dee. 'I promise we won't go further than the abandoned car. If our friend has managed to get past, there's no point in us chasing after him.' Her face was a picture of innocence, and Rob was probably the only one who didn't hear the subtle inflection when she referred to Ray as a *friend*. 'And if he has got stuck, he won't come back here unless we escort him. Trust me.'

Rob tugged the collar of his orange jacket, popping a couple of press studs. He stretched his neck, shaking his head slowly as if he was about to refuse, but in the next moment, he was digging his hand in his pocket. He dropped his keys into the palm of Dee's upturned hand. 'Don't make me regret this, Dee.'

'Let's get our things and move,' Kelvin said.

I was first to move towards the snug where I'd left my boots and jacket. Nan and Olly were close behind.

'Hold on,' Dee said, stopping us in our tracks. 'We're not all going.'

'Dee's right,' said Nan, side-stepping me so she could bar entry to the snug. 'Olly, go and wash your face and see to your wife. Paige, make hot drinks for our new arrivals.'

Olly wrinkled his bashed-in nose. 'But what if you need me?'

'I can't imagine needing you more than Izzy does right now.'

Olly shuffled his feet. 'I suppose, but please call me if there's anything I can do to help.'

'Just look after my daughter,' Nan said in a hoarse

whisper as emotions got the better of her.

'You can trust me,' he promised.

Nan nodded. 'I know I can.'

Once the rest of the group dispersed to get ready, washed, or, in Rob's case, wander around scratching his head, Nan continued to bar my way. She didn't look surprised that I hadn't backed down, nor did she appear in the mood to give in.

'You're not going,' she said, staring me down, even with one bruised eye half-closed.

'But Nan ...'

'Please, Paige. If we do catch up with your dad, there are things I want to say to him that I'd rather not say in front of you.' She clenched her jaw as if those unspoken words had already left a bad taste in her mouth, but she barely winced at the pain from her injured face.

'I have things I want to say too,' I challenged. 'You might be able to break all ties with Dad after this, but I can't, not completely. It's his blood pumping through my veins, and it's his genes I'll be passing on to my children one day. I'd say I have more reason than anyone to confront him. I hope he gets locked up forever for what he did, and if that happens, this will be the last chance I get to speak openly to him, or him to me. You can't deny me this.'

CHAPTER 50

SUE

Sue sat in the back of the rescue vehicle clutching Paige's hand while Kelvin was up front with Dee. Dee was driving, but Kelvin was also hunched forward as she steered the car along the single track down the mountain. The moon was long gone and heavy clouds were inky blots against a pre-dawn glow on the horizon. The headlights picked out the tyre tracks of the two vehicles that had travelled in opposite directions within the last half-hour. The snow had been compressed into strips of ice, and Sue could see where one car had skidded.

'He's going to slide straight off the road, isn't he?' Sue said, unsure if it were wishful thinking. She had said she wanted to confront Ray, but just the thought of looking him in the eye again made her want to vomit. He had used her as his alibi while he waited for Ellen to die. What kind of sick person does that? She supposed she should be grateful he hadn't used Paige instead. Sue squeezed her granddaughter's hand.

'It was bad enough when we tried to drive down yesterday,' Paige said. 'Dad was being reckless then, and when we started to spin ...' Her face creased with pain. 'I swear he sped up. Maybe he was worried about Jonah surviving and telling everyone what had happened. Maybe he thought we'd be better off dead.'

'And maybe you could spend the rest of your life trying to get inside Ray's head,' said Dee. 'But I wouldn't recommend it.'

'I'd rather try to understand Ellen,' confessed Sue. She had wanted to believe that her daughter and son-in-law were happy together, so much so that she had seen what she wanted to see. Ellen had disguised her unhappiness as effectively as Ray had concealed his true nature.

'I can see something ahead,' Kelvin said, craning his neck to see beyond the curve in the road that followed the contours of the mountain.

There was a cliff rising up on one side of the road, and a drop on the other that fell away into the valley that Sue could sense but not see in the grey light. She was sitting behind Kelvin and, looking over his shoulder, she spotted something too. Far in the distance, the twin red spots of tail lights. 'Yes, he's definitely there,' she said.

There was the click of a seatbelt as Paige stretched across her nan to see what they were looking at. 'I'm sure that's where we left the car. Is he stuck?'

'I think he might be reversing,' said Kelvin.

Sue squinted, and just when she thought she could make out the white reversing lights, the brake lights glowed brighter.

'He must be trying to manoeuvre past the other car,' Kelvin continued.

Dee accelerated a little. 'We should be able to catch him up.'

'Put your seatbelt back on,' Sue told Paige as she pushed her granddaughter gently back towards her side of the car.

'But I want to see,' Paige complained. She moved her head from one side of Kelvin's headrest to the other in an attempt to keep the car in her sights, but they were entering another bend that cut off their line of sight. 'Damn! We've lost him now.'

They didn't glimpse any more lights along the road, and Sue's heart sank as they pulled up near the abandoned car. 'He got past.'

'We should keep going too,' said Paige, refastening her seatbelt.

Dee pulled on the handbrake and rested her hand on the gearstick while the engine idled. 'There's a chance he might get stuck further on, either on this road, or on his way out of the valley.'

'We don't need to get into a race,' Kelvin said. 'The past has already caught up with Ray. It's time to leave the police to do their job.'

'Kelvin's right,' said Sue. She still had a family to look after and that included her new grandson. She knew he was in safe hands, and was glad Olly was there for Izzy, but she wanted to be there too. 'We can either waste more time following Ray, or we can go back to the pub and report his crimes. The police can pick him up.'

'But I have to speak to him,' Paige said, sharing Dee's frustration. 'I need to know why he took Mum away from us.'

Dee put the car in first gear and revved the engine; it was impossible to tell which way she intended to go.

'I know you're all desperate for answers,' Kelvin said, 'but even if we do catch him up, Ray doesn't strike me as the kind of person who's going to deviate from the stories he's sold you for decades.'

'Even with a knife to his throat?' asked Sue.

Kelvin twisted in his seat. 'Please, don't tell me you've brought one.'

'I wish I had,' she replied. She wasn't squeamish. She could do it. She could. If her heart were as black as Ray's. And then she saw the look of shock on her granddaughter's face. What had Ray reduced them to?

Kelvin exhaled sharply. 'That's it. Dee, we need to turn back. No one's in a fit state to confront Ray even if we could catch him up. He's gone. We have to accept it.'

Dee revved the engine again, her eyes glazing over as if she could see Ray in front of them and was preparing to run him down.

'Kelvin's right,' said Sue gently. 'It won't do any of us any good.'

When Dee didn't move, Kelvin put his hand over hers. She turned towards him, her eyes full of pain, but she gave way to love. 'OK,' she whispered, putting the car into reverse.

'Wait,' said Paige. 'Can we get my mum's ashes first?'

As Paige jumped out of the car to fetch Ellen's remains,

Sue got out too. The early morning air was numbingly cold and instantly turned her hot, wet tears to ice. Not wanting Paige to see her, she headed towards the edge of the road for her first glimpse of the new day dawning across the valley. Her borrowed boots were a size too big and the road surface was treacherous where the rescue vehicle had driven back and forth to move the obstruction, compacting snow until it was as smooth as an ice rink. She could see why Ray had struggled to get past.

Noticing one set of tyre tracks that had edged onto virgin snow, she imagined Ray's blind determination to escape. She followed the tracks, but only with her eyes. They had disappeared over the edge of the road.

CHAPTER 51

PAIGE

I'd retrieved Mum's ashes from Dad's car and was putting them in the back of the rescue vehicle when I noticed Nan taking in the view. She would have to wait a bit longer for the pale pink glow in the sky to turn into a proper sunrise, and even then, much of the valley was shrouded in mist. But the longer she stood there, her back straight and fixed, the more unsettled I became.

'What's up with Nan?' I asked the others who had remained in the car.

Kelvin and Dee had been sitting holding hands, and it was only when I'd slipped in behind them that they took notice of anyone else. Kelvin rolled down the window. 'Sue? Are you ready to head back?' he called.

When Nan didn't respond, I got back out of the car and made my way over to her. I kept my gaze fixed on the slippery surface, following Nan's footprints through snow, ice and then snow again. I didn't take note of the tyre tracks until I reached her.

'Oh,' I said.

Fifty metres below us was the underbelly of a car caught in a tangle of shrubbery and snapped tree trunks. I drew my eyes away only long enough to wave frantically at Kelvin and Dee. Soon all four of us were standing on the edge of the ridge.

It was easy to trace the trajectory of the car as it had left the road. As it had tipped and rolled down the mountainside, it had churned up snow and smashed into boulders during its rapid descent. The tree that had brought the car to an abrupt stop had been felled, and its misshapen branches surrounded the wreckage. The car was sitting on its crushed roof. Its windows were smashed and one remaining headlight pointed in the opposite direction to where Dad had been travelling.

'Can we get down there?' I asked, not giving myself a chance to consider if I wanted to see what lay below or not.

'We should try,' said Dee, testing her footing as she neared the edge.

'You can't just …' Kelvin said, but Dee was already on the move.

I quickly followed, stepping sideways as I kept to the trench Dee was making through the snow. The hillside was steep, and we both had to use our hands as well as our feet to climb down, but at least it wasn't a sheer rockface.

'I'll get flashlights and a first aid kit from the car,' Kelvin called after us.

Nan took longer to decide which direction she should

go, but I eventually heard her grunts and mutterings as she took the plunge too.

There was plenty of shrubbery to hold on to, and I quickly learnt to distinguish which ones had thorny stems. Halfway down, I grabbed hold of a boulder that wobbled precariously and I had to drop onto my bum until I was sure I hadn't started a minor avalanche. I could feel beads of sweat turning to ice on the nape of my neck.

When I was close enough to the car to hear the ticks of the cooling engine, I stopped to catch my breath. Nan was still on her way down, so while I waited, I took out my phone to use as a torch. Dee did the same.

'I don't think you should see this,' she said, warding me off when I pointed my light towards the wreckage. She crouched down to peer through the shattered windows.

We were on the passenger side so Dee had to lower herself onto her belly to see right across. She got back to her feet just as Nan joined us, huffing and puffing.

'Is he alive?' I asked Dee, unable to wait any longer. Did her reaction mean he was dead? Wouldn't she act with more urgency if he were injured? Did they want to save him?

Dee shrugged, 'He's not there. He must have been thrown from the car.'

We turned as one to survey the surrounding area. Bubbling clouds in the east had turned crimson at the edges, immersing the snow-covered valley in an eerie glow. The foreground wasn't nearly as picturesque. The deep gouge the car had cut into the mountainside was littered with dark silhouettes that might be rocks, or torn shrubs, or possibly a body.

A heavy raindrop hit my cheek, quickly followed by another. A thaw was on its way and our time on the mountain was coming to an end, possibly sooner for some than others. When I thought about Dad being dead, I tried to remind myself once more that the man I loved had never existed, but it didn't matter which way I framed it. The grief felt the same.

'Should we check the ground on the driver's side?' Nan asked Dee, who was back on her knees examining the mangled insides of the upturned car.

'The door's been skewered by a broken branch. He couldn't have got out that way,' Dee said, straightening up. 'Where's Kelvin?'

As we looked up the ridge, Kelvin appeared with two searchlights powerful enough to sting my eyes. He started to climb down.

'He's not here!' Dee yelled up to him. 'Check the whole area between us, and I'll look around the car!' To me, she said, 'Can you get back up to Kelvin and grab the spare flashlight? You need to scan each side of the car's path.'

'Sure,' I said, turning quickly.

As I scrambled up the slope, the rain became heavier. I stopped to pull up my hood and looked back to see Dee talking to Nan, and pointing to the front of the car. The single headlight lit up a path towards a mix of boulders and trees. There were dark spots on the ground where the churned up snow was mixed with mud. Except the mud looked almost crimson.

I was about to head back down for a closer look when Kelvin shouted above me. 'Here, I'll throw the spotlight to you. Don't worry if you can't catch it, it should be OK in the snow.'

He needn't have worried. I caught it, and immediately slid down the slope to catch up to Nan and Dee who had disappeared behind trees and beyond the reach of the car headlight. They had been following the track I presumed my dad had made after crawling out of the front windscreen, battered and most definitely bleeding.

I don't know how Dee had missed it before when she checked the car. Unless she hadn't missed it at all. She had warned me to stay away earlier, so of course she would send me back up to Kelvin to get me out of the way. As I picked up the trail of blood, it was obvious Dad's injuries were extensive.

Careful to keep the spotlight pointed at my feet for fear of what else it might reveal, I followed the bloody track. Beyond the first tree, I spotted two figures standing in front of a scattering of boulders, or what I presumed were all boulders until one of them spoke.

'Help me,' Dad gasped.

He was sitting with his back against a rock. His jacket gaped open and his hand was clasped to his left side. Blood that looked black rather than red oozed between his fingers, and the lacerations covering his face glistened with rain stained red. His eyes were open, and he was looking at Nan.

'Please. Do something,' he begged.

'Not until you admit what you did,' said Dee coldly.

'Dani,' his voice gurgled. 'I—I'm sorry—if I let you down. It would have broken—my heart—if you'd died.'

'But Dani did die. My name is Dee. And you are nothing to me.'

'I did—I did love you.'

'Love is supposed to nurture,' Nan interjected, 'not consume.'

'Sue, please. Don't listen to what she's been saying. Don't twi—twist what I had with Ellen. You're my family. You—you and Paige are all I have left. I need you.'

At the sound of my name, I felt my body drawn towards him. I was about to step forward, but the next question made me dig my heels into the snow, rooting me to the spot.

'Did you kill Ellen?' Nan asked, her voice like stone.

'No, it was an—an accident,' Dad panted. 'I told you.'

'You told me a story, Ray, just like you told a story about Dee,' she replied. 'And just because you got us all to believe you had nothing to do with Ellen's death, doesn't make it true. It makes the lie worse. It taints everyone with your sick reality. I feel tainted. I feel sickened that I never stopped to question what you said happened.' Dad whimpered and she had to raise her voice. 'How did Ellen fall?'

'Please,' he moaned, then released a guttural sigh. 'Yes, we did argue, but it was—it was in a calm way. So calm. She decided to leave, was in a rush. Maybe Dani said stuff that scared her. No need.'

'That's not a confession,' Dee said. 'That's a defence. And what you did to us both was indefensible.'

'Did you push my daughter down the stairs?' Nan said, her voice rising as fast as my pulse.

'No.'

I wanted to join the conversation, but it was as if I had taken a step outside my own body. I was watching actors on a stage. This wasn't my life. This wasn't my family. How could it be?

'Try again,' Dee was saying.

'Yes, sort of. I don't know. I had hold of the case. I might have pushed a bit, but I didn't touch her. I swear.'

'No, you didn't touch her, and that's the point, Ray,' Nan said, her voice scratched with pain. 'You stood back and watched her die.'

I heard a strangled sob issue from Nan's throat and put my hand over my mouth to stop myself doing the same.

'Why?' Nan said.

'Why, Dad?' I whispered too.

'I didn't deserve to lose her. That bastard Jonah turned her against me, with *her* help,' Dad added, using his waning strength to jerk his head towards Dee. 'They made me out to be the villain when he was the one breaking up a marriage. Ellen and I were meant to grow old together.'

'No, she was just supposed to grow old,' Nan corrected.

'At least you can't go on to destroy someone else's life,' said Dee, talking to Dad as if he were already dead.

'Please, no,' Dad said as if he too sensed he was slipping away. 'Help me. I'll do anything ... I'll say anything you want me to say.'

'Then admit what you did to Ellen, and then to Jonah,' said Dee. 'Admit what you did to me.'

'But I ...' The air Dad sucked into his lungs rattled. 'Fine, I did leave you to die, but only because it was what you wanted. You were hysterical. You begged for it to end.'

'Was Ellen begging you too?' Nan cried.

'That was diff— different.'

Suddenly, Dad's eyes rolled to the back of his head as if he was about to pass out. His face was bleached white in the growing light, while the blood trickling through his fingers shimmered red. Realizing he was running out of strength and might never make a full confession, I let the spotlight stretch across the ground until it lit up his crumpled body.

Nan glanced over her shoulder. 'Paige, you shouldn't be here!'

At the sound of my name, Dad brought his gaze back to us. He squinted against the beam of my spotlight. 'Darling,' he said. 'You came.'

'You were saying,' I prompted. 'It was different with Mum how?'

Dad's lips parted, pulling dried skin. 'Your mum had lost her senses. You know what Jonah was like. Do you honestly believe she would have been happier with him? She wasn't happy. We both saw that, we just didn't know why until it was too late.'

Before I could reply, Dee interrupted. 'I expect you took a lot of pleasure in killing him.'

Dad continued to squint in my direction; what focus he had remained on me. 'I heard what he was trying to tell you up on the ruins. He wanted to hurt you too. I couldn't let him destroy your life. I did what I did for you,' he said. His head lolled forward until his chin was resting on his chest. If he was going to say more, he couldn't raise the strength.

Panic bloomed in my chest. 'Is he going to die?' I asked.

Nan shifted from foot to foot. Despite herself, it was obvious she wanted to go to him. 'I could stem the bleeding, but I doubt it would do much good.'

'Please!' Dad cried, raising his voice but not his head. 'Paige, darling. I was only protecting you.'

'Shush,' said Dee in a soft, crooning voice. 'It'll be over soon.'

Dad gasped for air as he recoiled from her voice. 'Are you all going to just stand there? Please. Help.'

As he waited for an answer, Nan and Dee turned to look at me. It was going to be my choice. We could try to save him, or at best comfort him while he died. Or we could let him die alone.

My body swayed in indecision. For all the horrible, despicable things he had done, he was my father. In his own twisted way, he was trying to protect me, but was that enough? A shudder ran down my spine. My dad had always impressed on me to follow his example. I pulled the beam of the torch away from what was nothing more than a shell of the man I thought I knew, and played the light across virgin snow.

'I thought I saw something, but I must have been wrong,' I said. 'We should keep moving.'

CHAPTER 52

KELVIN

Kelvin couldn't explain his growing sense of unease as he watched his wife climb up the slope to meet him. She hadn't bothered to pull up her hood, and made no show of feeling the rain that beat against her face.

'Find anything?' he asked.

'We should go back to the pub,' Dee said, concentrating on the ground as she reached the road.

Sue and Paige weren't far behind, their ascent absorbing all of their attention. Not one of them had looked him in the eye.

Paige was the first to break away. 'Can I wait in the car?'

'I'll be over in a minute,' said Sue.

Kelvin dropped the first aid kit onto the snow. It was obvious it was no longer needed. 'You found him, didn't you?'

'Yes,' Dee replied. 'And we won't be bringing him up.'

Kelvin glanced over his shoulder at Paige's retreating

figure. 'Did she see the body?'

He turned back just in time to catch something in Dee's expression. Guilt? It was the same look on Sue's face, and he almost laughed at the absurdity of his next question.

'He is dead, isn't he?'

'He will be soon, I imagine,' said Sue.

'You mean he's alive, and you left him?' asked Kelvin, needing to spell it out for his own benefit. Dee went to take his hand, but he pulled away. 'Seriously?'

'Please, don't judge us, Kelvin,' Dee said. 'He's badly injured, and he deserves to die alone.'

Kelvin's jaw tightened as he looked back down at the car wreck. Fury burned in the pit of his stomach, but it wasn't directed at Dee or Sue. His anger was reserved for the man whose cruelty had reduced these compassionate and caring women to such an extent that they could do such a thing. And not only them, but Ray's daughter too.

'We couldn't have saved him,' Sue explained.

In his head, Kelvin finished the sentence for her. *Even if we had tried*. Because that was the inference. They hadn't attempted to help Ray. And now they were expecting Kelvin to do the same. His gaze remained fixed on the crash site. There was a dying man somewhere down there, assuming Ray hadn't succumbed to his injuries already.

'Did he say anything?'

'He admitted everything, and apologized for nothing,' said Sue. She glanced over at the rescue vehicle. 'I'd better go. I don't want Paige to be on her own.'

Kelvin stopped Dee before she could follow. 'We can't

just leave him.'

'Why not?' she asked. 'We could say we checked to make sure the road was clear and immediately turned back.'

'I can't keep something like this from Rob.'

'The last thing he needs is to tackle another search and rescue. It's better if no one knows about the accident yet.'

'Why? Are you worried Ray might actually survive?'

'Sue said he won't.'

'And she's sure about that?' Kelvin challenged. 'Because not that long ago she was saying she wasn't qualified to assess Jonah's injuries.'

'Ray wouldn't survive the journey back up here, let alone a transfer to hospital,' Dee said, but it sounded more like a prayer thrown out to the universe than any real conviction.

'Maybe not, but what will survive is the memory of what we do or don't do today. We'll have to live with this forever, all four of us. And once we tell one lie, it'll lead to another, and another, until someone slips up.'

'We won't slip up. None of us will want to talk about this once it's over.'

'You don't know that. How can you expect me to trust two relative strangers when for a while there, I didn't even trust you?' he said. He allowed his guilt to settle, and it weighed heavily on his shoulders. 'Ray was right. I did consider the possibility that you'd smothered Jonah. But I should have had faith in you. You're not a murderer.'

Dee wiped what could have been raindrops or tears from her cheeks. 'I don't blame you for doubting me. I should have spoken to you back in the summer after meeting Ellen, but I needed time to be sure my memories were reliable. I hoped if I could see her again, if we could talk properly about our experiences, I'd be ready to confront my past. And then Jonah turned up and told me she'd died.'

'So Jonah didn't actually remind you of someone, he simply reminded you that Ray was a threat.'

'And one I couldn't keep ignoring. I just wanted him away from the pub before I said anything to you.'

'I hate to say it, but Ray is still a threat. This', he said, sweeping a hand towards the wreckage, 'isn't who you are.'

Dee sniffed back her tears. 'I know I should be a better person, better than *him*, but his suffering pales into insignificance when you think about what he did to Ellen and Jonah. And what he did to us. We could have been a proper family if I hadn't let his words worm their way into my brain. There's a child-shaped hole he put in our lives that's always going to be there.'

Kelvin was about to dismiss the suggestion that their lives weren't complete, but this conversation was too important. What they said now would be remembered, along with the decisions they made. 'There are no holes, Dee, just a version of our life that we didn't get to explore. I promise you, this version suits me fine as long as you're in it.' He scraped a lock of wet hair from her face. 'This is where I get to protect you.'

'You're going down there, aren't you?'

'I won't be long.'

EPILOGUE

FIVE WEEKS LATER

SUE

As Sue knelt down on the damp grass, Olly supported her elbow so she didn't have to let go of the small oak box. The ground was damp, but there was a glimmer of warmth from the sun reflecting off the brass plaque etched with Ellen's name. From somewhere behind her, a baby whimpered and Izzy cooed until a sob caught in her throat. It was time to let go, and yet Sue clung on to her daughter's remains.

A breeze picked up across Allerton Cemetery, and Sue could hear the soughing of trees and the faraway rumble of the Hunt's Cross train. Ellen's grave was within walking distance of her house; it was a trip she would be taking regularly from now on. But to come back, first Sue had to leave.

A slender figure crouched down next to her and placed a hand beneath Sue's to share her burden.

'Let me help,' said Paige.

Her granddaughter was full of surprises. The harrowing events the month before had almost broken the child, but the young woman Paige had become overnight was strong, focused, more cynical perhaps, but cautiously determined. She had moved in with her nan and so far it was going well.

They leant forward and placed Ellen's ashes in her final resting place.

'I promise to look after Paige for you,' Sue told her daughter as her vision blurred with tears.

Paige put her arm around Sue's shoulders. 'And I'll look after Nan,' she said into the void. 'We're going to live our best lives because ...' She had to swallow hard. 'Because you didn't. I hope you never regretted having me, Mum.'

'She always said you were her greatest achievement,' came Izzy's voice.

'And she'd be so proud of you,' added Olly.

Sue's tears dripped onto the oak box as Paige continued to direct her conversation to her mum. 'I know I've not behaved very well, but I'm back on track, and I think you'd approve of what I'm doing now, even if this lot don't.'

There was a pause as Sue waited for her granddaughter to explain more, and when she didn't, Sue took a white rosebud from a spray next to the grave, kissed the warm, velvety petals and whispered one last, 'I love you,' before placing it on top of the wooden box.

With Paige's help, Sue rose to her feet, brushed her

knees, and turned towards the newest addition to the family. Izzy and Olly had named their son Cai, a Welsh name meaning 'rejoice', and when he was handed over to her, Sue's heavy heart lifted. Cradling her grandson in her arms, she left Izzy and Olly with Paige to say their own goodbyes.

'Would you like to add a rose?' Sue asked Kelvin and Dee, who were standing at the end of the row of white marble gravestones.

'Could I?' Dee asked hesitantly.

'You go,' Kelvin told his wife, choosing to remain with Sue.

'Thank you, Kelvin,' Sue said when they were alone.

'Dee wanted to come.'

'I wasn't talking about being here, although that's very much appreciated. No, I wanted to thank you for everything else you've done for us.' She glanced over at the undertaker standing nearby with the groundsman who would backfill Ellen's grave when the family had gone. Lowering her voice she continued, 'Most especially for going back down to check on Ray. Leaving him wasn't the right thing to do.'

'How could anyone expect you to give medical attention to the man who hadn't offered the same courtesy to your daughter? And there was nothing you could have done, Sue. He was cold when I got there.'

'Even so,' replied Sue, not willing to let herself off the hook so easily. She was comforted at least that she had a conscience, unlike Ray.

It would take Sue a long time to recover from the

trauma of that night, but thankfully their dealings with the police had been less fraught than they could have been. There had been no fabrications or omissions, and no fear of contradiction in their witness statements. The truth had freed them from the lies Ray had spent decades tying them up in.

'We did as much as we could for him,' Kelvin said, repeating what they had told the police.

'I would have hated pretending we hadn't found him. We needed to share Ray's final confession, and not just to the police,' said Sue, as she rocked her sleeping grandson. 'Izzy needed to know.'

'Needed to know what?' asked her daughter as she approached.

'That Ray admitted to everything he did,' replied Sue.

'I'd still like to know why,' she growled.

The tabloids had speculated that it was Ray's childhood that had moulded him, that his time in care had made him crave a family of his own that he would cling to at all costs. Sue had a simpler explanation. 'He was a heartless bastard, that's why.' She looked down at the sleeping baby and gave a silent apology for her language before returning him to his mother's arms.

'I can't help wondering what would have happened to Ellen if she'd resisted Ray's trap when she was still at uni,' Izzy said.

Thinking of what happened to Dee, Sue shuddered. 'I imagine I would have been here a lot earlier. It's a small comfort, I suppose. And she was happy for some of that time, wasn't she?' she asked, fearing she hadn't known her daughter at all.

'Yes, Mum, she was,' answered Izzy.

'And are you happy?'

As Izzy rocked her son, she looked over at Olly, who had just said something that made Paige and Dee laugh through their tears. 'I miss my sister,' she said with a trembling lip that she tugged into a smile, 'but otherwise, I'm blissfully happy.'

'He's a good lad,' Sue said, loud enough for Olly to hear as he and the others joined them.

'And he's sleeping through the night already,' Olly said, because of course he presumed Sue's compliment had been directed at her new grandson.

'Not him. *You*,' she said, stepping forward to hug Olly tightly. Fighting yet another urge to cry, she whispered, 'Will you forgive me?'

'I deserved your disapproval,' he whispered back, 'but I promise, I will do better.'

'And so will I,' Sue replied as she pulled away.

'Can we go to the pub now?' asked Paige.

Sue had spotted the groundsman slipping on his work gloves. Unable to watch what he was about to do, she bade farewell to Ellen and hooked her arm through Paige's. They had arrived in the undertaker's car but would be leaving on foot for a family lunch at the Hillfoot pub. After Olly had put the baby in his pram, they began to walk.

'So go on, what are you up to that I wouldn't approve of?' she asked, referring to Paige's earlier comment. 'Is it about your dad's remains?' They were expecting the coroner to release them any day now.

'I want him cremated, if he hasn't already burned in hell,' Paige said solemnly. 'And his ashes thrown into the Mersey so he can be swept away and forgotten. He'd hate that.'

'He would,' Sue agreed. It felt like a just end, and not something her granddaughter would expect her nan to object to. 'So if that's not it, what else are you planning?'

'I'm not going back to uni.'

'OK.' This was not news. After missing so much of her studies, Paige had been in discussions with her tutor about restarting her course in September.

'Indefinitely,' Paige added.

'What?' Sue asked in a high pitch that would have made a dog's ears twitch.

Izzy had overheard and came alongside. 'You're not going back to uni?' she asked. 'But you know how important it was to Ellen.'

'I do,' Paige said, slowing her pace, but only a little. 'And I think she'd understand better than anyone that I shouldn't feel trapped in someone else's dream. I'm not saying I won't focus on getting a degree and building a career eventually, but while I don't have any ties, I want to explore the world. I want to be reckless. Just a little bit,' she added quickly.

'And who will go with you?' Sue demanded. Her granddaughter would be coming into a significant inheritance when they sold her parents' house, and she had visions of some shady figure feeding her granddaughter silly ideas. Those kinds of people were everywhere.

'I'm going on my own to begin with, but there are plenty of like-minded people doing the same thing. I'll start off in Europe, then move on to Thailand, Australia, New Zealand.'

'No, Paige, you can't,' Sue told her.

Before her granddaughter's features could cloud over, Olly veered the pram towards them. 'It sounds like a great idea. And with today's technology, you'll never be on your own. We'll be on standby whenever you need us.'

Sue wasn't sure what to say, so kept quiet as Izzy bombarded Paige with questions. Her daughter and son-in-law seemed to be warming to the idea while Sue remained horrified. She had a mind to keep Paige locked in her room until she saw the error of her ways, but that thought pulled her up short. It was the kind of trick Ray would pull.

'I can look after myself, Nan,' Paige said as they reached the path that led out of the cemetery.

'I know. Just give me a bit of time to get used to the idea.'

Dee and Kelvin came up behind them. 'We're parked over there,' he said, pointing at his Land Rover. 'So we're going to head home now.'

'Oh, you can't go yet. The pub's only over the road,' Sue explained, pointing through the cemetery gates. 'Please, join us. Let us extend our hospitality for a change.'

'If you're sure we're not imposing,' said Dee.

'You're family now,' said Paige, looking to Dee in particular. She raised an eyebrow. 'Horrifying, I know, but it's not up for discussion.'

They continued in silence for a while, and Sue watched as Paige took over control of the pram from Olly. As they walked on ahead with Izzy, he began teasing her about her driving technique, their falling-out long forgotten.

Kelvin picked up his pace at the same time that his wife slowed hers, seeming to know that Sue and Dee needed time together.

'I wish Ellen had told me about your meeting in the summer,' Sue began, 'but most of all, I wish she'd trusted me enough to tell me how trapped she'd been in her marriage.'

'We all fell for Ray,' Dee said. 'It took years for me to work out that his love-bombing was a deliberate distraction to confuse and control. I don't doubt it was the same for Ellen, and for all of you.'

'And we might have continued under his spell for years if that storm hadn't stranded us in your pub,' Sue said. 'Ray had already started transferring his obsession to Paige. He had me convinced that she wasn't fit to live an independent life. He never would have allowed her to go off travelling, that's for sure.'

'Another good reason to let her go?'

Sue exhaled, knowing resisting her granddaughter's wishes would be futile. 'I'm not sure I could stop her,' she replied. She bowed her head. 'I wouldn't want to try. I'm done with interfering.'

'I may not know your family very well, but it seems to me that Izzy and Paige are strong-minded women, and I suspect Ellen was too. I doubt you interfered in their decisions half as much as you give yourself credit for.'

It was an obvious attempt to soothe Sue's conscience, but she was grateful nonetheless. 'I certainly wouldn't have approved of her affair with Jonah,' she said. 'What was he like?'

'It's hard to tell much from one conversation, but I don't doubt he loved Ellen very much.'

Sue's pace faltered. 'We said the same about Ray. Between the two of them, they treated her like a possession to be fought over and owned,' she said. 'But perhaps Ellen had already picked up on the similarities. It would explain why she didn't want to move in with him.'

'Jonah talked as if it had been set in stone that they would have a life together,' replied Dee. 'He was so angry that morning, but I suppose it was understandable given that no one else but me could see through Ray's charm.'

'I know we should be grateful to Jonah for helping us uncover the truth about Ellen's death, and he didn't deserve to die, but I can't forgive him for sending that anonymous email. If only he'd left it to Ellen to manage,' Sue said, voicing another 'what if' that would continue to haunt her.

'He thought he was engineering a confrontation where he would be there. He'd shared enough information about Ellen's secret rendezvous for Ray to catch them,' Dee explained. 'He clearly liked to make things happen. You only have to look at what he did to get your family to Mynydd Plentyn.'

'You'd think he would have learned that his actions had consequences, but he obviously didn't care about how

367

it would affect you, or Paige,' Sue said, concluding that Jonah was another man who put his own needs above all else. 'I do despair sometimes. Are there any decent men left in this world?'

Along the path, Olly was making Paige laugh again, while Kelvin followed behind, chatting to Izzy. Sue and Dee shared a smile.

'Oh, there are one or two,' Dee said.

A FINAL NOTE

PAIGE

The ashes floated on the water like scum, riding the waves until they were splashed back against the promenade wall.

'Are you ever going to leave me in peace?' I asked as I rested my elbows on the railings that lined this stretch of the Mersey. It was early morning, and the sun's beams were spreading out across the pink sky. With the exception of the occasional jogger, we were alone. My father and I.

No, he wasn't going to leave me alone. 'Not until you apologize,' I could almost hear him say.

He was going to have a very long wait.

It wasn't that I didn't regret what happened. Sometimes, my reactions are disproportionate, and that's something I'm going to have to work on. I need to work on a lot of things if I'm honest. Forgiveness for one.

I'd like to forgive Mum, not for having the affair, but for keeping it from me, along with what must have been a long-held urge to escape. I know if I'd been in her position, I wouldn't have told me either, but I just wish her last months on earth hadn't been one big lie.

And then there's Jonah. I need to forgive him for setting in motion the events that led to both my parents' deaths. When I'd fought through that blizzard to meet him, he'd made me believe I was running towards someone who would offer a listening ear and a shoulder to cry on, but Jonah had his own agenda. For weeks and weeks he'd built up my trust only to demolish it with a few words. 'You're not going to like me very much when I tell you how much I loved your mum,' he'd said, and he was right. I didn't like him. He was cruel and he was callous. But he didn't deserve to die.

Finally, I need to forgive Dad, if only in part. Despite all the horrific things he had done to Mum and Dee, he hadn't set out to kill Jonah, and when he tried convincing everyone I'd done it, it was only because he'd realized this was one murder he couldn't cover up. Having me locked up for a crime I hadn't committed was something he could have lived with, if only because it was one way of stopping me building a life of my own without him. And he would have stopped me by one means or another. He would tell me he was protecting me. And here's the thing, he did protect me.

When Dad knew he was dying, he took the blame for everything when he really didn't need to. He might be guilty of murdering Jonah, but he wasn't the one who triggered what happened that day. That was me.

I can remember the solid thumping sounds as I beat

my fists against Jonah's chest, but he stood with his arms folded, and didn't even flinch. When I'd stumbled away, I have no idea if he tried calling after me, but he certainly didn't follow, or check to see if I was all right after all the things he'd just said. I'd thought he was trying to tell me Mum had taken her own life, so when I stopped and looked back, I was furious to see that he'd simply turned his back on me. He was bent over the railings, presumably lost in thoughts of what else he could do to destroy my family, and especially my poor, innocent dad.

I couldn't help myself. I charged at him, and as I thumped my body against his, I heard the clatter of his phone dropping over the edge of the ruins. Instinctively, Jonah leant over to catch it, and when his foot came up, I grabbed it. With a strength I didn't know I possessed, I lifted his foot higher and higher until he did a forward roll over the railings. And then he was gone.

From what Jonah had said later to Dee, he hadn't seen who pushed him, and he must have presumed Dad had been up there too. And I think Dad had been there. Why else had he shared my desperation to drive through the storm to get home? Maybe he thought the guilt would get to me, and I'd raise the alarm that Jonah was missing. And the guilt did get to me in the end. That's why I joined the search, and if it wasn't for me, Jonah would never have been found alive. I didn't want to be a murderer. I am not my father.

But I do take after him more than I'd like. I accepted Dad's dying confession without acknowledging that he had only killed Jonah to protect me, and was protecting me still, and then I simply walked away. I was scared he might change his mind about taking the blame for Jonah's fall, or worse still, survive and use his knowledge to bind me to him forever. Self-preservation is a strong instinct, and apparently it's hereditary.

ACKNOWLEDGEMENTS

It was a pleasure writing this book, if not a little challenging sitting at my desk in the middle of summer trying to conjure a snowstorm. Although the setting is entirely imaginary, my love of North Wales is very real, and one of my earliest memories is of a school trip to Colomendy where we climbed Foel Fenlli only to be deprived of the spectacular views by thick fog. I'm pretty sure that was at the back of my mind while I was writing this book.

For dramatic purposes, I wasn't able to give Mountain Rescue England and Wales the credit they deserve. If you've read the book, you'll know it would have been a very short story if Sue and her family had been rescued within hours, but I'm in awe of the challenges Mountain Rescue volunteers face to save adults, children and often animals from otherwise inaccessible places. You have my deepest respect for the many lives you save.

A big thank you to my neighbours Patricia Fox

and Sue Brown for casting your eyes over the medical references in this book. Your nursing experience was a hidden treasure I didn't expect when I moved into my new house, as are your wonderful friendships. Any errors in the book are mine alone.

Thank you to Hannah Schofield at LBA Books for always being there to drive me forward and champion my books. As always I would also like to thank everyone at HarperCollins for their support throughout my writing career. Most especially to Martha Ashby who is responsible for not only whipping my stories into shape, but in shaping me as a writer. And to Belinda Toor for helping me sift through the many voices in this book and bringing to life the ones who needed to be heard.

To my daughter Jess, your love and support means more than I could ever express. I'm constantly amazed by what you've achieved and continue to achieve. You are my inspiration.

To my family and friends, thank you for being there through the highs and lows and for making sure that the long hours of writing alone never made me feel like I was ever on my own. Special thanks to my mum Mary, and sister Lynn for the open invitations to their caravans in Pantymwyn, which have given me plenty of excuses to visit North Wales over the years. And to my fellow writers Caz Finlay and Mary Torjussen, I am forever grateful for our little support group and your friendship.

Last but by no means least, a very big thank you to my readers. Whether this is the first of my books that you've read or simply the latest, I couldn't do this without you. Every time you recommend a book or leave a review, you probably don't realize how much of a boost it gives the author.